WHAT SHOULD WE DO ABOUT DAVEY?

Also by Julius Fast:

Watchful At Night
(Winner of the Mystery Writers of America EDGAR award
for the best first mystery novel)

Body Language

Sexual Chemistry

Talking Between the Lines

The Omega-3 Breakthrough

WHAT SHOULD WE DO ABOUT DAVEY?

■ Julius Fast ■

St. Martin's Press / New York

Design by Claire Counihan

Library of Congress Cataloging-in-Publication Data

Fast, Julius, 1918–
  What should we do about Davey? / by Julius Fast.
    p.   cm.
  ISBN 0–312–00698–5:$16.95
  I. Title.
PS3556.A78W5   1988   87–27118
813'.54—dc19

First Edition
10 9 8 7 6 5 4 3 2 1

For Barbara

▪ CHAPTER ONE ▪

It was February of 1936, the first day I walked into the third-term French class at George Washington High School, and I was just in time to hear Miss Applebaum say, "For this term, students, we will speak only French. These are the last words of English you will hear in this classroom."

Unfortunately, they were not the last words of English I heard from Miss Applebaum. I had flunked first-term French the first time; I took it again and creaked by with a 65 the second time. I flunked second-term French the first time I took that, and barely managed a 67 the second time. I tried to tell Pop that I showed improvement, that I was really trying, but I don't think I convinced him.

My pop isn't easy to convince, even when he's convinced about something. I think it's because he's naturally suspicious, since English isn't his native language. I never found out what his native language is. He can speak Yiddish, although my brother Sam's mother-in-law tells me it's not too good a Yiddish, and I suspect that his Russian isn't very good either, though he originally came to America from Russia by way of Ireland. I have a friend whose father speaks Russian, and he says Pop is no expert, which is probably where I get my own natural disability for languages.

Except English. I have a 70 average in English, which isn't bad for me. I'm great at composition, but lousy in grammar. In math and biology I'm up in the 90s, but French, eco, even gym—65 or 66 when I pass.

I'm probably the only boy in the third year at George Washington High School who's flunking gym, and my gym teacher is pretty sarcastic about it. He'll say things like "Look at you! Sixteen years old and over six feet, and built too. Why in hell, just tell me, why in hell can't you climb a rope? With knots in it yet!"

"It hurts my hands, Mr. Szylowski," I'd try and explain. "You see, I got this weak index finger from sucking it instead of my thumb when I was a kid—"

But he wouldn't let me finish. "Quinn! Get up that rope, get!"

But I never did get more than three feet off the ground. Gym just wasn't a strong subject with me. Like the first time I tried a one-knee bend. I got blood all over the mat from where I hit it when I fell.

My brother Sam says I'm uncoordinated, but Sam likes to say mean things like that to me. Pop doesn't mind my flunking gym. I think he feels it would be a little disgraceful for a nice Jewish boy to be good at something as physical as gym. But French he did mind, and I knew from the first day that I was going to flunk. How could I pass when I didn't even understand what the teacher was saying?

I figured that in four years of high school, if I kept on at this rate, I'd get at least two years of French credit, which isn't bad since I started French in the first term of my freshman year. Ordinarily I could never pass four terms of French, but this flunk-one, pass-one technique gave me an edge, and I was very good at translating from French to English. I wasn't any good at translating from English to French, or at grammar, or at irregular verbs, or even regular verbs.

I got through most of that term without any serious trouble, mostly by sitting in the back of the room and being absent whenever we had a test. Miss Applebaum didn't believe in homework. When I missed the midterm I got an "open," which means "you haven't flunked yet, but watch out!" I knew it would all explode when the Regents came around, but meanwhile I lived from day to day.

I was sitting in French one morning in April watching a fly amble over a patch of sunlight on my desk and kind of thinking of how disciplined I was sexually, and how only that morning I had broken my discipline.

I was really working at sexual control. A lot of us kids used to talk about how important that was, control, and since the only kind of sexual outlet I had was masturbation, my control was based on discipline.

With a partner you can pace your sexual performance to her

2

needs. I read that in a book I found in Sam's apartment hidden behind the bookshelf. The book was *Dr. Schwartzkopf's Marriage Manual*.

I figured Sam and Rhea, his wife, really must understand marriage because the book was almost worn out with use. Leafing through it I discovered that Dr. Schwartzkopf kept giving advice about partners, but I'd never had a partner, being technically a virgin, except maybe for my cousin Ruth, who had played around with me most of one Passover week I spent at my grandmother's house when I was nine. Only, with Ruth it was just playing, and I don't think there was ever any of what Dr. Schwartzkopf keeps calling penetration.

But without a partner, if masturbation is your only outlet, you can easily overdo it, so I was disciplining myself. Once in the morning before school and once in the afternoon.

The morning was easy. I slept in a double bed with Pop, but he was up at five showering and shaving, making breakfast, and preparing my sandwich for lunch. Then he'd leave for work at seven, so between seven and eight I was always alone in bed in the apartment—and it was very easy. Only this morning I had overslept, and I had to tear off for school, and I hadn't gotten a chance.

That was why, in French, which is the third period, I was sort of daydreaming erotically, since I was in the back of the room anyway, when all of a sudden Mrs. Applebaum called out, *"Levez-vous, s'il vous plaît, et conjugez le verb 'dormir,' M. Quinn."*

Most of it I didn't understand, but I did get Quinn, which is my name, and the *levez-vous*, which is the imperative form of the verb "stand."

It's funny that although I'm Jewish, I have a name like Quinn. There's a story connected with that because originally the name was Kvinski, with the *v* pronounced like a *w*. But my father stopped in Ireland for quite a few years on the way here from wherever he came from, and at Ellis Island, what with the Irish accent he had picked up, the Kvinski somehow became Quinn. At least that's the story the family tells, and it has a kind of logic to it.

I understood my name, but the trouble was I couldn't stand up, not with the physical result of my erotic dreams so obvious. I sat there figuring that in a few seconds it would be all right, but it wasn't. You'd think that the shock of being called would have done it, but sometimes it works differently, and instead I was worse than ever.

I just sat there, and I could feel my cheeks get red, and Miss Applebaum kept telling me to stand up, and then, because I didn't, she began to get very sarcastic in French, which wasn't too bad because I couldn't understand her, but her tone was pretty clear.

I can't figure out why all my teachers seem to react to me like that; I mean always getting sarcastic. It's not as if I talk back or anything, except by not standing up when Miss Applebaum told me to, which is really just a negative way of misbehaving, and I don't think it should be treated as seriously as Miss Applebaum did.

She took it as a personal affront and a clear-cut case of insubordination, and, as she later told Mr. Perry, the head of the French Department, with tears in her eyes, "It was the first time I was driven to speak English since the beginning of this term!"

Mr. Perry knew me from old, which is to say from first- and second-term French, taken twice over, and he also knew Dr. King, the head of the Biology Department. I was very big in biology, and Dr. King used to let me spend my lunch hour indexing his latest textbook, *Principles of Biology*. Mr. Perry knew about this because he used to come into the bio office and chuckle when he saw me at the desk, and say, "So you got the child-labor pool sweating for you again, Jim. Boy, how I wish I had your gall!" Dr. King's full name was James Byron King.

Now Mr. Perry looked at me and chewed his lip and shook his head and said, "I'll take care of him, Miss Applebaum." And then, when she was gone, he kept looking at me and finally shrugged and said, "Now what am I supposed to do with you. Davey? What in hell possessed you not to stand up?"

I couldn't tell him the truth, so I said, "I blacked out, Mr. Perry. Everything went blank."

"Yeah? Well, I'll tell you what. We'll give you enough detentions to lighten the blankness a bit. I want you in the detention hall every day after school for the rest of the term. Get it?"

4

So that was why I got to the Vanity Cleaners just on time, but with all my schoolbooks; I hadn't even been able to get home first and make the bed.

I knew Pop wouldn't like that, but I knew that Mr. Karasik, who owned Vanity Cleaners, would be even madder if I didn't get to work on time. I got the job delivering for Mr. Karasik from Pop, who gets me most of my jobs. On his way home from work he stops in at every store and asks them if they need a delivery boy. Pop is very persuasive, and as fast as I lose one job, he gets me another.

The job with Mr. Karasik wasn't too bad because delivering cleaning is easier than delivering groceries, especially since in our neighborhood they really haven't discovered the elevator, at least not in any of the five-story buildings.

Mr. Karasik calls himself a furrier, but he really runs a dry-cleaning store. He does have some furs that he stores and repairs, and the first order he had for me to deliver that day was a fitch jacket that had to go over to the west side of Broadway.

"You take care of it." Mr. Karasik warned as he smoothed down the fur. "You take good care of it. It's not mink, but anything should happen to it, God forbid, and it'll right away become mink. You understand?"

I said, "Yes, Mr. Karasik." And I smoothed down the fur myself, enjoying the soft feel of it.

Mr. Karasik slapped my fingers. "And don't handle it! Now hurry. Wait. As long as you're over there, pick up a suit from Mrs. Ryan at One Hundred Eighty-sixth Street. Here's her address."

I took off in a hurry as Mr. Karasik watched apprehensively from the doorway. I think each time I took out a suit or a coat he was sure I'd never come back. At least he always acted surprised when I did. "You're back already?" he'd say with the same sarcasm my teachers used. "It's only been an hour and the address was a whole block away."

He used to exaggerate and turn fifty minutes into an hour and two blocks into one.

The fitch jacket went to a Mrs. Bell, who lived on the fourth floor of a walk-up, and I kept thinking all the way up the stairs that today had really played hell with my sexual discipline because not only

5

had I missed the morning, but the afternoon as well, and the way things were going, I'd get home too late to do anything before Pop got there. If there's one thing I've always hated, it's getting caught at it.

Not that Pop or my brother Sam has ever been rough about it. In a home like ours, where there are no women, they just make a joke about things like that. But now that Sam was married, and Pop and I lived alone, I didn't feel that I should embarrass him by ever letting him catch me at it.

It's pretty hard not getting caught when you even sleep with your father. Sam used to sleep on the daybed in the living room, but Pop and I have been sleeping in one double bed since my mother died when I was only three. It's difficult to do much of anything in bed at night when your father is sleeping next to you.

I've always worried about having a nocturnal emission while sleeping with my father, even though Dr. Schwartzkopf, in his book, keeps saying how natural nocturnal emissions are, but I guess that's a silly worry because I haven't had one in my whole life like all the fellows I've talked to say they have. I guess it's because my sexual discipline never allows enough of it to get stored up to emit—nocturnally, I mean.

Anyway, I was in pretty bad shape that afternoon, and I remember hoping, as I climbed the stairs, that Mr. Karasik would be short a few deliveries so I could get home early.

I ran up the last flight because I think it helps your wind to sprint the last bit of a walk or a climb. At least that's what my gym teacher, Mr. Szylowski, says.

Mrs. Bell was all alone in the apartment, and at first she only opened the door with the chain on just enough to look out, but when she saw me, and I said, "Cleaners," and held the jacket up, she opened it all the way.

"Come on in. I'm glad you came now. I was just getting ready to take a bath. Here. Hang it in the closet. Wait a minute." She inspected the jacket carefully and then sniffed. "That's what he calls Hollanderizing? I could do better with a brush and comb!"

I hung up the jacket, trying not to look at her because she must have been right about that bath. All she had on was a kind of silk robe that wasn't really closed, with a sort of scarf around her hair. She had nice hair, pale blond and piled up on her head, and what I could see of her shoulders, especially when she was fishing in her purse for a dime to tip me with, was very soft and pink. The same thing began to happen to me that happened in French class, and I started edging toward the door.

She said, "Damn! I'm all out of change. How would you like a nice piece of cake instead?"

I said, "Gee, you really don't have to bother, Mrs. Bell."

She looked up at me, and then down and up again, and really seemed to notice me for the first time. She reached in front of her bathrobe to pull it together a little, and her eyes got a sort of funny look.

She closed the door and put the chain on, and I couldn't understand that, and she said, "Now you come into the kitchen and sit down, and I'll cut you a slice of homemade cake and pour you a glass of milk. Do you like milk?"

I followed her into the kitchen because if there's one thing I love it's homemade cake, especially if it's chocolate, which is foolish because I'm not supposed to eat chocolate. That was my brother Sam's wife's idea. She says chocolate is bad for the complexion, even though I've never had any trouble with my complexion. Still, there's always a first time.

Fortunately, Mrs. Bell's cake was white with a coconut frosting, and she sat across the table smiling at me every time I looked up, but not saying anything.

At first I thought she was as old as Rhea, Sam's wife. Rhea is twenty-five, but then I thought Mrs. Bell was much older, maybe even ten years older, but it was hard to tell with just that bathrobe on and no makeup. I mean I can usually tell a woman's age by how she dresses and how she wears makeup, but if she's not dressed it's hard to tell.

While I was chasing some crumbs around the plate, she put her hand on mine and squeezed it a little. "What's your name?"

I said, "David. David Quinn," and I swallowed because all of a sudden my throat was very dry.

7

She nodded as if she were pleased and said, "David, would you like to do me a big favor before I take my bath?"

I nodded back at her, afraid to speak because my throat was so dry, and I would probably have coughed. And I tried not to look at her bathrobe, which was very hard because it had fallen open and I could see just about all of her breasts, but seeing was kind of hard because of this pounding that had started in my ears.

"I have this box of books in the bedroom," she said, "that needs carrying into the living room, and it's too heavy for me."

I said, "Sure," and I started to stand up until I realized it was kind of like it had been that morning in French, so I slid out of the chair with my back to Mrs. Bell and said, "Where's the bedroom?"

"This way, David." She stood up and crossed in front of me, then led me through the living room to the bedroom. At the door she stood aside while I walked in. She couldn't help noticing that I was walking kind of bent over, as if I had a stomachache.

"Have you got a stomachache, David?" she asked anxiously.

I said, "Maybe it was the cake," and I ducked into the room quickly, looking around for the books. But I didn't see any, and all of a sudden I felt her right behind me, sort of bumping against me, but I couldn't move away because the bed was in front of me, and that was the only way to go.

"Now where are those books?" she said thoughtfully, but even as she was saying it in such a thoughtful, worried voice, one of her hands touched me.

Startled, I turned around toward her, and then I said, "Mrs. Bell!" because she had just dropped her bathrobe and was standing only an inch from me with nothing on.

I said, "Mrs. Bell, what about the books?"

And then she lifted her arms and put them around my neck and her breasts were so close I couldn't move away, and I kept wondering what Mr. Karasik would say if he found out.

She said, "Do you like me, David?" which was awfully silly, because with the kind of sexual outlet I had, what choice was there? Besides, she smelled so sweet and fresh, I couldn't imagine why she needed a bath, and I tried to answer, but the words just wouldn't come out.

8

I nodded, though, and she gave me a little push and I fell back on the bed and she fell on top of me, giggling. And then she was kissing me and her hands were very busy. When I could finally get the words out, I said, "I really don't know what to do, Mrs. Bell. I mean, I've never done this before, Mrs. Bell. You see, I'm technically a virgin."

"But you want to do it, don't you, David?"

I said, "You bet I do, Mrs. Bell. I haven't thought of doing anything else for months! I just don't know how."

She had a very sweet smile. "But that's what I'm here for, David. To teach you what to do." And she made it sound just like the coconut cake.

I guess the excitement of the whole thing was just too much for me, because she had hardly started to show me what to do when I did it. She said, "Oh, damn!" and I apologized and said I'd be all right again in a minute if she didn't mind waiting.

She looked a little startled, then smiled again and said, "You are nice, David, and while we're waiting I'll show you some little tricks just because you're so nice."

I tell you, with those tricks, which I had never imagined before but which were certainly nice, I was all right again in less than a few minutes, and I guess that was because of all the discipline I had practiced that day—or hadn't.

Afterward Mrs. Bell wrapped up another piece of coconut cake for me to take home, a big piece, too, and when I protested she held up her hand. "No, David. You deserved it. You were very sweet. I want to see you again, David."

I said, "If Mr. Karasik sends me," and she said, "To hell with Mr. Karasik. You get your ass up here tomorrow after school— when do you finish school?"

"Well, if I'm still working for Mr. Karasik, it'll have to be after that," I said regretfully. "Maybe five o'clock?"

I was feeling very happy when I got back to Mr. Karasik's store because I realized that this was an important step in my life. But what worried me was that everyone would know just by looking at me. I was sure I was different now, changed, maybe more mature. Anyone could see it.

What Mr. Karasik saw right away was that I had taken over an hour for one order, and that I had forgotten to pick up the other, so he fired me after some very sarcastic comments about my approach to life.

I didn't feel too bad about that because I knew Pop would find another job for me, and I also realized that now I could get to Mrs. Bell's right after school—after detention, that is.

▪ Chapter Two ▪

I didn't know if I should go to French class the next morning because I wasn't sure whether or not I had been kicked out by Miss Applebaum. Most of what she said was in French, which isn't one of my strong languages. I finally decided to go to Dr. King's office in the Bio Department again and ask him to ask Mr. Perry to ask Miss Applebaum if I should go back to class.

Dr. King was out, and Miss Caldecott, his secretary, was busy typing. Usually I kid around with Miss Caldecott because although she's as old as most of the teachers, she has a good sense of humor and laughs easily, which you don't find too often in older women— at least I don't. But today she was too busy to give me more than a quick smile, so I went on into the middle office where Dr. King keeps the files with the index of his new textbook. I thought I might as well do a little work while I was there, otherwise I'd be sure to get blamed for staying out of French deliberately.

Marcia Beck, who had a free period then, was arranging three-by-five index cards in alphabetical order in the middle office, and she said, "Hello, Davey. What are you doing here?"

"Waiting for Dr. King. Want me to help?"

"No. I'll do it myself," she said, then added challengingly, "I can do it easily."

There's this thing about Marcia that she nevers wants to let you

10

help her. Actually I think it's part of her lack of involvement with her peers, which Dr. Schwartzkopf thinks can create many marital problems in later life. Sometimes I feel sorry for her about it, but I never let her see I feel that way. I can really go for Marcia Beck, and I have ever since first-term French, which we took together. We both had a problem with French. Marcia had an over-all 98 average and couldn't get above 90 in French, which pulled her average down. My French pulled my average down, too, which gave us something in common.

I was very glad we had even that little in common, because it's very hard to make any headway with Marcia if you're a boy. She's always trying to prove she's a little better than you are, and with Marcia that isn't too hard. She has a very high IQ, and she's read about every book I've heard of, and she's the only girl in high school with bifocals—but she only uses them to read.

Marcia once got into a big argument with our physics teacher, who was explaining about the lens of the eye and how bifocals let you read print close to you and then see things far away. Marcia said she didn't need glasses to see things far away. She only needed her bifocals to read with. The teacher said that was impossible, and Marcia said even if it was impossible, it was still true.

I think that was the reason Marcia just got a 90 in physics when she was the only girl in George Washington High School to get 100 on the Physics Regents. Her physics mark and her French mark pulled her average below what she had expected.

"That's my trouble," she told me once when I was walking her home from school. "My real problem is that I expect too much of myself. Even a ninety-five is a disappointment."

"What you should do," I told her seriously, "is accept yourself for what you are. You're smart, and you look swell."

"Do you really think I look swell, Davey? I think my hair is too stringy, and my nose is terrible."

Marcia's hair is very straight and light brown and it falls to her shoulders. She's self-conscious about it, and she is always playing with it, putting a strand in her mouth and sucking it. But it's her eyes that get me. Marcia has green eyes, the kind of green that changes color whenever you look at them. With some of her dresses they look as green as grass, and with others they're almost muddy. Her nose is very straight, and she hates it because it comes right down from her eyebrows without a real dent between them, like on the Greek statues in the Metropolitan Museum.

She's very skinny, too, and her breasts sort of poke through her dresses like little fingers. One of the boys in bio, Saul Greenspan, nicknamed her Marzipan because he said she was good enough to eat, and the nickname stuck even though Marcia hates it. I never dare use it, though I know what Saul meant and I agree with him. She *is* good enough to eat!

That day as I sat there in Dr. King's office with Marcia, watching her put the file cards in order, waiting for her to push her hair back from her face and feeling funny each time she did it, I kept wondering whether or not she wore a bra. With Marcia you couldn't tell, but with some of the other girls you could put your hand on their backs, kidding around as if you were a clown, and say, "What's new, doll?" meanwhile feeling to see if the bra fastener was there.

But you couldn't do anything like that with Marcia. I don't know why. You just couldn't. Finally Marcia looked up at me with a little frown and asked, "What are you staring at?"

Very quickly I said, "What are you doing this summer, Marcia?"

She pushed her hair back while my stomach melted, and she said, "I have a job at this girls' camp as a waitress. They don't pay you, but you get tips, and they have clay tennis courts and a cinder track."

I forgot to mention that Marcia is a great athlete. She's a leader in gym, which is another thing we have in common. I mean she's able to give me very good advice on how to improve my own gym work. She asked, "What about you, Davey?"

I shrugged and said, "I don't know. Maybe I should try to get a job away from the City." I thought of Mr. Karasik and wondered when Pop would find out that I'd been fired. "Do they need any waiters at your camp?"

She shook her head. "Don't be dopey, Davey. It's a girls' camp."

"I'll take the job."

"Very funny." Tapping her teeth with her pencil, she stared at me. "But you know, there's a brother camp two miles away, and they take waiters. Why don't you try for a job there? It's under the same ownership."

I shrugged. "They wouldn't really give me a job, would they?"

"I'll ask Mom to talk to the director. Maybe they would. You know, Davey, that's your trouble. You don't have any confidence. Like just now. You start right off with they wouldn't give you a job. Just like that. How do you know they won't unless you ask?"

I nodded thoughtfully. "You're right, Marcia." And I leaned across the table listening to her. One of the things I like about Marcia is the incisive way she approaches what's wrong with me. She enjoys analyzing my shortcomings, and I enjoy listening to her. I consider it a good thing because it shows that she's beginning to become personally involved with my life. Actually, it's the only indication that she is involved.

The reason I mention this whole incident in the office before Dr. King came in is because while she was explaining my shortcomings I finally got up enough nerve to ask Marcia if she'd go out with me that Saturday.

She said no because she had this important report to do on Thorstein Veblen for economics, but maybe I'd like to come and have dinner with her family on Sunday afternoon.

I said sure, because Marcia's mother is a wonderful cook, and she always makes a big fuss over me, urging me to eat doubles and then triples of anything I finish, and I finish everything, though I notice that Marcia's family doesn't. They always leave a little on the plate, which Marcia says is a sign of being polite.

In my family it's a sign of being sick. In fact, when Sam still lived at home, if I didn't finish a real close second, I would find him reaching for what was left on my plate.

Of course things are different now that he's married. Rhea has her own ideas about eating. She's trying to train me, too, and I guess she's doing pretty well.

I was even happier about the invitation later in the week because things began to get sort of tense at home. I had to tell Pop about losing the job with Mr. Karasik, and that really upset him. "That's seven jobs in two months! Why? What did you do now?"

I said, "It wasn't my fault, Pop. His old delivery boy came back, and what else could he do but give him back the job. He said I was trying hard, Pop, but it was the only fair thing to do."

"David. You're telling me the truth?"

I looked hurt. "Pop! You know I don't lie."

Pop considered and nodded. "That much credit I'll give you. I sometimes don't think you've got the brains to lie. I almost wish you did." He sighed and said, "Well, tomorrow I'll speak to Mr. Heller, the butcher. Don't look so unhappy. Let's have supper."

I knew there wasn't much chance of his checking with Mr. Karasik. Pop uses the cheaper cleaner on our block. He only stepped into Karasik's to get me the job. I think it's a very good thing that Pop has this kind of absolute faith in my honesty because he needs something to hold on to. Pop is really very alone. I mean he doesn't go out with other men, and he never sees any of our relatives except my grandmother on Passover, and that's because I usually spend that week with her. Because of this I like Pop to have this idea about my being truthful.

Actually it isn't so, because I have a strong compulsion never to tell the truth if I can tell a lie instead. I don't know why I do it, but it usually saves a lot of trouble, like this whole business with Mr. Karasik.

It's pretty easy to get away with it with Pop, because while he's convinced that I'm truthful, he's also firmly convinced that I'm a little slow—in a nice way. The extra-change business is an example of it. One Saturday when Sam and Rhea were visiting, Pop sent me down to the grocery for a dozen eggs and a pound of butter.

"Don't go over to Broadway. Go by Mr. Gebhardt, the Nazi."

"He's not a Nazi," Sam said, but automatically, not really hoping to change Pop's opinion that every German was a Nazi.

"So go by Mr. Gebhardt who isn't a Nazi. The eggs is twenty-five cents and the butter is thirty cents a pound. Here's a dollar, so you should bring back forty-five cents change."

"If you keep treating him like a child, he'll never learn to handle money," Rhea said.

"Better he should be treated like a child, and he shouldn't be short-changed. Let him learn on his own money, not mine."

It didn't bother me, Pop talking like that, but I had ten cents of my own money in my pocket, and just because I know it gives him a kick, I put the ten cents in with the change. When I brought back the eggs and butter and handed him the fifty-five cents, Pop asked, "Where did you go?"

"To Gebhardt's, like you told me."

"And this is the change he gave you?" Pop's face lit up with pleasure. "Fifty-five cents?"

"That's right."

"It's ten cents too much. The Nazi cheated himself, and you didn't even notice it."

I looked at him innocently, and I said, "I didn't count it, Pop. Should I take it back?"

"Take it back!" He turned to Sam and Rhea and threw up his hands. "Even when he does something smart by accident, he wants to ruin it on purpose."

I didn't point out that it wasn't very smart of me if Gebhardt had undercharged me. I get enough of a kick out of seeing Pop feel so good. It kind of made his day. Sam, like Pop, was ready to believe I'd do anything. Rhea always looked at me in a funny way, as if she just couldn't believe what I was doing.

But the afternoon after I told Pop about Mr. Karasik, I was free. He hadn't gotten around to talking to Mr. Heller, so after school I was able to go right over to Mrs. Bell's. I didn't even stop at home to drop off my books. I was excited, but I was a little scared too. I tried remembering some of the things Mrs. Bell had shown me, and I wondered if I shouldn't go home instead and stick to my discipline. But then again, I figured that even if I was scared, there was always the coconut cake.

I was pretty hungry because what with my worrying about Mrs. Bell, and Miss Applebaum's being so angry, I had forgotten to take my lunch to school. Pop makes my lunch for me each morning before he leaves for work, and since he's not there to remind me to take it when I leave, sometimes I forget. It usually doesn't matter unless for some reason I don't go home, like today.

My pop gets a big kick out of making my lunch because no matter what he puts into the sandwiches, I always say it was great when he asks me how I liked it. Sometimes, though, this gets him exasperated. "You'd eat dreck, garbage, if I gave it to you, and you'd like it!" he said once. But most of the time he's sort of proud of the way I'll eat anything. "David," he told Sam and Rhea, "eats it, no matter what it is, what it tastes like, or what it looks like—he eats it!"

"You shouldn't let him," Rhea said. "It just gets him into bad habits."

"What kind of bad habits?" That was Sam.

Rhea shrugged. "Lack of discrimination is a bad habit. Part of maturity is learning to taste different foods, to develop a palate."

"I taste different foods," I protested, not so much because I wanted to prove anything, but because I thought it would keep the argument going. I always enjoy these analytical sessions about myself. I think I learn a lot, especially from Rhea, who studied psychology at Hunter College. That was before she married Sam, and she claims it got her through the first three years of their marriage.

To get back to my lunch, one time Pop decided that he was going to prove to Sam and Rhea once and for all that I'd eat anything and like it, so he made me a sandwich of two slices of rye bread with a slice of white bread for filling. At lunch I realized it was all bread; but I was hungry, so I ate the three slices with some ketchup and mustard I snitched from the cafeteria condiment table.

That night when Pop, trying to be casual, said, "So how did you like your lunch?" I realized right away by the look he gave Sam, who'd just happened to "drop in," what was up. So I looked innocent and said, "Great, Pop. It was a great sandwich."

Pop slammed his hand down on the table. "So! What did I tell you? Will he eat anything?"

But this day I had left my sandwich at home, so by the time I reached Mrs. Bell's apartment house I was weak with hunger. A lot of other things worried me, and I felt anticipation and even fear.

I took the steps two at a time to calm me down, and by the time I reached the top I was gasping. I stood in the hall and practiced hyperventilation, which I'd learned about from indexing Dr. King's biology book. It's very good when you're out of wind or practicing to dive. You take deep breaths of air again and again. Sometimes it can make you pass out, but usually it just makes you dizzy.

When I was pretty dizzy, but had my breath back, I rang the bell, and Mrs. Bell opened the door on the chain and peered out at me. "Why, David! I'd almost given up on you. I thought maybe you had to work."

She opened the door and let me in. "I was fired," I told her and pointed to my books. "I came straight from detention at school."

"And you're all out of breath too. You're a sweetheart, David. Put down your books and let me give you something to eat. I have a lovely maple-nut cake and some cold chicken. Do you like chicken?"

She must have known I was hungry by just looking at me. All of a sudden all my nervousness was gone. I said, "I love chicken, Mrs. Bell."

She told me to sit at the kitchen table and put out a plate of chicken and a basket of rolls, some milk, and a beautiful tan maple-nut cake. I ate everything and about three slices of cake while she sat there smiling at me. When I was finished I said, "I want to thank you, Mrs. Bell."

"Now don't thank me, David. I love to watch a man eat."

I said, "Not only about the food, but for all the things you showed me the other day."

"Well now!" She smiled, reaching out and touching my cheek. "Let's go inside, and I'll show you some more."

She made me take off all my clothes, and she sat there in her slip watching me. It was all kind of embarrassing, and I was glad that Pop always made me wear clean underwear every day, even if the shorts were worn here and there. "You wear clean underwear," Pop would say, "because you never know when you could be in an accident and have some strange doctor undress you. I'd really be ashamed to be called to the hospital and have some doctor I didn't know tell me my son was at death's door with dirty underwear."

I always thought that was silly, especially when I saw what some of the kids in gym wore, but now I could agree with him. When I was completely undressed, Mrs. Bell nodded and giggled a little. "Now I know you're a natural blond."

"A natural blond?"

She pulled her slip over her head and stood facing me. "See. Like I am, David. Now come here. Today I'm going to teach you how to kiss. You start like this, with your lips closed—but only closed at first, David. Then you open your lips and push your tongue out, like this. Watch."

It was all new to me, and really interesting, but finally I pulled loose and said, "Mrs. Bell, I don't think we ought to start with that."

"Why not, David?"

"Because the same thing is going to happen that happened before."

Frowning slightly, she drew back and ran her hand down my chest. "Yes, you're right, David. Now that's the first thing we'll have to work at. I don't think it's very serious, but there are a few little things . . ."

Mrs. Bell was a wonderful teacher; but I think, like Rhea used to say about my schoolwork, my problem was mostly motivation. When I used to fool around with the other boys, when I was just a kid, we all used to have contests to see who was the fastest. Mrs. Bell put another face on the matter and showed me that slow was even better, and it became quite a challenge.

I had just begun to get the hang of what she meant when the doorbell rang.

She jumped out of bed and ran to the door. Pushing aside the little peephole, she looked out, then came running back. "Oh my God, my God!" She grabbed her slip and began to pull it on. "Why is he home this early? He wasn't due till tomorrow!" The doorbell rang again, and she yelled out, "Yes, dear. In a minute." Then she looked at me and hissed through her teeth. "What the hell are you doing there naked?"

"Practicing to hold off . . ." I began, but she threw my pants at me furiously. "Get dressed and get out!"

"But if someone's at the door . . ."

"Through the window and down the fire escape, you foolish bastard!"

She ran out of the room and slammed the door. I got dressed

pretty fast, and I could hear her talking in the other room, and I could hear another voice, a man's voice that I didn't like the sound of at all. I grabbed the rest of my clothes, shoes and socks and jacket, and I pulled open the window and climbed out on the fire escape. I had just closed the window when through the curtains I saw a little bald man walk into the room and look around. He began to pull off his tie, and I drew back and pressed myself into the farthest corner of the fire escape.

Mrs. Bell came into the room behind him, and I could hear their angry voices but couldn't make out the words. He walked over to the window, and for a moment I was really scared, but he only pulled down the shade.

I crouched there on the fire escape, not daring to climb down the ladder because I have a terrible fear of heights. Finally the light in the bedroom went out, but I could still hear their voices, and I could tell that the man was very angry about something, and I wondered if he could possibly suspect that I had been there.

Crouching there, even with my fear of heights and worrying that I might be caught, I suddenly realized that I had been concentrating so hard on holding back that I ached all the way down to my knees. There was only one thing to do, and I did it right then and there, even though I was out on a fire escape four stories up. I just had to, or I would have burst!

Then I put on my shoes and socks and, still feeling a little strained, I climbed up the fire escape to the roof. I couldn't face the steps down to the alley with my fear of heights. Luckily the roof door to the stairwell was open and I got down to the street and back home without any trouble. I even had time to make the bed and clean up the apartment, but when I sat down to do my homework I suddenly realized that I had left my books at Mrs. Bell's!

I tell you, that was a pretty rough night. I didn't mind missing my French homework because I never really understood it anyway, but I was worried about eco, and I really looked forward to bio and math.

The first thing Pop said after supper was, "So sit down and do your homework, and I'll do the dishes. I didn't get to see Mr. Heller tonight, but tomorrow I'll stop in."

I said, right off the top of my head, "I don't have any homework tonight because tomorrow is teachers' exam day."

"Teachers' exam day?"

"The teachers take exams each term just to make sure they're on the ball," I said. Even to me it sounded logical.

Pop nodded. "It's a good idea. You see, in spite of all the tsuris you still get an education in America. In Ireland it was very bad. They used to have us all in one room, the children just learning to read and the ones starting for the university, all in one room."

"I thought you went to school in Russia."

"In the shtetl in the Ukraine we didn't even have school, school like here. I studied Hebrew in cheder, but I was only a child when I left Russia. That was right after the pogrom. I was so young. My aunt Hannah was in Ireland, and we went there for five years. I was thirteen when I came to America. I was younger than you are now, Davey, and all alone."

I knew this was the introduction to how hard he'd worked at my age, and maybe I ought to try working a little harder myself. Ordinarily I'd try to get out of hearing the story again, but tonight I figured listening to that was a lot safer than talking about school.

The next day, right after school, I hurried over to Mrs. Bell's, mainly to get my books, though I figured if she wasn't mad and wanted to teach me some more, that was all right too. I was developing a healthy respect for education, what Rhea would have called motivation.

I rang the bell to her apartment, and to my surprise it was opened by the short, bald man who glared at me. "What the hell do you want?"

I gulped and said, "I'm from the cleaner, from Mr. Karasik. He sent me to pick up Mrs. Bell's coat."

"Lisa," he yelled back into the apartment. "There's a kid here from the cleaners."

I heard a dish drop in the kitchen, and then Mrs. Bell came up behind him, and her face looked strange. "David!" she kind of gasped. "Oh my God, David!"

Very quickly I said, "She calls me David because she always

20

gives me cake for a tip. Did I leave my books here the other day when I delivered your coat, Mrs. Bell?"

"Your books?" She backed away, but he caught her arm and pulled her forward, and his eyes began to get a funny, bright look. "So he was here yesterday."

She started to say something, but I cut in quickly, "No. Not yesterday, sir. Last week sometime."

"And you left your books here then?"

I said, "Well, I deliver after school . . ."

Mrs. Bell had pulled her arm loose, and now she came to the door with my books in her hand. "You take them, David, and run along, and tell Mr. Karasik I don't need my coat cleaned again."

He grabbed the books from her and came out in the hall while I backed away. I didn't like those funny eyes of his. "So you were here last week? Look, kid, I know when these books were left here. What do you think I am, a half-wit? I tell you what, just set foot here again, just come near this neighborhood, and I'll cut your balls off and stuff them down your throat! Here! Here's your goddamn books!"

He began to throw them at me, one by one. I grabbed one, ducked another, and caught the next right in my head, a French text too! I grabbed the last book, my math text, at the foot of the stairs, and a quick check showed me that I had them all except my French notes, and they weren't worth much.

I figured I wasn't going to get much more teaching from Mrs. Bell, but on the positive side I had all my books. I tucked them under my arm and began to run home, partly because I could use the exercise, and partly because I was afraid Mr. Bell would come after me. At least I assumed the bald guy was Mr. Bell, or why else was he so sore?

I found out that he was Mr. Bell that night when Pop came home. I had supper all ready too, which isn't so hard because we have a pretty standard supper each night, either tuna-fish salad or salmon salad. I open a can and mix it with chopped lettuce and celery and salad dressing. Usually Pop makes it, but lately I've been taking over. That shows responsibility.

21

For a second course we have either spaghetti with ketchup on it, or boiled rice with ketchup, and for desert I usually make some Jell-O before I leave in the morning. On Fridays, for a change of pace, we have sandwiches, and since Pop gets home a little early, we eat them in front of the radio listening to Amos 'n' Andy and then H. V. Kaltenborn, Pop's favorite. Pop's always interested in the foreign news and what country Hitler is threatening. I listen just to keep him company and then we turn to WEAF and listen to *One Man's Family.*

I was just fixing the salad when Pop came in, and right away I knew I was in trouble. But he didn't say anything, not till he had finished supper and was done with the Jell-O, but he kept looking at me in a measuring way all through the meal.

Then, while I was putting some water on for his tea, he said mildly, "So you're growing up."

"Growing up?" I didn't know what to say until I found out how much he knew.

"You seem to know your way around with married women."

"Married women?"

"From what Mr. Karasik tells me, you're a regular Don Won."

"Don Won?"

"It's not enough you've got to deliver orders. You've got to give extra satisfaction."

"Extra satisfaction?"

"And stop repeating everything I say! David, what am I going to do with you?"

"Just because I leave my books at a house where I deliver an order . . ." I began, but he waved my explanation aside.

"All right. I know the whole story. The husband called up Mr. Karasik."

It was a tight spot, but on the other hand I hadn't really been caught at anything. It was all circumstantial, unless Mrs. Bell had told the truth, and why should she? I said, "I didn't do anything, Pop," and I looked him straight in the eye.

He said, "Who should I believe? You or Mr. Karasik?"

I considered that for a minute, then I shrugged. "I'm your son."

He sat there looking at me, trying, I suddenly realized with a rush

22

of relief, to keep a straight face, and then he began to chuckle, and then laugh, and then he got almost hysterical, smacking the table with his hand.

"Oh my God, at sixteen! At sixteen yet, and with a married woman! David, David! Wait till I tell Sam—another no-good. Oh my God!"

And he started all over again, laughing till the tears ran down his face. "If I could only have seen the husband, and that Karasik with his little pinched face, telling me you'd come to a bad end—a bad end!"

I figured it was all right. I like to see Pop happy, he so seldom gets a chance to laugh. I poured the tea, and just for good luck poured myself a cup too.

▪ CHAPTER THREE ▪

Sunday Pop decided we should have a family discussion about what to do with you-know-who. Sam and Rhea usually come for dinner on Sunday at about four o'clock, but since this was a special occasion, they came early.

"What I don't understand," Rhea said, lighting a cigarette after the table had been cleared and Pop was pouring coffee, "is what a woman that age could see in Davey."

They all looked at me and I didn't know whether to feel proud or ashamed of myself. I tried a little of both and brought out the Jell-O I had made that morning. Sunday, instead of the usual salad and rice or spaghetti, Pop makes a chicken or a pot roast and a soup to go with it. He's very good at soup, although he tends to get carried away and throw in everything in the kitchen. He has a heavy hand with the barley, and he insists that old wilted lettuce gives it a French taste. Then he'll add onions and sometimes potatoes and rice.

I put the Jell-O out, and Sam growled, "Jell-O again? Haven't you two ever heard of anything else for dessert?"

"It's very healthful," Pop said. "It makes the fingernails strong, and it keeps the weight down."

"And it wouldn't hurt you to get your weight down," Rhea said, frowning at Sam, whose waistline had been getting thicker and thicker since his marriage. Then she turned to me, still frowning. "I don't know. Davey doesn't even look as if he belongs in this family."

I knew what she meant because even though Sam is twelve years older than I am, he's bald as an egg and a head shorter. When he graduated from college and passed his CPA exam, he was neat and trim and had a full head of hair. He claims he started losing it when he married Rhea, but as I remember, he was getting thin on top before that.

Anyway, when Sam did have hair, it was black like the little fringe Pop still has. Me, I have light-blond hair and blue eyes, and I'm a little over six feet tall, which makes me tower over both Sam and Pop. That's what Rhea meant when she said I didn't belong in the family. She always says that, and sometimes it's a compliment and sometimes, like now, it isn't.

Pop came to my defense. "I don't know. When I was young, I used to be a good-looking man."

"But Davey . . ." Rhea shook her head. "What would a mature woman want with him?"

Sam shrugged. "That's not the point. Suppose she starts some trouble?"

"She should start trouble?" Pop said angrily. "A child like David she plays around with, and she should start? Besides, it wasn't David's fault."

"How do you know?" Sam asked.

"He told me."

"I did?" I said without thinking.

Sam threw up his hands and looked at the ceiling. "I give up!"

"All right." Pop pushed his Jell-O dish aside. "Let's get down to business. David, get the pinochle cards and shut up the mouth.

Rhea, put out the cigarette already. The two of you smoke like chimneys. Sam, spill me a glass water."

"Pour, Pop, pour," Sam said in an exasperated voice. "How many times do I have to tell you it isn't spill?

"Pour, shmour—play cards!"

I got a deck from the sideboard, and Pop started dealing a game of three-handed pinochle. "Crap!" Sam said disgustedly as he picked up his hand. "A handful of crap!"

Rhea said, "Sam! Please," but sort of absently as she arranged her hand.

Pop and Sam always think better with a pinochle game going, so I fixed myself another plate of Jell-O and started in on it while they decided what to do with me. "The problem is," Pop said, "I'm running out of jobs. I asked Heller, the butcher, and he's already got a boy, and the Nazi doesn't deliver. The fruit store won't take him back. Tell me, David, were you fooling around by the fruit store too?"

Indignantly, I said, "Pop!"

"All right, so where am I going to find you a job?"

"Do you need the few lousy bucks he brings in?" Sam asked. "If you're that tight, I can help out. Rhea's going back to social work next month. She's been offered her job with the city again."

Pop laid down three cards. "I don't need David's delivery money. My salary is enough for the two of us as long as they don't lay me off." Pop worked as a cutter in a dress factory in a downtown loft, but in the past five years it seemed he got laid off every time the slack season came. "What he makes I put aside for his education," Pop said, "though he seems to be getting quite an eduacation outside of school. This is a hand?" He put his cards down. "It's not so much the money, though that doesn't hurt. It's David. He needs a job to stay out of trouble."

They all turned and looked at me. I sat there feeling uncomfortable for a few minutes, then I asked, "Are you going to finish your Jell-O, Rhea?"

She pushed it across. "This family! You all eat so fast, it's a wonder you don't have ulcers."

I said, "Eating fast won't give you ulcers. Dr. King says emotional stress does it, and believe me, I'm under a lot of emotional stress even if I don't show it."

"Nobody likes a smart-ass!" Sam snapped. "Pick up your hand, Pop, and play."

They played another hand while I finished Rhea's Jello-O, then she looked at me with that funny expression and said, "I still don't understand what a grown woman would want with Davey."

"Shall I spell it out for you?" Sam said. "Or would you like to guess?" He pointed his cards at Pop. "You know whose fault it is? You spoil him rotten. When I was his age, I never got away with that kind of crap."

Pop said, "I'm melding," and added, as he arranged his hand, "but you got away with other things. The point is, David has to keep out of trouble."

Sam put his cards down. "Two jacks. That does it. If he's going to get into trouble delivering orders, why doesn't he get a real job that'll keep him busy?"

They all looked at me speculatively, and I said, "Hey, wait a minute! I'm only a kid. How can I get a real job while I'm going to school?"

Sam snapped his fingers. "Of course. The library."

Pop said, "The job you had in high school?"

"Yeah. When I was your age, Davey, I used to work in the public library after school, all through high school and even my first year in college. You know, I was a page."

I began to laugh because I thought it was some kind of joke, a page in a library, but he really meant it."

"I'll make a few calls. I think Miss Marx is still head librarian at the Mount Murray Branch. Let me pull a few strings."

"What kind of job is it?" I asked suspiciously. "What kind of work does a page do?"

"You know, you put books back on the shelf in order, straighten up the place, and sometimes even help at the check-out counter. It's easy work."

I wasn't so sure. There was something suspicious about Sam's cheery attitude. He never gave me anything good in his life, but I

26

didn't argue. At least this way I'd have a few free days without delivering orders. Saturday, too. That's always a big day for orders, and it usually knocks me out. Now I'd have a little time to myself.

Saturday, the Aviary Club had bird outings out at Van Cortland Park, and with my delivery jobs, I rarely got to go. The Aviary Club was a Biology Department club at school, and it was great. Saul Greenspan and I were the only boys in the club, and there were ten girls! The hikes were supposed to be for bird-watching, but mostly we fooled around and had fun. I don't think any of us knew a cedar waxwing from a robin, but we carried mimeographed slips with all the birds' names to list the ones we spotted, and while the girls were serious about it, Saul and I just put down any list of birds at random, whether we'd seen them or not.

I was thinking of the Aviary Club and this coming Saturday's outing while I was washing the dishes in the kitchen. I've noticed that Rhea is very big on setting the table and clearing it off, but I never remember her volunteering to wash the dishes. I guess she figures I'd be offended.

I had just stacked the last dish when the phone rang, and Sam answered it and called out, "It's for you, Davey."

"A woman?" Rhea asked quickly.

"Relax. It's a kid. Here."

I took the phone, and all at once, before she even said anything, I knew it would be Marcia, and I knew she was calling about dinner. She had asked me for this Sunday, and I had forgotten all about it.

"Davey? Where are you?" she asked, and that was kind of funny because I had to be home if she had called me there.

"I'm home," I said.

"But we're all ready to eat!" she wailed.

I turned my back to the living room where Sam, Rhea, and Pop were trying to listen, and I said in a hoarse whisper, "You didn't tell me what time."

"Oh, Davey, I said dinner. We always eat at six. You know how Daddy is."

I did know. Daddy didn't like me, and he was always glad of an excuse to be sarcastic. I don't know why he didn't like me, because I was always polite, and I always called him "sir," but somehow, whenever he looks at me, Mr. Beck gets angry. Marcia's mother is different. She really likes me and is always urging me to eat something.

I looked at the kitchen clock. It was just five to six. "Well, it's only five to. I'll be there on time."

"How?" Marcia sounded exasperated.

"I'll run. You'll see. I won't be late—not very."

"Davey, you're impossible!"

"I have to hang up, or I'll really be late."

I grabbed my jacket, and Pop said, "Where are you going?"

"I've got to get the homework from Marcia Beck. There's this big test on Monday, and Marcia has been helping me study. Besides, I need some fresh air. I'll see you."

"Why didn't you get the homework yourself . . ." Sam started, but Pop shushed him. "Let him go. He'll get some fresh air."

Homework is a magic word with Pop. It triggers a whole set of responses, like the bell did with Pavlov's dogs. I just say homework, and I can get out of anything, but I try not to overuse it. Another magic word is fresh air. Pop is convinced that if I do my homework regularly and get plenty of fresh air, nothing can possibly go wrong with me. Tonight I used both and it worked.

Marcia lives five blocks away in Washington Heights, but three of the blocks are uphill. I ran four blocks and sprinted the last one, and rang her doorbell at six on the button. That wasn't bad.

Her father opened the door, but instead of looking at me, he was staring at his watch. "He made it!" he called out in a disappointed voice.

Mrs. Beck came out of the kitchen and took my jacket. "I told both of you he would. Did you forget about dinner, Davey?"

"Oh, no, ma'am. It's just that I forgot about the time. We usually eat later at our house. I got to talking about this job my brother is going to get me, and the time went by."

"You're going to work with your brother? But what about school?"

"No, my brother's getting me the job—after school."

"Oh, what kind of a job?" Mrs. Beck asked. Mr. Beck didn't say anything. He just went to the table and sat down. Aside from not liking me, I think he's kind of rude because even if he didn't care about me, he should have waited for Mrs. Beck and Marcia. Pop always waits for Sam and Rhea when they're visiting.

"A job at the library."

Marcia came in then, and she had on a pink blouse and a white skirt. She looked just like a stick of marzipan. "Hi, Davey. You really got a job?"

"Well, not yet, but Sam says he'll get it for me by pulling a few strings. It's working in the library."

"Would you like to wash your hands, Davey?" Mrs. Beck asked.

"No, thanks," I said, holding the chair for Marcia. "I washed them at home before I left." After all, I had done the dishes. "I got here too fast for them to get dirty."

It was a joke, but Mr. Beck gave me another of those looks and started to eat. "I'm so glad you came," Mrs. Beck said. "I made something very nice. A pot roast, and we're having rice and potatoes and a special noodle kugel."

That was for Mr. Beck. He doesn't eat anything but meat and starches. Marcia says he hasn't tasted a green vegetable for as long as she can remember, but he certainly doesn't look undernourished. If anything, he's somewhat overnourished, probably because Mrs. Beck is such a great cook.

I had three portions of the pot roast, which was much better than Pop's, and I could really compare the two because I had finished his less than an hour ago. I also had two helpings each of the rice and potatoes and noodle kugel, which she makes with raisins and cinnamon and should really be dessert, but you eat it with the meat. For dessert she had ice cream with marshmallow sauce and chocolate, and even though Jell-O is a favorite of mine, I had to admit this was good.

Toward the end of the meal I noticed Mr. Beck had stopped eating and was just staring at me, but I didn't think anything was wrong, like my eating too much, because Mrs. Beck was still offering me more. Anyway, I felt that I really didn't have to worry about overeating because dinner at home had taken the edge off my appetite. I figured Mr. Beck was just peculiar, and I was convinced of it when, after the meal, he offered me a cigar.

I said, "No, thanks," politely, but I was really shocked. I mean, he shouldn't push cigars on a kid. I figured that maybe, because Marcia is an only child, her parents treat her differently, but after supper when we were alone in the living room and Mr. Beck was listening to Jack Benny on the radio in the room he called his study, Marcia said it was just his way of being sarcastic.

"But why to me?" I asked. "Why are they all so sarcastic to me?"

"If you don't mind my telling you," Marcia said, "it's your own fault. You have a masochistic streak that brings out the sadist in my father. It's a classical sado-masochistic relationship."

I felt a warm glow of pleasure at her neat way of putting it. I wasn't sure of what it all meant, but it proved that she had been thinking about me. "Why don't we take a walk?" I said.

"I don't know. I still have some work to do, and my drama report for English on *Hamlet*."

I said, "Great. I'll tell you all about it while we walk."

"You?"

"Sure. I read it last term."

"Oh—that would help." Marcia hesitated, and her mother came in with a slice of Dutch apple pie in a dish. "I found this left over in the refrigerator. Would you like it, Davey?"

I said, "Thanks," and I ate it along with a glass of milk she brought me "just to wash it down."

Marcia's father, who came into the room just then, saw me finishing it and said, "Oh my God!"

"Now stop it, Ralph!" Mrs. Beck said sharply. She turned to me. "Why don't you and Marcia take a walk and get some fresh air?"

"And get back before ten!" her father called after us.

We walked up to Fort Tryon Heights and into the park. It was that time of day when it's so blue you can't really tell the true color of things. Everything was a different shade of blue except the sky, which was pink and lavender, like a box of Valentine chocolates.

Marcia said, "Tell me what *Hamlet* was about."

Well, there was no problem there. If there's one thing I'm good at, it's telling stories. I have a natural talent for it. I told her the entire play, and I must say I told it well, weaving in all the tangled elements that make the play so confusing. I thought I was particularly good with Ophelia, but when I was finished, Marcia didn't say anything. She just gave a deep sigh, of sympathy with Hamlet's problem, I figured. I said, "Let's sit down here where we can see the river."

It was a beautiful view. You could see the whole river, from the George Washington Bridge way down to the harbor. And the lights! There were so many of them. Below the bridge the skyline of the City showed up dark against the lavender sky, only it was changing from lavender to deep blue.

"Is that all you got out of Hamlet?" Marcia asked, sitting down on the bench next to me. "What about the symbolism? Didn't it mean anything to you?"

"Symbolism?"

"Of course! The whole play is full of it."

I felt annoyed. After all my trouble, she had to bring up something like symbolism. Who cares about that when the story is good? But I decided not to argue. I put my arm along the back of the bench, very casually, not really touching her but so close I could feel the warmth of her body in my fingers. Then I kind of willed her to lean back with all my might. Sometimes, if you do that, a sort of telepathic power can affect the other person. In *Amazing Stories* it's called telekinesis.

It must have affected Marcia in reverse, because she leaned forward and gestured at the lights. "What do they mean to you, Davey?"

I knew what I was expected to answer because we had been through this kind of routine before; once in the seventh grade, when Marcia had tried to straighten me out about how important it was to get the best possible marks in junior high, and then again in the tenth grade, when she explained how high school was a sort of testing ground for tomorrow.

I started to say, "Just lights," but because I could see that she looked disappointed, I decided to show off a bit. I may not know French, but I do know physics. "I mean some are electric and some are fluorescent. That gives them the sparkling effect, that flicker with the neon adding the color, though actually I should say argon,

31

krypton, and zenon. Those are the other gases used for different colors, but neon is like a generic name."

"No, Davey," she said with a kind of tender disgust, and I knew I had loused up the whole thing. "I mean, what do the lights symbolize? I mean, in terms of what's really behind them."

It wasn't cold out, but I began to shiver while she was speaking. Sometimes I react to Marcia like that, sometimes when we're alone and I'm trying to get up enough guts to make a pass. I really wanted to touch her, to hold her even if I didn't actually kiss her, and the thought of her little breasts pushing out through her jacket and pressing against me made me feel weak.

I said, "Why are you always talking in terms of symbols? Why be so intellectual? Why not just feel things? If something's beautiful, enjoy it. Don't look for symbols." I thought that was all pretty deep, but mainly I said it because it gave me a chance to wave my hands and brush against her upper arms.

But I might just as well have been a tree branch, for all the notice she took. "That's the trouble with you, Davey!" she cried out. "The whole world is falling apart, and you talk about feeling things. Do you have any idea of what's happening in Europe? In Germany, in Italy? Do you realize Germany is going to annex the Danzig corridor, and Mussolini is bombing innocent people in Ethiopia? Davey, the world is going up in flames!"

"I've got enough trouble worrying about what's happening right here," I said stubbornly. "You have no idea of the job trouble I have, to say nothing of school!"

She brushed her hair back, and my chest got that sinking feeling like when you look down from a tall building, and the shivering was so bad I had to grit my teeth to keep them from chattering.

"Don't you ever read the papers, Davey?"

I said, "Of course I do. Pop brings the *Daily News* home every night. I read all about Helen Hayes getting sued as a love pirate!" What I didn't tell her was that the first thing I read in the *News,* and usually the only thing, is *Terry and the Pirates*. I'm crazy about Burma and the Dragon Lady! But I wouldn't tell that to Marcia. I don't think she'd understand.

She said, "The *Daily News!*" in a disgusted voice. "You aren't interested in what's going on here either," Marcia went on impatiently. "Where were you when we had the big peace strike at school?"

I took a big chance, and I grabbed her hand as if I were carried away by the argument. "What good does a peace strike do? All that stuff about boycotting imperialist Japan . . ." I wanted to show her I was up on current events too.

"Well, I'll only wear lisle stockings!" She pulled her hand loose to brush back her hair, and I swore to myself for being so klutzy. I'd grabbed the wrong hand! She was so excited, I was sure she'd have let me hold the other. "Even if the boycott doesn't work, at least I know that I'm doing something. I just wish there were something I could really do about Germany. Do you know, Mom still has relatives over there."

I nodded sympathetically. My arm was back on the bench, and I figured that now I could let it drop and land on her shoulder because she was leaning back, and if she objected I could always blame it on the heat of the argument. So I said, "Doing something about Germany means going to war, and how does that go with peace strikes?"

"You just don't understand."

I decided to give in graciously. "Well, maybe you're right about Japan." And I dropped my hand to where her shoulder should have been, but it wasn't. I almost tumbled sideways on the bench because she had jumped to her feet and was facing me with angry eyes, and I was wondering if that damned telekinesis was any good at all.

"Maybe I'm right! You always give in like that, Davey. Can't you think for yourself?"

That wasn't fair. That business about war and the peace strike was pretty good thinking, but I didn't want to get her angrier. Instead I grinned. "Why should I, when you think for me, and you do it so much better?"

That didn't get much more than a shrug, but I could tell she wasn't angry anymore. We started walking again, and I said, "You know, Marcia, I was just kidding around. I agree with all your ideas."

"All what ideas?"

I shrugged uncomfortably. I'd gone too far again. "You know, Italy, Germany, Japan . . ." And I took her hand, trying to be casual. I bent my elbow and that put our forearms together, and I felt a tingle go through me. But Marcia made a tsking sound and pulled her arm away.

"I'm perfectly capable of walking without support."

I said, "Boy, you sure are!" But she didn't get that, or pretended not to. Back at her apartment, I said good night, and was just about to take a chance on trying to kiss her, since she was between me and the door and was fishing in her purse for her key and couldn't have ducked inside, when she looked at me very seriously and said, "You know, Davey, in spite of all your faults, you know what I like about you?"

I moved in a little closer, but before I lunged, my curiosity got the better of me. "What do you like about me?" I asked.

"You respect my integrity. Good night, Davey."

I walked home trying to figure out just what the hell that meant. It wasn't late, and Sam and Rhea were still at the apartment, Sam and Pop playing two-handed pinochle, and Rhea listening to Lily Pons on WABC. I went into the kitchen to get some milk and a sandwich, and Sam came in after he had finished the hand. "I want to talk to you, Davey."

I said, "What about?"

He sat down on the edge of the table and scratched his head. "You know, I don't want you to get the idea that we're all down on you for what happened with that dame when you ran an errand for the cleaners."

I shrugged. "Well, it's my word against hers."

"Don't crap me, Davey." He grinned suddenly and, reaching up, ruffled my hair. "I'd rather you got your ashes hauled this way instead of getting some doll your own age in trouble. I just wanted to—well . . ." He twisted uncomfortably on the table and put his other foot on the ground. "You and me, we never talked about, well, you know, sex."

"Sex?"

"Sex."

"Oh." I swallowed the milk and said, "Well . . ."

34

Sam said, "Yeah. You know, there's a lot more to it than just shtupping someone."

I remembered some of the things Mrs. Bell had shown me, and I said, "I guess there is."

"I mean, there's VD and knocking someone up—you use anything, Davey?"

I didn't know what he meant at first, and then it dawned on me. I felt very uncomfortable talking like that with my own brother, and I just shrugged and tried not to meet his eyes.

"Well, do you?" Sam insisted.

"You mean to—to not to—that is . . ."

"Yeah, sure, that's what I mean."

I hadn't thought about it, and I never would have had the nerve to try and buy something like that in a drugstore. Sam shook his head. "You gotta use protection, Davey. You gotta worry about VD."

Since Mrs. Bell was married, I hadn't figured I had anything to worry about, and anyway, it looked as if I wouldn't be seeing any more of her, but Sam wouldn't let it drop. "Well, you should take a leak afterward. That's supposed to clean you out."

Embarrassed, I stared down at my sandwich, which reminded me I was hungry, so I took a bite. "Here," Sam said abruptly. "Take this and keep it in your wallet."

I took what he was handing me, and saw a pack of three condoms labeled Merry Widow. It gave me a start because my only contact with them had been when one of the kids in home room blew some of them up and floated them around the room before Mrs. Drochenko, our home-room teacher, came in. She pretended not to notice them, but then what else could she do?

I swallowed uncomfortably and said, "Gee, Sam. Pop wouldn't like me carrying these around."

"Well, don't use them when Pop's watching!" He gave a big guffaw and stood up. "Don't worry about Pop, Davey. He knows the score. Just be careful."

I mumbled, "Thanks, Sam." And then he went in to get Rhea and they left. I got my books ready for the morning and fell asleep that night dreaming that Marcia and I were holding hands and running down the long flight of stone steps that led from Fort Tryon

Park to Riverside Drive. It felt so good I decided to climb back up and do it again, but I woke up before I could, and I was cuddled into Pop. I had to turn the other way very slowly so I wouldn't wake him.

It took me a long time to fall asleep after that, and I kept watching the curtain at the window blowing into the room and listening to Pop snore. Snoring is a very comforting sound at night.

▪ CHAPTER FOUR ▪

My brother Sam kept his word and pulled a few strings here and there. "I can't get you in at the local branch," he said after a week of trying. "The librarian I know best is at One Hundred Fifty-seventh Street, and she'll have to request you there."

In the meanwhile I had to go down to Forty-second Street for an interview at the main personnel office where they asked me all sorts of questions, and I had to get forms signed at school for my working papers and then get a social security number. When I complained about all the trouble to Pop, he said, "You think it'll hurt you to work with books, David? Maybe a little will rub off on you. In this country, without an education you're nothing."

"I'm getting an education in school," I said before I could catch myself.

That was the cue Pop was waiting for. "A fine education. You're even flunking in art."

"Not flunking, Pop. That was just a deportment slip you had to sign."

What had happened was that I was giving my imitation of King Kong trapped on top of the Empire State Building. The movie was a few years old, but it was still showing around, and everyone was walking through the corridors at school hunched over with their fists dangling a few feet from the floor, grunting like Kong.

In art we have high stools, almost as high as the regular desks, and that morning, while Mrs. Burgess, our teacher, was out for a few minutes, I did my imitation for the class, mainly for Marcia, who couldn't stop laughing. The more she laughed, the better I got.

I climbed the stool the way Kong climbed the Empire State Building, and I had the little wooden mannequin we used to sketch from in my hand with my hankerchief around it. That was Fay Wray. I stood on top of the stool making buzzing noises like the airplanes and grabbing at them while I rumbled in my throat and occasionally drooled over little Fay.

Even though I usually keep to myself outside of school, I'm still pretty popular with the kids—mainly because of stunts like this. They were all shouting encouragement, and I was concentrating on the buzzing airplanes while every now and then I'd turn to look at Fay with pathetic longing—she was so small and I was so big! I was going great, completely lost in my role, when all of a sudden I noticed that the class was quiet, and Marcia, who was in the row facing me, had her hand over her mouth and was staring at the door.

I gave one last feeble buzz and a lunge, then turned my head to see Mrs. Burgess and Mr. Saperstein, the head of the Art Department, staring at me from the doorway.

I just crouched there until Mr. Saperstein said, "Well, yes, Mrs. Burgess. I agree the class is overcrowded, but their work habits are unusual."

I climbed down and put the wooden mannequin on an empty desk, tucking my handkerchief back in my pocket. Mrs. Burgess was very red in the face, and she didn't say anything else, just walked to her desk and began looking over the drawings that were there. But after class she called me up and handed me a deportment slip. "Have that signed at home and report to the detention room after school for a week. No—make it two weeks, Quinn."

I knew she was mad when she called me Quinn. Usually she calls me David, because I'm pretty good in art. I have a real talent for lettering.

I said, "I'm sorry, Mrs. Burgess, but I already have as many detentions as I can handle."

"Then start these next week."

"I have detentions for the rest of the term."

"I see." She shook her head. "I suppose some of you like to live dangerously. Maybe we can start next term off with a week of detentions. Get that slip signed."

That was why Pop could accuse me of flunking art. And for all I knew, I might flunk it. If I did, it would probably be the first case of anyone flunking art in the history of the school. I didn't think Mrs. Burgess would do that, but whatever mark I ended up with sure wasn't going to help my average. I wondered how important a good high school average was in the job market. There was a lot of unemployment around, but for that matter I was already a working man, even with my low average.

The one thing I had forgotten to ask was how much I'd get at the new job. I didn't find that out until I got a notice to report to the library on Monday. They were paying thirty-five cents an hour.

With two hours five days and eight hours on Saturday, it came to about $6.30 a week, which was about as much as I had pulled down delivering orders after school. "But it's respectable work," Pop pointed out. "You're getting culture with every book you put away."

"But I don't get anything for myself."

Pop nodded. He knew what I meant. With the delivery job I kicked in to Pop whatever the cleaner or butcher or grocer paid me for delivering, but I kept half the tips. That usually gave me a nice pocketful of change.

Pop said, "As of now, we'll increase your allowance. You'll get two dollars a week."

I said, "Carfare to the library is going to cost me sixty cents a week, and if I get milk for lunch each day, that's another quarter, and if I buy lunch out on Saturdays, that's another quarter, and a couple of candy bars during the week, maybe three, that's another fifteen cents. That's a dollar and a quarter, and it leaves me only seventy-five cents."

"It's amazing how quick you are at this kind of math, but math in school you can't do."

That hurt. Math had kept me going in terms of my average. I said, "I got ninety-five in math last term!"

"What happened to the extra five?"

38

You can't argue with Pop. "Make the allowance two fifty?"

"Two twenty-five. It's a deal." Pop put out his hand and I shook it. I knew it was the best I could get. Pop automatically bargains about everything. Even with shopkeepers. Whenever I need clothes, I meet him at the dress factory where he works. It's in a big loft near Thirty-second Street, and we take the subway down to the Lower East Side and go into one of the discount stores. Pop looks at the clothes, asks the price, and immediately offers a few cents less.

He did it once in Macy's with Sam and Rhea along, and Rhea wouldn't speak to him for a week. But you know, in nine cases out of ten, the storekeeper splits the difference. I should have known he'd pull it with me. Still, the allowance wasn't bad. The library was within walking distance of school and home, and I could save my carfare.

I reported for my first day at the library on Monday. Sam had given me all kinds of advice, and he'd tried to teach me a little about shelving books. "Whatever you do," he ended up, "be polite. None of this smart-ass stuff."

"I'm always polite!"

"That's what I mean."

"Leave him alone," Pop said. "They'll like David. I just think you should come home from school first and put on a clean shirt." That was another pet theory of Pop's. Everyone respected you if you wore a clean shirt. "It doesn't matter if the collars and cuffs are frayed a little as long as it's clean."

Sam shrugged. "Well, all I can tell you, kid, is don't shit on your own doorstep."

Rhea said, "Sam!" and Pop said, "Now what's that supposed to mean?"

Sam winked at me. "Davey knows." But I really didn't know what he meant.

The branch of the Public Library System where I was to work was an old-fashioned three-story building, and the children's department was in the basement, with its own entrance. In the back of the children's room was the magazine room, where all the periodicals were bound. Upstairs was the adult section, half a flight up from the street. Between the reference room and the top floor, off a landing, was the staff room. This had a little kitchenette and a couch where the librarians could lie down. It was, Miss Marx explained pleasantly, off limits to me.

Miss Marx had known Sam when he worked in the library, and she looked on him as the son she never had—at least that's what she told me in a moment of confidence. She was a white-haired little woman, nearly seventy, and she walked with two canes. She had a ranch, would you believe it, on the Hopi Indian Reservation or near it. She was kind of crusty, and most of the librarians didn't like her, but I thought she was great.

Harold Pennington, the other page, a mean little twerp who looked about ten but was seventeen, said she was a hard-up old maid. "She takes it out on everyone," he squeaked. That was my first Saturday at the library, and he was showing me how to bind magazines in the periodical room.

He ripped the cover off a copy of *Life,* drilled holes through the spine, and bent a heavy piece of red manila cardboard around to fit. Then he attached it with black shoemaker's thread and glued on the cover. *"Voilà! Un magazine."*

That was the thing that annoyed me most about Pennington. I could take the little squirt's bum jokes, like calling the fiction "friction," and twisting the names of books around so that for *Tale of Two Cities* he always said *Sale of Two Titties,* or his meanness, like telling the kids who were looking for books the wrong Dewey Decimal Number just to confuse them. I could even take his smoking in the men's room and stinking it up, or changing the date on the stamping machine when I had to take over the desk. I didn't like any of it, but none of it bothered me as much as his using French all the time. That killed me!

Pennington went to Haron High School and had a 98 average. He told me that three times the first day we met. He had never gotten less than a 100 in math or biology. Even with the library job he kept his average up. I felt bad about that but good about his corroded face. He had the worst case of blazing acne I'd ever seen. I've seen grown men shudder when they looked at him.

Besides all that, I didn't like what he had said about Miss Marx. Maybe she was an old maid, but she was pretty decent to me. The library frightened me at first. There were just so many books. I didn't think I'd ever learn where they all belonged.

"It all goes by the Dewey Decimal System," Miss Marx explained the first day I was on the floor.

I nodded. "We learned a little about it in school."

"Do you remember what you learned?"

"I'm not much good at remembering schoolwork," I said unhappily.

She smiled at that. "None of it?"

"Just the name. I always confused it with Thomas E. Dewey and Manila Bay."

"Two other Deweys, but it's a start. All the system is is a means for filing away books on the shelves and then retrieving them. Every book in the library is either fiction or nonfiction, pretense or real."

"Are all nonfiction books real?" I asked curiously.

She looked at me sharply. "As much as all fiction is pretense. Fiction is kept over here, A to Z by author. You see, there's no number on the back of a fiction book. Every other book has a code mark . . ." She took me from shelf to shelf, explaining all the numbers. "It's just a matter of fitting all the books in and edging the shelves."

The way she explained it made it very simple and fun too. I didn't have any trouble after that.

Besides Miss Marx, there were Miss Casey, the head of the children's room, very sweet and sort of vague, and Miss Percy, who ran the main floor. They were about the same age, thirty-something-or-other, but Miss Percy had gray-black hair and very sharp, alert eyes. She was as wide awake as Miss Casey was half-asleep.

Mrs. Jackson was in charge of the reference room, and she was a comfortable, round fiftyish. She had very dark skin, but she wore very light-blond and red wigs. There were others, at least two junior librarians in each department, but the four—Mrs. Jackson, Miss Percy, Miss Casey, and of course Miss Marx—were department heads.

Miss Percy was my favorite, I guess, because I used to kid around with her so much, and I even called her Percy. I liked the fact that she never touched up her hair. Somehow the streaky black-and-gray was just right for her face. "I was an old lady at thirteen," she told me one evening when we were alone at the front desk. "At least that's what my mother always told me."

"You're kidding me, Percy."

"Well, maybe not in so many words. My father was off in the army, during the war, and I had three younger brothers, just babies really. It seemed that everything was up to me, all the housework, the feeding, the cleaning. Mom had to go to work. We couldn't possibly get along on Daddy's army pay."

She used to go on like that for hours, telling me all about what it was like to be a teenager during the World War, and it wasn't so nice, to hear her talk. Still, she'd always end it with a joke, usually on herself. She was always poking fun at herself, and I don't know why, because except for her gray hair, she was a swell-looking woman.

Miss Casey, the head of the children's room, was altogether different. She was very pretty in a delicate way. Percy used to call her a washed-out Southern belle, with a sort of twist to her mouth, and I guess maybe that did describe her. She had come north a long time ago, but she still had a soft Southern accent. Her dresses were all flowery and made of some clingy material.

Sometimes, from the back, I'd get her mixed up with the kids. She was very thin and small, and she wore her dark-blond hair long, the way the kids do, and she used pink lipstick instead of red. Her eyes were a very pretty pale blue. The only trouble was, her face looked as if someone had started to erase it and then had stopped halfway. According to Pennington, she nipped gin all afternoon, but I never saw her do it.

But even with that sort of vague look, she was very much alive. I found that out the third Saturday I was working at the library. I was in the children's room cleaning up after closing when she came up behind me and said, "I have some pictures to hang in the upstairs exhibit room."

It had taken me a good half hour to clean up the mess after the last kid left. Most of the time I noticed Miss Casey watching me, and I kept wondering if I was doing something wrong, like shelving books in the wrong spot.

Anyway, I was glad to know she was looking at me because she wanted me to hang pictures, and I said, sure, I'd like to help her, with such enthusiasm that she looked surprised and then smiled at me, a slow, sort of pleased smile.

I kept remembering that smile because it took the half-erased look away from her face and made her seem a little too bright and glittery. I felt uneasy about it too, especially when we were both upstairs on the top floor. The reference room was closed, and there was only the downstairs adult section open. Miss Percy was working there alone, since Saturday night is pretty slow.

Miss Casey locked the door to the exhibit room and pulled the door shade down. "Just so no one will interrupt us, David."

I couldn't understand that because no one used the hall anyway, but I decided that her smile was sweet, and the way she chewed her fingernails while she studied the wall was kind of like a kid. She stopped me when I reached for the light pull. "Leave it off, David. There's still enough daylight."

She stepped back and frowned. "Now let's see. There's a stepladder in the closet." She stepped to the table and started leafing through the pile of prints I had brought up for her. "I want this exhibit to have significance for young people, to be political without being obvious. Now what do you think of this?"

She held up a poster of a woman leading a group of men in front of what looked like a steel mill. The woman had one fist up and seemed to be shouting. The colors were very raw, red and black. It sure looked significant, and I knew Marcia would have liked it. It kind of yelled out, "Workers of the world, unite!"

"I think it's . . ." I searched for a good word. ". . . kind of exciting." It was pretty political too, but I kept my mouth shut about that. As long as she liked it.

"Exciting!" She caressed the word. "Yes, I think it is exciting—and significant." She squinted at the wall. "Try it there, David. About five feet up."

I climbed the ladder and held the print against the wall while she got a box of hangers ready. "Yes, that's it. No—perhaps a bit higher. No, that's too high. Here, let me show you."

She came across the room, and before I could get down, she'd climbed the ladder behind me and put her arms around me to arrange the picture. I froze on the ladder and almost dropped the picture because she was so close. I could smell her, a sweet and clean smell like the sheets smell when I take them off the line on the roof. I stood there stiff as a board, while she moved the picture to just where she wanted it. Then she climbed down and said, "Perfect. Print it."

"Print it?"

She giggled. "They say that when they're shooting a movie and the take is perfect."

I fastened the picture and asked her, "Were you ever in the movies, Miss Casey?" I took a long time fastening the picture, trying to calm myself down.

"Not really in the movies. I did a little summer stock, and I had a few small parts in some plays back home with our local theater, but I just didn't have what it takes, I guess. It's a good thing I went to library school."

I put the ladder against the far wall and starting hanging the rest of the prints. They were all like the first, dramatic and very political, strikes and marches and a few from overseas showing Hitler's storm troopers and Mussolini's goons. I made a mental note to tell Marcia to come see this exhibit.

It was slow work, because I never seemed to get the pictures exactly where she wanted them, and she had to keep climbing up behind me to adjust them. Finally I said, "Gee, I'm sorry I'm so klutzy about this, Miss Casey."

She smiled and said, "I don't think you're a bit klutzy, David." She started down the ladder, and then gave a little cry as her foot caught, and she grabbed at me to hold on. She kept holding on till I turned around on the ladder to help her down. We were face to face then, only she was below me, and she moved her hand around behind me, and I was relieved, but only for a moment, because then she moved her head against me and both arms were around me.

I swallowed and said, "Can I get down, Miss Casey?"

Without moving, she said, "Why, David?"

"Because it's very uncomfortable doing this on a ladder."

"But you're not angry with me?"

I said, "Gee, Miss Casey, I'm not angry at all. In fact, I'm very glad." I said that because you could tell Miss Casey was old-fashioned, I mean her dress and that sweet, clean perfume she was wearing, and I didn't want her to be hurt. You could also tell she was the kind of person who liked gallant things, and while I'm not too good at saying them, I decided to give it a try.

She was smiling up at me, and she laughed just a little, and suddenly I didn't know what to say to be gallant, and in the condition I was in, it was sort of embarrassing—but not to Miss Casey. She climbed down and whirled around in a little dance step, her skirt flying around her, and then, as I stepped off the ladder, she pulled me to her, and I don't know who kissed whom, but it sure happened!

She said, very softly but with a funny kind of intentness, "I want you, David, right now, right here!"

Not only to be polite but because I really meant it, I said, "And I want you too, Miss Casey, but it's not very private here."

She grabbed the buckle of my belt and pulled me to her, her back against one of the tables. Her voice had lost the teasing, flirty quality, and it was very businesslike. "I locked the door."

"But the custodian . . ."

"He's having dinner, and Percy's busy in the adult department. Stop talking so much and hurry."

While she was saying that she bent back on the table. I was glad that Mrs. Bell had taught me as much as she had, and it wasn't all new to me. I was also glad that I was used to doing what older women told me to. I mean, I'm not a fresh kid. When a grown-up tells me to do something, I do it!

It's funny how different this whole business can be. I mean with different women. I kept thinking of that while we maneuvered around on the edge of the table. It had been very different with Mrs. Bell—maybe not better, but different. I'll say one thing for Miss Casey, when it got down to the nitty-gritty, she knew exactly what she wanted and didn't give me a chance to make any mistakes.

Afterward, when I had hung the rest of the pictures and straightened up the exhibit room, she became very vague and flirty again. When we were ready to leave the room she smiled at me sweetly and said, "Thank you, David."

Politely, I said, "You're welcome, Miss Casey. Anytime."

She took a last look around the room and sighed. "I do want the

45

exhibit to be contemporary and exciting. You did think it was exciting, David."

I wasn't sure just what she was referring to, but I said, "Oh yes, very exciting."

"Good. The library can be a dreadfully stuffy place, and so conservative. Well, I'll run down to the staff room and fix my hair. Thanks again, David."

"Not at all."

After she had gone I suddenly remembered what Sam had given me. I snapped my fingers and said, "Damn!" and I took the stairs to the men's lavatory two at a time. At least I could follow his advice and take a leak now.

Walking home along the Drive to save a nickel in carfare, I shrugged philosophically. What the hell. How many things could happen? I could get VD or Miss Casey could have a baby. I was sure Miss Casey wasn't the type to have VD, but I wasn't sure about the baby. Anyway, the whole thing was beyond my control now, and Pop had always told me it was wrong to worry about things you couldn't do anything about. I looked at the orange glow of the street lights reflected from the mist over Riverside Drive, and I thought, maybe I'm learning about life.

Then I figured if I cut east at 181st Street, I could stop at the deli and have a dog and a knish and finish it off with an ice-cream cone. That at least would take the edge off my appetite before supper.

▪ CHAPTER FIVE ▪

The job at the library wasn't too bad, and with all my detentions I was able to get most of my homework done before I left school. That was a help because it was hard doing my homework at home after three or four hours in the library. Lifting armfuls of books was like using dumbbells, and while my arms and shoulders began to swell up with muscles, it still left me tired—or maybe that was because of Miss Casey.

I had no idea there were so many art exhibits that had to go up and be taken down and rearranged. She'd come into the periodical room after the children's room closed and say, "Are you free to give me some help, David?"

Then up we'd go, and the whole thing would start again. She always began with me on the stepladder arranging pictures as if nothing had happened the last time. She must have had some kind of fixation about ladders, and tables too. The second time we went upstairs I put my arms around her as soon as she locked the door, or at least I tried to. She pushed me away almost as if she were insulted and said, "Now, David, we're here to hang pictures."

I felt terrible, really embarrassed, and for a minute I wondered if I hadn't made the whole thing up in my head. You read about kids doing that. I couldn't even look her straight in the eyes. But then she had me get out the stepladder, and she pulled down the door shade and began with the "No, it's too high—no, too low," and I had a terrible case of that thing we learned about in biology, déjà vu.

I was all confused when she came up behind me on the ladder, and then all of a sudden I knew it was all real, and I hadn't made any of it up. The other thing was the table. The first time it happened I figured it was because she was in a hurry. But the exhibit room had a couch along one wall, and when I tried to steer her toward it, she shook her head. She wanted the table again!

Once or twice, okay. But every time? Every Monday, Wednesday, and Friday, when the children's room closed? It began to make me wonder, and it was always Miss Casey and David, very formal, as if what I was doing to her on the table were something neither of us knew anything about.

I couldn't figure her out, and there was no one I could talk it over with. Saul Greenspan was my closest friend, but still, we weren't that close. Outside of the Aviary Club, which met in school at noon each Friday, we hardly saw each other. The things we had most in common were finches' eggs. The Aviary Club had a cage with four finches in a corner of the Biology Room, but the finches didn't do so well. They'd build a nest; one would lay some eggs; and before the

47

eggs could be hatched, the others would continue building the nest over the eggs. Saul and I would take the nests down a layer from time to time, but the eggs never hatched.

"It could be they're all female and the eggs are sterile," Saul suggested once, but we had no way of determining the sex of a bird when males and females had the same plumage.

Anyway, I didn't think I could discuss Miss Casey with Saul, because we hadn't even solved the case of the sterile finches. I didn't have any other close friends outside of school, though sometimes I'd get together with the other kids on the block, usually on a Sunday afternoon in an empty lot near our house. We'd play one-a-cat with a sawed-off broomstick, or else we'd sit around on the billboard and throw the bull. Some of the kids had built a platform on the struts behind the billboard, and only the older kids could climb up there, so it was kind of like a private clubhouse.

Whenever I joined the kids there, they'd be telling each other all sorts of lies about the girls they had tried to make it with. I knew they were lies, and so did the others, but you couldn't really ask them about something like Miss Casey. They'd never believe it to begin with, and I wouldn't blame them. I wouldn't believe it myself if one of them told me a story like this.

That's why I never mentioned Mrs. Bell or Miss Casey to the kids. All we talked about was how we'd like to make out with the girls in school, and Artie Wagner claimed he had, but I didn't believe him.

I couldn't talk about it to Sam either, especially since it happened in the library. He had gotten me the job there, and I thought he'd really be sore as hell if he found out what I was doing. That left only Pop to get advice from, and there were some things I just didn't talk to Pop about. I could never reach him on politics or how to make a decent soup without putting everything into it—and of course sex.

One evening, though, I really tried. We were sitting at the kitchen table, and I was doing my geometry, or I had started to do it, but I kind of got carried away by the problem of how many lines could be tangent to a circle, and I was trying to find out by constructing them, which, of course, is the wrong way to do it, but it makes a swell design. Pop was sitting across the table making fruit salad, which is one of his favorite jobs. He stops at the fruit store at least once a week and buys a whole load of "touched" fruit, fruit that is almost spoiled but not quite. At any rate, it's too spoiled to sell. The pears and apples have spots, and the oranges and grapefruits have little spots of green mold around soft circles. Biologically, I find it fascinating.

Pop cuts the bad spots away, then peels and cuts the fruit up into fresh fruit salad for the entire week. He says the spots don't matter as long as he's making salad out of it. "You think you get it any fresher in a restaurant?" he always asks defensively.

But it really used to bug Sam when he'd catch Pop doing it. That was before Sam was married. "For the few lousy cents you save . . ."

"I work hard for those few lousy cents," Pop said mildly, "and besides, fresh fruit salad every morning is healthy for David, and it's worth a little work."

"Then use fresh fruit, for Chrissake!"

"Don't swear. You can't tell the difference."

"Well, maybe you can't, but I can. Those rotten oranges you can taste a mile away."

Pop stopped it for a while, but after Sam got married and moved out, he began buying touched fruit again, first making me promise not to tell. It didn't matter to me. In fact, I kind of liked the sour-orange taste.

Now Pop sat there cutting the oranges, and I said, "Pop, don't you ever feel you want to go out?"

"I go out every day."

"No, I mean, you know, go out."

"So I go out every day."

"Well, what about a woman, Pop? Don't you ever feel you need a woman?"

He shrugged. "I used to have a woman in to clean once in a while while Sam was still living at home and I was working by Fine Frocks." Fine Frocks was the one good job Pop had had for as far back as I could remember. He was making fifty dollars a week, but it only lasted six months. "I don't need a woman now." He shook his head. "The house doesn't get so dirty with just the two of us."

I almost gave up. "Pop!" I said. "Don't you ever feel you want to go to bed with a woman?"

He put down the knife, and he was silent for a minute, then he sighed. "David, spill me a glass water, and run it until it's cold." When I came back with the water, he said, "Your mother's been dead over thirteen years." He took off his glasses, and I sat there waiting for him to say something else, but he didn't. I realized then that I couldn't get any advice about sex out of Pop. I just gave it up and coasted along.

The children's room closed early on Saturdays, and Miss Casey was usually gone by six. I still didn't understand her, even after two months had gone by. She just didn't act the way I expected her to. It wasn't only the crazy stepladder bit and the top-of-the-table routine, but she always wanted me to finish up so quickly, not at all like Mrs. Bell.

I began to wonder if what Mrs. Bell had taught me was all wrong. At least I thought I wouldn't have any use for it anymore. If Miss Casey was right, the idea was to finish as soon as possible, which was where I'd started. Only if I believed Mrs. Bell, that was all wrong.

And then I walked Miss Percy home one evening, and things began to fall into a different perspective. We had both locked up the desk in the main adult section, and I had stopped to talk to Mr. Duffy, the custodian. We'd talked about his son for a while because I enjoyed talking to Mr. Duffy. Mr. Duffy is divorced, and he has a mentally retarded son, Paul, who has been living with him for ten years. Paul had just started in a special school for retarded kids, and he was making a lot of progress. "Paul's a good boy," Mr. Duffy assured me. "Sure, he hasn't got it all up here, but he's good, you know?"

I nodded and he said, "Paul never hangs around with bad boys, you know? Never gets into trouble. He plays the piano, you know, good, too, and he looks at pictures in the magazines. I let him go through all the magazines in the periodical room, and he never hurts them, you know?"

"He plays the piano?" That surprised me.

"Sure. He plays good too, you know. They tested him at the

school and they said he was a musical genius, but now they're teaching him to read. Just a little, you know, but they're teaching him."

Paul had never learned to read, but I didn't think that was too bad. There's never anything good to read in the newspapers, and maybe if you couldn't read them, the world wouldn't seem so terrible.

But Mr. Duffy now, having a boy like Paul, ordinarily you'd think it was pretty sad, but it didn't work out that way. Paul was good company for Mr. Duffy, especially since he was home most of the time; I mean, living behind the library and being its custodian. Sometimes he'd show me pictures of Paul, and he was very nice-looking. He didn't look twenty, but he didn't have that funny look some mental people get. He just looked like what Mr. Duffy said he was, a good boy.

I was thinking of that when I finally got downstairs and I was relieved that Pennington had already gone. I thought I'd like to be alone and walk home. I wanted to think about Marcia by myself.

Mrs. Arnold, one of the reference librarians, was standing in front of the building, and she gave me a big smile, and then her husband drove up in a yellow Willys, a really nifty car. "Want a lift, David?" she called out, but I shook my head. "No, thanks," and I waved as they drove off. I really love cars, and I know every make, and I'm sure I could drive one if I ever got the chance, but that's not likely because Pop could never afford one.

I had just buttoned up my pea jacket, when I heard Miss Percy say, "Why, David; aren't you gone?"

I said, "Hi, Percy. How come you're so late?"

"Oh, a few little odd jobs." She frowned and chewed her lip. "I'll never get a cab now, and I hate to walk alone after dark. Which way are you going, David?"

"Uptown," I said, and she smiled. "Good. So am I. You don't mind walking with me, do you, David?"

I had to say no. "Of course I don't mind, Percy."

She linked her arm through mine and laughed, a sort of high-pitched laugh. "I hope none of your friends see us, David, and think I'm your girlfriend."

I didn't think that was very likely, because even if it weren't for her hair, which was pretty gray, no one was going to take Miss Percy for anything less than thirty. She lived all the way over on Riverside Drive in a very nice apartment house that overlooked the river. "I have a view of the Palisades and the bridge, and on a clear day I can even watch the ferry boat go back and forth."

She had been talking steadily all the way across town, and now, in front of her house, she opened her pocketbook. For one awful minute I thought she was going to tip me, but actually she was just getting her keys out. Still looking in her bag, she said, "David, would you like to come up for a minute?"

I said, "What for, Percy?"

She bit her lip, then found her keys and looked up with a very bright smile. "Why, I have some very nice banana cake, if you'd like some. After all, it was a long walk and you need your energy."

I hadn't eaten since lunch, and I knew Pop was probably dozing in front of the radio, and there was no telling when we'd get to supper, so I said, "That sounds great."

But it wasn't until we had gotten out of the elevator and Miss Percy had opened the apartment door that I began to wonder if all she had in mind was cake. Then I told myself, David Quinn, you're nuts. It happens once or twice, and you look at every nice woman as if she were a sex fiend!

I'd never seen an apartment like Miss Percy's before. The walls were all papered with a red wallpaper that had a bold sort of design on it in black, and the couch had a lot of old-fashioned carved wood but was upholstered in a modern-looking white-and-green-striped satin. It all fit together, though. There were books and papers and magazines all over the place, on shelves and on tables and even on chairs. There were hundreds of records, too.

She put one on the turntable and said, "This is a samba, David, the kind of music they play in Brazil. Listen to the beat, the one in the background. Do you like it?"

It was funny. When she talked about the music, her voice was different, sort of low and sad, with none of the high-pitched giggle left in it. I felt sorry for her without knowing why.

She took me into the kitchen, and she wasn't kidding about the cake. It was banana cake with a tall white frosting sprinkled with coconut. She cut me a big slice and poured a glass of milk. Then she took a small slice for herself and heated up a pot of coffee. I stared at the cake and remembered Mrs. Bell and her cake, and I had a funny feeling.

"I'll bet you drink milk. I'll bet you hate coffee."

"I don't hate it," I said, and I grinned because I remembered how on Sunday mornings when I was a kid Pop always used to make me coffee that was half milk and had a lot of sugar. I would dunk buttered hard rolls in it. They were delicious that way.

She looked down at her cake and very softly she said, "Don't smile like that, David."

I didn't know what she meant, but I was beginning to get an uneasy feeling. I said, "Like what, Miss Percy? Did I do something wrong?"

"Keep it Percy, David. Didn't we agree to forget the 'Miss'? Something wrong?" She hesitated. "Oh, Christ!" Suddenly she covered her face with her hands and began to cry. There's one thing that scares me, it's a woman crying; I guess because I just haven't had much experience with women. I mean, our house being an all-male place except for Rhea now and then, and she doesn't count because she doesn't live with us.

I took one last mouthful of cake, and I hurried around the table and said, "Don't cry, Percy." It sounded stupid, but I didn't know what else to say. She looked up at me and her eyes were runny with mascara but very soft, I guess because of the tears, and then suddenly—I honestly don't know how it happened, and I didn't suspect it would—she was standing up and in my arms, and I was kissing her.

Around about then I realized that it was going to be the same as it was with Miss Casey, only no tables, I hoped. I also remembered what Mrs. Bell had taught me about kissing, and I very dutifully began doing it.

To my surprise it was very effective, because Miss Percy got sort of limp, so that I actually had to hold her up, and she started making little noises as if I had hurt her, but when I asked, "Are you all right?" she said, "Oh, yes! Oh, God, yes!" which I took to be a good sign.

I don't really know how we got into the bedroom, but we did, and then she was unbuttoning my shirt and kissing my chest. She kept twisting and turning and saying how wonderful it all was, and things like "Oh, God!" and a few curse words that shocked me because you don't expect a woman to talk like that, especially a librarian.

I figured right then that she was more a Mrs.-Bell type than a Miss-Casey type, and I was glad of that because for one thing the tables in the bedroom all looked kind of flimsy. Anyway, she made me get all undressed, and she did, too, and it was very nice, because I was able to use everything I had learned from Mrs. Bell, and it was all appreciated. It's nice to be appreciated.

Afterward she kept telling me how beautiful I was, and that was kind of embarrassing, so I tried kissing her to keep her quiet till she calmed down, but all that did was to start the whole thing over again.

Later we had some more coconut-banana cake, and then Miss Percy insisted on walking me downstairs and halfway home. I was bothered by that, because I thought she didn't like to be out by herself after dark, but she just laughed when I mentioned it and grabbed my arm, pushing herself close to me.

"You're just afraid someone will see us and think I'm your girlfriend!"

I said, "That could happen too," and she laughed delightedly.

She left me at Broadway, and I walked the rest of the way home trying to puzzle things out. Mrs. Bell and Miss Casey, and now Miss Percy—all of them in so short a time, and I had gone for sixteen years without anything like this happening. Maybe it was just a coincidence, or maybe I was just lucky. I finally stopped thinking and hurried home.

▪ CHAPTER SIX ▪

"Your basic trouble, Davey," Marcia said, "is that you're too trusting. You're too naive. Whatever people tell you, you believe."

We were sitting on the grass in Isham Hill Park on Sunday morning breathing very hard because we had just finished a two-mile run along the park paths. At least I was breathing very hard. Marcia was in good shape, even though she claimed she had to build up her wind for summer camp. In addition to being a waitress, she was counting heavily on a strong track program for the summer, and she kept telling me about the camp's red-clay tennis courts.

My trouble was the two-mile run left me too breathless even to speak, much less discuss my problems. I just nodded and let my head hang, sucking in as many deep breaths as I could.

What Marcia was analyzing was why I had failed my last eco test so completely, even though I'd copied all the answers from Johnny Dorfman, and Johnny had passed. Somehow he knew I was copying and managed to use a phony test paper, something I just couldn't believe.

"You shouldn't have copied Dorfman's answers without thinking about them."

That was easy enough to say, but if you didn't know the material, what good did it do to think about it? Also I found that I tended to drop off to sleep in all my classes, tests or no tests, and I thought that maybe it was because of both Miss Percy and Miss Casey and seeing Mrs. Bell again.

I had run into her in the street one afternoon, and she had taken my hand, very friendly. "Why, David! What a coincidence!"

It wasn't much of a coincidence because I had been walking back and forth on her street for about fifteen minutes before I met her.

When I walked home from the library to save carfare, I would cut through her neighborhood. It wasn't too far out of the way, and I could get there by walking along the Drive where there was always fresh air blowing in from the river. I knew Pop would like that.

"Why don't I see you anymore, David?" she asked, still holding my hand.

"Well, school takes up a lot of my time, and I'm not delivering anymore. I've got a real job in the public library."

"Have you? Isn't that nice." She was sort of massaging my hand as she held it, and it made funny chills go down my back. I mean her hand was so soft.

"I hope I didn't cause any trouble with Mr. Bell," I said.

"Oh, him!" She shrugged him off. "He's on the road now, anyway. Why don't you come upstairs and have a piece of buttercrunch cake."

It was pretty late, but I didn't want to hurt her feelings, and frankly I had been thinking about her cake for weeks. This one was incredible. There were actually little flakes of crunchy candy inside it. She gave me a thick slice with a tall glass of milk and sat across the table watching me while I ate. I was beginning to realize that there's something about my eating that makes a certain kind of woman very happy, like Marcia's mother and Mrs. Bell.

When I'd finished the cake we both went into the bedroom and undressed, and then Mrs. Bell put the lights on because, as she says, "If a thing's worth doing, it's worth looking at."

It's funny how Miss Percy liked dim lights, and Mrs. Bell liked bright lights, and Miss Casey liked tables and ladders. It made me think, and it certainly kept me on my toes.

Mrs. Bell made me go over all the things she had taught me, and she was really surprised that I had learned them as well as I had. "Are you sure you haven't been practicing, Davey?" she asked teasingly.

I said, "You're just a good teacher, Mrs. Bell. I wish I had you for French."

But of course I had been practicing, and what with Miss Percy on Tuesday, Thursday, and Saturday, and Miss Casey on Monday, Wednesday, and Friday, and now Mrs. Bell whenever I could squeeze her in, my wind wasn't so good, to say nothing of my ability to stay awake in class. That was why I had copied Dorfman's answers without even thinking whether they made sense or not.

But I couldn't tell that to Marcia, so I let her finish analyzing my weaknesses while I got my breath back. I was beginning to think that Marcia was definitely interested in me, because, while she still wouldn't let me take her out on a regular date, she did let me do things with her, like pacing her while she ran.

"What about tonight?" I asked as we jogged back to 181st Street. "Would you come to a movie with me?"

"Tomorrow's school. You know I won't go to a movie on a school night, Davey."

"Then how about next Saturday night?"

She said, "Davey!" with an exasperated edge to her voice. "Can't we have a relationship based on friendship? Must you always try to make things physical?"

I said, "I only want to go to the movies with you. What could be more friendly? *La Maternelle* is playing on One Hundred Eighty-first Street." I knew foreign films were one of Marcia's weaknesses. She said they made Hollywood films look like silly fantasies— though, to tell the truth, I liked Hollywood films better. *Captain Blood* with Errol Flynn was on at the Loews, but I didn't dare mention that to Marcia. "We could have a Coke afterward and talk about it. It would help me with my French too. What do you say, Marcia?"

"Why don't you come to dinner instead, Davey?"

I don't know what it is about Marcia. She always tries to get me involved with her family. I said, "I can't on Saturday. I work too late, but I can pick you up after work and we can see a movie. Huh?"

"Well, I'll think about it."

"If you really believed in friendly relationships and all that stuff like you say you do, you wouldn't think twice about going to a movie with me, especially a foreign movie."

"That doesn't make sense. What has a foreign movie got to do with friendship?"

"Well, would Hollywood touch such a theme? Come on, would they?"

We were jogging along Fort Washington Avenue, and suddenly

Marcia stopped dead and stared at me. "What on earth are you talking about, Davey?"

I was a little flustered because I wasn't sure myself. Somewhere I had lost the thread of the argument. "All I want to know is, would Hollywood ever make a movie without sex?"

"Honestly, Davey! Now what has that got to do with going to a movie with you?"

"I guess it hasn't anything. Okay, I'll pick you up at nine-thirty."

"Oh, Davey . . ." But she didn't say no, and when I left her at her apartment house, I felt just swell. I had never gotten that far with Marcia before, I mean actually to get her to agree to go to a movie with me—or at least not to not agree. It was either helping me with my homework, letting me pace her while she ran, or dinner with her family, and I'm sure that was just her mother's idea.

I felt pretty good, and even Sam's sarcastic remarks when I got home about how I maybe ought to take a shower before my clothes walked away without me didn't upset me.

"I was out running. That's how come I got all sweated up."

"Running? On Sunday morning?" He looked surprised. "Since when are you trying out for track?" Sam knew about my gym problems.

"Not for myself," I said uncomfortably. "It was just a girl-friend."

"What?"

"I've got this girlfriend who likes to run the mile, and I was pacing her. That's all."

He just kept looking at me, which is something he does when he wants to annoy me, and finally he said, "So how's the library working out?"

"Oh, great."

"Miss Marx give you any trouble?"

"No. She's swell."

"Uh-huh." Then, very casually, in fact too casually, he asked, "I suppose Miss Casey's still there?"

I said, "Yeah. She's in charge of the children's room—and exhibitions."

He just kept looking at me, and I began to feel a little warm, and I knew I was getting red, so I said, "I'll take that shower. I guess I need it." But I kept wondering about the look Sam had given me. He couldn't possibly know about Miss Casey—or could he?

At dinner, Pop said, "It's been over two months and David still has the job."

"The trouble is, no one has any confidence in me."

Rhea said, "You only get confidence when you earn it," which wasn't a nice thing to say. I mean, coming from Sam I would have understood it, but I didn't need that kind of help from her.

"Marcia's mother says I can get a job this summer as a waiter in the camp she goes to."

Pop had met Marcia, and he looked at me, puzzled, and said, "Marcia's mother goes to camp?"

"No, not her mother. Marcia goes, and this summer she's going to be a waitress, only there's this boys' camp that the same people own, and her mother is asking the director if I can get a job there."

"But you've got a job in the library," Pop said.

"They'll give him the summer off," Sam said thoughtfully.

"It might keep him off the streets," Rhea added, as if I spent the whole summer out on the streets.

I said, "And I'll be out in the fresh air all summer. Could I, Pop?" But he shook his head. "I don't know. How much will it cost?"

"That's the good part about it," I explained eagerly. "It won't cost, and I'll even make money in tips. You can make a lot of money. Marcia told me about this guy, he made almost a hundred dollars last summer."

"And clothes?" Pop asked. "What about clothes?"

"I won't need much. Maybe some shorts and polo shirts."

"We'll see." That was always Pop's way of putting something off. *We'll see* meant *I'm too tired to say no now. Wait till I get my strength back and I'll give you a fair fight.* But I decided I'd keep after him in the two months left before the summer. If I could spend a whole summer in a camp close to Marcia, I just knew I'd be able to get somewhere with her.

What I hadn't told Pop and Sam was that Marcia's mother had arranged an interview for me with the camp director, Mr. Luft, on a

59

Saturday morning. I went down alone, but I knew how important it was to make a good impression. Pop always told me that. I put on my best pants and a shirt with a tie, and I have a nice corduroy jacket that Pop picked up cheap because it's an irregular, but you can't see the irregular part, which is under the arm.

I wore my loafers and socks too, and I combed my hair carefully because I wanted to make a good impression. I don't know what Marcia's mother told Mr. Luft, but he was very nice to me.

"We like our boys clean-cut," he said, "and I can tell you're a clean-cut type. We don't want any radicals in our camp."

I didn't know whether he wanted me to answer that or not. He was shorter than I, a stocky man in his forties with a completely bald head and cold, black, shiny eyes. I guess he was very political because he mentioned radicals six times, and he was very concerned about being clean-cut. Mostly I listened to him and tried to look as clean-cut as I could. I think that's a state of mind, and I concentrated on the right kind of thoughts hoping they'd show, and that my eyes would be as sincere as my mind.

"You look mature," he said after a while. "I like that. We want mature boys at Camp Harel. It's a man's job, waiting on tables, and what I want to avoid are these radical kids. Last year we had a kid who stabbed me in the back. He looked clean-cut, but by the end of the summer he had organized a waiter's strike." Mr. Luft's face reddened. "I don't want none of that!"

"I don't believe in strikes," I said quickly. I was going to add that Pop had a job in a non-union shop, but I thought I'd better save that.

"Well, good." Mr. Luft wrote something on a slip of paper and covered it with his hand. "Now I've written down what our boys take home in tips. I'm not going to tell you, but I'll show you the slip when we're done. The big thing is, you gotta be mature and no stabs in the back! You play ball with me, and I'll play ball with you. No strikes and no beards."

I said, "Beards?" No one I knew had a beard.

"You know what I mean. We had a kid who grew a beard last summer. Tried to call a waiter's strike when I told him to shave it off." He pushed out his lower lip, and suddenly I realized whom he

60

looked like—Mussolini! "That's not playing ball, and besides, a beard's not sanitary in the kitchen. Get it?"

I nodded, and he uncovered the slip of paper and took a look at it. I looked too and saw a one written on it. I said, "One?"

"One hundred. That's what a good, mature, clean-cut waiter can pull in tips at Camp Harel in one season. How about that?"

I said, "I'd be proud to be a waiter at Camp Harel, and I'm sure I can be mature and real clean-cut." Then we shook hands, and Mr. Luft said, "I like a firm handshake. It's a sign of a clean-cut boy."

When I went out, I passed under a sign with Camp Harel's motto on it. WE DEVELOP BETTER BOYS. It was lettered on the office door too, and Mr. Luft showed me a picture of the social hall, a great big two-story building with the motto printed on the front in letters six feet tall: WE DEVELOP on one side, BETTER BOYS on the other.

Marcia's mother told me I'd made a very good impression on Mr. Luft, and maybe with luck, if there was an opening, I could get the job. Marcia thought it looked good too. "You see, Davey, he's got this thing about clean-cut boys, but the camp is a Jewish camp."

I said, "Well, that's fine."

"I mean, they observe the dietary laws, and they have services on Friday night and Saturday morning."

I shrugged. "Pop will like that. We're not big with religion. We only go to synagogue on Yom Kippur, but he thinks I should be more of a Jew than I am, and anyway, I love kosher cooking."

Uncomfortably, Marcia said, "But that's just the point. Mr. Luft doesn't really think Jewish boys are clean-cut. He thinks they're troublemakers."

I shook my head. "You're mistaken. He liked me and told me I was real clean-cut. Your mother thinks he'll hire me too."

"Davey, this is hard to explain, but Mr. Luft thinks gentile boys are more clean-cut than Jewish boys—and that's why he wants to hire you."

"Because gentile boys are more clean-cut than I am? You're nuts, Marcia."

"Oh, Davey! He thinks you're gentile."

"Me? Why?"

61

"Well, you don't look Jewish. You're blond, and you have blue eyes, and your name is Quinn—don't look at me like that, Davey. I guess you could tell him the truth, but Mom didn't want to until I explained it to you."

I said, "I don't care, as long as I get the job. I'll pass as a goy."

"Oh, Davey, now don't make a case out of it."

When people say that I know they feel guilty, so I changed the subject. "Tell me how the camp got its name," I asked. "Harel sounds like an Indian name—or Hebrew."

"It's neither. It comes from Harry and Ellen Luft, Mr. Luft's parents. He is very devoted to them. 'Har' from Harry and 'El' from Ellen. Harry Luft died long ago, and the camp is a kind of memorial to him."

"Is his mother dead too?"

"No, she runs the Guest House across the lake, where the parents stay when they come up to visit, and his wife runs the girls' camp."

"So it's a family affair."

Getting the job was one part of the problem. The really hard part, I thought, would be convincing Pop. I didn't know how easy that was going to be. By the time summer came, Pop was ready to do anything to get me out of the City.

The whole thing started with Miss Casey's stomach upset. That was on a Friday evening, one of those nice spring evenings when hardly anyone comes into the library, especially into the children's room. Because of her upset stomach, Miss Casey left early, and Miss Percy took over. Percy doesn't mind staying overtime, at least that's what she told me. "As long as you're on too, David."

We were due to close at six, and the reference room was closed already. The rest of the library was empty except for Miss Marx in the adult room and one old man who was dozing in the children's picture-book section.

I was shelving books and kind of daydreaming, remembering that morning in school. It had started pretty bad, with Mr. Szylowski reaming me out for showing up for gym with shoes instead of sneakers. I had taken my sneakers home to run with Marcia, and I had forgotten to bring them back. I realized it when I was in my shorts, but I couldn't use that for an excuse, so I said, "The doctor ordered me to wear shoes all the time instead of sneakers, Mr. Szylowski. I have this foot condition . . ."

He said, "Not in my gym you don't wear shoes." His voice was a little high, and his face red, sort of, and I began to get uneasy.

"But the doctor told me—"

"I don't give a good goddamn what the doctor told you. You'll wear sneakers or stay to hell out of gym for the rest of the term!"

I couldn't believe my luck. I said, "Yes. Mr. Szylowski," and I started to turn away.

He bellowed after me, "Quinn! Where the hell are you going?"

I turned in surprise. "You just told me to stay out of the gym, Mr. Szylowski."

He got a crafty look in his eyes and said, "I suppose you haven't got your sneakers here today."

"No, Mr. Szylowski." I didn't like his voice.

"Well, I'll tell you what we'll do, Quinn. You'll go barefoot."

"But the doctor—"

"When you bring a doctor's note, then you'll mention the doctor, Quinn. Not till then. Understand?" He yelled suddenly.

I nodded, and his mouth worked a bit, then he said, "You know why I'm hard on you, Quinn?"

I said, "I don't believe you're hard on me."

"Oh, I am. Believe me, I am, and you know why?"

"No, Mr. Szylowski."

"Becaue I hate waste, Quinn."

"Waste, Mr. Szylowski?"

"That's right, waste. You got the body of an athlete. Look at those shoulders, those legs! Look at that stomach! Muscled, every inch of it. I spend months trying to get muscles like that on my football squad. And look at those biceps. Make a muscle, Quinn."

By now we had a big audience, all fighting to hide their grins. I couldn't look up, I was so embarrassed. "Make a muscle!" he yelled.

I clenched up my fist and lifted it toward him. "Not that, Quinn. Maybe I'm not Italian, but I understand those little gestures all right. Don't get fresh with me. I said, make a muscle."

I bunched up my arm. "It's from lifting all those books at the library where I work, Mr. Szylowski. Honest!"

"Don't tell me what it's from. It's from a goddamn natural build. You're a natural, one in a thousand. You know what I could do with you on my football team?"

"I have this bad finger, Mr. Szylowski . . ." I began, but he cut me off.

"I'll tell you what you have. You have an allergy to exercise. You have the material but no heart. Oh, get the hell out of my sight—no! Not out of the gym! Get your shoes off and work out on the mat."

I said, "Yes, Mr. Szylowski," and I went barefoot and almost broke my toe because Ralph Emory did a back flip and landed on his feet—and on my feet too. Thank God he was wearing sneakers instead of shoes.

That was the beginning of the day, and it was a pretty sad beginning. But at lunch I went into the bio office and worked on the index to Dr. King's book for about half an hour. Working on the index always soothes me. I don't have to think. Then Marcia came in, and for the rest of the hour we were all alone, and that was pretty terrific. Not that we did anything or even said much. I kept working on the index and Marcia was filing cards, for a while at least. Then she stopped and started talking to me. It seems she had heard about the gym incident, and she gave me some very helpful advice. I like to hear her talk, especially when she tells me what I did wrong and what I should do right. It shows I occupy her thoughts.

Finally she said, "Oh, yes, Davey. I forgot to tell you the best news of all. Mom says Mr. Luft will hire you for the summer. You made a very good impression on him."

"Gee, that's great." It wasn't only the idea of a whole summer with Marcia, but I was getting a little upset lately about the three-part parlay I had to keep up: Miss Percy, Miss Casey, and Mrs. Bell. It was beginning to get me down. I was even calling one by the other's name, and I found I was dozing off in all my classes, not only in French.

"The reason he hired you," Marcia said uneasily, "is like I told you. He thought a nice gentile boy on the staff would look good."

I grinned. "David Quinn, boy shaygets, strikes again." But Marcia didn't think it was funny.

After lunch, the school was given the rest of the afternoon off because of teachers' conferences. There was even an amnesty for detentions that day. I dropped my books at the house and kicked around the apartment for a while. It's funny, before I got involved with my triple play—Casey to Percy to Bell—I used to welcome any time alone in the apartment, if for no other reason than to be able to practice my sexual discipline. But now, somehow, I just didn't have the drive. I wondered if I was growing old. I've heard of kids using themselves up by twenty.

I finally decided to go out for a walk, and just by chance I happened to walk past Mrs. Bell's block, and I thought it wouldn't be polite not to drop in to see her, and so I did, and one thing led to another, and then we were in bed together again. Now what happened then I blame on Mrs. Bell's crazy business about the lights. If she hadn't wanted them on, then we would have gotten into bed in the dark, and I wouldn't have seen the candy bar on the end table.

It was half eaten, a Nestlés bar, and the wrapper was still on it. I was on top at the time, and Mrs. Bell, underneath me, had her eyes closed, which makes me wonder why she needs the lights anyway, and she was twisting from side to side, which she considers very provocative, but I find kind of distracting, but I didn't like to say so because I hate to seem ungrateful or critical. I mean, if she goes to all that trouble, then the least I can do is pretend I like it.

I was propped on my elbows, and I must admit my mind was wandering, partly due to Mrs. Bell's instructions on how to pace myself, and partly because I was just not too interested. I mean, after all, with the Casey-to-Percy-to-Bell routine going on for all these weeks—well, anyhow, I reached out and took the candy bar because it looked so good, and I don't have to worry about teenage acne, not really having any trouble with it. I propped myself on one elbow and began to unwrap it.

That was where I made my mistake, because Mrs. Bell heard the paper rattling and opened her eyes and saw what I was doing. "What the hell are you up to?" she screamed.

"There was this candy bar . . ."

She heaved up and I went flying. "Candy! At a time like this! Candy!"

"Well, I was hungry . . ."

"You were hungry! I'll tell you what you were—what you are. You're a goddamned kid, and I must be out of my mind!"

I didn't argue. I grabbed my clothes and dressed and beat it, and all the time she never stopped. I didn't get all of what she was saying, but the gist of it was that I was a kid, that she should have her head examined for having anything to do with a kid, and if I wasn't the hell out of there in five minutes . . .

What scared me was her upstairs neighbor, who heard the noise and began knocking on the floor, and Mrs. Bell got so mad she stuck her head out of the window and started screaming, and she hadn't even put on her robe.

I ducked out the door about then, and found I had held on to the candy bar all the time I was dressing. So I finished it and walked to the library along Riverside Drive.

That was the day Miss Casey had the stomach upset and Miss Percy was taking over the children's room. I had put the last truckload of books on the shelf, and I walked over to the old man who was dozing over a copy of the *Sunbonnet Girls on the Farm*. "Time to go, Pop. We're closing up."

He stood up unsteadily, a man about my father's age, but very shabby. His coat was ragged, and instead of a shirt he wore a gray woolen undershirt and a torn scarf. He needed a shave and a haircut, but something about him reminded me of Pop. A lot of old men, and some young ones, come into the library during the day to keep warm. Some read the papers and others the magazines, but most just pretend to read and doze off. Miss Marx never does anything about them. "It's bad enough now, after the depression," she told me, "but years ago, right after the war, it was terrible." She sighed. "So many homeless people."

I got the old man to the door, and Mr. Duffy, the custodian, was there, sweeping out the entryway. He watched me guide him out and when he wasn't looking I pressed a nickel into the old man's hand. "Get yourself a cup of coffee, Pop."

He seemed confused, but he pocketed the money and shuffled off.

Mr. Duffy shook his head. "There ought to be a law to keep those old bums out of the library."

"He wasn't making a fuss. How's Paul?"

Mr. Duffy's eyes lit up. "Hey, you ought to see him. He goes to school by himself now, on the trolley. How about that?"

I said it was great, and when he told me he was leaving the building now, I said, "Sure," and I locked the gate to the children's section. Pennington leaned over the staircase and asked if I had anything on tonight. I was cagey at first because I thought he wanted me to walk home with him, but it turned out he had a date and wanted me to close up the adult room. I said, "Okay, I'll be right up."

"What do you think about those lousy Athletes?" he called out.

I was startled, thinking for a minute he was talking about my gym class, but how could he know about that? I said, "Athletes?"

"Yeah, the Philadelphia Athletes. What a crummy team. They lost the first four games. Well, *au revoir*." He waved and took off, shaking his head.

I'm not much for keeping up on sports the way some of the guys at school are. They can tell you every fact you want to know about every team that ever played in every league. Me, I'm not even sure which league is which!

When I got back to the children's room, there was just one light on by the desk, and Percy was sorting out the last of the cards. I leaned on the desk watching her, getting a kick out of the way the shadows thrown by the desk lamp lit her face. She looked up and smiled. "All finished, David?"

"Locked up and shut up." I yawned, and then covered my mouth and said, "I'm sorry."

"That's all right. You look tired."

I said, "Boy, I can't wait to get home to bed."

She laughed. "I'll bet! On a Friday night? At your age? You're a big faker, David."

"No, honest. That's just what I'm going to do, go home and go to sleep."

She looked at me curiously. "Haven't you any girlfriends, David?"

I thought of Marcia and I shrugged. "Not really a girlfriend. Just a friend who happens to be a girl—through no fault of her own, believe me!"

"What about boyfriends? Don't you go out with the boys, David?"

I shook my head. "Not really." It's a funny thing. I'm pretty popular at school, and a lot of guys like to hang out with me, but except for Saul Greenspan, I don't have a real close friend, and anyway, Saul lives way out in the Bronx.

"Poor David." Percy reached out and took my hand, then turned it palm-up and ran her finger across the palm. I really shivered. I could feel that finger all the way down to my shoes. "You have a nice strong life line."

"Really?"

"Sure, and here . . ." She traced another line. "This is your love line."

"What does it show, Percy?"

"Well, it's very strong and very deep and quite full, David, and it starts at an early age."

I moved closer so she could really examine my palm. I get a charge out of anyone telling my future, and she pointed to a few short creases. "There's more than one girl, David," she said with a little laugh.

I was surprised at that because I couldn't believe I'd ever feel about another girl the way I felt about Marcia. "How about older women?" I asked, and she looked up with a grin. "I see a very caring one, David." Her grin faded, and we kept staring at each other, our faces less than a foot apart, her hand holding mine. And then I moved forward, and I guess she kind of moved forward at the same time, and our lips were so close, all I had to do was turn my head just a little to get my nose out of the way, and we were kissing each other, right there in the library!

Finally she pulled away a little and stared at me across the pool of light that spilled out of the desk lamp and said, "Well, David! Our first kiss in the library."

I said, "Gee, Percy!" and I reached for her hand, but then we heard footsteps coming downstairs, and Miss Marx called out,

"Sally?" which is Percy's first name, only I never called her that. She just isn't a Sally type.

She patted her hair into place and called back, "Yes, Miss Marx?"

"I'm leaving now, Sally. Is David still there?"

"Yes, he is."

"Well, remind him he promised Harold to close up the adult room. Have a nice weekend now."

"And you too, Miss Marx."

Then we heard the front door slam, and we stood there looking at each other. Then Percy laughed. "Oh, David, what am I going to do with you?"

I said, "You could try kissing me again."

"Not now. You have to close up the adult room."

I nodded and said, "What are you going to do, Percy?"

"I'm going up to the staff room, David." She took her bag and started for the stairs. Halfway up, she turned back and smiled and said, "Don't be long."

I figured then that she wanted me to join her, and I was glad of that. I locked up the children's room and raced through the adult section, pulling down shades and putting out lights. Then I took the stairs to the staff room two at a time.

There was a couch in the staff room, and she pulled me down on it. There was a little lamp with a fringed shade that threw a sort of golden glow over everything, just enough light to see by, and yet not too much. Percy was wearing one of those wide skirts that sort of fell up above her waist, and I had kicked my shoes and pants off and was halfway through some of the more recent things I had learned, when all of a sudden, *click!* the overhead light went on, and Miss Marx's voice cried out, "David! Sally!" Then, "Oh my God!"

I jumped up and she was standing in the door of the staff room, her mouth open and a horrified look on her face. Percy sat up, pulling her dress down stupidly, and said, "Jesus Christ!" and I scrambled into my pants and shoes as fast as I could.

"My umbrella," Miss Marx kept saying. "I came back for my umbrella. Sally, how could you?'

I finally got my pants and shoes on, and I didn't wait to say good-bye to either of them. I ducked past and raced down the steps, taking them two at a time. My jacket was in the children's room, and I grabbed it and took off without even putting out the front lights. As I went out the door, I could hear Miss Marx's voice getting higher and higher, and I thought, well, that does it. That really does it!

▪ CHAPTER SEVEN ▪

I didn't say anything to Pop about what had happened, because I figured that if he didn't know about it, I could still keep my date with Marcia. I stayed away from the library on Saturday. If I wasn't fired, I was as good as fired, and as long as I stayed away, I had some kind of psychological advantage—only I wasn't sure what kind. Then, to make matters worse, Marcia called off our date. She had an emergency meeting of the waitresses from Camp Rocky Clove, the sister camp to Camp Harel.

Somehow or other I knew I'd have to tell Pop I'd lost the job, except I couldn't think of any explanation, though usually I'm pretty good at improvising. The best approach, I finally decided, was to tell him I had done something wrong, lost some books or spoiled some magazines. He'd be mad, but not as mad as if he found out the truth. But the truth was just what he did find out. I had forgotten that Miss Marx was an old friend of Sam's.

After supper that Sunday night, when Rhea and Sam had come for the evening, I stood up quickly and said I had to do the dishes. But Sam, who had been looking at me all through the meal, said very quietly, "Never mind the dishes, David. Sit down."

Now when Sam calls me David instead of Davey, I know there's something very wrong, and I began to think fast, except that it really didn't do me much good. I mean, right away I knew what was coming. I think I knew it subconsciously all through the meal.

Pop said, "What's wrong?" and Sam stared at me and said, "You want to tell him, David?" I never before realized what beady eyes Sam has.

I tried the wide-eyed look, and "Tell him what?" but I knew that wouldn't work, and I just couldn't come up with a plausible explanation. I mean, what explanation was there? How do you explain something like that? Anyway, I wasn't going to try until I found out how much Sam knew.

"You can tell him," I said.

Rhea, who had started clearing the table, put back the dishes and sat down. "What's he done now?"

"I got a call from Miss Marx," Sam said. "The head librarian where David works . . . worked."

I wished he'd stop calling me David.

"Nu," Pop said resignedly. "So what did he do wrong now? He's lost the job? It can happen to anyone. Don't make such a tragedy out of it. He kept it over two months." Pop seemed almost pleased, as if he were personally vindicated, since he couldn't understand how I had held any job as long as this.

"Never mind the job." Sam scowled at me. "She caught him in bed with one of the librarians. I suppose that can happen to anyone?"

There was a long pause, then, almost plaintively, Pop asked, "Where do they come by beds in a library?"

"All right. So it was a couch. He took her up to the staff room."

"Oh my God," Rhea said, dropping the silverware she was holding. "Not again!"

Pop was chewing his lip. He raised his eyebrows a little and his voice was very soft. "It's getting to be a habit?"

I couldn't think of anything to say. I just kept my eyes on the table and listened. There was an awful lot to listen to, especially from Sam.

"I don't know what the hell you think you're up to, David, or where you think you're going. What are you, some kind of pervert? No one is ever going to trust you with anything. Suppose some other job you get calls back for a reference. What are they going to say? 'Oh, he's all right. He just bangs the help!'"

Rhea said, "Sam!"

Somehow, under all the anger and annoyance in Sam's voice, I thought I detected a note of real jealousy.

"But what would a woman that age want with Davey . . ." Rhea began, and Sam cut her off with "Oh, for Christ's sake, don't start that!"

Pop said, "What am I going to do with you, Davey?" And the way he said it hurt more than anything. I wanted to throw myself into his arms and cry on his shoulder the way I used to when I was just a kid, and knowing I felt that way made it even worse. In spite of myself I felt tears gather in my eyes, and I tried to wipe them away without anyone seeing by bending my head. But the funny thing was, as bad as I felt, I wasn't really sorry. I mean, I didn't feel I had done anything wrong.

Oh, I knew it was wrong. How could I help knowing that with Sam telling me so over and over, but I didn't really feel it. There's a difference between knowing and feeling. I knew right then and there that if I had the chance, I'd do the same thing over again, only this time I'd lock the staff-room door! I even knew that if I could get out later that night, I might walk over to Mrs. Bell's and see if she had forgiven me, if her shade was up or down in the bedroom. You could see the bedroom window from the street, and that was a signal we had to let me know I could come up without running into Mr. Bell.

The point is, I just didn't feel there was anything wrong with what I had done—except getting caught. And believe me, I knew there was everything wrong with that!

"I'll tell you what you ought to do with him," Sam said. "You ought to give him a good beating."

"Give David a beating?" Pop looked at Sam in amazement. "He's bigger than I am."

"Oh, for Christ's sake, Pop!"

"Sam, for this you don't beat a man."

"A man? Jesus!"

"First it's Christ, and now it's Jesus. You wouldn't think you'd been raised a Jew and even bar mitzvahed."

"Pop! What are you criticizing me for?"

"I'm not criticizing. I'm just pointing out that David is a man."
Pop looked at me and sighed, then repeated, "A man?" Only this
time it came out as a question.

"What I don't understand," Rhea said plaintively, "is why any
grown woman would do a thing like that with a boy like Davey."

"Oh, shut up!" Sam yelled.

Later, in the kitchen, when I was stacking the dishes, Sam came
in chewing on one of his black cigars. He eased his butt, which is
spreading quite a bit, up on the table and sat there puffing and
staring at me. "What made you use the staff room?" he said finally.

I soaped up the dishcloth. "I don't know." And then I made a real
stupid slip. I guess the whole thing had upset me so that I wasn't
thinking. "Miss Casey was always dragging me up to the exhibit
room on the top floor, and I hated doing it on those hard tables. The
couch in the staff room seemed like a good idea. Anyway, it was
Percy's idea."

He stared at me. "Miss Casey?"

"No, Miss Percy . . ." And then I realized what I had said.

In a tight voice he asked, "Who else?"

I shook my head. "I was only there a few months."

"You were only there a few months!" Sam had a funny red look
to his face that scared me.

"Are you all right?" I asked.

"Oh, I'm all right." His breath came out in a rush. "I'm just fine,
but I'm normal, Davey, so why shouldn't I be all right? Davey, what
the hell are you?"

I was glad he had dropped the David. That had bothered me.
"I'm sorry. I didn't mean to upset everyone."

"You're sorry? I just bet you are. What the hell have we turned
loose on the world?"

I wiped my hands and reached out to take a bite of a sandwich I
had made and put on the sink. Suddenly Sam knocked it out of my
hand into the basin. "And stop eating! Sex and food—that's all you
know!"

I looked at the sandwich in the bowl. "Why did you do that?"

"Oh, God!" He turned and walked out of the room, and a minute
later I heard him talking to Pop, and then the door slammed as he

and Rhea left. I took as much time as I could finishing the dishes and cleaning up the kitchen, and then I squeezed out the dishcloth and hung it up.

Inside, Pop was sitting at the table with the paper open in front of him. I got my schoolbooks out and sat down across from him. After a minute he looked up at me. "So, what are you going to do now?"

I thought he meant about getting caught. "Well, I can't go back to the library . . ."

"That I'm sure of, and I don't think I can get you another job delivering orders. It's all over the neighborhood, thanks to Kara-sik." He gave a deep sigh. "David, spill me a glass water and let me think—and be sure you run it until it's cold."

I got the water for him and said, "Pop, it's only a month or so till summer, and that job at camp as a waiter is mine if I tell them okay."

"An all-boys camp, is it?"

"Yes, Pop, and I'd get plenty of fresh air there. They got a sign, 'We Develop Better Boys.' I think they kind of train you to behave."

"You could use some training in that department, a better boy I'd give up on, but a better man . . ." He shook his head and turned back to the paper. "What can I say. Next Sunday we'll go downtown. There's a store near Essex Street where we can get you some clothes, and there's an old trunk of Sam's in the base-ment." He folded the paper and pointed to an ad. "I see Davega is selling shorts for fifty-nine cents and polo shirts three for a dollar. I guess that's what you'll need, shorts and shirts. So it's an all-boys camp?"

"I've got a list that Mr. Luft gave me, Pop," I said eagerly. "I won't need much."

"Believe me, you won't get much." He looked at his watch. "I almost missed Jack Benny! Turn on the radio."

I turned it on, trying to hide a smile of relief. All I could think was, a whole summer close to Marcia!

▪ Chapter Eight ▪

"What you need," Pop told me, "are some warm clothes. You could take your pea jacket, and somewhere I've got a nice sweater Sam outgrew."

"If Sam outgrew it, what good will it do me? I'm a head taller."

"You could at least try it on."

We were packing my trunk for camp, and Pop and I were arguing over everything that went into it—without much success on my part. "Why do I need warm clothes anyway?" I asked him. "For July and August? It's almost eighty-five degrees already, and on a day like this I don't need hot oatmeal for breakfast either."

Changing the subject like that usually threw Pop off, but this time he was ahead of me. "Everyone should have something hot to start the day. That's a fact I read in the newspaper, and don't be so smart about the weather. You're going up to the mountains, and it's cold up there at night. I know. When your mother was alive, and I was working by the Pitkin Brothers and making good money, I used to send the three of you up to the mountains every summer. Your grandma ran a hotel in Hawleyville. You wouldn't remember, of course."

I said, "What was she like, Pop?"

"Your grandmother? You know. We go out there every year at Pesach."

"No, I mean Mom, my mother."

Pop's face got that distant look, and for a minute I didn't think he'd answer me, but then he sighed. "I wasn't a world-beater as a husband. I gave your mother a lot of tsuris."

75

I couldn't imagine Pop hurting anyone, and I was fascinated. "How, Pop?"

He rubbed his head, which is pretty bald except for a fringe of gray hair. "Her brothers were big successes. Murray had his own business, and Jerry was a doctor. Even by the Pitkin Brothers, what was I making? Thirty dollars a week at the best of times. She sewed all her own clothes, your mother, and clothes for the children."

"But what was she like?" I asked again.

"A good woman, a shayneh . . . Here, give me the sheets. They should go on the bottom. What's next on the list?"

That was the most I ever got out of Pop about my mother, and it didn't tell me much. I once asked Sam, but he didn't want to talk about her. Once, when Sam wasn't around, Rhea, who had known her, told me that I was a mistake. "Not that they didn't plan to have you, Davey. Sam and Arthur were teenagers when Arthur died of influenza. Your mother felt it was a judgment of God because she had stopped having children. That's why she decided to have another baby, but it was a mistake. She was too old and her health was destroyed."

That was just like Rhea. She knew how to make a guy feel great! I was guilty about that for weeks. I was the cause of my mother's death! I couldn't get Pop to confirm the story, but neither could I get him to deny it. He just said Rhea had a big mouth and changed the subject. I could see he didn't want to talk about it.

The weekend before the trunk was to be picked up, Pop and I went down to the Lower East Side, around Orchard Street, to shop for clothes—and some food as long as we were there. Pop liked to shop there, and I liked going with him. There was a lot of life on the Lower East Side. The stores all had stuff out in front, barrels of pickles and herring, fruit and vegetables, fresh fish, and cans piled up in pyramids. Clothes hung in front of the shops that sold them, shirts and pants and even suits. And the people! They yelled at the storekeepers, and the storekeepers yelled back at them. The people were all over, on the stoops and in the streets, along with rows of pushcarts, and every once in a while a car would try to get through the crush, honking its horn, the driver shouting at the shoppers in the way, and the shoppers shouting back.

76

It was lively and exciting, and I had a lot of fun watching it all and seeing Pop so happy to be there, except when he was buying clothes. Then the bargaining really embarrassed me. This time we had checked over the list Mr. Luft had given us, and we had everything but white shirts. The list said I should have four. I was loaded with shopping bags and staggering along behind Pop when he finally found the shop he wanted, a store near Essex Street. The shirts were just right.

"So how much are you asking?" Pop said.

The owner, a big fat guy with a collarless shirt, a vest, and a bowler hat pushed back on his head, said, "I'm not asking. I'm telling you. A dollar a shirt, and you'll pay a dollar-fifty for the same quality in Macy's."

"And for four?" Pop asked, fingering the material.

"Four times a dollar. Can you figure that? Four dollars, in case you don't add too fast."

"Come on, David." Pop took my arm and started for the door.

I whispered, "Pop, they're just right, and the other stores were asking more. Why are we walking out?"

"Who's walking out, David? Keep the mouth shut, and let me handle this."

We were at the door, and I had opened it, when the fat man called out, "Three-eighty!"

Pop turned back. "That's ninety-five cents a shirt. If I were buying one shirt, okay. I'll give you three twenty-five for the four."

"You're trying to rob me!" the fat man yelled. "Get out of my store."

"A goniff like you, I don't need to buy from," Pop said furiously. "I'm going. Come, David!"

But the door hadn't closed before the fat man yelled, "Three seventy-five, and not a cent less!"

"Three-forty!" Pop snapped, his hand still on the door.

"Wholesale, I have to pay more!" The fat man looked around the shop as if he couldn't believe his ears. "Do I understand what I'm hearing? Three-forty for four shirts of the first quality? I'll show you irregulars."

"For irregulars I can go to the pushcarts," Pop said.

"Three-seventy, not a cent below that, on my mother's grave!"

They settled for three-fifty, and my face was red as the man began to wrap up the shirts. "So where are you from?" he asked Pop.

"You wouldn't know. A little shtetl near Kiev. And you?"

"From Galicia." He winked at me. "A good man, your father. He drives a hard bargain. Some more customers like him, and I'd be out of business." But he said it admiringly, and Pop laughed.

Outside I asked, "Pop, how could you do it?"

"What's to do. Listen and learn, Davey. Believe me, the Galitzianer got a good price for the shirts."

"But you were fighting like that over fifty cents!" I said.

"Fifty cents is nothing to sneeze at. Look, there's the appetizer store. I want to buy some knishes and whitefish and a couple of good schmaltz herrings. Sam loves them, and he's coming over with Rhea tonight. Would you like a knish? Potato or kasha?"

I took a kasha, and Pop said, "See, two knishes, two herrings, and a pickle. It doesn't even add up to fifty cents. Is that bad?"

"I was embarrassed, Pop."

"You'll finish the knish, and you won't be so embarrassed." He stopped at a pushcart that was piled up with eyeglasses, and he picked up a pair. A little man in black gabardine with a long beard was sitting beside the pushcart reading, and he didn't bother to look up as Pop began to try on glasses. "I've been having trouble reading lately," he told me.

"You're buying glasses from a pushcart?" I couldn't believe it. "You should have your eyes examined by an optometrist!"

"So what will an optometrist tell me? That I need glasses?"

Pop never read more than one or two lines of the newspaper each night before he nodded off. I've never seen him get past the front page. I couldn't understand why he needed glasses. Now he held a pair up, tried them on, and looked at the card of printing attached to the pushcart. "I think I'll take this pair."

"Pop!"

"Don't make a whole tsimmes out of it, Davey. They feel comfortable. So how much are you asking?"

The bearded man put his book down and took the glasses from Pop. He examined them and shrugged, then named a price in

Yiddish. It took fifteen minutes of bargaining, and I don't know what the final price was, but Pop gave him a dollar and got a lot of change back. "You know what I'd pay for such glasses by the optometrist?" he said in a satisfied way as we walked off. "It's criminal!"

I just shook my head. You couldn't argue with Pop. I gave in on the warm clothes too. Maybe he was right. Me, I'd never been out of New York City that I could remember, except when we went to visit my grandma, who lives in Edgemere. You can get to Edgemere by train, but the fare was almost a dollar. Pop used to take a subway to Jamaica, and then a bus the rest of the way. That came to ten cents, which I admit is a saving, but it took half a day.

But going to Camp Harel was a real trip. I was sent a ticket for the Hudson River Day Line, and one for the train we'd take at Catskill. I had to be at the pier at nine o'clock, and Pop was disappointed because it was a workday. "I should go down with you, David."

I said, "Pop! I'm sixteen years old. I can go alone. I'm not a kid."

"You'll take the subway. You'll know what stop to get off?"

"I'll be all right, Pop. None of the parents are allowed on the pier anyway." I drew that out of a hat, and it was pretty feeble, but Pop hated to miss a morning at work, especially when things weren't going too well at the dress factory. There had been a lot of layoffs lately, and he didn't feel his job was so secure, so he gave in, and the plan was that I'd go off alone in my new tweed jacket that was really an old one of Sam's, but Pop had lengthened the sleeves by adding leather cuffs, and he had put leather patches on the elbows, too.

"It's in style," he assured me. "I saw one just like it in the window at Lord and Taylor's." Pop used to check up on the windows of the fancy Fifth Avenue stores to keep up with the latest dress styles. I had to admit the tweed jacket looked good, and I had a pair of new tan pants, courtesy of Orchard Street. That had been an argument. Pop still wanted me to wear knickers, though I'd outgrown them at thirteen. Each time we bought long pants I had to go through the same arguments. Pop thought knickers were warmer and tougher—and they were, but on a sixteen-year-old?

The night before I was to leave for camp, Sam and Rhea came

79

over for dinner, and I had to model my "outfit" for them. "You could have gotten the kid a new jacket," Sam said, inspecting his renovated tweed.

"I don't know," Rhea said. "I think it looks good."

"The way he's growing," Pop said, "anything I got would be too short in a few months."

"He's over six feet tall," Sam said. "How much more growing can he do?"

"With Davey, you can never be sure," Pop muttered. Then the two of them began discussing me as if I weren't there.

Finally I said, "I like the jacket. Let's forget about it, huh?"

"I'll pack you a lunch in the morning," Pop said. "You're sure I shouldn't go with you to the pier?"

"For Chrissakes, Pop, he's sixteen years old. He can take the subway downtown. You'll be wiping his ass for him when he's married."

Rhea said, "Sam!" and Pop just raised his eyebrows and looked at Sam over his new Orchard Street pushcart glasses, then said, "Enough already! Where's the pinochle deck?"

Sam, grumbling, switched his attack. "Remember, you're only sixteen. Keep your nose clean up there. Just because you shtupped a few women doesn't mean you're a man."

I was pretty calm the day I was to leave, though I hadn't slept much the night before. I'd lain in bed listening to Pop's gentle snoring, and I realized that I'd be sleeping alone all summer. It hadn't hit me before, but a sudden wave of homesickness came over me, and that was crazy because I was still home. Finally I fell asleep, and when I woke up the room was quiet. Pop had stopped snoring, and I raised myself up on one elbow to check whether he was still breathing. The covers were over him and I couldn't tell, so I reached out and pushed him gently.

To my relief he snorted a bit, then said, "Huh? David? What— what?"

I said, "Go to sleep, Pop." And we both went back to sleep.

I remembered to take my lunch with me the next morning, and my tickets, one for the boat and one for the train, and a big yellow tag I was supposed to pin on my jacket. That would certify me as a waiter on the pier and boat. But going down in the subway I began to be uneasy, and I had a funny feeling in my stomach. Probably Pop's oatmeal.

It was even worse when I got to Pier 81. When I left the subway, I had to walk as far west as I could, and there were a lot of other people walking in the same direction. I wondered if they were all taking the Day Line. Were they campers and parents or counselors?

When I reached the pier, there seemed to be hundreds of kids of all ages and sizes. They were milling around, shouting at each other, and racing back and forth. The parents were yelling at the kids, and the counselors were blowing whistles and trying to organize the camp into groups around long poles with colored banners that matched our colored tags.

I finally saw a pole with a yellow banner, and I knew that was where the waiters were supposed to gather. I straightened my jacket and picked my way through the mess to it. A tall, thin, black-haired fellow in a plaid jacket was holding it up, and he looked relieved when he saw me. "You're the new guy, right? Quinn?"

"Dave," I said, and we shook hands. I had decided that Dave sounded much more mature than Davey, and less formal than David.

"I'm Shep, Shep Rosten, the headwaiter." He looked at his watch. "As usual, those bozos are all late. We board in fifteen minutes, and where the hell are they?" He looked around anxiously, standing on his toes. "No sign of them."

Well, I'd started off on the right foot, the only one on time. Pop would be proud of me. "I'll hold the pole if you want to look for them."

"Hey, great!" He grinned and handed me the flag, then took off. I was craning my head, looking around the mess of kids trying to see Marcia, when a woman, pulling a little kid behind her, came up to me.

"I just can't wait," she told me in an imperious sort of voice. "This is Norman. Will you take care of him?" She looked at the crowd and shuddered. "This is incredible! Now, Norman, stay with the nice man. He'll take you on board." She had blond hair and piercing blue eyes, and looked very elegant, but also very harassed. She looked at her watch. "I have an appointment to get my hair

81

done at ten. You'll mind Norman and see that he gets on board, won't you?"

I started to say, "I'm not a counselor, ma'am," but she was opening her purse. "I just can't wait. Here." She took a five-dollar bill out and handed it to me. "Just keep an eye on him. Norman, don't you dare cry. At least try to act like a man!" Then, before I knew what was going on, she had hurried off.

I looked down at Norman, and sure enough, the kid was in tears. He must have been about eight years old, a pink-cheeked boy with blond hair like his mother's, cut in, of all things, a Buster Brown haircut! Outside of the movies, I'd never seen a kid with hair like that. "Are you my counselor?" he asked, wiping his nose and tears with his sleeve.

"No, I'm a waiter," I said. "I'm Davey. Dave." I looked around to see if I could find a counselor to take care of him. "Where's your tag?"

"My mom forgot it." He held out his tickets. "I've got these."

This was great. My first tip, and I didn't know what to do with the kid. I could find a counselor and palm him off, but then would I have to hand over the five dollars? "Well, you stick with me, Norman, stick close, and I'll get you on the boat."

The boat, a big Hudson River Day Liner, was at the far end of the pier, steam coming out of its smokestack. It seemed enormous to me, at least four decks, and a big, enclosed side-wheel. It had its name on the side in black and gilt, *Alexander Hamilton*.

It was a funny thing. Having Norman hang on to me, and he did hang on, grabbing my jacket with one hand and wiping his nose with the other, made me feel a little less scared myself. Then two waiters came up to me, yellow tags pinned to their jackets. "You the new guy?"

I said, "Yes, and this is Norman."

One of them, a big guy with heavy shoulders, hunkered down on his ankles and said, "Hello, Norman. Are you a waiter too?" He winked at me. "Leave it to Luft to hire them young."

Norman began to cry again, and I said, "Cut it out, Norman!"

He looked at me, then put his thumb in his mouth. I said, "Come on, you're too big to suck your thumb."

He pulled it out guiltily. "Who's sucking it? I was just biting my nail."

"Well, you're too old to bite your nails." I reached down and touseled his head. "Norman's a stray camper," I told the heavyset guy. "I don't know where he belongs, but his mother asked me to look after him."

"I hope she shit on you."

I was startled. "Shit on me?"

"Tipped you."

"Oh. Well, she did. Do I keep it or turn it over to his counselor?"

"You goddamn well keep it!" He straightened up and stuck his hand out. "I'm Killer Cohen, and this is Squeak Zimmer."

"Dave Quinn," I said, shaking hands. I could guess why he was called Killer. He had a grip that almost broke my hand, though I tried not show it.

"Where are the rest of the guys?" Squeak asked. He had a deep bass voice, which seemed kind of strange for a guy nicknamed Squeak. There was something funny about the way he talked, a sort of held-in anger. He always seemed ready to explode. I decided that he wasn't a good guy to get mad at you.

"The headwaiter, Shep, went to look for them."

"Hey, there's Horse," Killer yelled, and began waving furiously. I shoved the pole with the flag up higher so it could be seen, and at the same time the Day Liner gave a blast on its horn, and the gangplank was lowered. Norman began to cry again, and I lifted him up in my arms and handed the flag to Killer.

"You'll be all right, Norman, just don't wipe your snot on my jacket. You'd think his counselor would notice he was missing and come looking for him," I said to Killer. "They all have lists."

"What the hell, bring him on board and we'll sort it out." Everyone was surging toward the boat, and the counselors were all yelling at the kids to stay in line. Shep came running back dragging another waiter. "Hey, two of you guys give them a hand with the food. Did anyone see Dinge?"

It was crazy, real bedlam, but somehow everyone got on board, me with Norman in my arms, asking every counselor I met if he was one of their kids, but no one would admit it. The waiters found a spot on the top deck near the back of the boat, and I wiped Norman's nose with the clean handkerchief Pop had made me take, and then I tucked it in his pocket and went looking for someone to palm him off on.

Finally, to my relief, I found Mr. Luft and two other counselors going over lists. I handed Norman over, and one of the counselors began complaining that he should have had a tag, and he belonged on another deck, and Mr. Luft started shouting, "I don't give a damn where he belongs. Get him tagged and back to his group." Norman began to cry again.

I squeezed his shoulder and said, "See you later, kid," and as I ducked away I heard Norman screaming, "I wanna go with Davey! I wanna go with Davey!" But luckily I got back to the other waiters without him.

On the way I kept looking for Marcia, and finally I saw her with a group of girls, waitresses, but they were all singing, and I couldn't get near her. I waved, but I don't think she saw me. Back at the waiters' group, the rest of the bunch had arrived, but Killer and Squeak and Horse had taken off. Shep was checking over a list he had while the boat was moving out into the river, the side-wheels turning, and the horn blasting away.

We were to take the boat up to Catskill, he explained, and there we'd disembark and take the Catskill Mountain Railroad up into the mountains. Once we were all checked off, we were free to roam all over the boat. At noon we had to gather on the second deck and help hand out the sandwiches and milk the camp had brought along.

Eppie, another waiter, a small, skinny kid, came running up to the bunch of us as we were sorting out the sandwiches. "Hey, there's a deck below with glass walls in the middle where you can look at the engine."

Killer looked up from the sandwiches and said, "No shit, Eppie!"

"Honest. It's an inclined, triple-expansion engine, an oil burner!"

The rest of the guys chorused, "No shit, Eppie!"

Eppie shook his head. "Morons!" And he stalked off. I wanted to see the engines, but I didn't go with him. The first lesson I learned then was not to show too much excitement about anything. It just gave the other guys a chance to make fun of you.

I was introduced to the other waiters, but I didn't really sort them out till later. Eppie's full nickname, Killer Cohen told me, was Epidemic. "The guy's a real plague!"

Another waiter was Horse Halpern. He was short and solid-looking and wore glasses, and most of the trip he spent in a deck chair with his feet up on the rail reading *The Night Life of the Gods,* by Thorne Smith, and it looked pretty spicy—at least from the cover, which showed a lot of naked people around a fountain.

Then there was Dinge Shapiro. Dinge was tanned almost black, and he had one of the foulest mouths I'd ever heard. But he wasn't mean, and like the others, he made me feel a part of the gang right away. "How come Mr. Luft sends the campers up by boat?" I asked him while we were sailing past the Bear Mountain Bridge. "Isn't it expensive?"

He said, "Shit, no! The fuckin' fare is nothin'. The Day Line charges two bucks a passenger, and Luft probably gets a group rate. Besides, if Luft sends us by boat, it's probably the cheatest fuckin' way to go!"

The last waiter I met was Small Fry. He had kept apart from the others for most of the trip. Small Fry was the youngest, only thirteen years old, and scared as hell.

"He should have been a camper," Shep told me later, "but his father is Mr. Luft's uncle, and the kid's been coming up here on charity. Luft wants to get as much out of him as he can, so he made him a waiter. I don't know how he'll make it this summer. It's no job for a thirteen-year-old."

I didn't feel too good about that. If it was no job for a thirteen-year-old, it meant it couldn't be too easy for a sixteen-year-old. I had looked on this as a vacation, but now I began to wonder. Still, once we got to camp, I found that with Small Fry around, the pressure was off me. Every mistake I made, and I made plenty in the beginning, was covered up by the mistakes Small Fry made. He'd break dishes, mix the meat silver with the dairy stuff, and take so long bringing the courses out that his tables would begin to chant out loud, "We want Small Fry! We want Small Fry!" And he'd rush around close to tears. I really felt sorry for the kid.

It was a funny thing about Camp Harel. All the counselors were called "Uncle." Uncle Sid, Uncle Sy, Uncle Bill, Uncle Julie. Everyone else, it seemed to me, had a nickname, at least all the other waiters did—except me. I was "the new guy" on the boat trip, and at first they called me David, though I kept introducing myself as Dave.

I didn't learn all the names that first day, or at least I didn't remember them, but Shep was great. He introduced me to everyone, and he explained exactly what my job was. He'd been going to Camp Harel since 1928. All of the waiters were old-timers, even Small Fry. They'd been campers for years, and when they reached sixteen, they became waiters. Waiters weren't paid, but tips could add up to a sizable amount, Shep explained. It depended on how popular you were.

At eighteen you could be a junior counselor, and at twenty you could be a real counselor and get a salary as well as tips. Shep had taken the headwaiter job, I learned, because it was the only waiter job with a salary. The rest of us would have to count on tips. Most of the counselors were teachers who had the summer off, but the head counselor, Tom Ciardi, was a West Point man.

I met most of the staff on the boat, while we were serving lunch sandwiches, and after. The camp doctor, Dr. Rosenberg, was a refugee who had left Nazi Germany but still didn't have a license to practice here. The camp rabbi, Dr. Kaplin, bothered me because he looked at me so intently that I was sure he had me figured for a fake, but I found out later that he was just nearsighted and hated to wear glasses.

"I don't really need them," he told me. "I can recognize everyone by their walk. Really, everyone has a unique walk."

The head counselor, Tom Ciardi, was the only gentile in the group. He had a very short haircut, the hair about one inch long, and a deeply tanned face. He was the straightest-standing man I'd ever met. At one point, when I was handing out sandwiches, egg salad and cheese, he took me aside, and in a quiet voice said, "Well, Quinn, it's good to have you on board. We'll have to stick together. We're really outnumbered."

It took me a minute or two to understand what he meant, and then

I got it. We were outnumbered by the Jews! I got away as soon as I could, and spent most of the summer trying to avoid being alone with him. What would I do if he made an anti-Semitic remark or told me an anti-Semitic joke?

I shouldn't have worried. As it turned out, I never heard an anti-Semitic remark from him, which is not to say there weren't plenty of anti-Semitic remarks going around—a lot of the counselors and waiters made them all the time and thought they were really funny. They also got a kick out of telling jokes about Jews in Germany.

Squeak told one on the boat going up, something about a little Jew pestering a ticket taker until the man lost his temper, then saying, "Tut, tut, anti-Semitism!"

All the guys laughed, except me. I felt strange as hell, and I just walked away. I had heard jokes like that before, told by Jews, and I'd laughed at them, but all of a sudden it was different. It was bad enough pretending not to be Jewish, but then to have to listen to a joke about Jews told by a Jew—I was really mixed up.

Shep came up to where I was leaning over the railing of the boat, and he said, "Don't pay any attention to Squeak. Everything he says is in bad taste."

Killer Cohen had walked over too, and he said, "A lot of us think it's funny to make fun of ourselves. If they knew what was really going on in Germany . . ."

"My aunt and her family are still over there," Shep said. "We keep writing to them to try and get out, but they hate to leave, keep putting it off."

Killer nodded at a group of counselors across the deck. "See that tall blond guy, Klaus? He's a refugee. A friend of Doc's. He was at camp last year, too. You should hear some of his stories."

The other waiters drifted over, and I listened to them talk, uneasy about saying anything myself. For one thing, I didn't know as much as they did about what was happening in Europe. I should have listened to Marcia more carefully. I felt uncomfortable about myself too. Talk about false pretenses!

By the time the boat reached Catskill, I had gotten to know all the waiters. Shep gave us table assignments and filled me in, as much as he could, about the camp. I liked Shep. He was older than the rest, about nineteen, and in his first year at NYU, but he never talked down to me, and he really seemed to like me. He was quieter than the other waiters. They were always clowning around, except for Small Fry, who usually hung out with the campers his own age.

I was pretty quiet myself, mostly because I was afraid to open my mouth and give myself away. What would I do, I wondered, if I was hurt and, off guard, I suddenly yelled out "Oy vay!" I had never said "Oy vay!" in my life, but I had a mental image of the whole camp hearing it and then turning and pointing at me. "He's a Jew!"

▪ Chapter Nine ▪

I really enjoyed that ride up the Hudson, and I was sorry when it ended, but I could tell the counselors weren't. They all had a kind of wild-eyed look, and a few were breathing heavily from chasing kids all over the boat. I never did get to talk to Marcia, but I figured with the whole summer ahead of us, it didn't matter. There would be plenty of other opportunities.

Just before we disembarked, Norman found me and said, "I don't like my counselor. I wanna go with you, Uncle Davey."

So I had become an uncle. I said, "Where's the hanky I gave you, Norman?" The kid's nose was running and his eyes were red. He pulled it out of his pocket, and I wiped his nose, then took him to his counselor, Uncle Art Aronsen, a big, heavy man with the smallest shoulders I'd ever seen.

"So there you are!" Uncle Art said with a sigh of relief. "I thought I'd lost you."

"I wanna go with Uncle Davey!" Norman began to cry again, and Uncle Art shrugged his shoulders. "You wanna take him?"

So I ended up carrying Norman onto the train and having him sit next to me for the long ride up into the mountains. The Catskill Mountain Railroad ran on single tracks. At first I worried about meeting a train coming in the other direction, but then I figured out that there was only one train up and the same train returned on the same set of tracks. It wasn't a bad ride up, except that the steam engine threw out a lot of dirt. You could feel it all along the plush seats, even with the windows closed, but I didn't mind since it was my first real ride on a train. I couldn't count the subway and the few times we'd taken the train to Grandma's. That was electric and all the scenery we saw was Jamaica Bay.

It was almost dusk when we arrived at the camp, and Norman, along with most of the little kids, was fast asleep. I managed to hand him over to Uncle Art without waking him up, and then Shep herded all seven of us waiters into the mess hall so fast, I hardly got a chance to see the camp itself. I had a quick impression of looming mountains and green lawns and a lake that didn't look anywhere nearly as big as it did in the photos I had seen in Mr. Luft's office in New York.

"They fake the pictures," Killer Cohen explained when I asked about it. "They have some trick photography in shooting the length of the lake, and it looks tremendous. The damn thing is only about an acre."

The mess hall was the bottom floor of the social hall, a big white clapboard building with the sign WE DEVELOP on one side of the top floor and BETTER BOYS on the other. Upstairs there were an indoor basketball court and a stage. On some Saturday nights they gave shows there and put folding chairs on the court for the counselors and visitors. The kids sat on the floor. But most Saturdays the shows were given at the girls' camp, Rocky Clove, which had a new social hall with a very professional stage.

I was given the Hunters for my tables, and Small Fry, who was still on the verge of tears, was given the Paps and a Bucks table. "They eat so slowly, he'll be able to manage," Shep told me, but I could tell from his worried look that he wasn't too sure about that.

I'd better explain about the groups at Camp Harel. The Paps, Papooses, are the smallest. They're four and five years old, and the Camp Mother, Mrs. Lowenstein, and her husband, Sol, take care of them. They live in the Paps bunk near the tennis courts. Mrs. Lowenstein is a big, motherly sort of woman, who always seems to be cuddling one of the little Paps. Mr. Lowenstein doesn't seem to be playing with a full deck. He smokes a big black pipe, and half the time, when you ask him a question, he puffs away at it instead of answering. The Lowensteins' two sons go to camp. They're twelve and thirteen, and I gather their tuition is the Lowenstein's pay. Mr. Luft is very fond of deals like that. They save a lot of money.

The Bucks are the next group. They're six and seven years old, and then come the Braves, eight, nine, and ten. Norman was in the Braves group. The Hunters, the kids I wait on, are eleven, twelve, and thirteen, which isn't a bad age. You can always bully them into behaving. The worst group is the Warriors, the fourteen- and fifteen-year-olds. They are really trouble. They can make a waiter's life miserable with their bread-throwing and food fights, but Shep waits on them, and he can handle them.

Camp Harel is very big with Indians. Not only do the groups have Indian names, but the mess hall has Indian murals on the panels that run along the top of the walls. Uncle Frank Eliscu painted them. He's the arts and crafts counselor, and he teaches at Pratt. His murals are great, with wigwams and battle scenes and campfires— except that he can't do feet, but that's no problem because all the Indians he draws are standing in deep grass.

Every Sunday night they have a big council fire at Camp Harel, and it's very solemn. The Warriors take care of it, and they dress up in loincloths and big feather headdresses that they make in arts and crafts. It's a serious occasion, and it's held up in the woods in a cleared circle surrounded by trees.

Every camper takes a blanket and wears it around his shoulders, and they all file in to the beat of a tom-tom. There's a prayer to Manitoba, and then a ceremony, and Indian songs and stories. It's really impressive, though the third week of camp there was a big hullabaloo because one of the counselors whose turn it was to tell a story read from Milt Gros's book, *Nize Baby.* He read in a Jewish accent, and it received a very dead reception. It was generally agreed afterward that he had disgraced the spirit of Manitoba.

"That kind of stuff is okay at Amateur Night," Squeak said indignantly. "But shit, at a council fire?"

On Monday nights there is Amateur Night, and on Wednesday

90

nights there is usually a campfire where we roast wienies and marshmallows and sing rousing camp songs.

That first day that we arrived at camp, we served a very light supper. It was milchedig, Shep explained to me. "There are two kinds of food in the Jewish religion, milchedig and flayshedig, milk and meat—and never the twain shall meet!"

I knew all about it because Grandma kept a kosher house, but Pop didn't, even though Grandma was very annoyed about it. But I played dumb while Shep showed me where the milk and meat dishes and silverware were kept, and where we put each when we returned the dirty dishes to the kitchen. They even had two sinks, which Grandma didn't.

The cook, Jenny, was a big, fat woman with the kind of face that should be jolly, but always looked worried and angry. When the last of the campers had filed out and we were sweeping up—"Don't forget the chairs. Sweep them off too," Shep reminded us—I heard a loud voice from the kitchen. "Nu, so where's the shaygets?"

Shep winced. "You've got to overlook Jenny," he whispered as he took me into the kitchen. "She has a good heart."

"Good-hearted" Jenny, in a white dress and apron, with a cook's hat on her head and her hands on her hips, faced me with a challenging look. "So this is the shaygets? It's not such a big deal."

I put out my hand, and she looked at hers, full of flour. "Never mind. We'll shake later—if you last." She turned back to the dough she was working on, and Shep pulled me out of the kitchen.

"She's all right." But he didn't sound as if he believed it.

"I know, good-hearted." I joked about it, but I felt pretty uneasy. It was that old business of grown-ups being sarcastic with no reason for it. I finished up my tables, wiping them off and setting them up for the morning, then, with the rest of the guys, I went up to the Hill.

Camp Harel is in a valley under Hunter Mountain, which is also called the Colonel's Chair because from town, Hunter, it looks like a great big chair, but I don't know who the Colonel was, nor does anyone else. Schoharie Creek runs along one side of the campgrounds, and it's been diverted into Lake Harel at the top of the campgrounds, and the water flows over a concrete dam at the bottom of the lake and back into the creek. All the campgrounds—the tennis courts and baseball diamond and basketball courts and the rest—are between the lake and the creek, like a big island.

The Hill is where the tents are, and the Bucks, Braves, Hunters, and Warriors sleep up there. It's across a wooden bridge over the creek and up a steep path. The tents are on top around a horseshoe. In the center is an open lawn that everyone uses for sunbathing, something that Rabbi Kaplin is mildly opposed to. Shep asked him why, once, when he caught a bunch of us lying out there in the nude. He just looked embarrassed and said, "Nudity is not allowed in the Jewish religion!"

I figured that left me out, so I just rolled over on my stomach while the rest of the waiters went back to their tents grumbling. The waiters' tents are behind the others. Each tent holds four cots and trunks comfortably, and six in a pinch. A line strung between the tentpoles holds our jackets and pants.

A favorite trick is to light a candle and hold it close enough to the tent roof to let the soot mark it, but not close enough to set the tent on fire. Then, by moving the candle, you can spell out your name and the dates you've been at camp. It's a big thing if you've been at Camp Harel more than three or four years. Then you write your name, like *Elliot "Squeak" Zimmer, 1930, '31, '32, '33, '34, '35.* That was right over my bed, and the second day in camp Squeak came into the tent with a candle to put a *'36* after the *'35.* I waited outside, expecting the tent to go up in smoke, but it didn't.

The toilets on the Hill are in two lines behind the tents on each side of the horseshoe, five on each side. The campers carve their names into the soft wood of the stalls while they're sitting on the crapper. It's a tradition like the candle marks on the tents. In fact, every spot in camp that's unprotected has some name and date carved into it. I even caught the kids trying it on my tables in the mess hall. They only stopped when I threatened to tell Mr. Luft.

The first time I went to the crapper, I saw *Sheldon "Killer" Cohen, 1932, '33, '34, '35. All-around camper, '33* carved on the right side. Killer was all-around camper in 1933, and that was pretty good. It meant he got a letter in every sport, a big gold CH that he sewed on his jacket. Part of the camp uniform was a blue felt lumber jacket.

Gold and blue are Camp Harel's colors, and one of the camp songs goes:

> Gold and blue, we're with you,
> And our cheers are for your men.
> So it's fight, fight, fight, you Ha-rel-i-ans,
> Victory again!

They sang that before any of the big baseball games we'd play with other camps. Mr. Luft was crazy about baseball. The guys told me he had rented an apartment on Edgecomb Avenue overlooking the Polo Grounds just so he could sit at his window with field glasses and watch the baseball games. "He's too fuckin' cheap to buy a ticket!" Dinge claimed.

Camp Harel had a regulation-size baseball field, and it took up most of the campgrounds. In fact, Killer told me he had been given a reduced rate as a camper in '34, when his father was having a hard time with his business. "Luft knocked a hundred bucks off the price. I only paid two hundred bucks for the summer on account of my pitching. I'm the best pitcher Harel ever had, and he didn't want to lose me." The way Killer said it was matter-of-fact, not boasting, just telling the truth.

In addition to all the playing fields, there were horse stables across the lake near the Guest House. Horseback riding cost extra, and only about fifty campers took it. Some kids, like Eppie, were horse crazy. He hung out there all the time, shoveling manure for free rides, and he smelled pretty ripe, too.

The fourth day of camp, Nancy Minogue arrived. She was the camp nurse, and she lived in Kingston and drove up in a swell car, a '28 Model A Ford Phaeton. It was eight years old, but it looked like new. It was mustard-yellow with brown trim, and she kept it beautifully waxed and polished.

I saw it parked outside the infirmary that afternoon, when I was walking back from the mess hall. I just stopped and walked over to it and ran my hand along the fender. We had never owned a car, but I knew every model that was made. The kids on our block used to have a car game. We'd each chalk a big square on the sidewalk and divide it into boxes, ten across and five down. That made fifty squares. Each time you spotted a different car, you chalked down its make and year, like a '34 Willys, or a '36 Chrysler Imperial, or a '35 Hudson Terraplane. You couldn't repeat the same year and model, and the first to yell out the name chalked it in his box. The first to fill all fifty squares won. I was good at that, and it got so I could recognize a Nash from a Pontiac three blocks away.

I was leaning over the side of the Model A Ford to see the dashboard, when a woman's voice said, "How do you like it?"

I turned around and there was the camp nurse in a crisp white uniform and a navy-blue cape lined in red and a little white cap perched on her head. She said, "I'm Nancy Minogue—and you must be David Quinn."

"The new guy," I said, and she laughed.

"Word gets around. Besides, I've been coming up here for four years and a new face stands out. Quinn? Well, we Irish have to stick together."

First the head counselor and now the nurse. I nodded at the car. "Some beauty."

Her face lit up. "Isn't it? The best model Ford ever made. I have eighty thousand miles on it, but I hate to give it up. I'm just gonna drive it into the ground." She wasn't very pretty until she smiled, and then her whole face changed. She was close to thirty, I figured, but her age was hard to tell, especially in that uniform. She had black hair and green-blue eyes that were so bright they startled me. "I tell you what. Someday I'll let you drive it."

"Gee, that would be swell!"

"What kind of car does your family have?"

"Well—we don't have a car."

"Oh, sure. I forgot. You're from the City. Well, I'll give you a ride in it this Sunday."

"Sunday?"

"Sunday morning. Tom Ciardi and I drive into Haines Falls to the Immaculate Conception for Mass." I just stared at her, and she looked puzzled. "You are Catholic, aren't you? Quinn?"

"Catholic? Oh, no," I said, and then began thinking fast. When I get trapped in a situation like that, my brain speeds up, and I can usually come up with a good story without any hesitation. I was a little shaky here, however, and I knew I was on treacherous ground.

I had forgotten all about the church business and I wasn't sure just what kind of a shaygets I was. "My father is Catholic," I said, "but my mother was Protestant, and when she died she made my father promise to bring me up Protestant."

"Isn't that sweet. Episcopalian?"

"I beg your pardon?"

"What church? If your mother was Irish, she was probably Episcopalian."

This was more complicated than I thought. I could feel the sweat on my forehead. "But she wasn't Irish." How many Protestant religions were there, and which was the safest?

"Methodist?"

I grasped at straws. "Yeah, Methodist."

"Well, fine. There's a Methodist church in Hunter. We'll drop you off there Sunday. At least you'll get a chance to ride in the Ford. I'll see you, Davey." And she turned and walked up the steps of the infirmary. I watched her, and as the wind blew her cape aside I caught a glimpse of her rear in that tight white uniform. Boy, was she sexy! Just looking at her reminded me that I had forgotten all about my discipline in the past few days. Too much had been happening.

I hurried up the Hill and stretched out on my cot in the empty tent. I must say that waiting on tables is not an easy job. There's so much running back and forth, and the kids make so much noise that you can hardly hear yourself think. Breakfast is worst of all, especially when we have boiled eggs, because you have to take orders for hard, soft, and medium, and there are always complaints like "I ordered medium and these are hard!" Or "I ordered soft and these are medium!"

Killer set me straight on that. "I get 'em all medium," he told me while we were waiting at the counter where you pick up your orders. "The ones who ordered hard figure they're underdone, and the ones who ordered soft think they're overdone. It saves a lot of trouble."

"Don't they yell about it?" I asked, looking back at my tables of Hunters. "They're always complaining."

"It's the nature of the fucking beasts," Dinge Shapiro said,

95

coming up behind me. "Fuck 'em, Davey. They yell about everything. Let 'em complain."

I was always a little shocked at the language Dinge and a few of the counselors used. Of course I'd heard worse at school, but I didn't curse much myself except for an occasional "Oh shit!" under stress, and Dinge's constant use of "fuck" bothered me. Otherwise Dinge was a great guy. He was one hell of a swimmer, a sport I wasn't too good at, but that was true of most sports. He could also dive beautifully. It was great just watching his jackknifes and swan dives off the high board.

"The great thing is," he told me, "the lake is all mud on the bottom, so diving is pretty fuckin' safe."

That afternoon, after talking to Nancy, I was lying on my cot alone in the tent, and I began thinking of Mrs. Bell and Percy, and suddenly nature began to get the better of me. I was wondering what to do about it, when Killer suddenly came in through the back tent flap. Before I could roll over on my stomach, he flicked his towel at me. "No banging the meat during rest hour!"

I sat up, hugging my knees to my chest. "I was just thinking . . ."

"That way lies madness." He hung up his towel and put his soap away, then stretched out on his cot. Shep, Killer, Horse, and I shared one tent, and I was glad of that. I liked Shep and Killer best of all the guys, and Horse wasn't bad. He took himself a little too seriously, and he always had his nose in a book, but he was very easygoing and a pretty smart guy. "You think too much," Killer went on, "and then you begin banging your meat, and that can make you crazy."

"Come on, that's not true!"

"Sure it is. I read it in a book."

"Well, I think you had the wrong book. Dr. Schwartzkopf says it's healthy. It prepares you for manhood."

Killer let out a whoop and sat up. "No shit? Then I must be one hell of a man. But there is a problem, it puts hair on your palms."

I wasn't about to fall for that by looking at my palms. I'd had the guys pull it on me at school. "My palms are smooth as a baby's ass," I told him.

Killer laughed. "Yeah, well, you're sure about Dr. Gloken-spiel?"

"I'm sure, and it's Schwartzkopf."

"How about that? I'll tell you the truth, Davey. I always thought it drove you crazy, but I never could stop doing it. I'd beat my meat morning and night, and I just figured if I had to go crazy it was worth it. It's good to know your doctor friend says it's okay."

"He's not a friend. He wrote a book about marriage, and my brother Sam, who's married, has a copy. I sneaked a look at it."

"Well, it makes sense. From what I've seen, every guy here bangs the Bishop and none are crazy—except maybe Eppie. But I think he was born crazy, at least crazy about horses!"

The guys talked a lot about masturbation, and they had some strange names for it—beating the meat, banging the Bishop, whacking off, pulling the pud, flogging the dog—boy, I think I heard a different one every day. It was all very imaginative, the kind of euphemisms Mrs. Rollins, my English teacher, used to talk about all the time and encouraged us to use.

And Killer was right about everyone doing it. At night, about ten minutes after the lights went out, you could feel the whole tent rocking, and then, bed by bed, it would quiet down. I got over my own shyness pretty soon, but the first time I did, Killer yelled out, "There goes Quinn! Hold on to your beds!" That took some of the heart out of it.

One of the things that worried me at first was being circumcised. As a resident Shaygets, the other guys expected me to have a foreskin, and I knew they were all eager to see what it looked like. Still, in high school, when we dressed for gym I noticed that almost all the gentile kids were circumcised too, so I just explained that my parents were hygienic when Killer mentioned it.

"You're lucky you're living in America," Shep said.

"Yeah? How come?"

"Well, in Germany, that's how they find out which Jews are pretending to be gentile. In fact, I read that some men have operations to put the foreskin back on."

Killer let out a moan. "That's awful. I'd die before I'd let anyone operate on my wang."

"I don't blame you," Shep said sympathetically. "That's where all your brains are."

Killer, stretched out on his cot, flicked his penis up. "You're just jealous because I'm so well hung."

"Hung, shmung. You can't match Horse."

"Hey, Horse," Killer yelled. "Show it to us. Davey's never seen it." To me, he said, "That's why we call him Horse. He's hung like one. Come on, Horse, show it."

"I will for a quarter." Horse looked up from the book he was reading and grinned. "That's the going rate."

"Aw, shit. It's not worth a quarter. I'll catch you in the showers for free."

The guys went on like that all the time, kidding around about sex, but I don't think any of them had any experience. Shep told me in confidence that he was still a virgin. "And I know Killer and Dinge are too, for all their bullshit."

I didn't say anything about myself. I figured if everyone else was a virgin, I'd better pass as one too. It shouldn't be too hard after passing as a shaygets.

"The Shaygets," incidentally, had become my nickname, but not to my face. A few times I overheard the guys talking about me when they didn't think I was around, and they always referred to me as "the Shaygets." To my face, it was "Davey." I just couldn't get Dave to stick. I guess I wasn't a Dave type.

The first Friday night we had dinner late, and before dinner there were outdoor services under the apple trees behind the baseball backstop. The only waiter who went was Shep because his father had died that past winter, and he was still saying Kaddish, the prayer for the dead, for him. Shep had told me that he intended to say Kaddish every night for the full eleven months after his father's death. When there were no services, on ordinary nights, the rabbi would go around lining up ten men for a minyan, the number of men needed to pray, officially.

The rest of us were busy setting up our tables that first Friday, but through the open windows of the mess hall we could hear the kids singing the Hebrew songs, and then their voices raised in the "responsive reading" where the rabbi read one line and the congregation read the next.

I went to the window and looked out. The kids were all seated on the grass, and Rabbi Kaplin was at a small table with a decorative cloth over it. One of the older boys was holding the velvet-and-silver-covered Torah that was kept in the counselors' room behind the mess hall. The air was full of that deep blue dusk that settled in the valley, and the white handkerchiefs most of the kids wore knotted on their heads in place of yarmulkes glowed like lights. I heard the rabbi read, "How goodly are thy tents, O Jacob," and the kids chanted back, "Thy dwelling places, O Israel." There was a soft and peaceful quality to everything, and I felt a strange sort of sadness go through me.

"Nu, so are you going to stand there all night?" Jenny, the cook, shouted from the kitchen. "Come on, I want the gefilte fish out on the tables before the little tramps come in!"

To Jenny, all the older campers were tramps. Usually she'd describe the "tramps" with a few choice Hungarian expletives. Once she got going, I'd wish I understood Hungarian. She'd mix the Hungarian with Yiddish, and I got a lot of that. Her Yiddish reminded me of the way my grandmother used to yell at me, and it made me feel warm and comfortable. The trouble was, I'd begin to smile, and she'd get angrier than ever. "So the shaygets is smiling," she'd announce angrily. "He thinks maybe it's a joke?" And she'd storm out of the room.

When I got to the kitchen, Mr. Luft was there yelling at Small Fry, who had been slicing challa for his table. "You dumb animal, that's no way to slice the bread! Thinner, for Christ's sake!" He looked up and saw me and caught himself. "Sorry about that 'Christ,' Quinn." Then back to Small Fry, who was close to tears. "You know how much you waste when you slice it like that?" He grabbed the knife. "Like this, you dumb animal!" And he proceeded to demonstrate the fine art of slicing bread for the rest of us who had gathered around. I'll admit he was a masterful bread cutter. You could practically read a book through his slices.

"It doesn't do any good, Shep told me later when he came in

from services and heard about it. "They just eat twice as many slices. It's another of Luft's crazy economies. Thank God he isn't in the kitchen all the time."

Luft had a lot of economies, and he was always bawling us out for bringing the pitchers of milk to the table too fast. "Let them wait a while. Maybe they'll kill their appetites." And when he was in the kitchen he'd poke his nose into all the pots and pans. "They don't need such big portions," he'd tell Jenny, but she'd just glare at him, her face red with the heat of the stove, her dress wet with sweat under her arms.

"Geh, geh!" she'd yell, and sometimes she'd pick up a cleaver threateningly. He usually went.

Another economy of Mr. Luft was doling out the supplies day by day. All the camp's staples and food were kept at the pantry and freezer behind the Guest House across the lake. Very early each morning, provisions were brought over, just enough for one day, another thing Jenny used to scream about. "That farshtinkener Luft, does he think I'll steal his lousy supplies?"

The hardest part about waiting on tables was keeping the meat and milk things separate. I'd get off easy when I made a mistake because as a shaygets I wasn't supposed to know about it. As Jenny used to mutter, "He's got a goyisher kop!" Which meant I had a gentile head and wasn't too smart.

But Small Fry was always in trouble, and often in tears. I must say, while Mr. Luft yelled at him something awful, Jenny was very patient and forgiving. In fact, the only time I saw her show any tenderness was with Small Fry when he got into a mess. She'd make excuses for him and baby him whenever she could, bringing him extra portions of any particularly good food or dessert, none of which endeared him to the rest of us. I've never seen anyone have a more miserable summer than that poor kid.

Except maybe Norman. He found me the second night at camp and came into my tent in his pajamas, his thumb in his mouth. "Hey, it's the kid!" Horse said, sitting up in bed. "What do you want?"

"I want Davey." His nose, as usual, was running, and I had to go through my trunk for a clean handkerchief, of which fortunately Pop had packed a lot. I wiped his nose and said, "Come on, Norman. You can't stay with me. What will your counselor say?"

"I don't like Uncle Art. I wanna be with you, Davey."

I said, "I'll take you back and tell you a story." I carried him back to his tent and tucked him in. Uncle Art didn't like it a bit, and after I'd told Norman and the other eight-year-olds the story of Jack the Giant Killer, Uncle Art took me aside. "What's the friggin' idea, Quinn? Buttering up my campers?"

"The kid came to my tent. He's homesick."

"He's a little pain in the ass. You let me handle him and keep your own nose clean."

That was gratitude! I guess he was sore about the five-dollar tip Norman's mother gave me, though I don't know how he found out. Anyway, I just ignored him and walked back to my tent. "Poor kid," I told Horse. "He's really miserable."

"Yeah. I know how he feels," Horse said. "They shipped me off to camp when I was six. My parents were sailing to Europe, and I was a nuisance. I really felt sick all that summer, scared and homesick, and everyone teased me. I was a marine, too."

"A marine?"

"Yeah, I wet my bed."

"What about your counselor?"

"He was a sadistic bastard. Teased me worse than the rest. That's why I feel for the kid. I got back at him, though." He began to laugh. "One afternoon I went up and peed in his bed, then made it up. Maybe we should tell Norman about that."

"Nah, he's too nice a kid . . . not that you weren't, Horse. Anyway, I don't think he's a marine. At least I hope not."

"Well, I can understand how he feels," Horse said as he put out his light.

I stretched out on my bed. "So can I. It's no fun being alone and away from home." I thought of Pop then, and how comforting it used to be to feel his body close to mine in bed at night and hear his soft snoring. I got a funny choked-up feeling, not so much for myself, I decided, but for Pop. I had never realized that my going to camp meant he'd be alone all summer!

▪ CHAPTER TEN ▪

The first Sunday morning at Camp Harel I woke up with an uneasy feeling. At first I thought it might be the chicken soup with matzo balls we'd had for dinner Saturday night. Horse called the matzo balls "sinkers," but I loved them. They were good and heavy, something you could sink your teeth into, and I had eaten a mess of them. I must say the camp food was delicious, even though the other waiters grumbled about it. But they'd never tasted Pop's cooking.

Anyway, after a minute or two I realized it wasn't the matzo balls that were upsetting me, but the fact that this was Sunday, and I was supposed to go to church with Nancy, the camp nurse, and Tom Ciardi, the head counselor!

Shep had arranged for Horse and Squeak to cover my tables, and I wouldn't have to serve breakfast or lunch if I was that late. I washed up and shaved with cold water at the big zinc-lined sinks near the crappers and felt a little better. The water on the Hill was all cold and always freshened you up in the morning—or at least it did those guys who washed. A lot of them didn't, figuring they'd swim later in the day, and that would be good enough. The only hot water was down at the showers next to the mess hall. The camp took showers there once a week on Friday afternoon.

It was quite a sight, shower time, all the counselors and kids in the bathhouse stark-naked, the kids lined up by tents, and the counselors scrubbing the younger ones down with soap and brushes while they screeched and slapped each other and raced back and forth on the slippery, wood-slatted floors.

The air would be thick with steam, and half the counselors would have their faces lathered, waiting to shave after the kids were done.

It was the only chance anyone got to use hot water. The rest of the week we all washed and shaved with ice-cold water up on the Hill.

We waiters always tried to get in first, using the excuse that we had to set up our tables, but Tom Ciardi would start shouting that there wasn't enough hot water, but then Horse would drown Tom out by singing. Horse had a wonderful baritone voice, and he would start singing the moment he hit the showers, and he was loud! Sometimes he was so good the counselors would stop soaping the kids and just stand there listening. "Beautiful Dreamer" was his favorite, but the one I liked best was "The Blind Ploughman."

"You could be a professional," Uncle Irv Sammis, who directed the Glee Club, told him one Friday, but Horse just shrugged.

"Not me. I only like to sing in the shower, and where did you ever see a shower onstage in the concert hall?"

But Uncle Irv still kept after him to come join the Glee Club, while Horse always put him off. "Maybe next week," or "I've got a sore throat this week, Irv. Later."

The camp ran out of hot water quickly on Friday nights, and Tom Ciardi and Mr. Luft were always trying to convince the older kids to take bars of soap and wash in the creek. The creek water was icy cold, too cold for the younger kids, so when the water did run out, the Hunters and Warriors ended up with creek baths. By then we waiters were out of the shower room.

That Sunday after I had washed and shaved, I combed my hair and slipped on my tweed jacket with the leather patches. I had thought it pretty snappy back in New York, but up here it looked shabby. All the other guys had new jackets, and a few had come up wearing suits. I had once owned a suit briefly when I was thirteen and about to be bar mitzvahed. Pop and Sam decided to take me downtown and buy me one on Orchard Street. We shopped around and found one for twelve dollars that looked great. "All wool," Sam pointed out.

But there was another for nine dollars, and I could see Pop was really interested in that one, so I said I liked it too. After all, how often would I wear a suit? It was a nubby gray tweed, and it looked fine at my Bar Mitzvah. Grandma came and brought some poppy-seed sponge cake, and afterward we had wine and cake at the apartment. I wore it one more time when we went to visit an aunt on Pop's side of the family, and then on the way home we were caught in the rain and soaked.

I hung the suit up in the bathroom to dry, and it did, but when I tried it on again the pants came above my ankles, and the jacket cuffs were halfway to my elbows. Pop tried to convince me it didn't look too bad. "I could maybe let the pants down a few inches . . ."

But the pants and jacket wouldn't close, and so that was that for the suit. Pop wouldn't throw it out. "You only wore it twice," he said indignantly when I wanted to get rid of it.

"But it's no good, Pop. It doesn't fit!" Well, we saved it anyway, and it's still hanging in the closet.

But at Camp Harel I realized that the clothes the other waiters had were not Orchard Street buys. They came from pretty fancy shops and looked great. Next to them my jacket was not only shabby, but cheap!

When Shep saw me looking in the mirror that Sunday morning, he asked, "What's wrong?"

"Do you think this jacket looks all right? For church, I mean?"

He was carrying his toothbrush and towel, and he put them down and stood back and put his head to one side. "Have you got another?"

"That's the problem. I should have brought up my corduroy. Maybe I'll just wear a sweater. I have a nice white one."

"Tell you what," Shep said. "Take my tweed jacket. It should fit you. We're almost the same size."

I wasn't sure, but Shep said, "Go ahead. We all borrow each other's clothes—when they fit. Try it on."

It fit pretty well, especially if I left the front buttons open, and it was a brown-and-rust check, so it went with my tan slacks. I felt pretty snappy when I joined Tom Ciardi and Nancy at the infirmary. Nancy was wearing a dress, a light, pink, chiffony sort of thing that came almost to her ankles, and she had a little jacket and a matching hat and she looked awfully cute—and young.

Tom was wearing a suit, but it fit him like a uniform. "He looks as if he has a ramrod up his ass," Dinge had said the first time he saw Tom. He had a real short haircut, about an inch of brush all over his head, with a bald spot at the rear. I could see that because we drove into town in Nancy's Model A and I had the rumble seat to myself.

"We'll drop you at the Methodist Church," Nancy called out over her shoulder, "and we'll pick you up at Musikants's at eleven."

Mr. Musikants ran the town soda fountain and the town bar, but only the counselors were allowed in the bar. It was just a short walk from the church, and Nancy and Tom were going on to Haines Falls, about five miles down the road.

I watched them drive off, then squared my shoulders and walked up to the church, only to find it hadn't opened yet. It was eight o'clock and the sign in front said services would be from nine to ten, so I had an hour to kill.

Of course I realized that I didn't have to go to church at all. I could just walk around town and pretend that I had been there, but I ought to go, I told myself. I should really see what this shaygets stuff was all about. Still, what if I made some stupid mistake? What if I had to cross myself? Did Methodists cross themselves?

I wasn't sure. Did you cross from right to left and up and down or left to right and down and up? The kids at Hebrew School, which I had to go to for a year before my Bar Mitzvah, had a joke about crossing themselves. They'd go, *"Kop, shmuck, tzitska, tzitska,"* which translates to "head, prick, tit, tit." That meant you started at the head, but which way did the rest go?

I walked up behind the church and sat in the grass in the small cemetery on the hillside. The gravestones were old, and some had fallen over. I don't think it was used anymore, it was in such disrepair, but it was very quiet and I could see the mountains all around and even the fire station on one of the ridges that led to Hunter Mountain.

I knew the girls' camp was right below that ridge, and that started me wondering about Marcia and what the chances were that I'd see her. So far, there had been no contact between the two camps, although the other waiters told me that next Saturday night there would be a play put on at the girls' camp. They had a very fancy new social hall, and the dramatic counselor, Uncle Arnie Schaeffer, had given out parts for the play to kids back in the city, and they had been rehearsing them. That would probably be the first chance I'd get to see Marcia.

At nine o'clock, sweating a lot and hoping I wouldn't stain Shep's jacket, I joined the line of people going into church. There weren't too many, and the minister, who stood at the door shaking hands, gave me a big smile. I was a new face. But nobody bothered me, and I slipped into a pew in the back. One of my big worries had been that you had to pay for a seat, but this church was free.

Now that's more than I could say for the synagogue where I was bar mitzvahed. There you had to buy a seat for any important holiday. Pop used to get two for the High Holy Days, the only time he went. The plan was, he and Sam would go in and sit down, and after an hour Sam would come out and give his ticket to me. I'd go in and pray for the next hour, and then Sam would relieve me. At least, Sam was supposed to relieve me, but the rest of the day would go by with no sign of Sam. When I'd protest to Pop, he'd say, "Because Sam is a no-good, does that mean you have to be one too? You'll feel better after you spend a day in the synagogue, Davey. Believe me."

I didn't believe him because I never felt better, just bored silly. Instead of praying, I'd leaf through the Bible for the jucier parts. I got to know the Song of Songs very well, and I think the story about Lot and his daughters is pretty spicy. The only excitement on Yom Kippur, the Day of Atonement, would be at the beginning, when we came to the synagogue. There would always be a woman outside shouting at the rabbi and the shammes, "A ticket? I need a ticket to get inside and worship God? This is what religion has come to! Money in the temple. Go ahead, charge us to worship the Almighty, blessed be His Name, charge us to pray!"

And the rabbi and the shammes would be trying to quiet her, "Shah—shah—it's a disgrace! Such carrying on!"

But they couldn't shut her up until she had her say, and everyone would pretend it was shameful to carry on like that, but they'd all love it. It added a touch of drama to Yom Kippur, and it was repeated at every holiday—not always the same woman either.

There must have been a whole group devoted to making a rumpus at the synagogue.

But here in the Methodist church, there was none of that. Anyway, they didn't charge. The inside of the church was dim and had a musty odor, as if it hadn't been opened all winter. There was a round stained-glass window over the altar, which sent a colored fluttering of light all through the church. An organ was playing and the music was deep and solemn. I saw a cross painted on the wall over the altar, but no statues of Jesus or any saints. I was a little disappointed because I had expected something more dramatic.

Then the organ stopped and the minister recited some prayer, and the choir of six men and six women filed up the aisle. They all wore long gowns and were singing a hymn as they walked, number 166 in the hymnal. I picked up the hymnal from the rack in front and followed the song, "Lord Jesus I Love Thee, I Know Thou Art Mine." I didn't sing at first. I'm not such a good singer. In music class I'm one of the listeners, and Miss Butel, our music teacher, walks up and down the aisle watching our mouths to make sure we listeners listen but don't sing out and throw everyone else off.

Singing has always been a problem with me. In Hebrew School we used to learn to read with our hands on the table, and the rabbi, an old guy with a long beard, would walk around the table with a ruler. When one of us made a mistake, *smack,* the ruler would come down on our hands. If we pulled the hand away before the ruler connected, we'd get two more, the rabbi holding our hands firm.

It helped me learn to read Hebrew. Those smacks hurt. But I never learned to understand the language. We were just taught to read phonetically. "It's not necessary for you to understand it," the rabbi would mutter. "The Almighty, blessed be His Name, understands, and that's enough."

When we started to learn the chants we would have to sing at our Bar Mitzvahs, I ended up with very raw hands. "Your son," the rabbi told Pop almost in tears, "is going to disgrace the congregation. He'll be the only Jew who recites his prayers instead of singing them."

"Why can't he sing them?" Pop asked mildly, while I sat there trying to avoid his eyes.

107

"Because," the rabbi said, raising his voice, "he can't keep a tune!"

So I recited the prayers at my Bar Mitzvah, and I became a man anyway. Now, in church, there was a lot of singing, and after a while I decided, why not? They couldn't tell, with all that singing, who was off key and out of tune, so I joined in and had a great time. I enjoy singing even if I can't. At least I enjoyed it until I realized that there were an awful lot of *Jesus Christs* in the psalms. "God, our Father," didn't bother me, nor did "Holy, Holy, Holy, Lord God Almighty." That had to be the same God, but I didn't feel right praising Jesus, so after a while I put back the hymnal and picked up the Bible, and that was a shock because it had the Old Testament in it, and I turned to the Song of Songs right away. It had helped me get through the Yom Kippur services and it helped me get through that hour in church.

My illusion about a free seat was shattered when they began passing plates around, and I could hear the clinking of coins. I'd have to put something in, I realized, and luckily I had some change in my pocket, a nickel and four pennies. When the plate came by I dropped the pennies in, holding my hand over them. The usher couldn't see how much I contributed, but those four clinks sounded reassuring and he smiled at me.

After the service I joined the line leaving the church, and then was upset to realize it was moving slowly because the minister was at the door saying a word or two to each person. When my turn came, he grasped my hand in both of his and gave me a big "Hello!" as if I were an old friend, but then he added, "You're new."

"I work at the camp," I said, and he nodded happily.

"Well, we're certainly glad to see you here. We're having cake and coffee in the basement. Maybe you'll join us?"

Much as I liked cake, I said, "Oh, I can't. I have to get back to work." And we both smiled until finally he let go and turned to the next person with that same cheerful "Hello."

I walked into Hunter and stopped at Musikants's for a soda. Musikants's is the hangout for all the counselors and waiters. The counselors hang out in the bar, but the rest of us go to the soda fountain. Uncle Arnie, the dramatic counselor, says Musikants's bar is the only way to endure the summer. "Three highballs and I can stand the little monsters. Four and I begin to think even Luft is human!"

The soda fountain is my favorite place. There's a big marble bar and behind it a mirrored wall with stained-glass panels that light up from behind, and there are shelves of clean glasses. There are three gleaming spigots coming up from behind the fountain bar to dispense soda, and below them is a row of smaller spigots for the different flavors.

Mr. Musikants's son, Hal, works the bar as soda jerk with a white jacket and white hat. He's very good. He can flip a scoop of ice cream into a metal container for a milk shake with a three-foot curve. He shows off a lot for the Rocky Clove girls, but he makes great sodas.

Eppie started the business of drinking half his soda and then complaining that it was too weak. He'd get a glop of extra syrup, drink half again and complain it was too strong. Hal would roll his eyes and give him a squirt of seltzer. After a while the rest of us tried it, until Mr. Musikants gave orders, "What you get is what you drink!"

I had a nickel soda that Sunday while I was waiting for Nancy and Tom, and Mr. Musikants's little daughter, Sonia, climbed up next to me to talk about her lost kitten. I thought of a dish of ice cream, but I didn't have any more change.

Not that I was broke. There was the five-dollar tip Norman's mother had given me, and the two dollars Pop gave me for spending money, but I had left them back at camp. I had tried to bargain Pop up to three dollars, but he'd stood firm. "What do you need with money? You'll get your food there, won't you?" I couldn't deny that.

Finally I heard Nancy Minogue's Model A honking outside, and I stood up and hurried out. "How were services?" Nancy asked as I opened the rumble seat and climbed in.

"Very nice, thanks," I said earnestly. "I had a long talk with the minister."

"Isn't that nice. We had a lovely Mass. That Father Donaghue is

109

a darling. Someday you'll have to meet him." She shifted gears and said something I couldn't catch as we started off. It was only two miles to camp, but halfway there Nancy pulled the car over to the side of the road and turned toward Tom Ciardi.

"Look, I told you to cut it out!" she said angrily. "Do I have to make a scene about this?"

From back in the rumble seat I couldn't see what was going on, but I could hear their voices very clearly. Ciardi turned to look at me, then back to Nancy. "Hey, come on, Nance—what's the big problem?"

"The big problem is I said no. I said it before and I'm saying it now. Keep your goddamn hands to yourself or get out and walk!"

"Fuck it! I don't have to take this shit!" He shouted suddenly, his face red, and he opened the car door and climbed out. "Thanks. I'll walk." I was really shocked to hear him use language like that in front of a woman.

Reaching over, Nancy slammed the door, then started the car with an angry screech of tires. But she went only a few hundred yards when she slammed on her brakes. "Davey?"

I said, "Yes, ma'am." I was too embarrassed to look at her. "Why don't you ride up front?"

So I climbed out, shut the rumble seat, and got into the front with Nancy. I could tell she was mad because she had her teeth clamped shut, and her face was very pale. She shifted gears, and we shot off, and for a while she didn't say anything. Then, to my surprise, we went right past the camp gates. I said, "Hey, Nancy! You missed the gates."

"I want to take a little ride, Davey. Do you mind?"

"Sure. I love riding in this car."

She almost smiled then, and she patted the dashboard. "Good old Model A! At least I can depend on it. Okay, here's the ride I promised you." She stepped on the gas, and the car let out a roar and began barreling down the road. At the crossroads she turned right, and about two miles beyond Camp Harel we passed the girls' camp, Rocky Clove.

A big sign framed in natural wood branches announced the camp name. It arched over two posts built of rocks with a wrought-iron gate between them. Beyond, I could see the playing fields on a

110

sloping lawn that ended in a row of white cabins. Beyond the cabins, a ridge swept up to the peak of Hunter Mountain.

On the right I had a quick glimpse of the new social hall, and on the left of the mess hall. Dozens of girls in green bloomers and blouses were running around the fields, and then we were past and through Rocky Clove Notch, the passage between Hunter Mountain and Rocky Mountain.

Nancy and I didn't talk, but the ride was swell. Scary, too, because the car swayed so, and the road wasn't always asphalt. Here and there it was dirt and ridged like a washboard, but that didn't bother Nancy. She was a real Barney Oldfield at the wheel!

She slowed down when we came to a little valley with a swamp on one side of the road and a neatly kept lawn with picnic tables on the other. She parked the car near an enormous rock. "That's Devil's Tombstone," she said as she opened her door and stepped out. The two of us walked over to the rock, and she showed me the outline of a face that did look a lot like a devil. "That's how it got its name. It's a favorite place for hikes."

She sat down at one of the picnic tables and held up the hem of her dress. "That son of a bitch tore it!" she said angrily. "My best dress!"

"You mean Tom Ciardi?"

"What other son of a bitch is there?" Her face was all screwed up, and for a moment I was afraid she was going to cry. I hadn't had any experience at comforting crying women, but then she bit her lip. "He's not worth getting upset about."

I reached down and looked at the tear. "It's okay, Nancy. It's right along the seam. You can sew that up easily."

She examined it closely. "You're right, Davey." She seemed to relax a bit, and she smiled at me. "How do you know about seams in dresses?"

"My pop makes them," I said. "He's a cutter and pattern maker. Sometimes he makes dresses for my sister-in-law. He's good."

"I'll bet he is." She dropped her hem and, leaning back against the table, fumbled in her purse for a pack of Camels. She lit one and drew in the smoke with a sigh of pleasure, then, looking at me quizzically, she offered me the pack. "Do you smoke, Davey?"

111

I said, "No, thanks." It's a funny thing that I don't smoke. Sam does, and most of the guys at school do, but Pop doesn't, and he once explained to me that if you blow cigarette smoke at a rattlesnake's head, the snake would die. That was good enough for me; besides, the one time I tried it I felt sick for hours afterward. "You gotta persist," Saul Greenspan explained. He had given me the cigarette on one of the Aviary Club's outings. But I didn't see any sense in persisting in something that made you sick.

"Damn that Ciardi!" Nancy said. "I'll tell you something, Davey; he'd never make a pass at one of the girl counselors. Oh no, he wouldn't dare try to screw around with a nice Jewish girl, but I'm fair game." She ground out her cigarette on the top of the picnic table. "Luft too! Anyone can make a pass at the camp shiksa!"

I wanted to say something funny about the camp shaygets to take the tension out of the air, but I didn't trust myself. I felt very uneasy listening to her, and I wasn't at all sure of what to say.

"I shouldn't bitch to you," Nancy went on, shaking another cigarette out of the pack and tamping it on the table, then lighting it. She had only taken three puffs of the first and had wasted the rest, and here she was on a fresh one. "I guess it's no big deal," she went on, but I tell you, sometimes I get so mad . . ." She was quiet for a while, puffing at the cigarette, then she said, "It's not that I don't like the job. I do. The work is easy, and I love it up here in the mountains, only . . ."

Very carefully, I said, "If there's anything I can do . . ."

She turned to me and smiled, and her face lit up and those blue-green eyes really seemed to glow. "You're a darling. Thanks for listening. If I need help, I'll call on you, Davey."

I thought she was teasing, but I grinned and said, "Sure. Anytime."

We sat there for another three cigarettes enjoying the scenery, and finally Nancy stood up reluctantly. "We'd better get back." Once in the car she turned on the ignition, then, facing me, she put a hand behind my head and gave me a quick kiss on the cheek. "You're a darling!"

We drove back to camp, and as we passed Rocky Clove I saw a group of girls crossing the road, and sure enough, one of them was

112

Marcia. I didn't even get a chance to wave, we were past them so quickly, and though I wanted to ask Nancy to stop and let me out and I'd walk back to Camp Harel, I couldn't think of any good excuse in time, and then it was too late!

Back in camp, I had missed lunch, but I was in time to clean up my tables and set up for dinner. I thanked Shep for the morning off and returned his jacket, but I kept thinking of Nancy all that afternoon. She had seemed so different out of uniform, in that summer dress. It reminded me of the dresses Miss Casey wore at the library, and that reminded me of Percy, and I realized that I really missed her—and for that matter Miss Casey and Mrs. Bell, too.

Then I wondered what Tom Ciardi had tried to do in the front seat of the car. I wasn't too eager to meet him just now, and I kept a watch out to make sure I could dodge him. Then I wondered what Nancy had meant when she said Luft too. I knew Mr. Luft was married, and his wife ran the girls' camp. I never thought he'd fool around so close to home. What had Sam advised me? Don't shit on your own doorstep! Well, at least I had followed his advice—not that I had much choice. The only women I saw were Nancy, Mrs. Lowenstein, the Camp Mother, and Jenny the cook.

I was a little late getting my tables set up, and the other guys had gone before I was finished. I was at the silver drawer, out of sight of the kitchen, when I heard Jenny say, "Shah, shah—now don't cry. It's all right, baby. Here, I'll get you another piece of pie."

I looked around the cupboard and there was Small Fry, his head in his hands, and Jenny was gently patting his shoulder. Poor kid, he must have gotten into trouble again. I didn't want to let them know I'd seen them, so I went back to the silver drawer and banged the silverware around a bit while I counted it out. When I finally carried the tray over to my tables, Small Fry was gone and Jenny was mixing something in a big bowl and grumbling in Hungarian. She gave me an angry look as I went past, but there was nothing unusual about that.

▪ CHAPTER ELEVEN ▪

"The trouble with you, Davey," Marcia whispered, "is that you're obsessed with the physical. You have no idea of how to improve your mind. I don't know when you last read a decent book—if you ever did!"

I used to get a kick out of Marcia's criticizing me. I always told myself that it meant that she cared, but this time it bothered me. Defensively, I said, "I've been in touch with more books last winter than you could imagine. Remember, I worked in a library."

"Oh, Davey, touching books is not reading them!"

"Hey, will you two quiet down and do something besides talking," Killer called out, and then there was some giggling and squirming from over on the right, but it was too dark really to see anything. We were in the haystack down below the waitresses' bunk and near the lake at Camp Rocky Clove—Killer and Squeak and Dinge and I, and, of all people, Small Fry!

I couldn't believe it, but it had really, finally happened, five of us and five girls. We had sneaked away after the Saturday show to meet the girls in the haystack, a pile of sweet-smelling hay inside a big shed between the waitresses' bunk and Rocky Clove's little lake. "A great spot for necking," Dinge had explained.

The way it happened was that Saturday morning, after breakfast, the four of us, Shep, Horse, Killer, and I were lying on our cots. Eppie and Squeak had come into our tent, and the guys were arguing about baseball, a subject I was particularly ignorant in. They had started with the National League, Killer claiming the Chicago Cubs had it sewn up because they were ahead of the St. Louis Cards.

"With Dizzy Dean, the Cards'll make it," Horse said stubbornly. "He happens to be just the best pitcher in baseball."

"Yeah," Eppie chimed in, "and there's Stu Martin on second base. The Cubs haven't a chance."

"Whaddayuh know about baseball?" Squeak flicked a towel at Eppie. "If it were horses, now . . ."

"Cut it out! I know plenty."

Squeak started singing, "Horses, horses, crazy over horses . . ." but Shep called out, "Leave him alone, Squeak."

Squeak said, "Okay, but I'm still rootin' for the Boston Bees."

Killer gave a raspberry. "The feeblest team in the league!"

"Yeah? Well, they're ahead of the Phillies and Dodgers."

"So who isn't ahead of the Dodgers?"

"If they had a guy like DiMaggio," Squeak said wistfully, "I bet they'd make it."

Shep had been trying to read a book, and now he put it down with a show of disgust. "Fat chance a guy has to read, with you clowns yakking. Who's DiMaggio?"

I was glad he asked, because all of it was Greek to me. I knew who Babe Ruth was, and that was all. There was a minute of quiet, as if none of them could believe the question, then Eppie said, "Wow!"

"The Yankees bought him from the San Francisco Seals," Killer said patiently, as if talking to a child. "In the first month of play the guy just batted four hundred. For Chrissake, Shep, Gehrig only batted three hundred and ninety eight!"

I decided I had to say something to show I wasn't another dimwit about baseball like Shep. The only safe ground for me was Babe Ruth. "He can't beat the Babe," I said knowingly.

"Well, no." Killer frowned. "But who can?"

I was saved any more observations by Dinge coming into the tent in a hurry. "Hey, guys, Shep and I have to drive a load of bread over to the girls' camp. Their oven's on the fritz. This is our big chance."

"A load of bread is our big chance?" Killer said, staring at Dinge. "You jest."

"Jest a moment." Dinge grinned, and we all groaned. "Now use your fuckin' head. Shep and I spend a half hour or so unloading bread—and talking to the waitresses! Get it?"

"You mean!" Squeak threw up his hands dramatically. "I'm speechless!"

"You'll be headless if you don't stop being a smart-ass. Look, you guys. Tonight there's a show at the girls' camp. We'll all be going over legitimately. We can sneak out after the show and meet the girls and head for the haystack."

"The haystack!" Killer's eyes lit up. "My wet dreams are about to come true! I want Zelda."

"You can have the whole bunch," Dinge said, "As long as I get the Southern belle." He rolled his eyes.

Laughing, Shep asked, "Who's the Southern belle?"

"Ruth Epstein!" Dinge kissed the tips of his fingers and threw his hand up. "She has this Southern accent that makes your balls freeze! Y'awl get me some hominy an' grits, man, an Ah'm youhs."

"Southern accent!" Horse laughed. "Come on, Dinge. My sister's a senior over there, and she told me La Epstein spent a semester at Alabama State and she comes back a Southern belle. Hell, I know Ruth. She grew up in the Bronx!"

"Bronx, shmonx!" Dinge grabbed at his crotch. "She's a dry fuck!"

I couldn't help asking, "What's a dry fuck?"

They all looked at me in surprise. "Hey, where have you been all these years?" Dinge said. "With a dry fuck you can pop off by rubbing against her. No bare skin. You keep your pants buttoned, and she keeps her dress down, but oh, boy!"

Shep shook his head disgustedly. "You guys are sick!"

Just then Small Fry came into the tent rubbing his eyes. "What's going on here? How can anyone sleep with all this racket?" He scratched his chest. "I think I got cooties. Someone took my soap."

"I did, Small Fry," Dinge said. "I'm headed for the creek for a cold douche before Shep and I head over to Rocky Clove. Then I'm going to borrow some of Squeak's stinky water."

"You lay off my cologne," Squeak said indignantly. "Now I know where it's going. I thought the damned stuff was evaporating!"

"You got good taste, Squeak. Hey, Small Fry." He winked at us. "You wanna come with us tonight?"

Small Fry looked surprised. "Come where?"

"Only if you're lucky!" Eppie burst out laughing. "Hey, get it? You'll come if you're lucky."

"We get it, Eppie," Shep said. Then to Dinge, "You really want Small Fry to come?"

"Well, sure. The kid needs to grow up." He put an arm around Small Fry's shoulders. "Obviously we can't fix him up with a waitress. There's a small age discrepancy. But one of the campers? A soph, maybe?"

"Cut it out!" Small Fry shrugged his arm off, then looked at us suspiciously. "Is this another gag?"

"No, honest," Dinge said seriously. "Shep and I are taking the station wagon over to Rocky Clove this morning, and we're going to arrange something with the waitresses, get them to sneak down and meet us in the fuckin' haystack after tonight's show."

"Now wait a minute." Shep put his book down and sat up. "First of all, count me out. It's against regulations, and my job is too important to me to get in trouble. I don't go along with this crap." He grabbed his shirt and walked to the tent entrance. With one hand on the flap, he turned. "Of course, whatever you guys decide to do, if I don't know about it I can't stop it." He grinned and left the tent, and Dinge slammed his fist into his palm. "Hot damn!"

"Hey, wait." Horse stood up. "I'm with Shep. Count me out."

"Me, too," Eppie said. "I'm off women this summer."

"You must be shtupping the horses." Dinge laughed and looked around. "Okay, that's me, Killer, Squeak, and Small Fry? Okay, Small Fry?"

Small Fry nodded. "Sure, if you can get me a girl."

"What about you, Davey?"

"There's a waitress named Marcia Beck. If she'll come, okay."

So that's what we finally decided. Dinge was all hot in the biscuit about Ruth Epstein. He had met her on the boat, and Killer had a thing going with Zelda Gruber. They used to date each other during the winter. Squeak had a crush on Ebbie Roseman, and they decided that Carol Marcus, who was a soph and thirteen, would be perfect for Small Fry. Dinge agreed to ask Marcia. "If she'll come," I said.

117

"Of course she'll come! What red-blooded Jewish girl would pass up the chance of a real-live shaygets?" Dinge said.

"I don't really know what to do, I mean with a girl," Small Fry said, sitting down on the bed when Dinge left. He looked a bit pale and scared.

"No problem," Killer said kindly. "Look, I'll show you. Hey, Squeak, come over here for a demonstration."

Squeak grabbed a white towel from Shep's bed and sat down next to him. "Who am I? Carol?" He arranged the towel over his head like a shawl. "Am I irresistible?"

"Yeah. Now, Small Fry, pay attention. When you get into the haystack with her, you start slow, real slow. Hell, she's only thirteen."

"So am I," said Small Fry. "That's why I'm worried."

"First you two find a private corner of the haystack, and you spread your jacket out. Gallant, got it?" He took one of Shep's jackets off the line and spread it out on the bed, then motioned Squeak to sit on it.

"Oh, thank you, kind sir." Squeak said in a falsetto.

"Then you talk."

"What about?"

"What can you talk about? Waiting on tables? School? Any shows you saw?"

"I never saw a show."

"All right, movies. How does she like Clark Gable? Talk politics. Will Roosevelt get in this term? Sports. How come that Nazi prick Schmeling beat Joe Louis? Anything to break the ice."

Small Fry nodded. "I wish I could take notes."

"It's dark in the haystack. How would you read them? Now listen and learn. Once you're talking, put your arm around her casually, not around her shoulders. Around her waist." He moved his arm around Squeak, and Squeak pretended to giggle. "Then you inch it around till you reach her breast."

He demonstrated and Squeak slammed his elbow down against Killer's hand. "Naughty, naughty!"

Small Fry's eyes widened. "You're kidding. You wouldn't do that!"

"Oh, Christ, I'm serious, Small Fry. This is educational. You go slowly, very slowly, and if she clamps her elbow down the way Squeak did, you try again." He had his hand around Squeak's waist, and he reached his thumb up toward Squeak's nipple.

"Don't you dare!" Squeak slapped at his hand.

"You see? Then you pull back and after a few minutes you try again, sneakily."

Small Fry shook his head. "I don't think I could do that."

"Shit! Sure you can. Now watch again."

I watched the demonstration for a while, thinking maybe it was good advice. I sure hadn't been able to make any time with Marcia in all the years I'd known her, but then I didn't have someone like Killer to coach me. I had to admit his approach was smooth. Once he even got his hand on Squeak's breast before Squeak realized it. Then Squeak stood up and dropped the falsetto. "Demonstration's over. You're enjoying this too much!"

"Come on back, baby," Killer coaxed. "I'm gettin' a hard-on!"

The trouble was, I realized, this approach would never work with Marcia. In fact, I was pretty sure she wouldn't go against regulations tonight and meet me. Marcia wasn't like the other girls, if I could believe Killer and Dinge. A dry fuck! I'd never heard that expression, but it sounded pretty exciting.

That was the longest Saturday of the summer. Morning services were indoors, and after rest hour we had a competitive baseball game with Camp High Point, hardball, too!

They arrived in buses during rest hour and we could hear them cheering from across the road.

> *Rah, rah, rah, rah, Camp High Po-in-t!*
> *Rah, rah, rah, rah, Camp High Po-in-t!*
> *Rah, rah, rah, rah, Camp High Po-in-t!*

It was a monotonous cheer, and they kept repeating it all day during the game, especially when one of their team scored a hit or did some exceptional fielding. While the buses were unloading, Killer began digging through his trunk frantically. "Oh, shit, I was sure I brought a camp uniform!"

"What do you need a uniform for?" I asked.

119

"I'm playing in the game, dummy. How can I play without a camp uniform?"

"But I thought it was inter-camp competition. Only campers allowed."

Killer straightened up. "So today I am a camper. Order of Luft." He charged out and began running around to the other tents trying to borrow a camp uniform.

That didn't seem fair to me, but Shep shrugged when I asked him about it. "That's the main reason Luft wants him up here. To play baseball. Most of the waiters are here for a reason. Horse has two paying sisters at Rocky Clove, and Squeak has a paying brother in the Hunters. That's the way it goes. Don't worry about it, Davey. So Killer plays baseball pretending to be a camper. Believe me, High Point has a few waiters or junior counselors in their lineup. By the way, you're taking one of Killer's tables today. He'll eat with the Warriors." Shep started for the tent flap, then turned. "Oh yeah, Dinge wanted me to tell you and the guys he fixed it all up with the girls."

I sat down on my cot, surprised. "With Marcia Beck too?"

"I suppose so." He smiled. "Watch your step, Davey. Don't get caught. Luft patrols the roads after eleven o'clock."

"How come you're not coming along, Shep?"

He stood at the door of the tent for a moment, then came over to my cot and sat down. "Aside from needing this job too much to take a chance—it's gonna pay my tuition—I can tell you, Davey, I don't see much profit out of spending the night in the haystack with some girl who won't let you get to first base. You just end up with blue balls."

I said, "Not Dinge. He claims his girl is, you know, a dry fuck."

"Dinge talks a lot, and maybe it's bullshit, and maybe she is, but even so, that's not my idea of a great sexual experience. Think about it, Davey." He stood up and stretched. "Well, I'm off to see the big game. Coming?"

I walked down the hill with him thinking about what he had said. The dry-fuck business, if it was true, did sound exciting, but remembering Percy and Mrs. Bell made me realize he was right. Even Casey with that crazy tabletop business hadn't been as

120

satisfying as the others. It seemed, I decided, that I still had a lot to learn about sex. One thing I was pretty sure of—I wouldn't learn much from Marcia.

The kids from Camp High Point were lined up on the right side of the baseball diamond, and we Harelians sat on the left. The game seemed pretty dull at first, most of the excitement coming from the cheerleaders. The High Point kids were great yellers, but we did pretty well ourselves. Our best cheer went:

> *With an* H *and an* A *and an* R,E,L,
> *With an* H *and an* A *and an* R,E,L,
> *Harel, Harel, rah, rah, rah!*

It doesn't sound like much when you first hear it, but after twenty or thirty times it begins to get a certain charge to it—especially if there's a good play going on. Trouble was, there weren't many good plays, at least not on Camp Harel's part. Even with my limited knowledge of baseball I could see that our team, except for Killer and a junior counselor named Lukie Wishnowitz, were a bunch of klutzes.

Then, in the top of the eighth, Killer came up to bat with two out and the bases loaded. The score was High Point 16, Harel 4. It didn't look too good.

"This is the time for a real cheer," Dinge said, gathering the seven of us waiters together. "We'll give Killer the waiters' cheer."

"What's the waiters' cheer?" I asked.

"Oh, shit, Davey doesn't know it. What the hell, you yell along with us." And as Killer stepped up to the plate, the group of us yelled out:

> *Succotash, succotash! A rag o' bone, a hunk o' hash!*
> *Sooop, sooop, gefilte fish, I ash yuh!*
> *Beans, potatoes, hip, hip, the waiters. Yeah, Killer!*

Killer grinned and swung the bat a bit, then stepped up to the plate, and at the same moment Mr. Luft came running over to us, glaring. "You stupid animals! What are you trying to do?" he hissed. "Why don't you just tell them he's a waiter instead of a camper?"

"With an *H*, and an *A*, and an *R,E,L*," Dinge yelled out, jumping to his feet in front of the camp, and the kids started off on the camp cheer, while Mr. Luft stormed away and glared back at us.

But it didn't phase Killer one bit, and I found out why he had made all-around camper. As the ball came over the plate on the first pitch, he stepped into it, swinging his bat and *Crack!* the ball sailed over left field in a long, lazy arc—and into the creek.

Well, the whole camp went crazy. Three campers and Killer came in, and the score was 16 to 8. "You've one more inning," Luft was yelling, "we've got a chance, goddamn it. Get out there and do your best!"

Harel's best wasn't good enough. They pulled in one more run, but High Point scored another two, and the game ended High Point, 18, Harel 9. "Oh, well," Killer said as we walked him toward the showers, "it's only the first game of the season. We'll get better."

"The trouble is," Dinge said, "they'll get better too."

We didn't have an answer for that.

Supper was a pretty gloomy affair, even though Tom Ciardi stood up and made a fine speech about how winning wasn't everything, and tonight he wanted us to make a good show of ourselves for the girls' camp.

The campers were trucked over to Rocky Clove right after supper as they left the mess hall. We had to clean up and set up and we didn't get over to the girl's camp till much later, especially since Dinge and Killer insisted on shaving. I had shaved two days ago, and with my blond hair I could go for a week without it showing, but those two had blue shadows two hours after shaving. This was the second shave that day for Killer because he had shaved real close for the game. It didn't look good to have a camper with four-o'clock shadow on his face.

Uncle Frank Eliscu, the arts and crafts counselor, was ferrying kids in the camp station wagon, and he let four of us ride inside on the last trip. The other four, Killer, Shep, Horse, and I, rode the running board. We hung on with one hand around the doorpost, and it was a wild ride over that bumpy road, with Uncle Frank driving like a cowboy and the four of us yelling like wild Indians.

We were too late to get seats in the social hall, so we stood near the porch to watch. Before the curtain went up, the girls sang:

We are the girls of Rocky Clove
You hear so much about.
The people stop to stare at us,
Whenever we go out.
We're noted for our winsome ways,
The things we like to do.
Most everybody likes us—
We hope you like us too!

It sounded pretty sexy, especially the last few lines, and they sang it in a kind of provocative way. Then Uncle Irv Sammis stood up and blew his whistle, and the Harel Glee Club filed up front. The Glee Club was made up of counselors and Warriors for the most part, but there were a few younger kids too, including, to my surprise, Norman Seidel! They all looked great, the counselors in white shirts and pants, and the campers in blue shorts and sleeveless jerseys with gold stripes down the shorts and a big *CH* on each jersey.

They sang "On the Road to Mandalay," and Uncle Art Aronson did the solo in a deep bass that made shivers go through me when he sang, "Ship me somewhere east of Suez . . ." They sang "The Green-Eyed Dragon with the Thirteen Tails," which was my favorite, and finished with "Recessional," which was very depressing. We all decided that Horse could have done a better job than the soloist, but he was leery of joining. "It takes up too much free time," he told me.

Then the lights dimmed and the curtain went up for the play, *Six Who Pass While the Lentils Boil*. It didn't make too much sense to me, maybe because it was difficult to hear everything out on the porch, but the scenery was great, and all the campers were enjoying themselves.

Before the curtain came down, Dinge pulled me aside and said, "Come on! Now's our chance," and while everyone was applauding, we sneaked off the porch and into the trees. In a few seconds we were joined by Killer and Small Fry.

"Squeak's down by the lake," Killer whispered. "Come on." And the four of us went through the woods that bordered the campgrounds. At the road we could hear the applause from the

123

social hall. "This is our chance to get across," Killer said. "We'll make it before the cars start pulling out."

We ran across and ducked through the bushes on the other side. I could feel the thorns tear at me, and Killer whispered, "Watch out for the brambles."

"Yeah, thanks," Dinge answered. "I'm all cut up, and now you tell me."

"Let me lead," Small Fry said confidently. "I'm terrific at woodcraft."

We stepped back as he slipped ahead, and we followed him through the bramble bushes down to the lake. He was right. Even in the dark he was able to find an easy path through. The haystack was in a shed just before the lake, and as we walked toward it, a tall, lanky figure stood up in front of us. Dinge let out a yelp, but it was only Squeak, and he shushed us. "You sound like a herd of elephants. Come on, the girls are waiting." He turned to Small Fry. "They couldn't get Carol, but it's all right. They got another soph, and she's even cuter. Alice Einstein, and she's smart. She dummied her bed so they won't get her at bed check." He urged us toward the shed. "Come on, the girls are waiting."

And sure enough, they were. I didn't get more than a glimpse of any of them, even the "Southern belle," whom I really wanted to see. Marcia grabbed my hand and pulled me into one corner of the haystack. We had hardly settled down when she started talking. "Now, Davey, I don't want you to get any ideas. I only came along to make sure you didn't get into trouble. This is a crazy thing to do, especially getting a kid like Alice for your little friend."

"He's big enough to be a waiter," Dinge said from the other side of the haystack. "So he's big enough to be a man, aren't you, Small Fry?"

One of the girls giggled, and then from Dinge's corner a heavy Southern drawl said, "Ah don' think it's nice to poke fun at yoah frien'."

Marcia lowered her voice to a whisper. "I really mean it, Davey. Whose crazy idea was this?"

I said, "That's okay, Marcia. We'll go back now, you and me, if you're worried. I don't want to get you into trouble."

I stood up, and she grabbed my hand and pulled me back down. "Don't be an idiot!" Then, whispering, she said, "The girls would think I was letting them down if I didn't go along with this, and I know I'm safe with you, Davey."

I thought, that's the trouble. She's perfectly safe. I could hear noises from Dinge's corner, and I wondered if he had started his "dry fuck" already. What about all that preliminary work Killer had talked about to Small Fry, and why was Small Fry so quiet? He was only thirteen, for God's sake!

"Did you hear me, Davey?" Marcia asked.

"Hear what?" I said, trying to get comfortable in the hay. It smelled peculiar, and it itched my nose. I felt as if I were just on the verge of a sneeze but couldn't get it out.

"I said I know I'm safe with you, Davey." She had forgotten to whisper, and her voice rang through the haystack.

"One hundred percent safe!" Killer called out, and there was a lot of laughing and giggling.

I leaned back in the hay and crossed my legs. "You don't have to worry," I said softly.

"I'm not worried!" Marcia said angrily. "Sometimes I just don't understand you, Davey." She took my hand and pulled me to a sitting position. "You could at least put your arm around me. I don't want the other girls to think I'm some sort of frigid woman."

I slipped my arm around her waist, suddenly realizing that being distant with Marcia worked better than trying too hard. I remembered Killer's demonstration and wondered if I dared move around to touch her breast. The idea of that left me a little breathless. But I decided I'd better play it safe. At the same time I was listening for the sounds from Dinge's corner—only there weren't any.

"You'd better kiss me," Marcia said in a resigned tone.

I said, "Why?"

"Because everyone else is doing it, even your little friend Small Fry," she whispered.

"How can you tell in the dark?" I still didn't make a move toward her, but I could feel my heart racing.

Instead of answering, she leaned forward and kissed me. It wasn't

125

much of a kiss, certainly not anywhere near the kissing Mrs. Bell had shown me, but coming from Marcia, it was pretty good. I put my free hand behind her head and kissed her again, trying to force my tongue between her lips. That was a mistake. She pulled free and wiped her lips. "Don't be disgusting, Davey!"

That's when she told me that my trouble was too much concern with the physical, and we had that little set-to about reading. After Killer had told us to quiet down, I remembered the book Shep was reading, and very casually I said, "As a matter of fact, I've been reading Huxley's *Eyeless in Gaza*."

"Really?" She didn't sound impressed. "Where did you get a copy?"

"The headwaiter, Shep, brought a copy up with him. I'm a lot more intellectual than you think, Marcia."

She sort of snorted, then said, "You'd better kiss me again. Everyone can see us, but none of that funny stuff."

The moon had risen over the tops of the trees across the lake, and its light filled the shed and the haystack with a silvery-white glow. You could see everyone, darker shadows against the dark hay, and a quick glance showed me that all four couples, even Small Fry and Alice, were busy kissing. Well, I might as well make Marcia look good to her friends. We began to neck in a very dispassionate way, mouths closed to avoid any of that "funny business" and no touching in certain places, as Marcia very quickly let me know.

It's a funny thing. I enjoyed it—more than enjoyed. I felt that weak, shivery feeling go through me, a sort of excitement that made me feel like getting up and running around, but something else was strange. In all the time we spent necking in the haystack, I never once got an erection! Now to me that was amazing. Maybe it was just because I loved Marcia so much I didn't want to spoil it with anything that "physical." But that's not really something I have any control over. It must have been my subconscious protecting Marcia, I decided as we hiked back along the road.

"How did you make out?" Killer asked Dinge.

He stopped and shoved his groin forward while we all looked. Sure enough, there was a wide wet stain down the front of his pants.

"They'll have to go in the wash, but it was worth it. How about you guys?"

"Oh, Zelda and I have an understanding," Killer said seriously. "We go only so far. Yodeling in the canyon—no sinking sturgeon."

"Yodeling in the canyon," Squeak explained to me as we walked along, "is heavy necking, hands on the breast, but no bare skin. Sinking sturgeon, well, that's going all the way."

"And you can forget that with any Rocky Clove girl," Killer said.

"Oh, I don't know," Dinge boasted. "I may sink it before the summer is out. That dame is something."

"So how did you do?" Squeak asked Small Fry. "You were quiet enough."

"I like Alice," Small Fry said seriously. "Sure we kissed a little, but we're both very young. You know, she's a very smart girl. She knows all about the expanding universe."

"Oh, shit," Dinge threw up his hands. "It's the expanding cock you should have concentrated on. What about you, Davey? How did the shaygets do?"

I said, "The shaygets decided the expanding universe is a foolish idea. The light of the stars reaches us thousands of years later, so how can we tell what's going on out there?"

Small Fry started to say, "It's the shift to the red in the light . . ." but Dinge grabbed a handful of dirt from the side of the road and heaved it at me.

"Bullshit. I saw you noodling with Marcia. How far did you get?"

"We won't get very far if we don't duck," Squeak yelped. "There's a car coming!"

We could see the headlights lighting up the road ahead of us, and we all five threw ourselves off the road and into the bushes, where we lay silently until the car had passed. "It's Luft," Dinge said as we climbed out and dusted ourselves off. "He's patrolling the roads. Let's beat it."

We made it back to camp, ducking in the back way, though we had to hide twice more when oncoming headlights lit up the road. On the bridge across the creek, we all decided to take a leak, and

Squeak grabbed Small Fry, who was about to pee off the upstream side of the bridge. "For Chrissakes, kid, don't do that. Pee against the stream and you can start a flood."

We peed downstream and had a contest to see who could pee the longest. Dinge won that. "I've been holding it in all night. Let's tippy-toe up the hill. All we need is for Ciardi to catch us now."

"Well, if you shut your mouth, maybe he won't," Squeak said. "Let's go along the side, through the bushes."

We got to bed safely, and as I pulled my blanket up, Shep woke up. "Have a good time?"

"It was great. I think Small Fry's in love."

Shep laughed. "You nut, get to sleep."

I did, but it's funny. I didn't dream of Marcia but of Nancy, of all people!

▪ Chapter Twelve ▪

Dear Pop:

Everything is fine. You should be proud of me because not only do I still have the job, but this week the campers voted me the fastest waiter, and that's a big honor. These kids eat fast, and the big trick is to have the next course on the table by the time they finish the first. It's not easy because in between they're yelling for more water and bread, and we have to slice the bread ourselves. Thanks for the sourballs, and don't worry. I have all the clothes I need and anyway, nobody wears shirts during the day, except at meals. I was short a pair of white slacks, but I bought them in the Army and Navy store in Tannersville. That's a town nearby. I bargained the price down to a dollar-fifty.

Love

Davey

That was a lie about bargaining the price down, but I knew Pop would be glad to hear it. It was true about my being voted fastest waiter. They took a vote by voice every Sunday night, and I won the second week, maybe because Red Mogulescu at my table liked me and got the Hunters to yell louder than the rest.

Small Fry was still having a rough time, but he was managing, and Jenny, the cook, had stopped babying him. That helped. The Paps didn't give him any trouble, but the counselors at the Bucks' table were real wise guys. One dinner they got a big washtub and put it under the table. They'd empty their pitchers of water into it and keep Small Fry running back and forth to the kitchen for more water. As soon as he'd turn his back, they'd empty the pitcher, and he'd have to run out to the kitchen and fill it again.

I stopped him in the kitchen and said, "You know what they're doing? They have a washtub under the table."

He looked at me in a funny way. "I could see that, Davey, but what they don't realize is that the more they keep me running, the later their food gets there, and the colder it is, and they can forget about seconds. There won't be any left!"

The kid was right. The counselors put up a big stink when there were no seconds, and they called Shep over. "What's wrong?" Shep asked innocently, because by then we all knew what was going on.

"He's too slow is what's wrong!" Uncle Milt Gordon, who was at the head of the table, complained. "He says there are no seconds left."

Small Fry smiled sweetly and pointed under the table. "If you guys hadn't kept me running to fill up that tub, I'd have gotten the seconds before they were gone. I just hope there's enough dessert left."

The table groaned, and Shep laughed. "Tough, Milt. You hazed the wrong guy." And he walked off. The word got around the mess hall, and when the meal was over the camp gave Milt's table the "raspberry." They did that by counting out loud, "Forty-eight, forty-nine, raspberries!" And then everyone would yell. Uncle Milt got red in the face, but that was the last hazing he tried on Small Fry.

The kids liked to yell out things during the meals. The table would decide on what to say, and the counselor would blow his whistle, and then the whole table would chorus out something. Like the time they served carrots and peas as a vegetable. Red Mogulescu's table, my Hunters, called out, "Eat every carrot and pea on your plate!" then collapsed in laughter. None of the waiters would let on that it was that funny. But then we had all learned that pretending something wasn't very funny was a sign that we were pretty smooth, very adult.

I had fallen into the camp routine very easily, and I liked it. We waiters had to get up earlier than the rest of the camp because we always ate before we served. The milk came in big metal cans, and we'd ladle it out into pitchers for each table, but it had to be stirred first because the cream always rose to the top.

Killer would always ladle off a pitcher of heavy cream before we stirred up the rest, and we'd have that on our cereal. That was one of the privileges of being a waiter. Another was eating first, and always being sure of enough food. After we'd clear the waiters' table, the campers would file in, and they would cover their heads with one hand and say a prayer in Hebrew while they stood behind their chairs. Then they'd scramble to sit down, and we'd really be busy serving until the meal was over.

Up on the Hill there would be clean-up and then inspection for the camp after breakfast, but not for the waiters. We kept our tent flaps down to hide the mess even though our tents smelled a little ripe. Usually, after inspection, we'd lie out on blankets in the grass in the middle of the horseshoe of tents, while the campers went off to their periods.

There was a very rigid approach to camping at Camp Harel. There were two morning periods and a general swim, lunch, rest period, three afternoon periods, a general swim, dinner, and then, some nights, free play till taps. On other nights there would be council fire, campfire, Amateur Night, and, on Saturday nights, plays, usually at Rocky Clove.

The campers went to each period in a group. Some mornings, for instance, the Hunters might have tennis and then baseball; the Warriors baseball and then tennis; the Braves boxing, then arts and crafts, the Bucks arts and crafts, then boxing. The Paps were outside camp discipline and either played in the sandbox or went wading or did whatever Mrs. Lowenstein, the Camp Mother, dreamed up.

Tom Ciardi made up the program, and each period ended with a bugle call. The bugle calls were Tom's idea, to give the camp a military snap, like marching from one period to the next in formation. Everyone hated that, but Tom was very insistent. The bugle calls weren't bad. We woke up to reveille, and we went to bed to taps.

I didn't mind reveille, because we waiters were usually on our way down to the mess hall by the time it blew, but I loved taps. The lonely sound of the bugle echoing from the mountains gave me gooseflesh. Skippy Mann, who was the camp bugler (a hundred bucks off his camp fee) was very good, and he drew his taps out, slow and gentle. Dusk came very early because the sun set behind Hunter Mountain, and even when the sky was clear blue, the camp would be filled with deep shadows, and taps would float over it with mournful notes.

I was usually sitting on the infirmary steps when taps blew, and I could watch the lake sparkling, and the stables across the lake and the mountains behind them. I had gotten into the habit of dropping by the infirmary each evening and talking with Nancy. She liked to tell stories about the crowd she ran with down in Kingston, and her stories were wild, especially the ones about Prohibition.

"We used to travel in groups," she told me. "Nurses and doctors, a bunch of us jammed into an open car, tearing over the back roads, drinking cheap gin, and sometimes, when the doctors could get their hands on it, ethyl alcohol with some glycerine to cut it and a drop of oil of peppermint to flavor it!"

"Couldn't that make you blind?" I asked.

She leaned forward, clasping her knees, and shook her head. "That's methyl alcohol, Davey. Ethyl is a hell of a lot purer and safer than the bathtub gin we used to get. We'd even spike it with a bit of ether to get a fast, clean drunk. No hangover! Christ, Davey, those were crazy days. We'd head for Albany and the Blue Grotto, a speakeasy we all loved, and we'd dance till it was light out, then ride back, all of us stoned, to get to the hospital in time for work."

"Could you drive like that, drunk?" I asked. "Was it safe?"

She turned and looked at me with her eyes wide for a moment, all the fun seeming to drain out of her face. "Was it safe?" she repeated. "No, Davey, it damn well wasn't. It was kid stuff. Who the hell knew what we were rebelling against? It wasn't safe.

"Once, on our way back, we smashed up the car near Saugerties, and we were all cut up, but Donna—they couldn't fix her face up right. Poor kid. And it was lucky we had the doctors along, or Rita would have bled to death." She stood up abruptly. "God, I need a little drinkey-poo! Good night, Davey." And she turned and walked into the infirmary.

But she was rarely as serious as that. Usually she was relaxed, and funny, too. I think maybe she'd have a few drinks before I came by, and that would loosen her up.

The four of us, Killer, Squeak, Dinge, and I, visited the haystack again a few weeks later. It happened because we four decided to walk into town after dinner. Small Fry didn't come because he was busy writing letters to his new girlfriend, Alice.

Eppie decided he would come into town with us, and we were all walking along the railroad tracks when Eppie stopped dead and clapped his hand to his head. "Oh my God!"

I was right behind him and almost knocked him over. "What the hell is it, Eppie?"

"Look, up ahead!"

I looked as the others came up behind me. "What's wrong?"

Eppie pointed dramatically. "See, up there? The tracks come to a point. Do you know what could happen to a train when it reached that spot? Bang! Right off the track. Detailment!"

"Eppie, you shmuck, didn't you ever hear of perspective?" Squeak shouted.

"Perspective?" Eppie was jumping up and down with excitement. "You think it's an illusion? Believe me, it's real. I'm going to get there before a train does and save the day!" And off he went, leaping and yelling down the tracks.

Dinge shook his head. "He thinks he's funny, but half the time he believes these fuckin' jokes himself."

I thought it was pretty funny, and as we hiked into town I kept laughing while the others told me Eppie stories, all the crazy things he had done. I began to understand his nickname.

As usual, we had sodas at Musikants's, and Sonia Musikants came down and climbed up on a stool next to me and coaxed me into telling her a story. This was a regular routine, and I'd make up fairy tales about princesses and dragons and castles on mountaintops and little boys with magical swords. She loved them, and her big dark eyes would be enormous, and she'd rest her chin on her hands and listen as if I were the smartest guy in the world.

I liked that. For one thing, I was pretty good at telling stories. I'd had a lot of practice with Pop. For another thing, I liked the extra soda her father would slip me from time to time.

That night, as we were getting ready to go back to camp, we met the girls on their way home from the movies. They'd just seen Shirley Temple in *The Littlest Rebel,* a movie we wouldn't be caught dead at. We walked them back to Rocky Clove and ended up necking in the haystack. Actually, the time in the haystack that night was more fun anticipating than anything else, at least for me.

Marcia was very strict about what I could do and what I couldn't, and mostly it was what I couldn't. She only went along to keep an eye on her friends—at least that's what she told me. As usual, she had spent the time away from me going over my faults, and a lot of the night was spent telling me about them, while I tried to ignore the scuffling and giggling from the other parts of the haystack. I found that I wasn't as happy listening to my faults as I used to be, and finally I said, "So how come you got such a kick out of Shirley Temple? I thought you only liked foreign movies?"

She said, "Oh, Davey, sometimes you're so obtuse!" And that was her answer. Not much of one, I thought.

The next day I asked Shep if I could borrow his book when he finished it. I had made up my mind to show Marcia that I wasn't the dummy she seemed to think I was. I was going to start by reading a few important books.

"Huxley?" Shep was sprawled out on his cot reading. "You want to read *Eyeless in Gaza?* Are you sure, Davey?"

I shrugged. "I should be improving my mind." That was a straight quote from Marcia. "Don't you think so?"

Shep put the book down and sat up. "I don't think you should read to improve your mind, Davey. That's a hell of a way to approach a book. You should read to have fun, because you enjoy it, because it excites you." He frowned. "Some guys are readers and some aren't. Take Killer. He's a hell of a smart guy, don't get me wrong. He expects to go to Cornell on a scholarship, and not an athletic one, but he isn't a reader. He reads what he has to. That's it. Now Horse, he's a reader. He reads a lot of junk, but I don't think I've ever seen him without a book, even when he eats."

I nodded. "You're right there. He props it up on the sugar bowl during meals."

Shep smiled. "When you do read, Davey, what do you like?"

I wasn't too comfortable answering that. The thing was, I'd read some books, but none of them were "good." "I like the Tarzan books and the Mars books, and H. G. Wells." I didn't mention that some of my favorites were the Tom Swift, Roy Blakely, and Pee Wee Harris series, and the Jerry Todd and Poppy Ott books. I was unhappy because I realized that Shep expected more of me. "I've read some good stuff too, Shep, for school. *The Scarlet Letter* and *The Tale of Two Cities,* and we studied *Hamlet* in English."

Shep nodded and opened his trunk. "Maybe it's time you did start on some of Huxley. I have one of his books I think you'll like a hell of a lot more than *Eyeless in Gaza*. It's *Brave New World,* and it's a story about the future, but it's a lot deeper than Burroughs or Wells. Try it, Davey."

I took the book and nodded. "I will, Shep." And I did, or at least I tried. It wasn't the easiest book in the world to read, but I decided to stick with it, and later on I really was fascinated by it, even though I didn't get it all. Late that afternoon, Killer came into the tent and stood looking at the three of us in disgust. Horse had come in earlier and was reading on his bed, and Shep was reading on his and I had joined the club, reading on mine.

"What the hell is this?" Killer asked. "A goddamn library?"

Horse looked up. "Hey, just because you're an illiterate bastard doesn't mean that we ain't educated."

"I can understand you and Shep reading on a gorgeous afternoon like this, an afternoon where the tennis courts are free, but Davey? Hey, come on, Davey. Let's play a few sets."

"Some of us are readers, and some aren't," I said, marking my place with my finger. I ignored Shep's grin. "Anyway, I haven't got a tennis racket."

"I'll borrow one for you."

I turned back to my book. "Wouldn't do any good. I have an injury in one of my fingers and I can't hold a racket, and anyway, I don't know how to play."

Killer stood there a minute or two, then he opened his trunk. "Well, I've got a little something to read myself. Dinge gave it to me. It's Harold Teen and Lillums in *The Artist's Model*. He took a thin, blue-covered comic book out of his trunk. "See, Lillums poses for Harold, who wants to be an artist. She poses in the nude, and he gets so hot and bothered, he . . . well, you guys aren't interested in this junk are you?"

That led to a free-for-all, and Horse ended up with the book while Shep and I sat on Killer. "That Dinge," Horse said admiringly. "Where does he get this stuff? Look at the shlong on Harold Teen!"

"It's almost as big as yours, Horse," Killer yelled. "Come on, give it back."

"Okay, let's knock it off," Shep said. "It's almost time to set up for dinner."

Usually, before dinner, Norman would sneak into the mess hall where we were eating, and I'd slip him a cookie. He was a little chubby, so I didn't think it would hurt him if it spoiled his appetite a bit. I couldn't get the cookies myself, because Jenny still didn't trust the shaygets, but Small Fry could wrap her around his little finger, and he always managed to get me some. But this meal there was no sign of Norman, and I was beginning to think maybe he was growing up a bit and didn't need me as much. Maybe the other kids had stopped teasing him.

I was wrong, though. I didn't see him at the meal, and I didn't want to ask Uncle Art where he was. I was not Uncle Art's favorite waiter, but as I was cleaning up I heard loud voices from the counselors' room behind the mess hall, and then Mr. Luft stuck his head through the door. "Quinn! Come on in here."

The other guys looked at me and Killer drew his finger across his throat, but I wasn't too worried. I hadn't done anything wrong—that I could remember.

Inside the counselors' room Uncle Art was facing Tom Ciardi and Mr. Luft across the table, his face red and angry. "Do you know where Norman Seidel is?" Mr. Luft asked me as I walked in.

I shook my head. "I haven't seen him all day. Why? Is he missing?"

"Damn right!" Uncle Art said angrily. "He's missing more than he's around. I spend half my time running after that little monster. No wonder the kids call him Blizzard. He's always lost in a fog!"

That wasn't true. I knew that good old Uncle Art had nicknamed him Blizzard. "Why the hell don't you keep an eye on him?" Mr. Luft was shouting. He was just as angry as Art. "He's your responsibility!"

"How can I discipline him? He runs off to Quinn there every chance he gets." They all turned to look at me.

"Lack of discipline is what's wrong with this entire camp," Tom Ciardi said grimly. "Now at the Point—"

But Uncle Art was too excited to listen. "The kid's a little whiner. You'd do better to send him home."

"If anyone gets sent home, it won't be the kid, Mr. Know-it-all," Mr. Luft shouted at Art. "When I need your stupid advice I'll ask for it. That kid is paying five hundred bucks for the summer! Understand that?"

That was when I realized Mr. Luft had a sliding scale for campers. Some, I knew, got in for two hundred, and here was one for five hundred! "Do you know who's shtupping that kid's mother?" Mr. Luft yelled. "A senator, that's all, a United States senator, and I don't need any dumb animal to tell me he's a whiner. I want that kid happy! I don't give a damn how whiny he is. He's your responsibility!"

Uncle Art stood staring at Mr. Luft for a minute, and I thought he would explode, then Tom Ciardi said, "Well, the big thing now is to find him. Let's get all the counselors and Warriors out looking. We'll organize this into a military-type operation. The waiters can give a hand, too."

He and Uncle Art walked out of the room, and I could hear him rounding up the waiters in the mess hall. "Do you want me to look for him, Mr. Luft?" I asked quietly. I was worried. I knew Norman cut periods, but he had never missed a meal before.

"Yeah, Davey. See what you can do. If that shmuck Art had done what he . . ." I didn't hear the rest because he walked out through the mess hall. I stood there for a minute, frowning. You see, I knew one thing about Norman. He was a creek baby. That's the kind of kid who loses himself as soon as the group moves off to any activity and winds up in the creek exploring the reeds and marshes. I'd found him there once or twice, but I'd never said anything. Hell, I didn't like sports myself, and I didn't think a little kid of eight should be forced to play baseball or to box or swim if he didn't want to. Not for five hundred bucks, anyway, and besides, he was supposed to be having fun.

So I ducked out the back entrance and down to the creek. I could hear the noise of the search parties being organized, but I ignored them and followed the creek upstream along the bank, past the bridge to the Hill and then to where it opened up on one side into a small marsh with cattails and other bushes and overhanging willows, and sure enough, I found him there, hunched over a little pool watching some insects skid around on the water.

"What are you doing, Norman?" I asked, squatting down next to him.

"Hey, Uncle Davey!" He looked up at me, delighted, "Did you ever see insects walk on water, really walk on top of the water?"

I nodded. "I sure have, and I see you have too."

"What keeps them up, Uncle Davey?"

"Surface tension." I remembered that from biology. "It has to do with the molecular structure of the water, but what are you doing here now? You know you missed dinner, and the whole camp is searching for you?"

His lower lip pushed out. "I don't care, Uncle Davey. I hate Uncle Art, and I don't want to go back, ever!"

I stood up and held out my arms. "Come on, I'll give you a lift back on my shoulders."

"I don' wanna go back!" He blubbered a little, but came to me anyway, and I hoisted him up and carried him back on my shoulders, along the creek and into the mess hall by the back way.

As we went it grew darker, and we could hear the shouts of the search parties and the glow of their flashlights like fireflies across the creek.

When I walked in, Mr. Luft had a group of counselors in the counselors' room, and they were bent over a map of the camp on the table busy dividing it up into territories to continue the search. There was a big fuss then, and Norman was petted and praised by Mr. Luft, and then he told me to get him a meal, which I did even though Jenny gave me a hard time. "It's not for me," I told her. "It's a little kid who missed dinner. Would you let a little kid go hungry?"

"A *klug tzuh* Columbus!" she shouted, but she put something together, and I sat with Norman at the waiters' table while he ate it. Mr. Luft came in and sat down next to us. "Aren't you happy, Norman?" he asked.

Norman sighed, a real heavy sigh, and shook his head. "I don't like Uncle Art," he whispered, looking around to make sure we were alone.

I said, "Hey, Norman, he's all right. He likes you."

"No, he don't. He makes fun of me all the time, and he got the kids to call me Blizzard, and he teases me because I wet my bed once." He began to cry. "He says I'm a marine, and all the kids laugh at me."

Mr. Luft's face was darkening, but before he could say anything, Norman said, "I want to live in Uncle Davey's tent. Please, Mr. Luft, can I stay with Davey? Please?"

And that was how it came about that eight-year-old Norman Seidel was moved into our tent. His cot was put between mine and Horse's, which didn't make any of the others too happy.

"How the hell am I going to beat my meat with an eight-year-old in the tent?" Killer muttered.

"You'll do it very carefully, and quietly," Horse told him. "Come on, he's not a bad kid."

"There's no such thing as a bad kid," Shep said. "There are only bad counselors."

"Norman's almost an orphan. He's only got one parent," I said. "His mother."

138

We were all quiet for a while. I was thinking, the kid's like me, but I've got Pop. What would it be like to have a mother and no father? Then Killer said, "What the hell, we'll educate the kid, teach him about life."

I said, "Listen, guys. Norman may have a snotty nose and whine a little, but he's a very sweet kid, and he won't be any trouble. I think we should all sort of act like—well, like fathers to him."

I surprised myself with that, but Shep put an arm around my shoulders and said, "Davey, you're right. We'll be surrogate fathers to the miserable little brat."

Uncle Art was relieved to have Norman out of his hair, and sore that he'd lose out on a tip from Norman's mother. I wondered which senator was "shtupping" her, and I tried to remember what she looked like. It seemed to me that she was very thin and had light-blond hair like Norman's, but I had been very anxious that day, and now I just couldn't remember her face.

So Norman moved in, and to everyone's surprise, it wasn't too bad. After a day or two he became a sort of mascot to the waiters. He ate with us and helped us set up and clean up, and in the mornings he'd sweep out the tent and even make the beds while we were lying out in front sunbathing. By special dispensation of Mr. Luft he was allowed to skip periods, but Dinge decided to teach him how to swim, and we were all amazed at how well that worked. Dinge was half fish anyway, and in the water he had all the patience he needed. Within a week Norman had progressed from the dead man's float to a good dog paddle, and by the end of the summer he had developed a neat crawl and was beginning to dive.

Killer took him in hand as far as baseball was concerned, and when Norman finished cleaning up our tent, Killer would get him out onto the grass circle where we sunbathed and bat fungoes to him. It was something to see, Killer, naked, hitting the ball while little Norman would run after it, red in the face and sweating like crazy. He wasn't much good, but he loved it and was eager as hell, and surprisingly he knew more about the game than any of us, even Killer. Like the time the guys were arguing over the All-Star lineup for that year, and Killer said Gehrig was on second base.

Norman piped up, "No, he isn't. That's Gehringer. Gehrig is on first, and Appling is shortstop and DiMaggio is right field . . ."

"That's enough, Norman," Killer said. "No showing off."

Most eight-year-olds in the camp were pretty wiry, but Norman had his share of baby fat. His blond hair in a Buster Brown cut looked a little girlish, and we knew that eventually we'd have to do something about that, but we kept putting it off. He sunburned easily too, and half the time we spent yelling at him because he forgot to wear a shirt and his shoulders would burn, and then we'd rub butter into his burns while he tried to be brave. I don't think Norman had ever tried to be brave before, but he did well at it, and eventually even his runny nose stopped.

The nicest part of having Norman in the tent, as far as I was concerned, was his cuddling in at night. Most of the counselors used to tell the kids good-night stories, and I didn't want Norman to be neglected, so when Norman told me his mother used to read him the Oz books, I made up a story called the *The Lost Subway Train in Oz*. I had read *The Wonderful Wizard of Oz* and *Tik Tok of Oz* and I knew the characters. In my story a car on the BMT gets lost driving in the wrong tunnel and ends up in the Nome King's underground kingdom. The kids on it have all sorts of adventures, and since Oz is a magic fairyland, the subway car begins to talk and develops into a staunch friend who protects the kids.

Norman loved it, and he'd come into my bed and cuddle in while I told the story, and then he'd fall asleep and I'd carry him over to his cot and tuck him in. But sometimes I'd doze off too before the story was over, and we'd sleep like that, and there was something nice about him next to me. I was more and more homesick for Pop as the days went by.

It was a funny thing about my story, *The Lost Subway Train in Oz*. Shep and Killer and Horse, if they were around, used to stop reading when I started telling Norman the story, and they'd listen too, and then, after a few days, they always managed to be there at story time, and soon the other waiters took to dropping in.

"We've got to know the story," Squeak explained, "just in case Norman asks us questions, or you get sick."

"The truth is," Shep told me one day, "you're a born storyteller, Davey. You're very good at it."

I was really surprised and pleased. I couldn't remember when anyone had last told me I was good at anything, except being voted the fastest waiter. I certainly wasn't so good at schoolwork, not French and eco. I got high marks in biology, but Marcia was so much better that no one ever told me I was good. Pop, in fact, used to play everything down. If I brought home a 95 in English, bio, or math, my three best subjects, he would say, "So how come you couldn't get five more points and make it an even hundred?"

I'd try to make him understand. "Pop, they figure no one is that perfect."

"Not even you, David?" Which was Pop's way of being sarcastic. The fact was that Marcia did pull down hundreds in bio and eco. But the day Shep told me I was a born storyteller—which I had always suspected because I lie so convincingly—we were hitchhiking to the Ashokan Reservoir.

I should explain that the waiters got one day off a week, usually Wednesday, which was Hike Day, and since the whole camp was off hiking—even the Paps, though they'd go all but the last quarter of a mile by truck—and lunch was sandwiches, and dinner was a light meal, we could do with half the staff, so those of us who had the day off would leave right after breakfast.

Shep asked me if I'd like to hitchhike down to the Ashokan Reservoir near Woodstock and see how New York City purified its water. "We'll take sandwiches and picnic out. But you've got to dress well," he told me. "No shorts. Slacks and a sport jacket and tie are best. That way drivers figure you're respectable and safe to pick up. Cripes, Davey, I've hitchhiked home from college and over most of the state. You meet some interesting people."

We did. The first car to pick us up outside of Hunter was Nancy in the Model A. She was heading into Tannersville to pick up some "Boozy-poo," as she put it. "I don't like to buy it locally. People talk, and it gets back to camp. Gives me a bad reputation. My, you boys look good."

I had borrowed Squeak's dark-blue blazer, which almost fit me, and Dinge's shirt, which was pale blue, and a blue-and-white striped tie from Shep. But I was wearing my own new white slacks. "Those colors make your baby-blues shine, Davey!" she said as I climbed into the front seat, while Shep took the rumble. Nancy didn't stop chattering all the way to Haines Falls, and she let us off regretfully. "I wish I were headed for Kingston, boys. I'd love to give you a hitch, but I have to be careful taking the old Model A up and down the mountains. It hasn't many climbs left in it. Bye now, don't do anything I wouldn't do!" And she was off, the old Ford bucking as she shifted gears.

Shep was grinning, and when we were alone on the road he punched my arm. "Hey, she likes you, Davey. You could make time there."

"Me? You're crazy." I acted more surprised than I was. Nancy had been more and more friendly since that first ride to church. We went each Sunday now, without Tom Ciardi, and I rode up front and we talked about everything. Nancy was easy to talk to, a lot like Percy, and I had some funny thoughts about her, but I still remembered Sam's advice, "Don't shit on your own doorstep." So I had been very polite and formal, which only seemed to make Nancy even friendlier.

After Nancy let us off, we had to wait only five minutes before another car picked us up, a big black Packard with a uniformed chauffeur driving it. There were a man and woman riding in front with the chauffeur and a young girl in back. The chauffeur got out and opened the back door on our side and waved Shep in. When I started to get in with him, he stopped me.

"We're together," Shep said, and tried to climb out, but the chauffeur pushed him back, closed the door, and led me around to the other side. He opened the door on that side and gestured for me to climb in. We ended up with Shep on one side of the girl, who looked to be about ten, and me on the other.

There was something funny about her, though. I noticed it as I settled back and thanked the couple in front. Her head was too big, and she was smiling, but without any real expression, and she kept turning from Shep to me.

"Now, Alice dear," the woman in front said in a high-pitched voice, "you've got company. Isn't that nice?"

Alice made some kind of noise and spit dribbled down her face. The lady, still smiling at all three of us, reached back and wiped it off. The girl, I realized, was some kind of a moron, and we were stuck in the car with her! All kinds of crazy thoughts ran through my head. She could be a killer, maybe with a knife hidden under her dress, or even worse—but what could be worse?

The woman went on talking brightly about how Alice loved company, and it was so lonely for her driving long distances, and they had come all the way from Montreal, and wasn't it nice of these dear boys to keep her company. "Wasn't it, dear?" she said, turning back to her husband.

All he said was "Shut up," and the chauffeur sort of grunted, but I could see his eyes in the rearview mirror watching us, and I didn't like the look in them. I looked at Shep and shrugged, and he looked as nervous as I felt. We passed through Haines Falls and then started down a long, twisting mountain road, and I realized that the chauffeur was driving in the left lane around blind turns, and that made me even more nervous. As we rounded one turn a car came dead at us, and with a blaring horn pulled over to our right and barely made it around us.

Shep yelled, "Hey, shouldn't you be on the other side of the road?" but the chauffeur didn't answer. The curve had swayed the girl against me, and I could feel her thighs pressing against mine, and then she looked at me and reached out to touch my face. It was really weird!

"We get off here!" Shep called out suddenly, and the Packard stopped in the middle of the road with a squeal of brakes. On one side the mountain dropped away into a tremendous gorge, and on the other side it climbed up in a staggering series of cliffs. The road had been cut right into the edge of the mountain.

"Here?" the woman asked. "Here? There's nothing here."

"Let 'em go," her husband growled. "I told you it was no good."

We both climbed out as quickly as we could, one on each side, praying no other car would come up or down that narrow road. "We have to meet someone in the woods," Shep babbled. "We're hiking, you see, going mountain climbing . . ." But before he had finished talking, the Packard took off with a scream of tires. We looked at each other, and then burst out laughing, the kind of laughing you do when you're frightened and relieved.

143

"Now that's what I call really weird!" Shep said.

We started hiking down the mountain road. "That girl!" I shook my head. "She was a moron, wasn't she?" I had never seen anyone like her except maybe one of the kids on the block back home. Philip Bernstein's brother had that same big head, but he talked. Not that he made much sense, but he wasn't like Alice.

We kept talking about the ride, how scared we'd been and how spooky the chauffeur was, like Boris Karloff, and as we hiked along we took off our jackets and loosened our ties. There was no chance of hitching a ride. The road was too narrow for any car to stop; in fact, we were scared every time one passed. We'd just barely get out of the way. "That Alice," I said to Shep. "She reminded me of little Audrey and all the moron jokes."

"Little Audrey?" Shep asked.

"Yeah, you know, she saw a bear hugging a tree, and she laughed and laughed because she knew only God could make a tree."

Shep laughed and then sobered up. "We shouldn't make fun of her. I kind of felt sorry for that mother. I guess she figured we'd be company for the kid, but it was really scary!"

We had come to a part where the road made an abrupt turn, and a small bridge crossed a rushing creek. We looked over the side of the bridge and saw that the creek fell over a cliff face to make a waterfall into a big natural pool below, a pool big enough to swim in. "Hey, come on, Davey," Shep said. "To hell with Ashokan Reservoir. Let's stop and picnic here."

So we climbed down the side of the road, sliding and slipping to the edge of the water, and then we decided to swim because it was so beautiful, even though we didn't have any bathing trunks. "No one can see us," Shep pointed out. "They drive right over the bridge. They'd have to stop and look over, and there's no place to park, so let's go."

We stripped and piled our clothes on the bank, and then jumped into the water. I tell you, if I could have, I'd have jumped right out again. It was freezing. Icy cold. We yelled and splashed, and I headed for the bank, but by the time I reached it I was warm enough to keep swimming.

We spent about half an hour in the water, swimming and climbing up the bank behind the waterfall and jumping through it into the pool. I'm not so great as a swimmer, but this didn't take much skill. There wasn't room enough for any real swimming. We just splashed a lot and horsed around to keep warm. There was a big, flat rock just out of sight of the road and in full sunlight, and it was nice and hot from the sun. We finally climbed out and stretched out on the rock to dry.

The rock was blue slate, and it felt good against our skin, especially after the icy mountain water. We could look up and see the side of the mountain covered with wild pink roses and beyond the roses the dark pine trees climbing toward the rich blue sky. Below us the creek ran down a gorge that grew steeper and steeper until it looked like a miniature Grand Canyon.

That was when Shep told me I was a born storyteller. "What college are you going to?" he asked then. "You ought to pick one that has a good English Department. I have a hunch you could write."

"I'm good at English—and bio too," I admitted, "but I can't go to college."

"Why not?"

I shrugged. "Well, my marks aren't good enough to get into City College. English, bio, and math are my best, but I flunked French as often as I passed it, and I'm lousy at eco and history—can't remember dates—and I flunked art, of all things. My King Kong routine took care of that."

"King Kong?"

I told Shep about my imitation of Kong, and he got hysterical. "Hey, you have to do that at Amateur Night. But even if you don't qualify for City College, there are plenty of other places, and with the economic mess the country is in, they'll be glad to take you, marks or no marks."

I shook my head. "Me and Pop can barely make it as it is. Since the depression he doesn't make much, and there just isn't any extra for college."

"What about scholarships?"

"You're kidding! With my marks?"

"I meant athletic scholarships. You must be a great athlete,

145

Davey, with that build. What's your sport?" He reached out and put his hand on my chest, then moved it down to my stomach. I felt a sudden, uncomfortable sensation, and I sat up quickly and grabbed my knees.

"It's chilly, isn't it? I don't have any sport, really. I'm lousy at athletics."

Shep put his hands behind his head. "Maybe it's just because you don't try."

I picked up a pebble from the rock and tossed it into the pool below. A bunch of orange-and-black butterflies, there must have been twenty of them, fluttered up from the blue slate and red clay rocks, then settled back. "Monarchs," I said. "Do you know, Shep, they migrate just like birds."

Shep sat up next to me. "No kidding. Where to?"

"Somewhere in Brazil. Nobody knows."

"Really? I thought they only lived a day or two, butterflies."

"These migrate, down there and back. What are you going to college for, Shep?"

"Me? Pre-med. Eventually, if I can get past the Jewish quota, I'll go to med school."

"The Jewish quota?"

"Sure. Every med school has a quota, how many Jews they allow in. It used to be only the top students, the A students. Now there are so many Jewish doctors at the top of the graduating class, they only allow the Bs in, and I'm an A Student!" He sounded bitter. "You're lucky, Davey."

I tossed another pebble down and shivered even though it wasn't cold in the sun. I watched the tumbling waterfall as it crashed into the pool. "Why am I lucky, Shep?"

"Because you're not Jewish. You don't have to put up with shit like quotas."

"Fat chance I'd have of getting into med school anyway. Besides," I said, and it came out before I knew what I was saying, "I am Jewish."

"What?" Shep turned to face me, his dark face gathered into a frown. "What the hell do you mean?"

"Just what I said." I felt afraid of what I was saying, and yet I

146

had such a wonderful rush of relief. "I'm Jewish. My name is Quinn because at Ellis Island they changed it from Kvinski when my Pop came over here, dropped the "ski" and changed the spelling. I'm no more a shaygets than you are!" I looked at him angrily. "So what are you going to do about it?"

He just stared at me for a long moment, then his mouth twitched. "And Luft? Luft hired you because he thought you weren't Jewish?"

"Sure. I'm a Shabbes goy! I give the camp class." I stood up and yelled out, "A Jew! I'm a goddamn Jew." And the gorge echoed, *Jew, Jew, Jew.*

"Davey! Oh, shit, Davey!" And then he was laughing and pounding the rock. "Oh, shit, what a gag!" And he laughed so hard he began to choke. I pounded him on the back a few times and he coughed and shook his head. "Oh, Davey, I love you! Really!"

I was laughing too, and then I yelled out and jumped into the pool below, and Shep dived in after me. We started clowning around in the water, splashing and ducking each other. Then we climbed out and pulled on our undershorts, shaking to get as much water off us as we could.

We sat around until we were dry, and I told him the whole story, and Shep promised to keep my secret. "Christ, if the other guys only knew. You ought to tell them, Davey. It's just too good to keep to ourselves. Kvinski, aka Quinn! And that schmuck Luft hiring you as a gentile!"

"It's always been Quinn, since I was born, and I didn't know Luft was hiring me as a gentile. Not right away. You don't know how hard it's been, Shep. Honest."

He sobered up. "I can believe it. Don't worry. I won't give you away . . ." And he began to giggle again, and it started all over. Afterward, when we had dressed, I knotted my tie, the one Shep had lent me, and I said, "The only thing that's been getting me down is that I really don't belong here."

Shep was opening our sandwiches. "Shit, egg salad. Why don't you belong here?"

"I love egg salad." I took the sandwich. "Because we're poor, Pop and me, and everyone here is rich."

"Rich?" Shep shook his head. "Hell, I'm not rich, and Dinge isn't, and neither is Killer."

"Rich to me. I've heard you talk. You live on West End Avenue, and Dinge lives in White Plains, and Killer's folks have an apartment in Flushing and a summer house on Long Island. He told me about it. Shep, that's rich to me. I had to bargain my father up to two dollars spending money for the summer. If Norman's mother hadn't given me that five bucks, I wouldn't be able to go to Musikants's with you guys for a soda."

"I never realized that," Shep said slowly. "I—all of us—we always figured—well, to tell you the truth, Davey, you're so goddamn good-looking, so tall and blond—hell, we all envy you, all of us. Besides"—he began to grin—"you're a shaygets!"

I said, "Watch your step or I'll throw you into the pool with your clothes on!" And then we began to wrestle a little, not seriously because I'm really bigger and stronger than Shep, and we finished our lunch and hiked back up to the road.

On the road, waiting for a ride either way, Shep put his arm around me and said, "I'll tell you one thing, Davey. I like you a hell of a lot. We're gonna be friends, real friends!"

I felt a warm feeling go all through me. I'd never had a real close friend before. Oh, I was popular enough at school, and everyone liked me, but a real friend? No, not till now.

■ Chapter Thirteen ■

Five of us, Killer, Dinge, Shep, Horse, and I, were lying out on the grass circle in the sun. Shep was reading his new Huxley book, and I was almost finished with *Brave New World,* which got better and better as I got into it. "He knows a hell of a lot about biology," I told Shep.

Shep put his finger on his place and said, "He would, Davey. He's a Huxley."

It hadn't occurred to me until then that he was related to that Huxley. I went back to the book, and Horse smiled at me. "When you finish that, Davey, I have a good Thorne Smith for you to borrow."

"That should be more your speed," Killer said, looking up from the magazine he and Dinge were going through. "Or maybe you'd like to borrow one of our *Spicy Detective Stories*. Listen to this description of the girl. If this isn't great writing, I'll eat it." He started to turn the pages when Shep said, "Put it away. Here comes the kid."

Killer turned the magazine face down as Norman came up to us. "Hey, Norman," he said in annoyance. "I thought I told you to make my bed."

"I started to, Killer, but I gotta change your sheets."

Killer sat up. "What's wrong with my sheets?"

"You must have blown your nose on them. They're all shmutzy."

"Blown his nose!" Dinge let out a yell. "The guy's had a wet dream! I didn't think it possible, the way he beats his meat."

"Okay, cut it out," Shep said. "Not in front of the kid."

"Why not?" Dinge sat up. "C'mere, Norman, and sit down. It's time you learned the facts of life. Do you ever play with yourself?"

I said, "Stop it, Dinge. He's only eight years old!"

"I never do," Norman said seriously. "Honest."

"Cut the shit, Norman. Everyone plays with himself." Dinge looked at us and winked. "I do and Killer does. That's what's in his bed."

Killer said, "For Christ's sake, he's only a kid!" and Shep stood up. "You guys are too much." He turned away in disgust and walked off to the tent.

"A kid has to learn," Dinge said angrily. "You want to make a pansy out of him?"

"Maybe you're right," I said, frowning, "but there are better ways to teach a kid about that."

"Bullshit! Norman, everyone plays with himself, even Davey."

Norman looked at me uncertainly. I said, "It's all right,

149

Norman." I was sore as hell at Dinge for doing this, but at the same time I knew I had to follow through now. It was a little like telling a kid there was no Santa Claus. Sooner or later he'd find out from the other kids, if he hadn't already, and it was better if he knew what was right and what was nonsense. The trouble was, I wasn't all that sure of everything myself.

I said, "Dinge is teasing, but sure, everyone does it, all the guys. It's all right."

Norman drew back and looked at me. "Honest?"

Horse said, "Dinge, you're a real crud!" To Norman, he said, "It's true, kid. Davey is right."

"The thing is," I explained slowly, "not everyone is a nut like Dinge, and we shouldn't talk about doing it, or let anyone catch us at it." I wanted to make sure he understood that. "That's very important. Remember, it's as natural as—as taking a crap!"

"You've got a way with words," Horse said, shaking his head.

"And that stuff in Killer's bed?" Norman asked curiously.

"Tell him, Davey," Dinge said sarcastically. "Give the boy the fuckin' facts of life."

I glared at Dinge. This was getting real crazy. "Well, when you're older, some stuff will come out every time you do it—"

"And that's how babies are born," Killer and Dinge sang out in chorus.

Norman looked at them indignantly. "My mommy told me all about babies being born. They grow in the mommy's tummy, and then they're born."

Horse said gently, "You're right, Norman. Don't pay any attention to those clowns. They're just trying to get our goat."

"You ought to teach sex to kids, Davey," Killer said. "You're real good at it."

"You've got a career!" Dinge added.

"Screw you both!"

Norman was quiet, then, avoiding my eyes, he asked, "All the boys do it? Play with themselves?"

I said, "Oh, sure."

He nodded, and I could almost see wheels going around in his head. "And the girls? Do they do it?"

150

Before I could help myself, I said, "Oh, shit!" I didn't know how to handle this!

"I'm going to put my sheets in the laundry," Killer said, getting up.

"I've got to write a letter." Dinge rolled up his magazine.

"Come on, you started this," I told them angrily. "You guys stay here!"

"Nobody knows if girls do it, Norman," Horse said quietly. "That's one of the great mysteries of life. Anyway, what Davey means is that you shouldn't worry or feel guilty about doing it. If you do it, you do it—okay? Just don't yak about it like Dinge and Killer. You don't hear Davey talking about it all the time, do you?"

Norman shook his head. "I won't even tell Mommy."

"Good boy."

"And what's more," Dinge said, settling down on the blanket again, "it's not Mommy and Daddy. That's fuckin' baby talk. You call your mother Mom, or Mother, never Mommy."

Norman nodded seriously. "Okay."

We watched him walk off, and I said, "Thanks a lot, Dinge. I really needed that."

"Hey, come on, Davey. You want the kid to grow up or not?"

"Sure, but slowly, shmuck, slowly!"

"Get the shaygets! Shmuck, yet. You'll be talking Yiddish in a few weeks."

"Hanging around with you guys, I'll be talking dirty."

"Now that reminds me of a great joke. You guys want to hear it?"

We all yelled, "No!" as Shep and Killer came back and dropped down next to us. "I see you've all set the kid straight."

"You should have stayed," Horse said. "Poor Davey was on the spot."

"About that joke," Dinge went on. "There's this kid who was always beating his meat, night and day."

"Like you?" Horse said, going back to his book.

Dinge threw a clump of grass at him. "Shut up and listen. So his old man takes him to a fuckin' doctor to have a talk. They weren't as smart as Davey. They wanted him to cut it out. Son, says the doctor,

151

each time you come, you waste some future child. He might be a doctor or a lawyer or a statesman—even President!

"The kid's impressed, and he goes home, but he can't stop whacking it, and he ends up with a handful of come."

"Disgusting!" Horse said.

"Yeah, well, he looks at the fuckin' stuff in his hand and says, 'My God, you might have been a doctor or a lawyer or a President.' Then he flips it all onto his other hand and says, 'On the other hand, you might be a pervert or a crook or a murderer, so what the hell!'" Dinge slapped his knee and began laughing hysterically.

"That's funny?" Horse asked. "You're sick, Dinge."

"Besides, he might have had a daughter," I put in, pretending to be serious. "You know about the X chromosome?"

Shep laughed. "So Huxley's finally penetrating. But seriously, guys, what Norman needs isn't sex education. He needs a nickname. The trouble with Norman is his name, Norman."

"Well, they started calling him Blizzard," Killer said. "You know, he's always lost in one."

"He's not anymore," I said, "and that was good old Uncle Art's doing. Why don't we give him a nickname, a decent one? One he'll like."

We were all quite for a few minutes, considering that. "How about Speedy?" Horse said.

"He isn't." Shep shook his head. "Don't give him a nickname he isn't. He'll hate it. You know how Squeak hates his."

"Yeah. You think I like Horse?"

"Well, you're hung like a fuckin' horse," Dinge said. "So it fits. I don't mind Dinge."

"If you were a Negro, you would," Shep said.

"Yeah, well, I'm not a nigger. When I'm out of the sun, my skin is alabaster white. What about Happy?"

"Happy? That's a hell of a name to live up to." Shep shook his head.

I said, "Butch. What about Butch?"

Killer yelled out, "Yeah! Hey, that's great. We'll call the kid Butch. Hey, Norman! Come out here, Norman!"

Norman came running out of the tent. "What do you want, Killer?"

"We want to give you a nickname, Norman. Do you want a nickname?"

Norman looked apprehensive. "I don't want to be called Bliz!"

"Shit, no. This is a good name. Now you kneel down like the knights do. Give me that stick, Dinge." Norman kneeled uneasily, and Killer tapped his head lightly with the stick. "I dub thee Butch. Butch Seidel. You're no more Norman. It's Butch from now on. You hear that? Rise, Butch."

Norman stood up grinning. "I like that, Killer. Am I really Butch?"

Killer frowned at him. "Well, you will be. Shep, where's your scissors?"

"In the tray of my trunk. Why?"

"I've got an idea." Killer ran back to the tent, yelling as his bare feet hit the pebbles on the path, and he returned in a minute with the scissors. "Come here, Butch."

Norman came to him, and before we realized what he was up to, Killer had grabbed a handful of Norman's Buster Brown cut and sniped it off! "We'll make you a man, Butch."

"What the hell are you doing?" I lunged toward him, but Dinge caught me. "Hey, no! He's right. The kid'll always be a fuckin' pansy with hair like that. Let Killer cut it."

I couldn't believe the lousy job Killer did on the kid's hair. We all shook our heads in disgust. "Take him into town," Shep told us. "You've got two hours before lunch."

"What if Luft sees him?" Dinge asked uneasily.

"Take him out the back way. There's a barber near Musikants's."

And that's what we did. Norman-Butch was happy as a bedbug, while Dinge, Killer, and I took him through the back woods behind the tents out to the highway and then into Hunter. The barber shop next to Musikants's was called Pete's Hair-Cutting Salon, and Pete took one look at Norman-Butch and upped his price to seventy-five cents, which was robbery. We all chipped in, since there was no way we could get it out of Norman-Butch's canteen account, and when he was finished we were just amazed. He had a real "Butch" haircut, an inch of blond hair standing up like a brush all over his head. It made him look about ten years old, and he was swaggering when we left the shop and started back.

"What you need to do to earn it," Dinge said thoughtfully, "is something real butch. We gotta work something out." And all the way back to camp, which we reached just in time to set up, we tried to figure out what Norman could do to earn his new nickname.

What Dinge and Killer finally decided on, without telling the rest of us, was that Norman would go down the big slide at the waterfront. We had two docks at the lake, end to end. There was a small dock for the younger kids, the waders, where the water was two or three feet deep, and there was a small five-foot slide there. The Paps and Bucks and most of the Braves usually swam there, or waded around and went down the slide into the water.

Right next to it was the big dock where the water was twelve feet deep, and there were two diving boards, a low one and a high one, and the big slide. This slide was eighteen feet high and piped water splashed down it to cool it off. The water also guaranteed a very fast ride!

Only the Warriors were allowed to use it, and the waiters, though I stayed away from it. It was scary. But by now Norman was at home in the water under Dinge's teaching, and when Killer and Dinge suggested the slide, he agreed. Their plan was to do it during swim period when everyone would see him. I didn't like the idea, and I argued against it.

"It's too dangerous. He's only eight."

"For Crissakes, what the fuck's dangerous about it?" Dinge asked. "He can swim, and I'll be in the water in case anything goes wrong."

"Yeah, what could go wrong?" Killer asked.

"One drowned kid, that's what!"

"Besides"—Dinge smiled at Norman—"he wants to do it, don't you, Butch?"

Norman nodded, eyeing the slide uneasily, and Killer said, "Maybe he should rehearse it?"

"I don't think so." Dinge shook his head. "This is a one-time thing. The fuckin' counselors are going to be sore as hell as it is." He hunkered down and put his hands on Norman's shoulders. "What do you say, Butch? This is your big chance to gain lasting fame and camp immortality."

Norman looked up at the slide, and then looked away very quickly. His voice was shaky. "Okay!"

"There! The kid has guts. Now wait till general swim."

We hung around the dock, trying to look casual, knowing that if Uncle Paul Mandelberg, the swimming counselor, found out about Norman's projected slide, he'd put a stop to it. I kept thinking maybe I should tell him myself, but I knew Norman wouldn't forgive me. Scared as he was, he had to go through with it. Then, once all the kids were in the water, yelling and splashing, and Uncle Paul, on the edge of the diving board, was blowing his whistle, Dinge decided it was time.

It's a funny thing about Uncle Paul. In all the time I saw him teach swimming and supervise the waterfront, I never once saw him go into the water. He always wore red swim trunks and a white sailor hat and a whistle on a cord around his neck, and he was burned almost black by the sun, but he was never wet.

Killer and Dinge had planned it well. Dinge slipped into the water, and Killer ran out to the diving board and pointed out over the lake. "Hey, Uncle Paul, look. Is that a turtle out there, by the boats?"

Uncle Paul blew his whistle and all the kids quieted down, and then Dinge yelled out, "Hey! Look at Butch! He's doing the high slide! Come on, Butch! You can do it."

In a minute the camp took up the yell. "It's Butch! It's Butch! He's on the slide." No one had called poor Norman Butch before, but we could see him swell with pride. He shoved himself off, down the slide, and with a yell shot down the length of it and slammed out about six feet over the water before he splashed down.

Dinge swam toward him at the same time, but Norman came up splashing and paddling, the first Brave to dare the high slide! The whole camp was cheering him. "Great going, Butch. How about that Butch? Did you see him?"

Uncle Paul looked bewildered. "Who the hell is Butch?" he asked Killer.

Killer pointed to Norman climbing up the ladder, his face one great big smile. "Meet Butch, Uncle Paul!"

155

From that day on, Norman was Butch to all the kids, and he began to strut around as if he really owned the place. He got into more and more games as the days went on, and the other kids began to fight to have him on their teams. Not that he was any good at athletics, or only a little better than he had been, but he was confident, and now he had a personality. Butch, the tough kid who had gone down the eighteen-foot slide.

"I think," Shep said one day, "that you guys may have created a monster. Have you noticed, he's stopped making our beds? Why don't you have a talk with him, Davey?"

Dinge and Killer were in the tent, and Shep and I were out in the circle getting some sun, our favorite occupation. I seemed to tan easily, and I was a deep brown all over, but Shep, who was so dark, kept getting red and burned, and then he'd wear a shirt for a few days and it would all disappear. Dinge, of course, had the darkest tan of anyone, but Killer was like Shep. He'd get red and then pale again.

Killer had a funny build, heavy shoulders and a narrow waist, but a very big head. He usually slumped a little, and his head seemed to hang forward as if it were too heavy to carry. You'd never think, looking at him, that he was as terrific an athlete as he was.

I didn't particularly want to talk to Norman because I was enjoying his new personality. I got a kick out of seeing him swagger around, and I knew he was having a wonderful time of it, but I agreed that maybe a little humility was a good thing. So I picked up my blanket and walked back to the tent, and just as I walked in, Dinge, who was stretched out on my cot writing postcards, let go with an awful fart.

Norman jumped up and ran over to him and began punching him, while Dinge put up his arms in a sort of mock defense and yelled out;

> Aily, baily, bundle of straw,
> Farting is against the law.
> Hit me now, hit me then,
> Hit me when I fart again.

Dinge finished and sank back on my cot, grinning. This aily-baily business was something Killer had come up with. The rule was, if any guy farted, the others could keep punching him until he recited the entire verse. It helped a lot, because Dinge was one hell of a farter. He could fart at will, and with the tent flaps down it made things uncomfortable. As a matter of fact, Dinge once won a bet from Squeak by insisting he could fart the first six notes of "My Country 'Tis of Thee."

I sat down on Norman's cot and said, "Now, Butch, what's this I hear about you not cleaning up the tent?"

Norman pushed out his lower lip and avoided my eyes. "I don't have to."

"Why not?"

"That's what Skippy Mann said. He saw me sweeping out the tent, and he told me I didn't have to. I was a paying camper."

"That makes a lot of sense," Dinge said. "But if you're a paying camper, what the fuck are you doing in the waiters' tent? Maybe you should move back with Uncle Art and the Braves."

Butch dissolved into Norman immediately, and his eyes filled up. I dug into my trunk for a handkerchief and handed it to him. "Okay, Butch. No tears. You can stay with us, but you have to do your share of the work. Okay?"

Norman nodded. "Okay, Uncle Davey. I will."

"Oh, yes," I said as he picked up the broom. "Another thing. That aily-baily business is only around here. I don't ever want you to try it at home."

"Even if someone farts?"

"Even it someone shits!" Dinge said. "How many times have we gotta tell you, Butch, some things are for men only."

Norman nodded seriously, the tears gone. "I get it." And he started sweeping.

That was how we kept the new Norman under control, and it worked. He was still happy, and swaggered around the other kids, but he understood his place in the scheme of things just as he understood which kids he could push around and which he couldn't. As for me, I wasn't sure which Norman I liked best. There was something kind of nice about the old Norman, like having a kid brother.

As for myself, I was startled one day to realize it was August 1st and half the summer had gone. I was really enjoying camp. The days, when we weren't working, were spent loafing. We hung out on the Hill, sunbathing and bullshitting with each other. I never talked so much about so little and enjoyed it so much. The guys were great. Killer and Horse and Shep and I were very close since we were in the same tent, but we'd often get together with the others, especially Squeak and Dinge, who, in spite of his foul mouth, was a lot of fun. Eppie was a loner, and Small Fry hung out with the Hunters and his old buddies.

Shep and I had become very close friends. We took our days off together, and went into town together at night. I learned a lot from Shep, especially about books. I finished *Brave New World* and borrowed another book from him, *Of Mice and Men*. The best thing about them was the long talks we'd have afterward.

I also found out how Eppie, short for Epidemic, got his name. One Sunday Norman came running up the Hill and into the tent yelling, "Eppie's up the flagpole! Come and see."

"Up the flagpole?" I couldn't figure out what he meant, but I pulled on a pair of shorts and sneakers and ran down the Hill with him. Sure enough, Eppie had taken some boards and a hammer and shinnied up the pole, about twenty-five feet, and nailed the boards to the pole. Then he draped his legs around them, and took out a sandwich he had brought along and started to eat it, while half the camp gathered around to watch.

"What the hell is going on?" Tom Ciardi said, pushing his way through the crowd. He looked up at Eppie, then took his whistle out and blew it. "All right, get down!" But Eppie ignored him.

Dinge pushed through to my side. "Isn't it great?" he whispered.

"What's he doing?"

"He decided to sit on the fuckin' flagpole like Shipwreck Kelly. He says he's going for a record."

Killer, who came up then, said, "Some record. No one else is stupid enough to do it. He's already made a record."

Shep joined us. "The kid's an epidemic, I swear!"

"What are you going to do?" Killer asked.

"Me? I'm only the headwaiter. I'll tell you what I'm going to do.

I'm giving one of his tables to you and one to Davey until he gets down. Come on, Shaygets, let's set up."

That had become my nickname since I told Shep the truth about my religion. Before that everyone used it behind my back, now Shep used it all the time, and it was catching on. But he kept his promise and hadn't told anyone yet.

"What about Eppie?" I asked. "What'll Mr. Luft do?"

"My prediction is," Shep said, "that Luft will manage not to be around. He'll let Ciardi handle it, and Eppie'll stay up there as long as the little idiot wants to."

"He won't be fired?"

"You got to be kidding," Killer said. "He has job insurance, two sisters and a cousin at Rocky Clove. Do you think Luft will risk three camp fees? Eppie can get away with murder!"

So we set up, and I took over one of Eppie's tables, and Killer took over the other. The flagpole sitting only lasted a few hours. The campers got bored with watching, and Eppie got bored with sitting. When he showed up in the mess hall for dinner, Mr. Luft was dishing out the ice cream, a once-a-week treat. Mr. Luft always served it himself. He was very particular about food. All the supplies were kept at the Guest House. His mother ran that, and every day she shipped over just enough food for one day, in spite of Jenny's protests.

"The shmegegge thinks I want to steal his food," she told us once in great disgust. "The way he hands it out, a meal at a time— God forbid the hotel should ever burn down, the camp would starve! Why we can't even have enough flour, I don't know." And then she lapsed into Hungarian, which I always found fascinating to listen to.

On the night of Eppie's flagpole sit, Shep took him aside and said, "I'm docking you a day off. Killer and Davey had to cover for you while you pulled that stupid stunt."

Eppie shook his head sullenly. "No, you don't. I'll talk to Luft."

"Yeah, talk, but I'm the headwaiter here."

Eppie went up to where Mr. Luft was dishing out the ice cream and asked, "Mr. Luft, I want my day off next week. I want to hitch up to the Thousand Islands."

Mr. Luft straightened up and hefted the ice-cream scoop, and for

159

a moment I thought he was going to brain Eppie with it, then he seemed to get himself under control. In a tight voice he said, "You do that, and stay a day on every goddamn island!" And he handed the ice-cream scoop to Shep. "You finish!" And he stormed out of the kitchen.

"This is a new first," Shep said, staring at the scoop. "Letting me dish out the ice cream. Okay, guys. This is a chance to reward our friends and punish our enemies. Line up with your trays and let's go." He just ignored Eppie, and sure enough, he did dock Eppie a day off. Not that it did much good because Eppie crawled under the Pap bunk and stayed there the whole day. He refused to come out.

That night, after the camp filed out, Shep dished out ice cream for the waiters and Jenny and the kitchen help, great big bowls of it, and then sent the can back to the hotel with Elmore, one of the dishwashers. Elmore was the third dishwasher we'd had. I don't know where Mr. Luft hired them, but all were skinny, ragged-looking guys who, according to Shep, were drying out. They only lasted until they could get hold of some alcohol, and then they'd go off on a binge and we wouldn't see them again.

With the second guy it had been Jenny's vanilla extract. Then Mr. Luft would have to bring another one up from the city. "I think he hires them from the Bowery," Shep said. "Lost guys, drunks, whatever is cheap." The rest of the kitchen help, two women, came from Hunter and were good hard workers.

Since Mr. Luft usually dished out the ice cream, we would get ours after the campers, and it was a small amount. Seconds in ice cream were rare and went to the campers Mr. Luft favored, those who had scored winning runs at baseball, or the team that had won in inter-camp basketball, or, as Dinge put it, anyone who had sucked up to him that week. But with Shep dishing it out, we waiters got seconds and even thirds, each portion an enormous bowlful.

In fact, as I left the mess hall, I felt sick to my stomach, and up on the Hill I threw up in the crapper. That scared me because I was hardly ever sick, and I wondered if I wasn't coming down with something, especially when Dinge, seeing me come back from the crapper, said, "You must be real sick. You look like shit warmed over."

I stretched out on my bed and felt a little better, but then I wondered if I shouldn't go down to the infirmary and let the doctor check me out. I didn't have too good a feeling about hospitals, but this was an infirmary, not a real hospital, and after all, it was free medical attention.

The only time I'd ever been to a doctor was to my mother's brother, my Uncle Jerry, but the family called him Uncle Doc. That was back when I was seven and had my appendix out. Pop couldn't afford the doctor or hospital, so Uncle Doc arranged with a friend to do the operation at Jewish Memorial Hospital over by the river, and I remember when Pop came to pick me up to go home, after about a week, the hospital bill hadn't been paid. Uncle Doc had somehow forgotten about it, and Pop didn't have the money.

I was all dressed in the downstairs waiting room sitting on a bench while Pop argued with the nurse in charge. Then he called, "Come on, Davey," and I stood up, but the nurse said, "You just sit there!" and I sat down, and Pop raised his voice and said, "Come ahead, Davey!" and I stood up, and the nurse shouted, "You sit there!" and I began to cry.

I really don't remember for sure how it all ended. I thought I'd have to stay in the hospital and never go home with Pop, because even at seven I knew he didn't have the money to bail me out. But I think he finally called Uncle Doc, and the whole thing was settled. Anyway, I did go home.

It didn't leave me with too good a feeling about hospitals, but this was an infirmary, and I trusted Nancy and Dr. Rosenberg. Dinge walked me down and waited in the outside room with me while two kids were examined for sore throats, then packed off with lozenges and excuses to keep them out of general swim the next day. Nancy, looking very efficient in her white uniform, came into the waiting room and looked at us in surprise. "Now what's with you two?"

"I'm here as a patient, I think," I told her. Then, as the Doc came in, I explained about the ice cream and my stomachache.

"Well," Doc said as he took me into the examining room, "three bowls of ice cream will do it every time. How's the stomachache now?"

161

I said, "Not bad." And he said, "Pull up your shirt." He probed and poked a bit and listened all around my chest and back with a cold stethoscope, then shrugged. "It feels all right and sounds good, but just to be on the safe side, take his temperature, Nancy."

He began putting away his instruments while Nancy stuck a thermometer in my mouth. Looking at his watch, he said, "I have a poker game going tonight in the counselors' room. I think I'll just make it."

Nancy took the thermometer out of my mouth while Doc's back was turned. I saw her glance at it, then, to my surprise, turn it upside down and shake it. She looked at it again, winked at me, and handed it to the Doc. "It's over a hundred."

"Damn!" He took the thermometer and examined it and shook his head. "I guess I'll have to stay."

"Don't be silly," Nancy said briskly. "I can handle this. I'll put him to bed here, and you can look in in the morning. A few aspirin and he'll be normal. You know these summer fevers."

Doc frowned and argued a bit, but Nancy was firm. "I'll need my toothbrush and pajamas," I told her, and I went out to Dinge and asked him to get them for me. "I have to spend the night here. I've got a fever. Oh yeah, and my wallet, too. It's in the top tray of my trunk."

He said, "Sure, Davey. I'll get them. Don't worry, and I'll tell Shep. You want any visitors tonight?"

I had an idea of what Nancy was up to, and all I needed was visitors! I said, "No. I'm going straight to bed. Just my stuff, Dinge."

"Sure." Then he hesitated at the door. "Your wallet?"

"In case I need some money," I said vaguely. You can never tell." The last thing I was going to tell Dinge about was Sam's contribution to my sex education, the condom he had given me to keep in my wallet!

Finally Dinge got back with my pajamas and toothbrush and my wallet, which I slipped into my pocket. Then, after he left, Nancy closed the infirmary door and locked it and pulled down the shades. She had me put my stuff on one of the cots, and then she said, "Now for a little drinky-poo, Davey," and I followed her into her room. It was painted a pale yellow, much more cheerful than the dark green and cream of the rest of the infirmary, and she had hung white, lacy curtains at the windows. There was a dresser with a frilly lamp on top, and a big iron bed against one wall.

Nancy patted the bed and said, "Sit down, Davey. We'll have a drinky-poo and a little talk." She went into the front room while I sat down on the bed very tentatively, and she came back with a bottle of gin and two glasses. She poured some gin into each glass and handed me one, then put out the lamp. The only light in the room came from the front of the infirmary, a dim glow that made everything dark and fuzzy.

Nancy sipped her drink and let out her breath in a grateful sigh. Then she said, "Bottoms up!" and emptied it in one gulp. "Mmm, that's better." She smiled at me. "Drink up, Davey, while I make myself comfortable. This uniform is like a straitjacket."

I smelled the drink and then tasted it. It was pretty strong, almost as strong as the slivowitz Pop used to break out on special occasions, but Nancy frowned. "Don't sip the damned stuff, Davey! Bottoms up."

I said, "Sure," and I tipped the glass and swallowed the whole thing in one gulp, and I thought for sure my insides would explode. But after a minute a nice, warm feeling spread through my stomach. Nancy went into the bathroom, and when she came out she had her uniform on a hanger and was wearing a sheer sort of kimono with some feather stuff around the neck—and nothing underneath it!

She sat down on the bed next to me and lit a cigarette from a pack on the night table, inhaled, and let the smoke out. Then she put the cigarette down and turned to me with a smile. "Surprised, Davey?"

"A little bit."

She narrowed her eyes and looked at me in a calculating way. "I don't know why you should be. You've been coming on to me all summer."

I was really shocked. "Me?"

"Or maybe you didn't know it." She reached out and ran her hand up my chest inside my shirt, and her fingers moved over my nipples. I swallowed and reached out to put my arms around her, but she drew back and, in a businesslike way, said, "Let's get that shirt and your shorts off, Davey." I pulled my polo shirt off and unbuttoned my shorts, and Nancy looked at me and raised her eyebrows. "Well, you are ready."

I reached into my pocket before I put the shorts down and took out my wallet, and then surreptitiously tried to take out Sam's protection, but to my dismay something had happened to it, and it crumbled away in my hand.

"What the hell are you doing?" Nancy asked impatiently.

"There's this thing my brother gave me . . ." I started to explain, but she snatched the wallet away and looked at it, then laughed. "For Chrissakes, Davey, you don't need that, not with me. Come here!" And she dropped her robe and pulled me toward her, and it was all pretty great. In fact, it reminded me of some of the things Mrs. Bell had taught me, but Nancy had some different techniques that really startled me, like her being on top. I had never dreamed that was possible.

"You just lie there and let me do the work, gorgeous," she said softly, and she took another drag on her cigarette and did some very unusual things that left me breathless.

Afterward, sitting up in her big iron bed, she lit another cigarette and said, "Davey, you're not the little innocent I thought. Someone's been at you, haven't they?"

I didn't know what to say, but finally I admitted that I wasn't a virgin. "I hope it doesn't make any difference," I said.

"*Au contraire,* my love," she said, stroking my chest, and then my stomach, and then, when I began to respond, she said, "Well, maybe I can show you a few things you've missed." At her insistence we both had another small glass of gin, and then she did some really remarkable things I never dreamed a woman would do, but the gin that had given me such a warm glow at first now made my head very fuzzy. I felt as if I were packed in wool and didn't hear too well.

I don't remember getting into my pajamas and lying down, but the next thing I knew I woke up alone in a hospital cot, the covers over me. I had a pounding headache and I was terribly thirsty. It was still dark outside and raining gently. I got out of bed, and through the door of her room I saw Nancy sprawled out on her bed. I tiptoed past her, and in the front room I found some aspirins in the medicine chest and I washed two down with a glass of water.

I couldn't go back to sleep, so I slipped into my clothes and left the infirmary very quietly. I walked through the gentle rain to the dock at the waterfront, and I stretched out on the diving board, staring at the rain-stippled surface of the lake, waiting for the headache to pass.

I felt very strange, not at all the way I had felt with Mrs. Bell, or Miss Casey or Percy, sort of sad, and restless too. After a while the headache subsided, but the rain felt so good on my arms and legs that I stayed there wondering what would happen if I dozed off and spent the rest of the night sleeping there. But then I realized the board was too hard, and I'd probably catch a cold or something, so I stood up and walked back to the bridge, peeing off the downstream side, and then climbed the Hill to my tent.

I was shivering by then, my clothes soaked, and I took them off and dug a clean pair of pajamas out of my trunk, moving very softly so I wouldn't waken the others. Then, as I started to get into bed, I realized that Norman was sleeping in my cot. I eased myself in beside him, and he groaned a little and turned, but I patted his shoulder and whispered, "It's all right."

The cot was warm, and the kid's body was just what I needed to warm me up. I fell asleep like that, and the last thing I thought was, "I've got to get my pajamas out of the infirmary."

▪ CHAPTER FOURTEEN ▪

Saturday morning, before services, the Glee Club rehearsed in the social hall above the mess hall. This Saturday all of the waiters cleared up in a hurry and raced upstairs to watch and listen. Uncle Irv, who directed the Glee Club, had prepared something special for tonight. The program included "The Blind Ploughman," a camp song, "Hail Men of Harel, Hail" and a modern song, "The Boulevard of Broken Dreams." But the grand finale was to be the big event of the evening. It was an original set of lyrics to a Gilbert and Sullivan tune, and it was called "Camp Harel's Lament." It started with the entire Glee Club singing:

> *At sundown, we're rundown*
> *Each day of the week.*
> *All called out, and balled out,*
> *We've gotten so rotten,*
> *We're afraid to speak!*

Then the solos came. Uncle Art with his deep bass voice sang:

> *Oh, the days are awful, but the nights are joyous,*
> *For we spend them reading Keats and Stevenson,*
> *And we shun the female sex 'cause they annoy us,*
> *Oh, a counselor's life is not a happy one!*

Then Horse, who had finally given in and joined the Glee Club just for this performance, had the next solo:

> *At the table little kiddies eat like horses,*
> *And they're through before the meal is half begun,*
> *Appetites like these are grounds for good divorces,*
> *Oh, a waiter's life is not a happy one!*

And then the final solo was sung by our own Butch. Uncle Irv had discovered that he had a sweet voice and perfect pitch. His verse went:

> *From July the first until September morning,*
> *We must play and still our play is never done.*
> *Reveille finds us stretching and a-yawning,*
> *Oh, a camper's life is not a happy one!*

It sounded great, and Norman was so proud of himself he could have burst. Horse and Art had some trouble with their parts and had to keep going over them, but our Butch piped up in his clear little voice and did a perfect job each time.

166

"If he only doesn't get stage fright," Shep said as we all walked up the Hill after rehearsal.

"Butch?" I said proudly. "Not anymore. The kid is really sure of himself."

"We've done a good job," Horse decided definitely. "You got any of those lozenges, Shep? My throat feels tight."

"Jesus! You'll be able to sing, won't you?"

"Maybe I better stop off at the infirmary," Horse decided. "I'll let Doc look at my throat."

I let them go alone. Not that I didn't want to see Nancy, but we had both agreed to keep our "affair," as she called it, quiet. I was seeing her almost every night. I'd sneak out of the tent after "lights out" and ease down the side of the Hill below the path, where I was sure I wouldn't meet anyone. Once Shep, waking up at night to go to the crapper, noticed my empty bed, and I made some excuse the next morning about wanting to take a walk and watch the stars. After that I dummied my bed with a rolled-up blanket and a pillow. I was always back in bed by one or two o'clock, and outside of some dark circles that were growing under my eyes, nobody noticed anything.

Nancy always insisted that I have a little "drinky-poo," but I couldn't stand the taste or the funny, detached feeling the gin gave me, so I'd take my glass into the lavatory, empty it into the toilet bowl, and then fill it with water. So far she hadn't caught on.

Now I made my bed and rolled up the flap on my side. Norman, since becoming Butch, had gotten as sloppy about cleaning the tent as the rest of us. None of us cared much, but when things got too ripe I'd roll up the flaps and tie them to let in some fresh air. I was trying to decide whether there was time for a quick sunbath out in the circle, or if I should get down to the mess hall before services started. Then Skippy Mann, the bugler, came up on the Hill and yelled out, "Hey, Davey, there's a convertible Rolls-Royce in front of the mess hall!"

That made up my mind for me. I grabbed my shirt and hurried down the Hill. Sure enough, there it was, a Phantom Three convertible with the most beautiful lines I'd ever seen. There was a chauffeur in a blue uniform and cap sitting in the front seat, ignoring the group of kids clustered around the car.

I prowled around it, stroking the bumper and hood and peering inside to see the dashboard. What I would have liked was to get under the hood. This baby had a V-12 engine modeled after the Rolls-Royce aircraft engines! The chauffeur sat there staring straight ahead, pretending he was alone. Then a cool woman's voice asked, "Do you like it?"

I turned, startled, and saw a tall, thin woman with light-blond hair wearing a wide-brimmed hat and a black-and-white dress. She was smiling at me in an amused way. I guess she had seen me ogling the car. She was very beautiful, and she held herself very straight, but she did look familiar.

"Well, do you like it?" she repeated.

"I love it!" I said, looking back at the car. "I've never seen a Phantom Three before."

At that moment Norman came tearing out of the bathhouse in his bathing trunks. "Mom, hey, Mom! You gotta watch me!" he was shouting as he ran up to us.

Mom! Of course. This was Norman's mother, and if I had known that, I would have made myself scarce up on the Hill. But maybe she wouldn't recognize me. I started to turn away, and Norman yelled, "Uncle Davey! It's my mom. She's come to hear me tonight. Mom, this is Uncle Davey. I wrote you about him."

She turned toward me, and the amused smile faded. "You're the one who cut Norman's hair?"

It was a question and an accusation all at once, and there was an icy quality to her voice. I remembered the harassed woman at the dock who had slipped me the five bucks, and there was no resemblance. This lady was tough!

"Well actually . . ." I started, "we had to take him to the barber. What happened . . ."

But Norman wouldn't let me finish. He grabbed her hand and was dragging her toward the dock where the kids were finishing their general swim. "Hey, Mom, you gotta watch me swim. You gotta, and I went down the big slide—only the Warriors use that!"

"That's nice, Norman." She followed him, turning to look back at me. "You and I must have a little talk, Mr. Quinn."

168

"It's not Norman," Norman whispered urgently. "It's Butch. My name is Butch now. Uncle Davey gave it to me, and wait till this afternoon. I'm in the Braves' softball game."

He dragged her off to the dock, and I saw him run out on the diving board and belly-flop into the water as she winced. Then, as he climbed up the ladder, she looked back at me with those same cold eyes. I smiled weakly, waved, and walked into the mess hall without even looking at the Phantom Three. I was in for trouble!

But I couldn't forget the Rolls that easily. Everyone was talking about it, and even Jenny was dragged over to the mess hall windows by Small Fry to peer out at it. "So what's the big geshrie? It's an automobile."

"It's a Phantom Three Rolls-Royce," Small Fry told her. "That's one of the most expensive cars made."

"Expensive, shmensive. To me the noodle kugel is more important. If I don't get it out of the oven right now, it'll be a real tragedy."

I almost agreed with that. A Phantom Three Rolls was special, sure, but Jenny's kugel was fantastic. In fact, everything she cooked was fantastic. True, I wasn't such a good judge. Anything was better than Pop's cooking, but Shep, who claimed his mother was a wonderful cook, agreed that Jenny was better. "There's a rule for pastry, kugel, and matzo balls," he told me. "The heavier the cook, the lighter the food. My mother is just too thin, but she's getting there. Since my father died she's put on ten pounds, and her cooking's picked up."

It was funny how Shep could joke about something like his father's death, and yet I knew he'd loved him and missed him. He said Kaddish every night and went along with the rabbi rounding up the necessary ten guys for a minyan.

I managed to avoid Mrs. Seidel, Norman's mother, that afternoon, even though it meant missing Norman's performance at right field. He was still as lousy as ever at sports, baseball in particular, but now he was eager and popular, and he managed to get chosen for most of the games in his age group.

The Rolls was gone that afternoon. "My mom is staying at the

Grand View Hotel," Norman told me. "She says the Guest House is too primitive. What does that mean, Uncle Davey?"

"The Grand View!" Dinge whistled. "That's real classy, and three times what the Guest House costs. Very fancy, Butch."

The Grand View Hotel was on the road to Camp Rocky Clove, up on the side of Hunter Mountain. It had a white-pillared porch that wrapped around the hotel, and it looked very impressive. "It's Greek revival," Shep had told me one night when we were hiking back from the girls' camp, and we'd looked up to see it all lit up with colored lights. Couples were dancing on the broad porch, with music drifting down into the valley. "But they charge an arm and a leg."

Evidently an arm and a leg meant nothing to Norman's mom, and again I wondered which senator was shtupping her. Whoever he was, he hadn't come with her, but I had a hunch the car and chauffeur might be his. Still, her staying at the Grand View was a piece of luck for me. It made it easier to stay out of her sight. The one thing that bothered me was that she was sure to complain to Mr. Luft about Norman's haircut, and eventually Dinge and Killer and I would get hell. So far, if Mr. Luft had noticed it, which I don't think he did because so many kids had crew cuts, he hadn't said anything. I guess he figured as long as Norman was happy, why rock the boat?

I spent most of that afternoon hiding out in the back woods, just exploring and looking for blueberries. If we could get enough, Jenny would usually make a pie for us, complaining all the time. Mostly, though, it was an excuse to avoid Mrs. Seidel. Dinge and Killer managed to go off on a trip to town, and the rest of the waiters swept the tents and made their beds for the first time that week, then made themselves scarce.

It wasn't until that night at Rocky Clove that I saw the Rolls parked in the lot in front of the social hall with all the other parents' cars. Four of us had ridden to the girls' camp on the running boards of the old station wagon while Shep drove. He was the only waiter with a license, and Mr. Luft let him drive us over after cleanup. Shep and I had taken Horse's tables that night so he could arrive with the Glee Club. That was why we got to Rocky Clove a little late, but still in time to hear the Glee Club sing the new song with Horse and Norman doing their solo bits.

I stood on the porch and grinned with pride as Norman's sweet little voice rang through the social hall, and what a hand they got! I was turning away when I came face to face with Mrs. Seidel. She was out on the porch too!

She was wearing a white suit with long pants, and she had a big saucer-shaped white-and-black hat on, and her hair was pulled back in a bun. It was the way old-maid teachers wore their hair, but there was nothing old-maid about her. In fact, she looked sexy as hell, except for those eyes, which seemed to bore right through me!

"I wanted to talk to you, Mr. Quinn," she said softly.

"Wasn't Butch great?" I answered enthusiastically.

"Actually, it's about 'Butch' that I want to talk. Not here," she said as I began to stammer some excuse about his hair. "At my hotel. I'm staying at the Grand View. When is all this over?" She waved her hand at the social hall where the girls were now singing, "We effervesce! We're bubbling over with happiness!"

I said, "About nine-thirty. The kids have to be in bed by ten— usually."

"Well, I want you to meet me at eleven at the hotel. I'll be on the porch." She half turned away, then turned back. "Be there!"

It was an order, no kidding, and I nodded and watched her move into the social hall. I didn't hang around to see the play, which was *The Robe of Wood* by John Golden. I had watched a few rehearsals anyway, and the part of Soo Sin Fah, the Lily Flower of Shun King, was played by Zip Golden, who just happened to be the prettiest boy in camp. Dressed in a Chinese kimono and black wig, he was going to be a sensation, but I was too depressed to watch.

I walked off the porch, and had hardly gotten two feet away when Marcia ran into me. "Why, Davey! Aren't you staying to see the play?"

I shrugged. "I saw the dress rehearsal at camp. Why aren't you in there?"

"I was on my way." She hesitated. "Is something wrong, Davey?"

"Wrong?" I shook my head. "Oh, one of the parents is sore at me."

"No, I mean between us, Davey. You haven't been over here in two weeks." Her voice was unhappy. "And you haven't asked me down to the haystack either."

I suddenly realized that she was right. For the past two weeks I had been too involved with Nancy to get over to Rocky Clove—and I was surprised to realize that I hadn't even missed seeing Marcia! I looked at her in the dim light that filtered out of the social hall. She was as pretty as ever, and her little breasts poking through her blouse still reminded me of marzipan, but the old excitement just wasn't there! Usually, in a situation like this, especially with Marcia asking me why I hadn't seen her, I would have felt shivery and tense, but now? I wasn't sure what I felt. Was it Nancy? But when I had been parlaying Mrs. Bell, Miss Casey, and Percy, I had still felt excited at seeing and being with Marcia. Maybe it was Mrs. Seidel. Maybe I was just too anxious about what was going on.

Then, to my surprise, I heard myself say, "I tell you, Marcia, I don't get a kick out of spending a couple of hours in the haystack with you, holding back and not even kissing you unless you feel like it, and you don't feel like it that often, to say nothing of touching you!" I was really surprised at myself. The words tumbled out without my being aware of them.

Marcia stared at me, and her eyes seemed to sparkle in the dim light—or were those tears? Behind us I could hear the beginning of the play, the mean old Mandarin threatening Soo Sin Fah—"Soo Sin Fah has a golden dagger. Its jewels are exquisite!" That was Rudi Levin, made up to look like a very old man.

Then, before I knew what was happening, Marcia took my hand and put it on her breast! I could actually feel her nipple under my fingers! She wasn't even wearing a bra! Not that she needed one. "I never knew how much you wanted to—to touch me, Davey," she said softly.

"Jesus Christ!" Shocked, I pulled my hand back as if I had been burned. "What are you doing, Marcia?"

She smiled and moved toward the porch. "I'll be down at the haystack later."

I said, "Oh, shit! I can't. I have to meet Norman's mother at eleven to get bawled out. Tomorrow, Marcia?"

She nodded, or I thought she did. It was hard to see in the dark, and she went up the steps to the social hall where a wave of laughter suddenly came out. Something funny must have happened on stage.

I kicked at the dirt and walked down the path toward the road. My one chance to get somewhere with Marcia, and I couldn't take it—or did I want to? I suddenly didn't know. I wasn't even sure what I had felt when I touched her breast. Just shock, I realized, but there should have been something else. I should have grabbed her and kissed her. Wasn't that what she meant? But why had she done it? For two years I had been trying just to put my arms around her, and nothing had happened, and now—now what?

I couldn't bear to go back on the social-hall porch, so I went down to the gate and out onto the road. Then I started walking back toward Camp Harel. It was a nice clear night with a big, fat moon, almost full, and over beyond Hunter Mountain I thought I could see the flicker of the northern lights. Shep had pointed them out to me once, but with the moon as bright as it was, they were hard to see.

I felt very restless and unsettled, and I looked up at the Grand View Hotel uneasily as I passed it on the road below. What was Mrs. Seidel going to do? Bawl me out? I could take that, but what if she got me in trouble with Mr. Luft? What a dope I'd been to let Killer cut Norman's hair!

At the gates to Camp Harel I paused, then I realized that I didn't want to go back there either. I kept on walking, not on the road, but on the single railroad track that bordered the creek. The ties were too close for my pace, so I tried balancing myself on one of the rails with my arms outstretched. It was kind of like tightrope walking. Looking ahead, in the moonlight, I could see where the rails came together, and I thought, maybe Eppie wasn't so crazy after all. Maybe they did meet. Where? At infinity?

Finally I crossed the bridge that led into Hunter and walked down the main street to Musikants's. Inside I got a big hello from Mr. Musikants, and Rosalie, who waited on tables in the bar, gave me a hug and said, "Wait till Sonia hears you're here."

Hal said, "Where's the gang? Hey, what are you doing here on Saturday night? Isn't there a play on?"

I shook my head. "I don't know, Hal. I think life's got me down."

He couldn't stop laughing at that. Big joke! I went back to the booth with a sundae and after a few minutes little Sonia came down and sat across from me. "Isn't this the night you go to the girls' camp?" she asked.

I said, "You know everything about the two camps, don't you? Are you going to be a camper there?"

"Nah, my daddy couldn't afford it. Anyway, Hunter's great in the summer, and in the winter we close up here and drive down to Florida." She folded her arms on the table and leaned her chin on them. "Come on, tell me a story."

"Which one?"

"The one you tell the kids in camp, the one about the subway train in Oz. I rode on a subway last year, Davey."

"Yeah? Well, let's see—where was I?" Between bites of the sundae I told her the story. I loved to watch her eyes while I talked. They grew big and dark and excited, and even though she knew I was making it all up, she still kind of believed it. Later Mr. Musikants brought me another sundae, "On the house." And he sat down to listen to part of the story. When I finished with a cliff hanger and a promise of "more next time," he shook his head.

"That's a rare gift, Davey. I tell you what, could you make up some kind of—well, a new sundae? Something the camp kids would like?"

I said, "Gee, Mr. Musikants, I've never tried that."

"Of course I wouldn't expect you to do it for nothing. I tell you what. Every time you make up a new sundae with a tricky name, I'll give you a free sample of it. How's that?"

We shook hands on it, and I started work that night. Sonia brought me a large piece of shirt cardboard and some crayons and I named the first sundae Dinge's Virgin on Toast. It was all white, two scoops of vanilla ice cream on a sliced banana with crumbled mints over it and marshmallow over that and topped with a cherry. With Sonia's help I drew a large picture of the dish and labeled the name in my best Art II lettering. I was proud of it when Mr. Musikants pinned it up over the soda fountain, and I finished off the sample he made for me. "What I think it needs," I said thoughtfully, "is some kind of sauce over the ice cream."

"Chocolate?" he suggested.

I shook my head. "It should be all white. I'll think about it." And I did on the way back to camp. I didn't have a watch, but it was ten when I left Musikants's and I figured I'd get to the Grand View by eleven if I walked at a comfortable pace and took the shortcut along the railroad track.

Mrs. Seidel was waiting for me, sitting in a wicker chair on the broad porch that surrounded the Grand View Hotel. Inside the floor-to-ceiling windows I could see couples dancing, and I could hear the band playing. I climbed the front steps and stood there for a moment, listening, before I saw her.

"Come over here and sit down, Mr. Quinn." Her chair faced a little table, and she gestured at another chair across from it. She was wearing the same white suit, but now she had a white fur piece around her neck. It looked swell, better than anything I had ever seen in Mr. Karasik's cleaning store. I sat down gingerly, and she said, "Would you like a drink?" A waiter had appeared at the table, though I could have sworn we were alone on the porch.

"I'll have a Coke," I said, realizing that my lips were dry, and she nodded at the waiter. He was back in a few seconds with the Coke, and when I dug in my pocket for change, she waved it away and signed the check. She was drinking something that looked like water from a stemmed glass, but it had an olive in it, and remembering Nancy's gin, I decided it probably wasn't water.

For a moment we were both silent while she sipped her drink and stared at me. I went over half a dozen excuses in my mind and finally decided to tell the truth. What the hell, the most she could do was yell at me—or get me fired. "About Norman's hair," I started. "I know you're upset, but . . ." But what? My voice trailed away, and I took a deep breath. "He doesn't mind."

"No, he doesn't," she said finally. "But since he's only eight years old, I don't put much trust in what he minds or doesn't." She paused, then shook her head. "No, that's not true. I was furious today when I first saw him, and I was ready to explode, but I watched him all afternoon and tonight . . . you're not Norman's counselor, are you?"

"I'm not a counselor," I admitted. "It's a little complicated. I'm

175

a waiter, but on the dock when you gave me that tip I didn't have a chance to explain—and Norman took a liking to me."

She smiled then and I began to relax. It was the first time I had seen her smile, and it changed her whole face, made her softer and even prettier. Maybe she wasn't going to chop my head off. "Yes, he certainly took a liking to you. All I've heard is Uncle Davey this and Uncle Davey that. But what I don't understand is why he's sleeping in your tent with all you older boys. Why isn't he with children his own age? I can't think that's healthy."

This was going to be tougher than I thought. I began to explain just what had happened, trying to be fair to Uncle Art and Mr. Luft, but it sounded strange even to myself. "We sort of took Norman under our wing," I said slowly. "The bunch of us, and we nicknamed him Butch. It's—well, a tougher name, and Dinge—he's one of the waiters—taught him to swim, and Killer taught him baseball, and even Small Fry taught him woodcraft." I had to smile as I remembered how Norman demonstrated to me the way he could walk through the woods without crackling the underbrush. "The haircut was a part of it, and he's much happier now, honest!"

She nodded and sat there sipping her drink, not tossing it down the way Nancy did. When she had finished she signaled the waiter somehow because he was back with another almost at once. Finally, in a soft voice, she said, "I told you I was furious when I first saw Norman." She hesitated. "Butch. I was, but by tonight I was— well, delighted. You've done a wonderful job. Norman doesn't have a father and he needed one terribly."

"Your husband," I started without thinking, but she waved one hand in a dismissing gesture.

"I haven't got a husband," she said flatly. "Norman was—a love child. That's a Victorian phrase, I know, but that's how I always think of him, my love child. I know I've babied him and petted him too much, and I was devastated at sending him up here alone for the summer, but I didn't have much choice. I had to be free—I had to!" Her voice had become very intense, and now she looked away, down the valley where you could see the twinkling lights of the camp.

"He's found a father in you, Mr. Quinn. I realized that after an afternoon with him—and it's what he needs. I don't know how to thank you, except . . ." She had opened her purse and fumbled around in it, then brought out a wad of bills and handed them to me. I was startled and drew back, even pushed the bills away, but she said, "Consider this a tip. I would have given it to his counselor if he had stayed with him."

I felt terribly embarrassed and awkward. "I didn't do it for money," I protested. "Norman—he's like a kid brother to me. I really—like him." I wanted to say "love," but that sounded strange. "I do."

"I know you do. That's very obvious. Now, take the money, please, or you'll start embarrassing me. And it's not to share with the other waiters."

She must have read my mind. "They all helped."

"And I'll take care of them. Believe me." She finished her drink and stood up. "It's late, Mr. Quinn, and perhaps you'd better be getting back to camp."

I stood up feeling faintly disappointed, though I'm not sure what I had expected. I just wanted to spend more time talking to her. When she wasn't angry, there was something about her voice that made me shiver. I put the money in my pocket and mumbled, "Thank you," and started to turn away. Then, to my surprise, she came around the table to me, took my head in her hands, and, reaching up, kissed me on the cheek. Then she turned and went into the hotel. I just stood there, surprised, still feeling that kiss on my cheek and smelling her perfume, a very sweet smell like the vanilla extract Jenny used, but deeper and nicer. Then I walked down the steps and started back to camp.

In the parking lot, I saw the Phantom Three and I walked over to it and stood looking at it for a moment. There was a light on a pole, and I took the roll of bills out and counted them. It was fifty dollars! I was really stunned. I had never heard of a tip anything like that. Shep had said, "Sometimes you get five bucks, but don't expect more than two or three." That was for the waiters. I knew the counselors got more, but from what I'd heard, never more than five, or maybe ten for the summer, but that was rare. I counted the money again, and I couldn't get over it.

Then, making sure no one was around, I opened the door and slid in behind the wheel. I must have sat there for ten minutes, just turning the wheel and making humming motor noises, though I imagine the Rolls was real silent. Finally I left the lot and headed back to camp. I passed the infirmary on my way to the Hill, and I almost stopped, but I didn't want to be with Nancy that night. I didn't know what I wanted. All I could smell was that vanilla perfume, and all I could think was which senator was shtupping Mrs. Seidel?

▪ Chapter Fifteen ▪

From the fire observatory on top of Hunter Mountain you could see for miles and miles, range after range of mountains, blue nearby and then violet in the distance. Between each range there was a low bank of fog, thinning out as the noon sun reached it.

Shep and I had climbed up here on our day off after getting an early start. The entire camp had taken a trip in trucks to Camp North Star to play them at baseball, with Killer becoming a camper for the day. Killer had developed a "dry spitter" pitch that he was eager to see in action. This time Mr. Luft himself had bought Killer a camper's uniform. The trucks took off early and were due back late, after dark, and we waiters were to serve a light cold supper when the campers came home.

Now Shep and I sat on the top steps of the tower chewing blades of grass and staring at the mountains. We couldn't get into the observatory itself because the ranger was off somewhere and had left it locked, but the view from just below was almost as good.

"They're called the Blackhead Mountains," Shep told me. "All this section above Kingston and Saugerties."

"You're kidding."

"No, really."

"Blackhead, like in pimple?"

"Cut it out, Davey!"

"Anyway, I thought they were the Catskills."

"They are, but this section is the Blackheads. That's Slide Mountain off there, The Indians hunted all through here summer and winter, not like the Adirondacks. They couldn't hunt there in the winter. Too cold. They'd pack up and move down here, and below." He waved vaguely toward Slide Mountain.

"You know a lot about this area."

"I should." Shep shrugged. "I've been coming up here for how long? Let's see, since twenty-seven—nine years now."

"Will you come back as a counselor next year?"

"It depends. I need money for college, and I don't think Luft is going to shell out enough. I may look for a job in the city—if there is anything. Jobs are hard to find."

"It's funny, I still can't get used to the idea that you guys could need money."

"Well, none of us are exactly broke. In fact, some of the guys are pretty well-to-do. Take Horse, his family owns a shoe factory up in Connecticut. Walkwell Shoes. Don't buy 'em. They wear like cardboard." He laughed. "Dinge's father is a lawyer, and he does well. Let's see, Squeak's folks own a chain of groceries out on Long Island, and Killer's father is a doctor."

"My pop is a cutter and a pattern maker in the garment center, only he doesn't do so well. He works in a nonunion shop."

"He should organize the place. That's the only way to get a decent salary."

"Not my pop. He's not the type. It's funny, but when I read that book you loaned me, *Brave New World*, that whole business of twinning the single egg cells to get hundreds of workers who all thought alike, who wouldn't rebel—that scared me."

He looked at me curiously. "Why?"

I chewed my lip. "It's hard to explain. Thinking about Pop and how he wouldn't join a union—well, in the book the workers lose their identity. That's terrible."

"But they're happy."

"Maybe that's what scares me." I had trouble saying exactly

179

what I meant. "I want to be happy, sure, but—well, I want to know and understand what makes me happy. Just to be happy, even when things are lousy, like Huxley's workers—I think they lost their souls, Shep!"

He nodded. "That's interesting. You did get a lot out of the book."

"It's more than that." I had an idea at the back of my mind, but I couldn't quite get it into shape. "Take Eppie and all his stunts. Eppie seems to be two guys. He's crazy with us, but he's responsible as hell when he works with the horses. Red Mogulescu told me that. What I'm getting at is, he has this choice of being two different people. All of us have that. Dinge and his foul mouth is one person, but Dinge in the water is another. Take Norman and Butch. One and the same, but different. All of us have that. What frightens me about Huxley's brave new world is that his workers don't have it!"

"But the . . . what are they, aristocrats? The privileged class in that brave new world have it. The hero has it. That's the point of the book. That's what gets him in trouble. He won't conform."

"But everyone else does." I was quiet for a moment, then I said, "My pop not joining a union—maybe he's doing it to get a job, but he's not conforming."

"I think I see what you're getting at," Shep said slowly, "and I understand it. It's something to think about. Davey, you said you read *Hamlet* in school."

I laughed, remembering that night with Marcia explaining the story. "I read it, but maybe I missed the symbolism."

"I doubt that. Anyway, you should try *The Tempest,* especially after Huxley."

"Okay, it's next on my list, after Dinge's *Spicy Detective Stories.*"

"God! That Dinge!"

I said, "What was your father, Shep?"

"He was in real estate. He owned some apartment houses in Manhattan. Mom runs them now, and sometimes I help by collecting the rent. They're real tenements. After my father died things were in a mess and we lost a lot of property. There's enough

180

left to live on, but money is tight. That's why anything I make here has to go to tuition."

"It's funny," I said thoughtfully. "I hear some of the guys talking about how they hate to go into their father's business. Me, I wish Pop had a business I could go into!"

Shep looked at me curiously. "What are you going to do with yourself, Davey? I mean, after high school?"

"I wish I knew."

"I don't think you should give up on college, Davey. You could start saving whatever you make here, and if you work after school— who knows? You might get a decent-paying job, and anyway, my father used to say that things were headed up, that President Roosevelt was good for the country and we'll pull out of this mess."

I looked at him curiously. "I don't know much about politics. We sort of ignore it at home. Pinochle's another matter, but politics . . . the only person I hear any political talk from is my brother Sam, who's always yelling about how bad the New Deal is."

"What you ought to do," Shep said, "is read about it for yourself. You shouldn't listen to your brother and other people all the time. Make up your own mind. I don't think you realize how smart you are, Davey. You should read more, learn more."

I looked out at the mountains. "It's a funny thing, Shep; about reading, I mean. We have a bookcase in the living room with glass doors and Pop keeps it locked."

"Why would anyone lock up books?"

"Pop figures they must be worth something. He picked them up for very little at an auction. There are some sets with real leather bindings. I was never allowed to look at them unless I asked permission, and then he'd give me the key, and I had to read them in the living room. I couldn't take them out of the room."

"What books were they?"

"One was a set of the *Book of Knowledge*. There were great stories in it, and pictures too. That's where I read the fairy tales I tell the kids. The other was Ridpath's *History of the World*. I never really read that, just browsed through it and looked at the pictures, but the *Book of Knowledge*—I was crazy about that."

"Maybe because it was under lock and key."

I looked at him. "What do you mean?"

He frowned a little. "School's too easy."

"Not for me!"

"I don't mean it that way. I mean we're forced to go to school, forced to learn and read, and that makes us hate it. If we can't get at books, if they're forbidden somehow, we really want to read them."

I nodded. "I think I know what you mean. My brother, Sam, has a book about sex and marriage, and he keeps it hidden behind other books. I found that quick enough and read it from cover to cover, but I never looked at his other books."

"You nut!" He laughed. "But you're right. That's my point."

We both sat there silently for a while, then Shep stood up. "Come on, let's get going."

We started down the tower steps, and Shep said, "You keep reading, Davey, not the crap Horse lends you, but some good stuff. You've got a good brain, even if you act dopey sometimes!"

I said, "Thanks. Is that a compliment?"

He punched my arm. "You bet. Come on, I'll race you down the mountain!" And he took off, jumping and leaping down the trail. I tried to keep up with him, but I wasn't as surefooted, and I was scared stiff of falling and breaking an arm or leg. Somehow, though, I made it down, panting for breath, a good five minutes behind Shep, who was waiting, stretched out in a little patch of meadow at the end of the trail.

"Another thing," he said as I dropped down next to him. "You're out of condition."

"I never was in condition!"

"I mean someone with your build ought to be more athletic. You've got the potential and the coordination. All you need is heart."

That sounded like my old gym teacher, Mr. Szylowski. "It's like a song, Shep." And I sang out, "You gotta have heart, all you need is heart, you gotta have heart to fart!"

Shep shoved me. "Be serious, you dumb klutz. I'm trying to help you!"

We began wrestling in the grass, and finally I pinned him down. We had been laughing, but suddenly he stopped and looked up at me with a funny expression, and his body relaxed. I loosened my hold,

182

but he didn't fight back. He put one arm up around me, and I pulled loose and jumped to my feet. "Everyone is trying to help me," I said, brushing the grass off. I avoided his eyes as he stood up. "The thing is, I'm perfectly happy, but you tell me to read and be athletic, and Marcia tells me to be more concerned with what's happening in the world—why can't I just be myself?"

Shep brushed himself off. "That's okay if you know yourself. I don't think you do, Davey."

I said, "Hey, can't we talk about something that's fun? What'll we do this afternoon?"

"Okay. I'll back off. You wanna go to Hunter? Tannersville? Down to the gorge? How about Devil's Tombstone? It's only a few miles down the road from Rocky Clove. We could hitch or walk."

I shrugged. "There's nothing much there. I went there once with Nancy in her car."

We started down the trail to the road, and Shep looked at me curiously. "What's with you and Nancy?"

I avoided his eyes and pulled up a blade of grass as we walked. "Why should there be anything with me and Nancy?"

"I thought we were pals, Davey. Why don't you level with me?" When I didn't answer, he said, "A few of the guys are talking about you sneaking down there after lights out."

I shrugged. "We're good friends. After all, we're both goyim."

"Very funny!"

"Well . . . we talk things over. Nancy's a very intelligent woman."

"Uh-huh, I'll bet." He grinned at me and punched at my arm. "Okay, you keep your secrets, but I notice you and Marcia aren't seeing much of each other. Rumor has it she was down to the haystack with Squeak."

I was really shocked at that. "Squeak! I can't believe it."

"Yeah, well, there's no accounting for taste, but I thought you were soft on her."

I said, "She's okay. Come on, let's head back for camp—or maybe Hunter. I've got a great idea for a sundae, and I have this deal at Musikants's . . ."

We ended up in town, Shep reading the magazines in front of the store, and Sonia and I sharing a booth while I told her another episode of the *Lost Subway Train in Oz*. I had the train learn to go without tracks so I could get him out of the tunnel he was in. The train was definitely a he, and I had the Nome King shrink him down to human size. It's hard to tell a story when one of the characters is an entire subway train!

On the way back to camp I told Shep I'd have to remember this latest episode to tell to Norman and his friends.

"He's got plenty of friends now," Shep said thoughtfully. We were both walking along the tracks, each balancing on a rail and holding hands for steadiness. "All the Braves like him. We ought to move him back with the kids his own age."

I felt a sudden sense of loss at the idea of Norman moving out. I was really used to the kid. "You think so?"

"Sure, he should be with kids his own age. All he's learning from us now is dirty talk. I caught Dinge telling him how to get whacked off by a fly!"

"What? What the hell is that?" I almost fell of the rail.

"According to Dinge, you catch a fly and pull off its wings, then you get into a bathtub with a hard-on and let the tip of your shlong stick up above the water. You're sure you want to hear this? It's really disgusting."

"It sounds disgusting. Tell me more."

"You put the wingless fly on the tip of your shlong and let it walk around, bzzz, bzzz, until you pop off."

I stopped and stared at him. "You mean Dinge actually does that?"

"Who knows? I think Dinge would stick his cock into anything he could, anytime. I don't even like the way he looks at Norman sometimes."

"Shit, you're right. We'll have to move him, and keep an eye on Dinge! Now that you mention it, I heard him asking the kids in the shower if they'd like to learn how to play Pick Up the Soap!"

When we got back to camp we found it almost completely deserted. The rabbi was there and Doc Rosenberg and Nancy. The arts and crafts counselor and his assistant were preparing an exhibit and hadn't gone on the trip, and two of the waiters had hung around, and there was Mr. Lowenstein, the Camp Mother's husband. We all had sandwiches together, and then Horse drifted in. He had been to Haines Falls and was all excited about the library there.

As usual, in the evening, the rabbi started rounding up ten men for the minyan so Shep could say Kaddish for his father. I really admired the way he stuck to it, never missing a day. "I believe in it," he had told me very seriously one day. "I believe that Kaddish lights the dead's way into the next life. I intend to say it every night for eleven months!"

Shep really loved his father, and sometimes I wondered if I'd feel like that if Pop died, but I couldn't ever think of Pop's death seriously—or maybe I didn't want to. I remember once when I was eleven years old and playing down near the Hudson River at 200th Street I saw a crowd of people gathered at the end of the dock. I walked down there curiously, wondering what they were doing, and when I came close I saw that they were all gathered around a man stretched out on the dock, soaking wet, a piece of cloth covering his face.

"What happened?" I asked one of the kids in the crowd.

"Some guy who drowned. They just fished him out. Must be a suicide."

I pushed through the crowd, horrified, and stared down at the man. All I could see were his feet and hands. His shoes were gone and there were holes in his socks. Suddenly I had a terrible premonition that it was Pop! He had fallen into the river, or he had been laid off and had jumped in. There was no logic to what I felt, just a terrible fear, and before I could stop myself I'd bent down and pulled the cloth from the man's face.

A strange bluish face and staring, sightless eyes lay under the cloth, and there was a gasp from the crowd, and someone called out, "Hey! What the hell are you doing?"

But I didn't care. It wasn't Pop, thank God, and I pushed back through the crowd and ran off.

It's funny I thought of that when Shep told me how much Kaddish meant to him. I didn't believe in religion, really, though I wasn't so sure about God, but if there was a chance that it was true and saying Kaddish worked—could I take a chance on ignoring it?

I was stretched out on my cot thinking about that when Shep burst into the tent, a wild kind of look in his eyes. "Davey! I can only find nine guys for a minyan. I need ten."

I sat up. "What are you talking about, Shep?"

"I have to say Kaddish, and I can't make a minyan. Besides me and the rabbi, there are only seven guys in camp!"

"Did you check all the tents?"

"Everywhere. I'm one short, Davey!" There was a plea in his voice, and I felt a sudden chill go through me.

"Jesus, Shep! I can't!"

"Why not, Davey? You'll have to tell them eventually."

"Why? Why should I tell them? Shep, I can't do it. I just can't!"

"Oh, shit!" He turned away furiously and started running down the Hill. I ran after him, calling, then, as I hit the gravel path, I realized that I didn't have any shoes on. I limped back to the tent and pulled on my sneakers, but then I just sat there. Didn't Shep understand? Why had I ever told him I was Jewish? How could I go down now and say, "Hey, guys, I'm no shaygets. It was all a big joke. I'm really a Jew." And if I did, would they believe me?

In the end I just sat there while the light faded and eventually I heard the trucks returning with the kids singing at the top of their voices:

> *Fight on, you Harelians,*
> *Hit the ball, pile up the score.*
> *Fight you on, Camp Harel,*
> *Bring the laurels home once more!*

I went down as they were all piling into the mess hall for a late supper. Camp Harel had won, and Killer had pitched a hitless game with his dry spitter. Everyone was excited and bubbling over with the victory. I set up my tables and tried to talk to Shep, but he avoided me, and when the meal was over he ducked out before I could reach him. Skippy Mann, the bugler who also handled the mail, stopped me and said, "There's a letter for you, Davey."

I was surprised. I'd only gotten three cards since I came up here, all from Pop, and all pretty brief. This was a letter, and it had Sam's name and address. I felt my heart skip a beat and I tore it open, sure that something terrible had happened to Pop. This was my punishment for not helping Shep!

But I realized that was silly. The letter had been mailed a few days before. It was from Sam, all right.

Dear Davey:

I hope you aren't screwing up on the job. For one thing, we need the money now. Pop was laid off. When you get back, we'll have to figure out some way you can make a buck. Anyway, since Pop isn't working, I'm going to borrow a car and drive him up to visit your camp. He says he's lonely and wants to see you. God knows why. (Ha, ha.) We'll be there Sunday.

Sam

I just stared at the letter. This was Wednesday. I had four days before Pop arrived. I really wanted to see him. I had missed him more than I thought I would, but what would happen when Pop showed up with his accent? How was I going to explain Davey Quinn, boy shaygets, to him?

▪ Chapter Sixteen ▪

Four days till Pop arrived with Sam. I knew how Jimmy Cagney and those other guys on Death Row felt waiting for the chair. I had all sorts of crazy ideas. I'd send a telegram home, "There's an epidemic of polio here stop don't come stop love Davey." But that was over ten words. I could take out the "love" and one of the stops. Or I could hitchhike down to Haines Falls and wait in the road till Sam's borrowed car came and flag them down and tell them the camp burned down. Anyway, where had Sam borrowed a car? And when had he learned to drive?

Or maybe I should quit right now and take a bus home. There was one that went from Hunter to New York. I could tell Pop the camp had closed early, or a flood had washed it away. Didn't Shep say there was a flood every few years?

We had stopped on the bridge one night a few weeks ago, and he had pointed down to the concrete piles the bridge was built on. "That nut Luft. Every time there's a flood, the bridge is washed away, and he rebuilds it and pours more concrete in and makes the ends shorter and the piles thicker."

"That should help," I said.

"Like hell it does. It makes it worse. It simply offers more resistance, and the creek piles up behind it until there's enough force to smash the bridge down and carry it away. If he had any brains, he'd make the bridge longer instead of shorter, he'd open up this part of the river so there was less resistance. But not Luft. He's too damn stubborn!"

I agreed with Shep then and now. Mr. Luft was stubborn, and yet I had to respect him. He'd taught me a lot of things, like how to slice bread real thin, and how to cut butter. The butter came in one-pound blocks, not in a tub, and to serve it we had to cut each block into four long quarters and then cut each quarter into pats. The first time I was getting ready to cut mine into pats, I saw Small Fry at the counter making a real mess of his butter. It stuck to his knife and ended up in crumbs.

Mr. Luft walked in and watched for a minute, then grabbed the knife from him. "You dumb animal! Can't you use your brain? Do it this way!" And he took the paper the butter was wrapped in and put it around the knife blade. Would you believe it? The knife cut right through the butter without crumbling it or messing it up. I learned from that; don't be the first to try anything. I was glad it was Small Fry who caught it instead of me.

I couldn't wait to show Pop that trick. At home he'd send me to Mr. Gebhardt for a quarter pound of butter, and at Mr. Gebhardt's the butter came in tubs. "Make the Nazi give you one piece," Pop would warn me. "I don't want the scraps left over from when he cuts it for his other customers." But it was cutting up that one piece at home that always gave me trouble. Now I knew how to do it, except I wasn't sure that the paper Mr. Gebhardt used to wrap the butter in would work as well as the thin paper the pound packages came in.

And thinking of Pop reminded me again of the day of reckoning that was approaching. I thought of all the schemes to stop him from coming, but I didn't follow up on any of them. I wanted to ask Shep's advice, but things were kind of cool between us after that business of the minyan. I tried to apologize, but Shep just shrugged. "It doesn't matter, Davey." But I knew it did matter to him, we both knew it. I really felt lousy about it, about disappointing Shep and now losing him as a friend. We had had so many long talks together, and the talks had meant a lot to me.

Not that we always discussed something great or important. We'd talk about ordinary stuff, like what we were going to do after school, how the camp was run and how we'd run it if we got a chance, and what a jerk Tom Ciardi was with his West Point crap. We talked about why some guys like Killer were such great athletes, and why other guys like me hated athletics, but when we talked about me it was never the way Marcia did, tearing me down. Shep just seemed to take me the way I was. Oh, sometimes we'd talk about the things I might do, about college and reading, but talking to Shep made me think I could do a hell of a lot more than I did.

Talking to Marcia, on the other hand, always made me realize all the things I couldn't do. But to be fair, I had always enjoyed listening to Marcia talk about my problems, and in fact I had encouraged her to do it. I used to think it meant she was thinking about me, and the same was true for Sam and Rhea. I enjoyed being the center of a family discussion.

Well, I'd sure have a chance at that when Pop arrived. I had a feeling I'd be right at the center of things, and I didn't like the feeling one bit! That Friday I decided that maybe I could ease the shock a little if I began spreading the idea around that I wasn't a real shaygets after all. I'd start with the guys in my tent.

We had more room in the tent now because we had finally moved Norman out, back to one of the Braves' tents. We thought he would take it hard, but we all agreed that it was better for him to be with guys his own age now that he was such a little big shot. I tried to figure out some way of doing it without breaking his heart, but when the time came, it was obvious that Norman's heart was not breakable.

"Butch, how would you like to move back with the Braves?" I asked.

"Not in Uncle Art's tent." Norman frowned at the four of us. "I can't stand that son of a bitch."

"Hell no, Butch!" Killer said. "There are two other Brave tents."

"Sure." Norman shrugged. "It's okay with me, if you don't mind, Uncle Davey." He looked at me questioningly. "You won't think I'm running out on you?"

"I'll live with it, Butch. Anyway, you'll have more fun with your own group, won't you?" To tell the truth, I did feel he could have put up more of a fuss. "I'll be around, especially for stories."

So it was decided, and we checked it out with Uncle Frank Eliscu, who had a Braves tent, and he was delighted. Norman's mom's visit in the Rolls had upped his status, in terms of eagle shit, which was what the counselors called tips. Before he left, Norman shook hands with all of us, and in his best Butch manner said, "I won't forget you guys. You were real friends to me when I needed it."

"How about that?" Horse grinned as we watched Norman and his new tent mates carry his bed and trunk across the circle. "The kid's come a long way. We ought to go into business. 'We make over kids!' How's that for a slogan?"

"We develop better boys," Killer said. "That's Harel's motto. Maybe we ought to open a camp in competition. Give us your sissies and weaklings. We'll turn them into real men!"

"Norman wasn't a sissy," I said defensively. "He just needed confidence. Anyway, I'm going to miss the kid."

Dinge, who had walked in while Norman was moving, said, "It's a good thing he's out of here. I thought for sure Davey was going to bugger him one of these nights."

"Me? You're the one I was worried about!" I threw a pillow at him, and that started a free-for-all, and of course one of the pillows split, and there were feathers over everything, and we spent the next hour picking them up one by one!

With Norman gone, there was extra room in the tent, and the other waiters took to hanging out with us. That Friday, when I decided to tell the guys the truth about me, Squeak and Dinge were in our tent. Eppie was across the lake in the stables pitching horse manure, and Small Fry was playing basketball with the Hunters. Squeak had received his weekly batch of comics from home, from a Long Island paper that carried *Buck Rogers in the Twenty-Fifth Century* and *Brick Bradford*. I had been following them all that summer, but I didn't have the heart to read them now.

"I've got something to tell you guys." I felt myself tighten up as I said it, and I thought maybe I shouldn't go through with this, maybe it's a big mistake. Then I saw Shep looking at me in a kind of peculiar way, and I said, "Hey, come on, will you guys quiet down for a minute?"

"Okay," Killer said. He and Dinge were on his bed trading magazines, and they both looked up. "Let's hear from the Shaygets."

I scowled. "That's just it," I said carefully. "This shaygets business."

"We're sorry about that," Horse said quickly, putting a page of the comics down. "We shouldn't call you Shaygets. It's not that we're making fun of you . . ."

"Yeah, some of my best friends are goyim," Dinge put in.

"Cut out the kidding. This is serious. I have a confession to make." Nobody said anything, and I bit my lip. How the hell did I say this? "I'm not one, a shaygets . . . I mean, I'm Jewish."

"I knew it," Killer said. "The reb's converted you. I always said, give him half a chance . . ."

"Cut it out, Killer. I was born Jewish. I lied to get this job—or at least I didn't tell the truth, which I guess is the same thing."

Killer sat up. "You're really serious? You're Jewish? You're not shitting us?"

"I'm serious. Our family name was Kvinski. At Ellis Island they changed it to Quinn. It's as simple as that. When I went for my interview with Mr. Luft, he assumed I was a goy. I didn't straighten him out because I wanted the job, and once I got up here, once I got to know you guys, I didn't have the guts to tell you the truth." I looked at Shep. "I'm sorry about the minyan."

Shep stood up and came over to me and gave me a friendly punch

191

in the arm. "Davey, I'm proud of you." He turned to the other guys, who were staring at me. "Davey told me about it a while ago, but I respected his secret. I think all of us should."

"Funny, you don't look Jewish." Horse grinned.

"You put it over on Luft," Dinge said slowly. "My God, that's funny!" He started to laugh, and after a minute the other guys joined in, rolling on the beds and laughing so hard they were almost crying.

I had to smile too. "You won't tell?"

"I'd die before I told!" Dinge laughed. "But I'd love to see Luft's fuckin' face if he ever finds out."

"Well, he won't find out from me," Horse said. "I think it's great."

Squeak had laughed with the rest, but now he was frowning. "I don't know. Isn't it"—he shrugged—"sort of dishonest?"

"Oh, shit," Dinge said. "You think Luft's honest? Anyway, it's not dishonest. Who's Davey hurting?"

"That's hardly the definition of honesty," Shep said, "but the choice is Davey's. I'm just proud he had the guts to tell us, and he trusts us." He stuck out his hand. "Forget about the minyan, Davey. We're friends!" And all the other guys shook hands with me solemnly and swore wild horses wouldn't drag the truth out of them.

I felt all choked up. It was only later, when I was off by myself, that I faced up to the truth. I hadn't told them because I had guts or trusted them. I had told them because I knew everyone would find out Sunday, when Pop arrived, and I wanted to soften the blow.

That was why I told Nancy the truth that night. I had, as usual, sneaked down to the infirmary after lights out, and she had taken out her bottle of gin and poured us two enormous "drinky-poos," and I, as usual, had gone to the bathroom and changed mine for water.

"What I don't understand, Davey," Nancy said before I told her, "is why you always have to pee before making love. It isn't possible that a kid like you has a prostate problem."

I didn't answer that. I said, "Listen, Nancy, I've got to tell you the truth."

"Always tell me the truth, kid, but come over here first and tell it

192

to me on the bed—and for Christ's sake, take off those shorts. Let's see if you're still fond of me."

I slipped my shorts off and sat down next to her on the bed. "Nancy, I'm Jewish. I've been lying about being a Methodist. I'm not even a Christian."

"No shit?" She ran one finger down the line of hair that went from my chest to my groin. "The trail of the lonesome pine!"

I said, "Did you hear me, Nancy?"

"Davey, I don't care if you're Jewish, Moslem, or Hindu, as long as you can get this cute little fellow up. Come on!"

So that was that as far as Nancy was concerned. Walking back to the Hill across the bridge that night, I thought maybe it would be that way with everyone else, that no one would care what religion I was, but I knew that wasn't true. I stopped to pee off the down-creek side and was buttoning up my fly when Tom Ciardi and a couple of the counselors came across the bridge. They had been in town drinking, and they were staggering a little and singing, off key:

> Heigh-ho, Kefusalem,
> The harlot of Jerusalem.
> Heigh-ho, Kefusalem,
> The daughter of the rabbi!"

"Hey, Quinn," Tom Ciardi yelled. "Did you piss off the right side? We don't want a flood." He started to unbutton his fly, and I waved and hurried up the hill. I wouldn't mind a flood, I thought. I wouldn't mind the whole damn camp being washed away just so long as it kept Pop from meeting Mr. Luft!

No such luck. They met all right, early Sunday afternoon. I had stayed away from Rocky Clove Saturday night because it was raining and the play that the girls' camp was putting on wasn't that good. I'd seen the rehearsals. It was by a poet named Edna St. Vincent Millay, and was called *Two Slatterns and a King*. It was all talk and no action. But the real reason I didn't go was because I wanted to avoid Marcia. Things had gotten very awkward between us, and since she had been going around with Squeak, I didn't know how she felt about me. The best thing, I figured, was to stay away.

Saturday night I watched the last truckload of kids drive off, and then Shep and the waiters followed in the station wagon, Dinge and Killer riding the running boards. I sat on the porch of the mess hall for a while watching the rain fall. It had been a wet week, and according to Shep, who said he could predict the weather by the clouds over the Colonel's Chair, we were going to have another few soggy days.

I didn't mind the rain. It kind of matched my mood, and then I heard someone playing the piano upstairs, a sad, lonely kind of blues. I listened to it for a while, then, curious to see who else had stayed in camp, I climbed the stairs. There, in the empty social hall, the rabbi, of all people, was sitting at the upright piano playing a ragged kind of tune.

He turned around when he saw me, and he smiled but didn't stop playing. "You like blues, Davey?"

I came forward and sat down on the apron of the little stage. "Yeah, when I feel like this."

He kept playing. "Is something wrong?"

I sighed. Rabbi Kaplin was the last person I could tell my problem to. I was sure he'd never understand. After all, I had sort of betrayed my people. I said, "No, not really. I just feel blue."

He nodded and switched to another song, one I recognized. "Yeah, I know that feeling. It seems to me I get it every Saturday night after two days of services. I should feel uplifted, nearer to my Maker, but I never do. I wonder why?"

It was funny. Rabbi Kaplin had just the slightest touch of an accent, and yet he reminded me of Pop. He wasn't that old, of course, though I couldn't tell just how old he was. I've always had that trouble with adults, telling their age. "Where did you learn to play?" I asked.

"In the borsht belt. You know where that is, Davey?" When I shook my head, he explained, "Around Fallsberg. That's about twenty miles south of here, toward the city. There are a lot of Jewish hotels there, and I worked summers playing with the bands. It sent me through Yeshiva. I don't get much of a chance to play now. I usually wait until the camp is deserted. It's not considered—well, proper for a rabbi to play jazz."

"I don't mean to be rude," I said uncertainly, "but you don't seem—well, like a typical rabbi."

194

He laughed. "What's typical in a rabbi, Davey? But you wouldn't know. Let's see, we're not like priests. We're not intermediaries between the Lord and men. Rabbi is more of a title given to learned men who teach the Torah and other books. Oh, we perform marriages, we teach and offer advice and comfort to people. So you see, I'm an ordinary person who knows a little more than the average guy." He finished with a flourish on the piano.

I nodded. "The other day, Rabbi, when Shep couldn't make up the minyan . . . what happened?"

He looked at me in surprise. "Nothing. We had a minyan the next day."

"Do you think—I mean, would it have hurt Shep's father's chances of getting into Paradise?" I realized how silly that sounded even as I said it, and the rabbi laughed, then stopped playing and swiveled on the piano stool to face me.

"You know, that's all superstition, Davey. Even the concept of Paradise is superstition. It's not written in any holy book that man will get into Paradise, no matter how many Kaddishes are said for his departed soul. It's superstition, but . . ." He spread his hands. ". . . a nice superstition."

"I don't understand."

"Well, the Jews don't have a Heaven and Hell like you Christians believe in. To us, worshiping God and leading a good life should be ends in themselves. Can you understand that?"

You Christians was all I heard, and I stood up and nodded. "I think so. Thanks, Rabbi Kaplin."

He said, "Anytime, Davey," and he went back to playing the piano. I walked up to the Hill slowly and stretched out on my bed. Tomorrow, I thought. Tomorrow it all happens. As Dinge would say, "The shit hits the fan!"

Sunday morning I told Nancy I wasn't going to church and wouldn't drive into town with her. "You remember what I told you?"

She laughed. "You're a crazy kid. You told Luft yet?"

"No, not yet."

"I'd like to be around when you do."

"I wouldn't," I muttered.

"Well, we'll put off the driving lesson till another time." And she took off in the Model A. I watched her go regretfully. She had been teaching me to drive each Sunday, and I was getting good at it. I had the shifting down cold. "The trick," she'd told me in the beginning, "is to go slow. Any idiot can drive fast. It takes skill to drive slow, and don't ever ride your clutch."

I straightened up and hiked over to the Guest House across the lake, a small white clapboard building next to the stables. At the desk I asked if I could make a room reservation for my father and brother. I had been putting it off, hoping they'd be full up, and there'd be no room, but there was no problem. The Guest House was half empty that weekend. Just my luck! Then I went back to the mess hall and began setting up for lunch.

After lunch, just as I finished sweeping, I looked out the mess-hall window, and I saw an old Chevy pull up near the camp entrance. Sure enough, Pop and Sam and Rhea climbed out. I had forgotten all about Rhea. She was just what I needed to make my day complete!

I put away the broom and sprinted toward them. Maybe, somehow, I could keep them from meeting Mr. Luft. I could see him over on the baseball diamond with Tom Ciardi, checking for pebbles near home plate. If only he stayed there!

I came running up just as Sam started to take two suitcases out of the trunk of the Chevy, a beat-up 1930 sedan. I said, "Nice car, Sam," and the three turned to look at me.

Pop said, "Davey!" and we both stood there looking at each other, then Pop held his arms out, and I grabbed him and hugged him.

"All right, already," Sam said. "You can give me a hand with these."

"Don't take them out," I said. "The Guest House is across the lake."

I let Rhea give me a peck on the cheek. "You're all sweated up, Davey," she said disapprovingly. "Don't you wear a shirt? You're half naked."

"That's the way we dress here," I said. "How was the drive up?"

"Not bad. I did seventy on route Nine W in spots, before Rhea got excited." He patted the Chevy. "It's a good car. We ought to think of buying one, Rhea."

"That's just what we need, especially now that your father's been laid off."

"I'll find work," Pop said cheerfully. "I've been laid off before, and I'll be laid off again. So where are we staying, Davey?"

I showed them the way to the Guest House, and rode the running board over there while Rhea protested that it wasn't safe. "I only got one room, but I'm sure they'll have another available," I told them as we unloaded the car.

"One room for the three of us? Good old Davey," Sam said. "Acting true to form."

I didn't want to tell him I'd forgotten about Rhea, so I carried in the bags, and of course they had an extra room. They also gave us a special rate when I explained that I was a waiter at the camp. But even with the special rate, Rhea wasn't happy. "I had no idea it would be this—well, primitive! Look at those walls!"

"So it's not the Ritz." Sam shrugged. "How about showing us the camp, Davey?"

"Not me." Rhea grimaced. "I'm exhausted from that ride. I'm going to take a nap."

"A nap! For Christ's sake, we just got here, and we're leaving tomorrow. Don't you want to see the place?"

"I've seen enough," Rhea snapped, taking a handkerchief from her pocketbook. "As a matter of fact, I think I'm allergic to something around here. You go ahead. I'll see you later."

With Sam muttering as he followed us, I led Pop outside and gestured toward the lake. "That's Lake Harel, and that's the mess hall and social hall, the building with the sign, 'We Develop Better Boys.' And that's the baseball diamond, over there, and there's the tennis courts and the Papooses' bunk where the little kids stay, and way back there, across the creek, that's the Hill where we sleep, where the tents are. Would you like to go into town now?"

Sam stared at me. "We'd like to see the camp, Davey. We had something like a guided tour in mind, not a view from across the lake!"

"Of course," Pop said, calming Sam down. "Davey was getting

197

started. He looks good, Sam, doesn't he? All nice and brown—there's certainly plenty of fresh air here." He sniffed. "And horse manure. I smell horse manure, Davey."

I said, "That's the stables, Pop. The camp has some horses and a few of the kids take riding lessons, but that costs extra."

"Come on," Sam said. "I need a walk. Let's go." And he started off around the lake. Well, this was it. I might as well go through with it. I led them over to the front of the mess hall, and when I saw Mr. Luft leave the baseball diamond and head for the mess hall, I figured I could miss him if I got them out to the dock right away.

"And this is where we swim," I said, grabbing Pop's arm and walking him toward the dock." The only one there was Dinge practicing back flips from the high diving board.

"The mountains remind me of the Old Country," Pop said, gesturing toward Hunter Mountain.

"What's with the Old Country?" Sam frowned. "You come from the Ukraine. Are there mountains in the Ukraine?"

"We lived in Ireland for five years," Pop said. "In Ireland there were mountains—like these, but greener. Of course I was younger than you, Davey, when I came here, and I earned my own living. Thirteen, and I was on my own already."

I saw Mr. Luft walking toward us, and I grabbed Pop's arm. "Let me show you the baseball diamond."

Dinge had climbed up on the dock, and he grinned at us. "Hi, Davey."

"This is my father and brother, Dinge. This is Dinge."

Dinge said, "Hi. I'm too wet to shake hands. Nice to meet you, Mr. Quinn. Davey's a great guy." I was proud of him. He said it all without using fuck once! He looked toward Mr. Luft. "Does he know yet, Davey?"

I said, "No!"

"Well, take care." He walked out on the board, teetered up and down a bit, then did a perfect swan dive."

"That boy can dive!" Sam said admiringly.

"Yeah, well, come on. I'll show you the baseball diamond." Mr. Luft had almost reached me as I dragged Pop and Sam on past the shallow water dock and cut past the apple trees to the baseball diamond.

"Vus fur a name is Dinge?" Pop asked as we walked away. "The boy is a shvartzer?"

I said, "No, Pop. He gets very dark in the sun. He tans easily."

"What did he mean, does he know yet?" Sam asked with his usual suspicion.

"One of the waiters is sick," I said quickly. "Dinge will explain it to him. See those apple trees? We have the Friday night and Saturday morning services under them, if it isn't raining. Then we have them inside, like yesterday. You're lucky today is so nice. It's been raining on and off all week." I led them around the backstop. "This is the baseball diamond. It's regulation size and they play hardball on it. One of the waiters is a fantastic player, that's Killer, and he puts on a camp uniform when we play other camps and pretends to be a camper."

Pop shook his head and tsked a little, and I looked back to see Mr. Luft talking to Dinge and looking at us curiously. I led them toward the Pap bunk and the infirmary. "The little kids stay in this bunk, and there's the Camp Mother to take care of them, and that's the infirmary. The camp nurse lives there and the doctor sleeps up on the Hill with the rest of us . . ." I was babbling a little, and Sam was beginning to get suspicious of this quick tour.

"Hold up, Davey. Take it easy now. You can't drag Pop around like this."

"It's all right," Pop said. "I want to see the camp. Friday and Saturday services, and they keep a kosher kitchen?"

"Oh yeah, they even have separate dishes for milk and meat meals." Just then two of the Warriors came jogging by and one waved at me. "Hi, Shaygets!"

Sam turned to stare at them. "Shaygets? Did he say shaygets? Why did he call you shaygets?" He and Pop looked at me, and I said, "Well, it's sort of complicated." And then Mr. Luft walked up.

"Davey?" He looked at Pop and Sam, and I knew that this was my moment of truth.

I said, "This is Mr. Luft, Pop. He owns the camp and he's the director."

Pop put his hand out and said, "I'm glad to meet you, Mr. Luft. I want to thank you for giving Davey such a nice job, and your camp—it's, taka, a beautiful place. You can smell the fresh air."

I had had some wild idea that I could get away with it, that Mr. Luft wouldn't guess Pop was Jewish, but until that minute I never realized how heavy Pop's accent was. Maybe I could tell Mr. Luft later that I was adopted . . .

"Has Davey been behaving himself, Mr. Luft?" Sam asked.

"Mr. Quinn?" Mr. Luft asked in a bewildered voice. "You're Davey's father? Really?"

"Of course," Pop said, smiling at me fondly. "Davey tells me you keep a milchedig and flayshedig kitchen here. That can't be easy in a camp this size."

Mr. Luft seemed to be in a state of shock. He looked at the three of us, and I could see the storm building up in his face. Before he could explode, I said, "I wanted to show them the Hill, Mr. Luft," and I started off toward the bridge.

Mr. Luft's mouth tightened up, and I knew that look, but a group of Braves came by just then, and one of them grabbed Mr. Luft's hand. "Are we having ice cream tonight, Mr. Luft? What flavor?" Mr. Luft scowled at me a minute longer, then put on his best "camper" smile and, ruffling the kid's hair, moved off with them. "Strawberry," he said, pulling himself together and sounding almost cheerful. "Now who won the game this afternoon? Who gets doubles?"

Somehow I managed to get Pop and Sam up to the Hill and I introduced them to the waiters who were in the tent, and I carefully avoided Tom Ciardi on the way down. I told them how we peed off the bridge after dark. "It's a camp custom," I said. "We always pee downstream."

Sam looked shocked. "Is that the water that goes into Ashokan Reservoir? The water we drink in the city?"

I said, "I don't think so. It's flowing the wrong way. It goes toward Hunter. I think it goes into Schohari Reservoir."

"My God," Sam yelled. "We drink that water too!"

"By time it reaches New York," Pop pointed out, "it's purified."

Sam made a face. "I could be drinking Davey's piss!"

Pop said, "Enough already. Davey says all the boys do it."

"You think it's any better drinking all their piss?"

Pop said, "It's late, Davey. We'll go back to the hotel. Did you bring the pinochle deck, Sam?"

I finally got them back to the Guest House. At least with Sam bothered about our fouling the creek, he wouldn't notice how careful I was to avoid Mr. Luft and the counselors. But for all the good that did I might have saved myself the trouble. I was just setting up for dinner when I looked out the mess-hall windows and there, out on the lawn, were Pop, Sam, and Rhea, all talking to Mr. Luft!

▪ CHAPTER SEVENTEEN ▪

I went back to one of my tables and sat down, and Shep, who was setting his up, looked across at me, then came over. "What's wrong, Davey? You look weird."

"I'm in very deep trouble," I said. "My pop and my brother and his wife are here for a visit."

Killer had come up behind Shep, and he sat down at the table, then one by one the other waiters stopped working and came over. "Is that so bad?" Shep asked. "I mean, what can happen?"

"They're talking to Mr. Luft right now," I said, pointing toward the Guest House.

"Well, your father's not going to say, 'Davey's Jewish'," Killer said. "What do you care if they talk to Luft?"

"With my father's accent," I explained, "no one could take him for anything but Jewish. Mr. Luft met us on the campus and my father told him keeping a kitchen milchedig and flayshedig must be hard. You should have seen Mr. Luft's face!"

"What do you think he'll do?" Horse asked. "He won't fire you this late in the season, will he?"

I hadn't thought of getting fired till now. I said, "I was worried about him telling Pop what I did, pretending to be a shaygets. Pop won't like that, and I'm not gonna like being fired."

"He can't fire you for being a Jew," Eppie said. "That's anti-Semitism."

"Sure he can," Small Fry said glumly. "He can do anything. He's an absolute despot."

"So who's a Jew?" Jenny said from behind us. She had come to the serving window and was leaning her fat arms on it, her cook's hat wilting on her head. "Who's an anti-Semite?" Only she pronounced it "onteesemeet."

I said, "I'm a Jew, Jenny."

"The shaygets is a Jew! Oy gevalt!" She put one hand to her head and rolled her eyes. Then, grinning, she asked, "So when did you convert?"

"I was always a Jew," I said. "Mr. Luft just thought I was a gentile, and he hired me because of that."

Her smile faded. "He hired you because he thought you were a shaygets? Is that man a paskudnyak? I ask you!" She shook her head slowly. "And Davidul is a Jew!" She looked at me grimly for a minute, then began to smile. "You see, I always knew you were too smart for a goy." She moved away from the serving window, and I could hear her telling the rest of the kitchen help, "Would you believe it, our Davidul is a Jew!"

I had to smile. "Leave it to Jenny. "Now I'm a hero—a hero without a job."

"Aw, come on," Dinge said. "So he bawls you out. That's the worst he can do. He wouldn't fire you."

"Of course he wouldn't," Horse said definitely. "Would he, Shep?"

"With Luft you can't tell." Shep looked thoughtful. "Except if we all stuck together . . ."

"You mean like a union?" Horse said slowly.

"Exactly. All for one and one for all!"

"We could all go on strike." Killer grinned at me. "Hey, we'll

202

picket the mess hall. He'll have to keep Davey. Who'll wait on the kids?"

"Wait a minute," Small Fry said anxiously. "I can't do that. He's my cousin. My parents would kill me!"

"Well, we'll count you out. You've got a good excuse," Killer said. "What about the rest of you guys?"

I looked at them anxiously as one by one they nodded agreement, until it was Squeak's turn. He frowned and said, "As long as they don't think we're Reds."

Dinge said, "Oh, shit, they know we're not Reds!"

Horse was all for it, and so were Dinge and Killer. Eppie was the most excited of all. "If we stick together," he kept saying, "there's nothing he can do but give in. We'll have a real waiters' union. We can negotiate all sorts of demands, better working conditions, two days off a week—we need a union representative . . ."

"Now wait a minute," Shep said. "You can't rush into this without knowing the consequences. If we lose, we lose our jobs and our tips—remember that."

They were all quiet for a minute, then Dinge said, "How can we lose as long as we stick together?"

"Look, I don't think we'll lose," Shep said. "All I'm saying is, *if* we lose, are we all prepared to be fired?"

Killer didn't hesitate. "Of course we are." He looked at Dinge, and Dinge nodded. "I'm with you."

"And so am I," Eppie cried out.

Horse put his hand out, and the four of them clasped hands. "One for all!" He grinned. Shep, his face serious, put his hand on theirs, and then Squeak shrugged and said, "What the hell!" and added his hand. I put my hand on top of Squeak's. Deep inside I wanted to say something like "Hey, guys, I can't let you do this. I'll take my medicine alone," but I didn't have the guts. I really wanted to keep my job!

Small Fry, biting his lip, suddenly put his hand on mine. His face was pale. "Okay! To hell with Luft. I'm with you too!"

"You don't have to, Small Fry," Shep said.

"I want to," Small Fry said tightly. "Look, if I don't stand up to the guy sometimes—well, I'm just with you!"

Jenny, looking out of the serving window, yelled, "All right already! Stop holding hands and put the chopped liver out. It's almost supper time." I have to explain that most Sunday nights were milchedig meals, no meat, but Jenny made a wonderful artificial chopped liver. She used cooked stringbeans for a base and Rokeach fat, which tasted like chicken fat but was milchedig, and onions and hard-boiled eggs, and it fooled me the first time I tasted it. I could have sworn it was chopped liver.

Anyway, we began setting it out when suddenly the door banged open, and Mr. Luft stormed in. Everybody froze, and I put my plate of chopped liver down carefully. "Quinn!" he yelled, and I turned to him. "Yes, sir." I always called him "sir" because I knew he liked it, but this time he didn't like anything.

His voice sounded tight and really mad. "I talked to your father, Quinn. A nice man. A very decent man. I didn't tell him about his son. I didn't tell him that you were a snake in my bosom, how you stabbed me in the back. I couldn't hurt such a decent man, and you, Quinn—" I wasn't Davey anymore. "Where did you come by your double-dealing?"

"I didn't mean to double-deal, sir," I said earnestly. At least he hadn't told Pop. Maybe things weren't so bad after all. "I honestly didn't. You never asked me if I was Jewish. You just took it for granted."

"You let me take it for granted. I thought you were clean-cut. I gave you credit for being clean-cut, and what did you do? You stabbed me in the back!"

I shook my head. "Please listen to me, sir. I didn't mean to stab you. Honest! I've done my job here . . ."

"You've done it, and you're fired, Quinn. You can pack up your trunk and go. That's it. I'll let you explain what you've done to your father. Let him see what a double-dealer his son is. Let him hear it from his son's mouth. I won't shatter the illusions of a decent old man!"

Well, that was it. I turned toward the door and looked back at the guys, and I felt as if I were going to cry. They were all standing there looking scared and uneasy. Jenny and the other kitchen help had come into the dining room and she was wiping her flour-covered hands on her apron.

204

Then Shep stepped forward and said, "Wait a minute, Davey. Mr. Luft, we don't want you to fire Davey. He's a good waiter, one of the best, and he doesn't deserve to be fired just because he's Jewish."

"Where the hell do you come off telling me what I can do and can't do?" Mr. Luft thundered.

The outside door opened and Tom Ciardi stepped into the room. "What's all the noise about?"

"This—this snake in the grass is being fired, that's all!" Mr. Luft said dramatically, pointing to me. "He's Jewish!"

Jenny shook her head. "A klug tzuh Columbus! The boychik is Jewish!" she said sarcastically.

Killer and Dinge started to laugh, but stopped when Mr. Luft glared at them. He turned to me. "Get going, Quinn."

"Wait a minute," Shep said. His voice was a little unsteady and his fists were clenched. "If you fire Davey, we all quit!"

"We're sticking together," Horse said quietly, stepping forward.

"Yeah! We're a waiters' union!" Eppie cried out.

I thought Mr. Luft would pop. His face got red and then white. "A union? You're telling me you've got a union! I'll—I'll—all right, okay, you're all fired, all of you. You too, you little dumb animal!" And he pointed to Small Fry. "You ungrateful little sneak. I took you off the streets for six years and made you a camper for free, *for free,* and I had to turn away paying campers because there was no room. You're fired, all of you!"

We hadn't expected that, and nobody said a word. "You!" Mr. Luft pointed at Tom Ciardi. "Find me eight counselors who'll wait on tables."

"I can't spare eight men," Tom Ciardi said slowly. "Be reasonable."

"Don't give me 'reasonable'! Give me junior counselors or Warriors who want to make some tips. Tell them it's for the good of Camp Harel; just get me eight of them."

"Okay." Tom Ciardi grimaced and started for the door, and then, breaking the silence that had fallen, Jenny called out, "And find a cook too."

"What?" Mr. Luft whirled toward her. "What did you say?"

"A cook. You know what is a cook? Someone to put the kugel in

205

the oven, because if it doesn't go in in ten minutes, there'll be no noodle kugel for tonight's meal. Also the fish."

"What? What?" Mr. Luft started to choke, and I wondered if I shouldn't pat him on the back, then I thought, maybe not. "What? What?"

"You're maybe having trouble with your ears?" Jenny said, dusting the flour off her hands, "Or with your kop, a real goyisher kop. You'll fire one of my boys here because he's Jewish?" We had become her boys instead of the farshtinkeners which she usually called us. I straightened up, and so did the other waiters. "You're trying to be a real Hitler, an anti-Semite. I should work for such a man? Who needs it? I've got my own restaurant by Schermerhorn Street. So it's closed for the summer. I'll open early this year. Go, go! Find yourself another cook."

She began to untie her apron and turned toward the kitchen. Mr. Luft bit his lip, then said, "Jenny, wait, you don't understand." But his voice was wheedling, and I caught Shep winking at me.

"I understand, believe me. I'm not such a dope like I look. Big Fat Jenny understands. You hire a shaygets because you think he's classy—such an attitude for a Jewish man! If you hired him because he was a good waiter, but what did you care from waiting? He should just look good. Now you fire him, even if he's a good waiter, because he's Jewish." She threw her arms up. "Oy, Gottenyu!"

I will say one thing for Mr. Luft. He knew when to admit defeat gracefully. He turned to Tom Ciardi. "All right, never mind the counselors." To us, he said, "Get back to work. We'll forget the whole thing."

"And Davey?" Shep asked.

"Davey, Davey! All I hear is Davey. Let Davey do his job and he can stay the rest of the summer."

Jenny sighed. "Ah, a mechaieh! And, Luft!" He had turned to go, but now he turned around. "When we sign a contract for next year, I want these boys back, Davidul too."

Mr. Luft smiled, and I admired that. It took a lot of effort. "We'll straighten it all out." To Shep, "And don't forget to go over to the Guest House for the ice cream."

Eppie piped up, "About our days off . . ." But Shep put his

hand over Eppie's mouth before he could say any more. As Mr. Luft
walked out of the door with all the dignity he could muster, Shep
shook his head. "Don't you know enough to quit when you're
ahead?"

The guys started yelling. Then, abruptly, we all formed a circle,
put our heads down and shouted:

> *Succotash, succotash, a rag o' bone, a hunk o' hash,*
> *Sooop, sooop, gefilte fish, I ask yuh!*
> *Beans, potatoes, hip, hip, the waiters!*
> *Yea, Jenny, yea, Jenny, yea, Jenny!*

"All right, all right . . ." She actually blushed. "Get back to
work. I got to put in the kugel. Shepeleh, I need more sugar from
the Guest House when you get the ice cream. Believe me, next year
it's written into my contract, I want a week's supply of food kept
here! No more running this low." And she bustled off to the kitchen.

▪ Chapter Eighteen ▪

Sunday night at Camp Harel is Council Fire Night, and I took Pop
and Sam and Rhea to watch it. The council fire was lit back in the
woods, and the kids trailed in solemnly, each wrapped in a blanket
while the Chief of each group wore an authentic Indian headdress
made in the craft shop.

After everyone was seated, there were Indian prayers, and then
wrestling contests, Indian style. One of the Hunters recited a long
portion of *Hiawatha,* and then two of the Warriors sang a song about
an Indian maiden from the Land of the Sky-Blue Waters, and Uncle
Arnie Schaeffer, the dramatic counselor, read a monologue about an
Indian hunter and a herd of bison.

It was all very impressive, but I managed to get Pop and the
others away early. Usually, after the kids left, all the counselors

gathered around the smoldering fire and peed on it to put it out. Not only did it smell lousy, but it really spoiled the ritual.

Rhea complained about the mosquitoes all the way back to camp, and I'll admit they were something fierce, especially with all the rain we'd been having. But you have to take some bad with the good, I told her.

"You've become a philosopher," she said, and I decided to take it as a compliment.

"Yes, we have some pretty serious discussions in the tent after dark," I told her with a straight face.

Under his breath, Sam said, "Yeah! I'll bet."

Back at the Guest House, Pop said he really liked the council fire. "So there were a few mosquitoes, Rhea. They have to live too."

"Not on me!" Rhea snapped.

"Anyway," Pop said, "the stars were so bright. You don't see stars like that in the City."

"Pop, they're the same stars," Sam said, annoyed.

"But Pop's right," I told them seriously. "The air here is cleaner, and the stars, and the moon too, are brighter. Sometimes you can even see the northern lights. Anyway, you're lucky. This is the first night without rain we've had all week."

Rhea shivered. "It's cold, Sam. I'm going in."

I said, "How is the Guest House food? It's great at the camp. Jenny is a wonderful cook."

"What do you know about food?" Sam said. "Give you a bowl of Jell-O and you're happy. This kosher food sits on the stomach like a lump of lead. Good night." And he followed Rhea into the Guest House.

Pop reached up and patted my shoulder. "Don't pay him any attention, Davey. Sam is a born krechtzer. He's not happy unless he's complaining. The Guest House food is very good." He shrugged. "Not as good as your mother's cooking used to be, but good."

I was about to ask him about my mother, but just then taps sounded from the Hill, late because of the council fire, and Pop smiled and nodded. "That's nice, very nice. Good night, Davey." And he turned toward the porch.

"I'll see you in the morning, Pop." I kissed him good night and walked off toward the Hill. Things were really working out. I still had my job and Pop hadn't found out about my life as a shaygets, and he was having a good time. But with all of that I couldn't figure out why I felt so uneasy.

The next day, after breakfast, I arranged for Sam and Rhea to use one of the tennis courts for a few hours, since there was no tennis instruction that morning. I borrowed rackets for them and Rhea was happy for the first time since their arrival.

There is a lot of red clay in the valley under Hunter Mountain, and Camp Harel has two great clay tennis courts. They used to have three, but Mr. Luft has a thing about concrete, and after repairing the bridge's pilings one winter, he found he had a lot of concrete left over, so he made a concrete court out of the third clay court.

It was only used one week, Nancy told me, because she ran out of bandages. Every kid in the camp who used the court went around with scraped raspberries on their knees and elbows. Mr. Luft took down the net and tried to convert it into a skating rink, but that turned out just as bad in terms of raspberries. Now he was wondering if he could use it as a new kind of foundation for a building.

"It should revolutionize architecture," Shep told me dryly. "The first flat basement in existence!" We all called the court "Luft's folly."

With Sam and Rhea taken care of, I asked Pop what he'd like to do.

Pop adjusted his straw boater, which looked very snappy with his summer suit. "Well, we have to leave after lunch. Sam only got one day off. Myself, I got an extended vacation. Show me the stables, Davey."

That surprised me. The stables weren't far from the Guest House, and there were eight horses. I had never gone near them, but Eppie hung out there when he wasn't under a bunk or up a flagpole. He'd shovel horse manure and brush down the horses, and in return he got some free rides.

We walked over, and Red Mogulescu, who took care of the horses, was in his office, a little room off the stables, while Eppie, true to form, was shoveling manure in one of the stalls. Pop walked up and down past the stalls, nodding at the horses and smiling. When he reached out to stroke the nose of one, I cried out, "Watch out, Pop! It could bite."

"Shah, Davey. I know how to pet a horse."

"Since when are you interested in horses, Pop?" I was still nervous about them biting. They were awfully big and restless.

He turned to me and raised his eyebrows. "I grew up by horses."

"Aw, come on, Pop! What are you talking about?"

"Davey," he said patiently, as he reached out and stroked another horse's head, brushing away the flies, "My father was the overseer on a prince's ranch in the Ukraine. I learned to ride when I was a child."

"Okay, let me get this straight." I thought I was good at stories, but Pop was a master, I decided. "You were thirteen when you came here, right?"

"Of course, and I used to ride by Whitestone when I worked in the tin factory. They had stables there and I rode along the river, the Sound. You know, Davey, I rowed to Whitestone from the Bronx each day, and back. I'd take a trolley to—"

"Wait a minute!" I interrupted. "Wait a minute. You were five years in Ireland before you came to America, right?"

"You think they don't have horses in Ireland?"

"Pop! In the Ukraine, you were how old when you left? Eight?"

"Of course. If you're so good in math, how come you can't get better marks in French?"

This was turning into another example of Pop's logic. I said, "Okay. You were a great horseback rider. Where should we go now?" The smell of manure was getting me down. I had never been in the stables before.

"What I'd like, Davey," Pop said as we walked out of the stables, is to take a little horseback ride."

I looked at him as if he were crazy. "A horseback ride? You?"

"You too. You come with me. I'll show you how to ride. Is it all right by the camp if one of the guests wants to ride?"

I figured the only way to end this nonsense was to call his bluff, so I said, "Wait here, Pop," and I walked back to Red's office and knocked. He said, "Come in," and I explained my problem. Red was the only counselor nobody called Uncle. He was very thin but muscular and always wore riding breeches and an open shirt. He ate at one of my tables, and we liked each other.

"Your father?" He looked past me to where Pop was stroking another horse's head. I could understand his surprise. Pop, in his summer suit, boater, and tie and collar looked completely out of place in the grimy stables. "Are you sure, Davey?"

"I'm not sure at all," I said. "I think he's kidding me, but I want to call his bluff. I'll pay you later, Red, but I don't want him to know there's a charge. He'll use it as an excuse to get out of this. Anyway, I don't think I'll have to pay. Once you offer him a horse, he'll find some great excuse, like who goes riding in a summer suit. I know my pop!"

Red laughed. "If he does go, there won't be any charge for you, Davey. Just a few extra desserts. Let's see. I have two very gentle geldings, Brownie and Whitey. We don't use much imagination in naming horses here."

"Two?" I said as we walked toward Pop.

"Sure. You don't want your father to ride alone."

"I don't want him to ride at all," I muttered. "I'm just trying to get him to stop telling stories. Me, I don't ride anything I can't put an ignition key into!"

I introduced Red, and he showed Pop the horses he had selected. Pop nodded and looked back at the horse he had been stroking, a big black monster with a white splash on his forehead. "What about that one?"

Red shook his head. "Blaze is pretty rough, Mr. Quinn. I have trouble handling him myself. I only let the most experienced campers on him."

Pop shrugged. "Experience I've got, believe me. You saddle him up." He pointed to Brownie. "And Davey could maybe ride that one?"

Red hesitated. "You're sure?"

"Positive!" Pop unbuttoned his jacket and vest and took off his collar, tie, and boater. "You have a place I can hang these?"

Well, in the end I was the one who was embarrassed. When Blaze

211

was brought out and saddled, snorting a bit for effect, Pop calmed him down with some sugar cubes he had taken from breakfast, patted him gently, whispered some Yiddish in his ear, and before I knew it, he was up on him, in the saddle!

I was terrified. I expected the horse to rear up and paw the air like the ones in the Tom Mix movies, but old Blaze put his head back once and made a feeble bite at Pop's knee, and then Pop jerked him forward and grinned at me. "Now, Davey, are you ready?" Boy, was he enjoying this!

Ready! I had never been on a horse except the ones on the merry-go-round at the boardwalk in Edgemere when my Grandma used to take me there. I got up, finally, with a lot of help from Red and a lot of advice from Pop and some horse laughs from Eppie. "Don't hold on to the saddle," Pop said gently. "Just the reins. Sit up straight, Davey. Remember, you're the boss, not the horse."

I grabbed on to the front of the saddle for dear life. Blaze took off walking up the trail behind the stables, Pop sitting on him as if he were a part of the horse, and Brownie followed, me jouncing and bouncing at every step. I tried standing up in the stirrups to avoid the bouncing, but Pop, looking back, said, "Don't fight it, Davey. Relax!" And he patted Blaze and whispered more Yiddish to him, and the damned horse tossed his head and smiled as if he understood and liked it. So Pop was lucky. He had found a Jewish horse. Me, I bounced along in stark terror. How the hell had I gotten into this?

We walked the horses up the trail through deep forest, and then along a ridge with a beautiful panorama that I was too frightened to enjoy, but Pop loved it and kept telling me, "Look, Davey. Enjoy! You don't see this by One Hundred Ninetieth Street!"

Finally, after what seemed forever, we reached a small glade on top of the ridge, and Pop took pity on me. He dismounted and tied Blaze's reins to a shrub, then helped me down.

"I'll walk back!"

"You'll sit down and rest for a while," he said gently. "Horseback riding is good for you, Davey. You should learn how."

"A Jewish boy has no business on a horse," I muttered. I tried to sit down on a rock, but I winced and stood up. I stared at Pop.

Where was the sweet old man I knew? "I can't believe it. You can really ride."

Pop laughed and tied Brownie to another branch. "So your old man hasn't got one foot in the grave." He stretched and groaned. "Oy, gevalt! I'm stiff. It's been how many years? Thirty, maybe, since I rode."

"So you rowed across the Sound to Whitestone. You never told me that."

Pop sat down on a rock and looked up at me. "You never asked me, Davey."

"How could I ask you something I didn't know? Was that after you were married?"

"No. When I was married, I was working on the cable cars on Broadway. I was a gripper on the cars."

"A gripper?" My mouth was open. "Pop, what's a gripper?"

He reached forward and pulled an imaginary lever toward him. "The gripper stopped the car by releasing the cable or started it by gripping the cable."

I shook my head. "No shit!"

Pop looked shocked. "You're talking like Sam! Since when do you curse?"

"Pop, I've got good reason to use strong language. You were a gripper on a cable car?"

"On the Broadway run, all the way uptown to Two Hundredth Street. When I married your mother, I needed something that paid better. One of your mother's brothers, a no-good, but rich, had a dress factory, and he took me on as a cutter. I also learned pattern making. He went out of business, but I got another job, and since then I've been working by dresses."

I said, "How come I'm seventeen and you never told me this?"

"Seventeen? Davey! You had a birthday last month and I forgot all about it!"

"That's nothing, Pop. Jenny baked me a cake—that's the cook—and the guys sang 'Happy Birthday.' They do it each time someone has a birthday. Then, before I knew what I was saying, it just popped out of me. "Pop. I haven't told you the truth."

"Davey! I can't believe you ever lied to me." But he was smiling when he said it, and I had a sudden uncomfortable feeling that made me wonder how much I had really gotten away with over the years. I always thought Pop was sort of dim about me. Now I wasn't so sure. "So what haven't you told me the truth about?"

"This shaygets business, why the kids call me that." I swallowed. "Pop, when I went for the interview with Mr. Luft, he thought I wasn't Jewish . . ." Slowly, and without meeting his eyes, I told Pop the whole story. He listened to me soberly without saying anything, then he stood up and stretched. "We should start back now, Davey." He began to untie my horse. "I'll help you up."

I bounced back down the trail behind Blaze, both Pop and me quiet. I didn't know what I had expected, a bawling out? Shock? Anger? Anything, but not this silence. I felt a lump in my throat that I couldn't get rid of. Had I really hurt Pop that much? I wanted to ask him to forgive me, to explain again how it had all happened, but all I could do was concentrate on the damned horse and try to keep my rear end from being hammered apart. That little rest hadn't done me any good.

After we had returned the horses, and Pop had put his tie and collar on, we started back to the Guest House, and I tried again to explain how it had all happened, but at the fence he held up his hand and stopped me. "Davey!"

I looked at him, and to my bewilderment saw that he was trying to hide a smile. Finally he gave up and, leaning against the fence, he started to laugh. "Davey, Davey—what am I going to do with you? You're too old to hit."

What a relief! I felt my whole body sag. "Then you're not mad at me?"

Finally he stopped laughing. "I'm only glad you told me yourself, finally."

I stared at him. "Pop! You knew!" I said accusingly.

"Why shouldn't I know? Your Mr. Luft told me about it yesterday. He couldn't wait."

"But he promised me he wouldn't! He said you were a fine man and he didn't want to shame you."

"Shame me! That man is a farbissener, a mean man. Davey, the one fact you have to learn in this life is not to trust a no-goodnik like

214

that. From the first minute I met him I saw what he was like, talk nice to the guests and mean to his help. No, you didn't shame me, but such a tsedraytelt tsimmes you got yourself into. Why don't you use your head sometimes. Shaygets! Sure, you acted like a goyisher kop!" He started to laugh again. "So they all thought you were a goy. I'll tell you, Davey, when I worked by the cable cars, all the other men were Irishers. I think my name, Quinn, was why I got the job. I kept my mouth shut as long as I could, but they soon found out the truth. In those days I didn't speak as good as I do now."

He pulled the big gold pocket watch that he wore on a chain out of his vest and looked at it. "There's still time before lunch. Let's walk over by the camp, and you'll show me some more."

Sam and Rhea were off the tennis courts, and I was just as happy to be without them. We walked around the grounds and I introduced Pop to Jenny, who told him in Yiddish what a fine boychik I was. I understood enough to make that out, but Pop pretended she had told him how much trouble I caused. At the infirmary I introduced him to the Doc and Nancy, and she told him too, a little too enthusiastically, I thought, that I was a fine boy, and he could be proud of me. We met the rabbi too, and he joined in singing my praises. I wondered how the news of my return to being a Jew had spread as fast as it did. Everyone in camp seemed to know it.

By now Pop was looking suspicious. "One person praising you, all right, but everyone? Something is wrong, Davey."

I was very indignant. "Pop, I'm a very popular guy here. I'm a good waiter, and I don't get into trouble. Honest, you should be proud of me."

"I am, believe me, Davey. That nurse, the pretty shiksa with the big eyes, Davey, what's going on with her?"

I froze and tried to keep my voice level. "Nothing, Pop. How could you even think it? She's old enough to . . . to . . . ."

"The others were old enough too. Tell me the truth, David."

When I was David instead of Davey, I was in trouble. "Have I ever lied to you, Pop?"

"Have you ever been caught lying to me, you mean. All right. I won't ask."

I said, "Yes, Pop."

"Yes what? I shouldn't ask, or you're fooling around?"

I looked down at the ground and said, "I guess I'm fooling around."

"Oy!" Pop sighed, a real sigh from his shoes up. He took off his boater and fanned himself with it. "What are we going to do with you?" We walked on quietly then, across the campgrounds and back to the Guest House, where Sam and Rhea were waiting on the porch.

"You won't tell Sam?" I asked uneasily.

"It's none of Sam's business." Then he said softly, "At least be careful. Don't get into trouble. I know, I know, it's like asking the wind not to blow!"

"Pop, I'm sorry."

"Don't do it, and don't be sorry."

After lunch, when the time came for them to leave, I shook Sam's hand and kissed Rhea on the cheek and gave Pop a big hug and kiss. I said, "Thanks, Pop."

"What for?" Sam asked suspiciously.

"For teaching him to ride a horse." At Sam's bewildered look, Pop said, "Go ahead. Get in the car." When Sam had left us, he asked, "Davey, do you need some money?"

I saw the gleam in his eyes and I knew he was getting ready for one of our real bargaining sessions. This was what I had been waiting for. I said, "How about a hundred dollars?"

"What?" That was the first time I had really seen Pop shocked. Then he shook his head. "Stop fooling around."

I said, "No fooling, Pop," and I took a wad of bills out of my pocket and handed them to him. "Tips. They've been piling up since Norman's mom tipped me. That's why this is such a good job, Pop."

"A hundred dollars!" He stared at the money and then at me. "You made this honestly?"

"No! I stole it, Pop! Of course it's honest. That's what we count on. The campers' parents give us five or ten dollars for the summer, except some tightwads only give us two. I'll get more, Pop, honest." I was beaming at him.

"I can't believe it." He counted it out and started to put it in his pocket, then hesitated. "Don't you need any, Davey?"

I shrugged. "What for? Anyway, I have a few bucks in the tent, and I'll get more. Take it, Pop."

"Well—I won't say it's not handy now, being laid off . . ." Sam tooted the horn, and Pop waved at him. "Shah already!" I said, "One thing more, Pop."

"Nu, what's that?"

I stood up straight. This was going to hurt him, but I had decided I had to do it. "When I come home, I want to sleep by myself, on the daybed in the living room. Okay?"

He took my face in his hands and slowly pulled my head down. "A grown man is entitled to sleep alone." Then he kissed me, and hurried off to the Chevy. I waved as they drove off. I liked that, "a grown man."

While we waiters were eating supper that evening, Shep asked me how I had made out with my pop, and I told the guys the whole story. They couldn't believe it until Eppie confirmed it. "Shit, that old man of Davey's mounted Blaze like a cowboy and rode Western style, firm in the saddle—which is more than Davey could do."

I shrugged. Let them laugh. I was happy, and it would be a long time before I got that close to a horse again. I still had a sore backside, but it had been worth it. We were clearing up after the meal when Small Fry took me aside and said, "Guess what, Davey. I have a date with Alice Einstein."

"Alice? But she's only a soph. How can she get out?"

"She's going to take a chance and dummy her bed and sneak out. Isn't that great? Davey, I'm taking her to the haystack, and I swear, tonight I'll really do more than kiss her. Talking back to Luft gave me so much confidence, and I owe it all to you."

"Well, don't get her in trouble," I said.

He drew back offended. "Davey, we're only kids!"

That night Nancy said, "I liked your father, Davey. He's a real gentleman. Nice manners. I can tell you're his son."

I said, "Gee, thanks, Nancy," and when she started to get undressed, I said, surprised, "No drinky-poo?"

"Don't make fun of me, Davey. Tonight I'm going to stay completely sober. I really want to enjoy this."

That made me uneasy. "Enjoy what?" I asked as I took my sneakers and socks off.

"Don't be so dopey. You know, Jewish men are a lot sexier. This is going to be a wonderful night!"

Well, it paid to be back as one of the chosen people. To my surprise it was a wonderful night, and a tiring one. The rain had started again, and as I heard it spattering against the roof, I said, "Thanks, God," sleepily. "Thanks for holding it off for Pop's visit." Then I drifted off to sleep to the sound of Nancy's gentle snores.

I was sure I'd wake up in time to sneak up on the Hill, but I didn't. For the first time I slept in Nancy's bed all night. I didn't know that Small Fry had come home from his date as happy as a bedbug because he had kissed Alice five times, one French kiss, too, and he'd been so excited that he peed off the bridge on the wrong side, upstream!

I slept on, while Schoharie Creek rose and rose and grew fiercer and fiercer as the mountains released all the rainwater the soaked ground could no longer hold. Then, somewhere around three in the morning, the creek carried away the bridge and half of Camp Harel!

▪ Chapter Nineteen ▪

I stood on the porch of the infirmary, stunned, and I stared at the campgrounds or what had once been the campgrounds, then I ran to the other side of the porch and looked back at the Hill. It was an awful sight. The entire bridge was gone, swept away downstream toward Hunter. Half of the slate walk that led up to the Hill was gone too, the white railing dangling down over the red mud of the hillside. At the top of the Hill I could see a group of campers and counselors looking down at the flooded campgrounds.

All this had happened while I was asleep! I couldn't believe it. I couldn't believe that the creek was that strong, that deadly. And what about the campers? Were they all safe? Oh, God, what if one had been down here, washed away? But this had happened late at night while everyone was sleeping. Maybe nobody had been hurt. Maybe it was just the campgrounds that had been destroyed.

I turned away from the Hill and looked over the remains of the campus. At least the infirmary wasn't damaged. The Paps' bunk and the mess hall with the social hall above it all stood on a narrow island now, with the raging creek on one side and the raging lake on the other. At the top of what had once been Lake Harel, the flood had swept away the iron gate that controlled the entry of water into the lake, and at the bottom of the lake it had torn away the dam that contained the lake.

The baseball field, Mr. Luft's pride and joy, was covered by running water almost a foot deep. The backstop, the apple trees, the two docks, and half the slips with a few rowboats still remained. The rest was gone, all swept away!

I felt sick and anxious and excited all at the same time. I started down the steps, and behind me Nancy opened the infirmary door and came out on the porch. "Holy Mother of God! Will you look at that!"

I said, "I'm going to the Paps' bunk to see if they're all right."

She stared around without answering, then, as I reached the ground, she said, "Put something on, Davey. You'll catch your death of cold."

I was wearing shorts and sneakers without a shirt, and a light drizzle was falling. I didn't feel cold, but I was shivering. "I'll be all right."

"Wait." She ran back into the infirmary and came out with a white sweatshirt. "Put this on. I haven't got a poncho or raincoat that would fit you."

I shrugged into the sweatshirt and splashed through the water toward the Paps' bunk. We were on an island, but the island was covered by a few inches of water racing past very swiftly. Walking was difficult because there were deep holes in the path that I kept stumbling into, and there were rocks and pebbles underfoot that I could feel through my sneakers. Once I tripped and fell and the water caught at me, rolling me over before I could get to my feet. That shook me up!

I called out, "Are you all right in there?" when I reached the Paps' bunk, and Mr. and Mrs. Lowenstein came to the door, behind them a bunch of excited children.

"Thank God you've come, Davey," Mrs. Lowenstein said. "We thought no one would get through. How did you manage it? Oh dear, you're bleeding!"

I looked down at my knees. "Just a scrape where I fell. Is there any water inside?" But I could see there wasn't. The bunk was at least two feet above ground. Like the infirmary, it was built with the supporting beams laid on big flat rocks without any real foundation. The flood had loosened one of the rocks at the rear and that part of the bunk sagged, but the rest was high and dry.

"We're all right," Mr. Lowenstein said. He had lit his pipe, and he was puffing at it nervously. "The kiddies are scared, but I think the bunk will stand against the flood even with that sagging back." He sounded uneasy in spite of his reassuring words. I noticed that his hand holding the pipe shook as he talked.

Mrs. Lowenstein seemed much more in control. "The only thing we're worried about is feeding the children."

I said, "I think I can make it to the mess hall."

"Now be careful," Mrs. Lowenstein warned. "If you tripped and fell, you could be carried away!"

I could almost believe that, even if there were only a few inches of water rushing over the path, especially after my fall on the way to the Paps' bunk. But I had to check up on Jenny and the kitchen help. They slept in the rooms above the kitchen, and while the mess hall looked safe, I was still worried, and scared stiff as I stumbled past the tennis courts toward the mess hall. The courts had been washed clean of all clay and the concrete court was buckled and twisted.

I couldn't figure out how an enormous slab of concrete like that could be tossed and twisted about while the wooden buildings resisted the flood, but when I reached the mess hall I realized why. The posts on which all the camp buildings were built offered very little resistance to the water. The slabs of concrete offered the most. Shep had explained that to me. That was why the bridge had been torn loose. Mr. Luft and his concrete!

At the mess hall I called out, "Jenny?" and I stomped the mud

220

and water from my sneakers and sloshed into the building. She came running in from the kitchen, her face as white as the flour she always seemed covered with. Behind her the dishwasher and the two women who helped in the kitchen crowded in. "It's me, Davey."

"Davidul! Gott tzedanken." Jenny enfolded me in a warm hug, then stepped back. "You're soaking wet. Come by the fire already. I've started the stove, but who knows who I'll cook for or what? Where are the rest of the boys?"

"They're all up on the Hill." I explained about the bridge being swept away. "We're isolated here, Jenny. We can't get to the Hill and we can't reach the Guest House. I'll take some food back to the Paps and maybe we can get them down here later for lunch."

She put her hands to her head. "Gottenyu! What will we do if the water comes in here? We could all be drowned in our beds!"

The dishwasher, a tall, skinny man who had just come to work a week ago, another of Mr. Luft's "finds," said, "Shee-it. I'm getting the hell out of here."

I said, "Not unless you can swim like a fish. There's water all around us, and you couldn't stand up in it a minute."

One of the two women who helped Jenny began to cry. The other, Miriam, shrugged. She was from Hunter and slept in at camp, but she knew the land and the weather. "It won't come no higher, the water. Fact is, the rain stops, it'll go down."

"And if, God forbid, the rain doesn't stop?" Jenny asked.

"Now that the brige and dam are gone," Miriam said knowingly, "it'll stay like this for two, maybe three days."

"Three days!" Jenny looked dismayed. "What am I going to do, Davey?"

I didn't understand her. "Just make me a tray of food to take to the Paps. Don't worry, Jenny. It'll be all right." I don't know why I was so reassuring. In a way I was excited. This was one terrific adventure, but on the other hand I was scared stiff. Suppose Miriam was wrong and the water did rise? We could all be drowned unless they could get us off, and I wasn't sure who "they" were. The counselors and kids were up on the Hill. Sure, they could go up the back woods to the road and down to Hunter, and if the bridge at

Hunter was still standing, they could come back on the other side of the lake to the Guest House and stables. And there were Mr. Luft and the staff at the Guest House—Jesus! I realized suddenly that if Pop had stayed another day, he'd have been caught in this.

"Here, already, let me dry you." Jenny brought me a big fluffy towel and began drying me off.

I said, "Don't bother. I'm going right out again. I want to see if Mr. Luft has figured out how to get across to us. You fix the food, and I'll come back and get it."

"Alevai I could fix you some food. I should only have some here. What food, Davidul? That momzer Luft keeps the food at the Guest House. It comes each day in drips and drabs. What food can I give the little Paps? Some cookies left over from Sunday night? I haven't even a can milk or a pound butter to bake with. Go, go catch me some fish from the farshtinkener creek. I'll fry them for the little darlings!"

And she sat down on a chair and began to cry. I was startled. Of course. I should have remembered that Mr. Luft kept as little food as possible in the camp. Each morning at about five the station wagon brought the day's supply from the storeroom and freezer in the Guest House, and old Mrs. Luft, his mother, doled it all out in careful rations. Jenny had complained about it often enough. "Haven't you got anything left over?" I asked. "Nothing the Paps can eat? Some old bread or cookies?"

"Do you think those chozzers leave anything behind when they finish a meal?" she cried out. "There's hardly a crumb here. A few slices of stale bread maybe. Not even enough cereal. And milk—where will I get milk?" She got to her feet heavily. "Let me look and see what I can fix up."

I shook my head. "Jesus, Jenny, maybe we can get a boat or something across. You wait here. Don't worry. We'll work something out."

"Don't give me bobbe-myseh, Davidul. I'm not ten years old. Go, see what's doing, but we won't work anything out. Believe me, we'll stay here." While she talked she rummaged in the cupboards and gathered a trayful of food, some cookies and slices of bread. There was a roll of strudel and she cut it up into small pieces. I

222

could see it hurt her to give less than her usual generous servings. She took down a canister of flour and peered into it. "A little, but what can I make without butter or eggs? Matzos! I'll bake some matzos. Go, Davidul, take the food."

I hurried out of the kitchen, the tray covered with cellophane I'd found in the counselors' room. At least that would keep the rain off. As I slogged back to the Paps' bunk through the water and rain, I looked out at the lake. What a sight! It was enormous. If Mr. Luft could take a picture of Lake Harel now, he wouldn't need to fake the photograph. The flood had swept away the far side of the lake, and instead of the normally calm surface, there was a raging torrent of water rushing along. The two docks, the one for swimmers and the smaller one for nonswimmers, were still in place, and so was the big slide, but half the boat docks had been torn loose and only two rowboats remained in their slips. Maybe we could get one across, but I didn't know how.

By time I got to the Paps' bunk, I was soaked through and through, and I was shivering, but the food was dry. Nancy had managed to make it down from the infirmary, looking unruffled in her crisp white uniform and blue cape. She and Mrs. Lowenstein were making up the beds, while Mr. Lowenstein was reading to the Paps. I took Nancy and Mrs. Lowenstein aside and explained about the food.

"Bread and strudel?" Mrs. Lowenstein looked at the tray. "What kind of meal is that?"

"I'm sure it's the best Jenny could come up with," Nancy said cheerfully. "Let's give it to the children now and tell them it's a treat."

After they had divided the food, Nancy offered me a slice of bread, but I shook my head. "I'm not hungry, honest. I'm too excited to eat."

"Don't be stupid, Davey. You're going to need your strength."

"We're counting on you to get us out of this," Mrs. Lowenstein added.

Oh, great! I was just the one. "I'll go out to the dock and see if I can call across."

"You be careful now," Nancy warned me. "That water looks scary. Why don't you stay here till it goes down."

"That could be a couple of days." I shook my head. "The Paps will be starved."

One of the Paps heard me and immediately began to cry. "I'm hungry! I'm starving!" The others took it up, and one five-year-old began to wail, "I want my mommy!"

Mrs. Lowenstein picked him up and patted him gently. "Now, now. Let's have the treat Uncle Davey brought us." She shook her head at Nancy and me and put her finger to her lips.

I got the message, and I started slogging back toward the mess hall. I kept looking down at the water running over the path. Was it less than before or more? Was the water going up or down? Then I heard a scream from the Paps' bunk and I turned, startled. Mrs. Lowenstein was on the porch waving to me, and I saw that one of the posts in the rear of the bunk had slid off the rock and the whole rear end had dropped at least a foot.

I hurried back and Mrs. Lowenstein took me aside. I could tell that she was frightened, but she was trying to keep calm in front of her husband. "What should we do, Davey?"

Why me? Why didn't she call on her husband? He just stood there looking puzzled, puffing that damned pipe!

Nancy was rounding up the children in the front part of the bunk, and I said, "Look, we'll have to get them all to the mess hall. That's too big and heavy for the flood to damage, and it's on solid ground, higher than this place."

"How will we get them there?" Mrs. Lowenstein asked anxiously.

"Tell them to put on their slickers and boots," Nancy told her calmly. "We'll carry them."

Well, let me tell you, that was easier said than done! The little Paps were all bundled up in their yellow slickers and rain hats, most of them looking like the Uneeda Biscuit Boy, and we started out with the first load. I carried two, one on each arm, and they were having a great old time laughing and teasing me, not a bit scared anymore. It was all a big adventure. Me, I was scared shitless! Suppose I slipped again or dropped one? I didn't know if the water would rise any higher, and I wasn't at all sure the mess hall was that safe. Sure, it was big and solid, but the bridge had been big and solid too, and look what had happened there!

Nancy and Mr. Lowenstein carried one kid each, but when we reached the mess hall I noticed that Mr. Lowenstein was very white and breathing hard, and he had to sit down on the porch for a few minutes before he could climb the stairs to the social hall. We left him there with the four kids, and I found a basketball they could kick around.

Jenny came out on the porch as we took off for the second load. "Be careful, both of you!" And she began muttering in Yiddish. On the way back, Nancy grinned at me. "Having fun, Davey?"

"Fun? This is a nightmare, and those little voncen keep squealing and squirming when I carry them."

"Voncen?"

"That's Yiddish for bedbugs."

Nancy laughed. I was scared, sure, but I was excited too. She just seemed excited. "You think this is bad? I'll tell you flood stories that'll knock your socks off. They called the whole gang of us at Kingston Hospital up to Albany a few years ago . . ." And she launched into a gory story of a flood that drowned twenty people. I didn't need to hear that, believe me!

All in all, we made four trips. I carried two Paps back on the second trip, and Nancy took one. The third trip I went alone while Nancy caught her breath. "I wish to hell I could get a nip of booze, Davey," she said to me while Mrs. Lowenstein was rounding up my two passengers. "Do you think I could slip over to the infirmary while you carry those two kids?"

"Are you crazy? Just rest and forget the booze!"

That third trip alone with two kids was the hardest. I was getting tired, and there was no one to keep me company. I was really scared that one of the kids would slip out of my arms. They squirmed like little puppies. Finally I dropped them off at the mess hall and started back. Across the lake I could see a bunch of people, and it looked as if some of the counselors and waiters were there. They must have made it through the back way. That meant the bridge at Hunter was still standing.

On the last trip, we started off each carrying a kid, Mrs. Lowenstein, Nancy, and me. These were the last, and the oldest—and heaviest! The Paps' bunk had slipped down even lower, and most of the inside was awash with a few inches of water. Mrs. Lowenstein had dragged all the trunks up to the front to keep them out of the water, and she had a paper bag full of her own clothes. "God knows when I'll see my things again," she muttered as we trudged along. How could she worry about clothes at a time like this? I was just grateful that this was the last trip, and I was carrying only one kid. My arms and shoulders felt ready to fall off.

When we got them safely inside the mess hall, I started across to the dock. "Where are you going, Davey?" Nancy asked sharply, turning back to look at me.

"I want to see who's across the lake. They have to get some food to us."

"Let's wait till the water goes down. It's too dangerous out there." She looked at the water swirling over the campus. "It must be a foot or two deep!" She was standing on the porch, holding the upright post with one hand.

"The water's not that deep, and it may not go down for days," I told her. "That's what Miriam says, and she lives around here. Do you think the kids can make it for a few days on Jenny's matzos?"

"Matzos?"

"That's all she can make!" I turned around and headed out to the dock. I didn't really want to. I wanted to believe that we could wait till the water went down, and if it were only the grown-ups who went hungry, I might have. I was tired, really tired, but still too keyed up with excitement to pay any attention to my tiredness. That sounds crazy, but I was sort of up and down, scared and exhilarated at the same time. This was one hell of an adventure!

It wasn't too hard getting across to the docks. The water was only an inch or two deep over that part of the campus, but I could see that it had stripped away all the grass and topsoil and left only pebbles and rocks. Wait until Mr. Luft saw his treasured regulation-sized baseball diamond!

At the docks I could really see what damage had been done. The far side of the lake was gone, and the railroad tracks were hanging in the air. The ground underneath had been washed away, and so had the road beyond. All that was left were the Guest House and the stables. The water in front of the nonswimmers' dock seemed calm,

226

but about thirty feet out the lake became a real torrent, raging down toward the point where it joined the creek. I saw Mr. Luft in front of the Guest House, and there were a few counselors there and Killer and Shep. I could see the station wagon on the lawn and realized they were loading it with food for the campers up on the Hill. I shouted to them, and Mr. Luft and Tom Ciardi came as far forward as they could to the edge of the rushing water.

"Are the kids all right?" Ciardi yelled.

"They're fine. We carried them to the mess hall, but we need food!"

"What?"

"Food! Food!" I yelled, and I knew that they heard me. Then Shep and Killer came up, and they all seemed to be having a discussion. Then Shep yelled out, "Davey! Is the rowboat all right?"

The rowboat! Were they crazy? There was no way that a rowboat could be taken across that rushing water. I walked over to the big dock and beyond to the boat slips, or what was left of them. Two rowboats were still tied to the nearer slips, protected probably by the jutting dock. They were full of water, but they looked sound. I opened the oarbox on the dock and saw that there were still oars in it, but who could row a boat in this flood?

"The boats are okay!" I yelled.

"Davey!" It was Mr. Luft. I wasn't Quinn anymore. "We're going to throw a stone across with a string attached. You pull it in, and we'll tie a rope to it."

I yelled back, "Why?"

Shep answered. "So we can make a ferry, Davey, and ferry food across!"

I looked at the rowboat and at the water. That made sense—if anyone could throw a stone that far, and I doubted that. I knew I couldn't. I waved to show I understood. It was lucky they had Killer there, I thought. He had a terrific pitching arm, but it probably wasn't good enough.

They tied a rock to a thin cord and he threw it toward the dock with all his strength, but it fell short by about twenty feet. He might

227

have made it with a baseball without a string, but I wasn't sure of that. It was just too long a throw.

He tried again and again, and each time he missed. Then Tom Ciardi tried, but he couldn't even reach Killer's distance. It was no use, I realized. The distance from the dock to the other side of the lake was just too long. If I were out in the water . . .

I looked at the rushing river and shivered. The water on the nonswimmers' side was usually two or three feet deep, and now it still looked that shallow, if the relatively calm surface was any clue. The real rough stuff began about thirty feet out. If I waded out to the edge of the shelf of shallow water, I might catch the stone Killer was throwing—might, because I was such a lousy catcher, and a lousy swimmer. What if I slipped and fell into that rushing water? Good-bye, Davey!

But there was no other way they could get food to us. Then I saw the lifesaver that hangs on the swimmers' dock with the coil of rope attached. I took it down and played out the rope. There was enough to reach halfway across old Lake Harel. It would easily reach to the edge of the waders' shelf.

I didn't let myself think, because I knew if I did I'd never go through with it. I tied one end of the rope to the big slide, and I tried to slip into the lifesaver, but it wasn't big enough. Instead I tied the rope and the lifesaver around my waist, and then, before I got too scared, I took off the poncho I was wearing and went off the small dock into the shallow water.

I could hear my heart racing, actually feel it. The water was icy cold, and it came up to my chest. Some of the shelf had been washed away because the shallow water usually only reached my waist. I prayed it would be no deeper all the way to the rushing water, and I started out slowly, feeling my way along the bottom with my sneakers, almost inch by inch. The water tugged at me, but I could withstand the tug even when I slipped. Luckily I didn't lose my footing completely. It was scary, though. Then, after what seemed hours, I reached the edge of the shelf. Here the tug of the water was fierce, but I was able to keep my balance.

I waved to the group gathered on the shore watching me. "Killer! Try it now!"

He came as close to the water's edge as he could and threw. It was going to make it! The stone came straight to me—and I missed it. Not only did I miss it, but as I lunged for it my feet slipped and I went down into the rushing stream.

I gasped as I went under the icy water, and I took in a mouthful of it. Flailing my arms, coughing and struggling to keep my head above water, I was swept downstream, and then, with a yank that almost pulled me in two, the rope held. The current had carried me into deep water, and the rush of it, combined with the pull of the rope around my waist, slammed me sideways into the big dock. Coughing and spitting, I struggled to stay afloat.

I grabbed at the dock and somehow managed to pull myself up and out of the water. It took me a few minutes to get the water out of me and the breath back in. My hands were bleeding, and my side burned with the force of the blow against the dock. I could hardly breathe and I should have been terrified, but instead I was suddenly angry, furious. This goddamned river wasn't going to get me, I told myself furiously. I'd do it again and this time I'd catch the stone. I pulled the rope and stormed back to the nonswimmers' dock, and I saw Nancy come hurrying toward me from the mess hall.

"Davey! What the hell are you doing? Mother of God, you're all bloody!"

I didn't answer her. I pulled the rope onto the dock, then went back to the ladder and started down into the shallow water.

"Davey, don't! Are you crazy?"

"We're going to make a ferry."

"You're going to make a corpse!" She saw the men across the lake and shouted. "It's too dangerous!" But her voice wouldn't carry that far. "Stop him!" But by then I was into the water, and I couldn't see her, though I could hear her shouting that I was all kinds of a fool, and I'd be killed, and it would be her fault for not stopping me, and how did I think she'd feel about that?

I couldn't figure why she thought it was her fault, but I couldn't be bothered to think about it. The icy water took away the pain of my cuts and bruises, and again I felt my way out to the edge of the shallow shelf. The water seemed to me a lot deeper this time, but when I finally got a footing near the edge I yelled, "Okay, Killer!"

"Get it this time, Shaygets," he called back, and he let go a perfect pitch. I gritted my teeth and reached for the stone—and of course missed it again, but I caught the cord that it carried, and then I lost my footing!

The river swung me against the dock again, another smashing blow that took my breath away, but I had sense enough not to swallow any water this time, and, wonder of wonders, I held on to the cord!

I pulled my way to the ladder, and when Nancy reached down to help me up, I handed her the cord. "For Christ's sake, hang on to this. Don't bother about me. I can get up."

She took the cord and almost dropped it. "Davey! I can't hold it. The water dragging at it is too strong."

I grabbed it away from her and, still hanging on to the ladder, I tied the cord to my life preserver. "Please, God, don't let it break!" I prayed as I climbed up onto the dock.

"I'm sorry, Davey." Nancy looked at me in dismay. "My God, you're a mess!"

I laughed and held up the cord and there was a loud yell from the other side. With an effort, I pulled the cord free of the water, and suddenly the fierce tugging was gone. I tied the cord to a leg of the slide and waved to the other side. "Send over the rope!"

Well, I thought the worst was over, but there was still plenty of trouble ahead. They put a stronger cord on the end, and I pulled that over, but every time it touched the water, it was almost tugged out of my hands. I realized we needed to get it above the water, and the top of the slide was the obvious place.

I was beginning to feel all the aches and bruises and cuts, but I tried to ignore them. Once the cord was over the top of the slide and out of the water, we began to pull in the rope. It wasn't too hard as long as we kept it above the water. They sent over a light clothesline first, and then a heavier rope. There was plenty of that in the stables.

It took half the day, but finally we had two lines across the lake, and I managed to get one tied to the front and the rear of one of the rowboats after I bailed it out. We rigged up a working ferry system, the boat held by one rope and guided along by the other. The empty boat was pulled to the other side, and it worked in spite of the tearing current. The first ones back were Killer and Shep with a boatload of food. They jumped out and began punching me in the arm and slamming me on the back. "Hey, Davey! That was wonderful, just swell! You were great!"

I yelled out, "Don't!" I hadn't realized how sore I was until they started pounding me. "I hurt all over!"

Nancy took over then. "I don't want any horsing around from you boys. Get that food to the mess hall, and you, Davey, come to the infirmary with me. I want to fix up those cuts. For all I know, you've broken a few ribs. I wish to hell the doctor could get over here."

While Killer and Shep carried the food to the mess hall, Nancy and I slogged our way to the infirmary, my cuts and bruises aching more at every step. The infirmary was still intact, though the Paps' bunk had sunk even lower in the rear. The rain was still coming down, a very light drizzle, and the sky was filled with blue-black clouds. There was no sign of the sun.

I don't remember much of the rest of that day. Nancy cleaned out my cuts and pulled a few splinters from my side and decided I had no broken ribs. She used iodine and adhesive tape on the cuts. It stung like hell, but it was a good sort of pain, and I took three white pills that she gave me and fell asleep.

While I slept, Shep and Killer made a half dozen trips in the rowboat ferry and brought over enough food to satisfy Jenny and give the Paps a good hot meal.

▪ Chapter Twenty ▪

I woke up late that night to the smell of coffee and hot, fresh rolls and Killer's grin. He was sprawled out in a chair by my bed. I sat up and winced. "Wow! I hurt all over!"

"Davey, you were swell, just swell. What a show you put on!"

"Hey, it wasn't any show. That water really slammed me around." I eased back on the bed. "Is everything okay?"

"Sure. You're the camp hero. The Paps are camping out in the social hall. They made tents of their blankets and are happy as bedbugs. Shep drove the station wagon and a load of food to Hunter and across the bridge there, it's still up, and the counselors and Warriors are trekking food in the back way to the kids on the Hill. Uncle Irv is teaching them how to build tepees in the back woods and live Indian style, with nice hot meals from the Guest House. Everyone's having a swell time, except Butch."

"Is he all right?" I asked, alarmed.

"Hell, yes. He's just been looking all over for Uncle Davey. He's sure you were washed away in the flood. He won't believe you're safe until he sees you."

I smiled. "Good old Butch." I sipped the coffee, which I've never liked, but which tasted great now. I remembered the coffee Pop used to let me have every Sunday morning when I was a kid, his special kind made just for me, about one inch of coffee and the rest warm milk with four teaspoons of sugar. He'd butter a hard roll on the outside, and I'd dunk it in the coffee. I loved it!

I smeared butter on the outside of one of Jenny's rolls and dunked it in the coffee. It tasted great. I hadn't realized how hungry I was. I finished all four rolls and three cups of coffee, and felt I had had a good appetizer. I could really manage a meal now.

Against Nancy's protests, I started back to the mess hall with Killer. "Yeah," he told me as we splashed through the water. "Butch really missed you." Then he stopped and frowned. "Hey, where the hell were you last night? How did you wind up down here?"

For once I didn't have a quick answer. I grabbed at my side and said, "Gee, Killer. It really hurts."

He was all sympathy at once, and he let me lean on him all the way to the mess hall. Leaning like that hurt more than walking alone, but it made him forget the question!

Still, it was a question that kept coming up in the next few days, and I became pretty adept at sidestepping it. As for the flood, it lasted two more days, and then subsided as quickly as it had come. I slept in the infirmary legally because I was a wounded hero, and one morning I woke up to brilliant sunshine, no rain, and the creek almost down to its normal level.

Mr. Luft had a team of workmen in from the nearby CCC camp at once, damming up the head of the lake. The water dropped and by evening the lake was just a muddy pool. They built an emergency bridge over the dam at the foot of the lake, and then the trucks rolled onto the campus.

I must say they worked fast. They strung a temporary suspension bridge over the creek that same day and the campers tumbled down the Hill and across it for their first civilized meal at the mess hall. The kids had a ball racing back and forth over the suspension bridge which scared the hell out of me. It was just planking held by two ropes, and it swayed when you crossed it.

The second day after the flood, everyone pitched in to pick up the debris of the flood. The canoes were found halfway to Hunter, and bits and pieces of the campus, nets and fences and equipment, were salvaged from all over. The rest probably ended up in Schoharie Reservoir.

Color War, which should have been the last week of camp, was called off, and the season wound down in a listless way. "It's just as well," Shep said. "Color War leaves all the kids exhausted and half of them wind up with colds. We send them home like that and it loses a hell of a lot of campers."

"If that schmuck Luft would wake up and have Color War next to the last week, the campers could go home rested and looking good," Killer put in.

"If he stopped pouring cement into the creek and just built a simple bridge, we wouldn't have this mess," Horse said.

We were sitting around the waiters' table before supper, and Jenny, from her serving window, called out, "If, if, if! Ven di bobbe volt gehat aiyer vet zi geven a zayde!"

Dinge slapped the table. "That's great, Jenny. Hey, Shaygets, it means if the grandma had balls, she'd be a grandpa!"

I said, "You don't have to translate, Dinge. I'm Jewish now."

"Gee, I forgot. You don't look Jewish."

Killer called out, "How's this, Jenny. If the bobbe volt gehat wheels, she'd be a trolley car!"

"Smot Alex!" But she smiled and turned back to the kitchen. Later that day she took me aside. I was her favorite now, even displacing Small Fry. "Davidul, I want, when the summer is over, you should come to my restaurant on Schermerhorn Street in Brooklyn and I'll cook you a real meal, you and your father—such a nice man. Such manners."

"Jenny, all your meals are great."

"Great? With the dreck they give me, how can I cook decent? Look!" She pointed dramatically to the enormous tray of noodle kugel she was preparing. "On Schermerhorn Street, they come from all over the city for my kugel. Here I have to use packaged noodles. That momzer Luft won't let me make my own. There's no time, he says. I told him I'd get up earlier, four o'clock if I have to, but no. He brings me dried, packaged noodles. Pheh!"

I said, "Jenny, with any noodles, your kugel is wonderful."

Pacified, she said, "You like it, huh?"

"I love it. I wish I could make it at home."

"You? You cook at home, Davidul?" She hit her forehead. "Of course. You have no mama, a shame."

"We don't really cook much," I explained. "Pop makes a tuna salad or a salmon salad on weekdays, and we have spaghetti or rice with ketchup, but on weekends he makes a chicken or a pot roast. And I make Jell-O for dessert. I'm good at that. Sometimes I make two flavors and layer them."

"Oy, gevalt!" She looked at me tragically. "On such food you had to grow up? No wonder you look like a goy. Tuna fish, Jell-O! If I'd known sooner I'd have taught you a little something. At least you can learn how to make a kugel. Watch me. Here, there's the noodles, you cook in boiling water with salt, a lot of water, and here's the raisins and cheese and whole eggs and tzimmining . . ."

"Tzimmining?"

"Tzimmining, tzimmining!" She held up a large tin of cinnamon impatiently. "You can read, Davidul?"

She named each ingredient and showed me how to mix and bake the kugel, and afterward I thought, if I could do that for Pop some night, what a terrific surprise! I went up to the Hill, over that miserable bridge again, and I wrote the entire recipe down. What was more, I had the address of Jenny's restaurant. When Pop found work again, I was going to insist we go there, or maybe with some of my tip money I'd take him there—if he'd let me spend it. The tip money was really coming in now. As Dinge said, "The eagles are shitting all over the fuckin' place!"

There wasn't a great deal going on those last few days, and nobody cared if I hung around the kitchen learning Jenny's tricks. Of course they were tricks for cooking for over a hundred people, but I figured I could extrapolate and scale them down to two—maybe.

Mr. Luft didn't bother me. As a matter of fact, in his eyes, from then on, I could do no wrong. He kept introducing me to strangers as the "clean-cut young man who saved our Paps!" And he hinted that next year, if Shep didn't come back, I might even be headwaiter. But most of the time he was on the phone reassuring parents that their kids were all right, not washed away in the flood. In spite of his reassurances, about a quarter of the parents drove up before the end of the season to take their kids home by car. Mrs. Seidel, Norman's mother, was one, and she insisted on slipping me another twenty-five dollars. I felt very guilty about taking it.

"You know, I'm not his counselor," I protested. "He's back with his own group, and I don't even wait on his table."

She just looked at me out of those piercing eyes, and I swallowed and folded the money into my pocket. "I know what you've done for Norman," she said as she was about to climb into the Rolls.

I said, "Well, Butch. Have a good winter." Now, I told myself a little smugly, the real Norman will come out. None of this Butch stuff. He'll hate to say good-bye. But I was disappointed. He climbed out of the car, stuck out his hand and shook mine. "See you around, Uncle Davey." And the little wretch turned away without a tear!

Killer and I watched them drive off, and I shook my head. "You'd think he would at least put on a show, cry a little."

"What are you bitching about?" Killer said. "The eagle shit, didn't she? How much?" When I showed him what I got, he whistled. "Twenty-five smackers! Have you been shtupping Mama, Davey?"

"You're crazy," I told him.

"Yeah, I guess so. You're like the rest of us, a summer spent without sinking any sturgeon. The nearest any of us got was Dinge, and that was only a dry fuck."

We all promised to write to each other, and we agreed to meet in the city in two weeks, downtown under the clock in the Biltmore lobby. I wasn't sure I could cough up enough money for an evening with the guys, but Horse said, "Don't worry. I know this restaurant near Times Square, the Canton Village, where you can get a complete dinner for thirty-five cents, a nickel tip, and five cents each way on the subway. That's half a buck. We can have a ball around Times Square."

So we all agreed to meet in two weeks. None of us got a chance to talk to the girls at Rocky Clove again, because all coed activities were called off for the duration. It was really a winding-down time. We packed and goofed around and watched the CCC guys repair the camp.

"It's a good life, the CCC," Dinge decided. "Like camp for grown-ups. I ought to fuckin' try it."

"You work that hard?" Killer hooted. "You wouldn't last a day!"

Since the train tracks were still washed out by the flood, when the time came to leave camp, we took buses down to the Day Liner in Catskill. Before we got onto the buses, Nancy took me aside. We had said our real good-byes the night before in the infirmary, but now she said, "I have a good-bye gift for you, Davey."

"Gee, you shouldn't do that, Nancy. I didn't give you anything."

She reached up and ruffled my hair. "Oh yes, you did." She handed me a small box. "Look at it."

I opened it and saw a little silver medallion with a chain. "Gee, it's pretty. What is it?"

"A Saint Christopher medal. I want you to wear it. It'll keep you from harm. Promise me, Davey." She took it out of the box and slipped it around my neck. "It has a carving on it of Saint Christopher carrying our Lord."

I thought, "Your Lord, maybe, not mine anymore!" I didn't know what to say. How could I possibly wear this? Pop would think I'd converted!

"Promise me, Davey?"

I said, "I'll try."

"No. Promise!"

"Okay." What the hell, I'd broken promises before, and if it made Nancy happy . . .

"I know I won't see you again. I don't think I'll be back next summer." She shrugged. "Well, that's the way it goes. I've got some advice for you, Davey."

I said, "What, Nancy?"

She smiled. "Don't drink bad gin, make love very slowly, and stick up for yourself! That's all, baby." Then, before I knew what was happening, she stood up on tiptoes, grabbed my head, and gave me a big smack on the lips, right there in front of all the campers and counselors!

When I got on the bus I was greeted with a chorus of whistles and catcalls. I sat down next to Shep, with Killer and Dinge in the seats ahead of us. They both turned around to stare at me and I could feel my face getting red. After a minute Killer said very softly, "Okay, Shaygets, you never told us how come you weren't on the Hill during the flood."

"What did you do to deserve that kiss, Davey?" Shep asked.

"It was the flood," I lied. "Because we were working together trying to get the rope across, and the rowboat and everything."

"Oh, sure, sure," Dinge chimed in. "Can the fuckin' bullshit. Where were you that night?"

I looked out the window as the mountains moved past, so dark and green against the brilliant-blue sky. I had one last look at the campus and the social hall above the mess hall with the big sign— WE DEVELOP on one side, BETTER BOYS on the other—then the trees blotted out the view, and we were on the road to Hunter, Tannersville, Haines Falls, and then Catskill.

"So where were you that night, Shaygets?" Killer asked again, and I fingered the Saint Christopher medal through my shirt.

"That's for me to know and you guys to find out!" I grinned at them and leaned back and closed my eyes.

▪ Chapter Twenty-One ▪

It was September of 1936 when I walked into the third-term French class at George Washington High School for the second time. If my luck held true, this was the term I'd pass. I had flunked a term, passed a term since I started French in the second term of high school. I had flunked last term under Miss Applebaum, but this time, I told myself firmly, I was going to pass. Camp had given me a new outlook on life, a new determination. I wasn't a kid anymore. I had grown up this past summer. I was seventeen, but much older, I told myself, more mature.

This was my senior year, and I still had two chances to pass fourth-term French, this term and next term. I had what Dr. King, the head of the Biology Department, called reinforcement.

Miss Engels was the teacher this term, and she sure didn't remind me of Miss Applebaum. For one thing, she was younger and a lot prettier. She looked like the woman in the Tattoo Lipstick ads. Her light-brown hair was up in a roll, and her lips were very full, and deep red. She had dark-blue eyes and just the trace of a lisp, which sounded sort of cute in French. She didn't try any of that "We'll only speak French" stuff, but she said she was going to get all of us good French dictionaries as one of our textbooks. "And when I give a test, I'm going to let you use these dictionaries."

That was a shock. A whisper ran through the class, and one of the girls raised her hand. "You mean we can use a dictionary on our tests, Miss Engels?"

"That's what I said." She smiled. "I'll give you something to translate, from English to French, or from French to English, and I can judge how well you do by how much you translate. Of course there will be a strict time limit, and a dictionary won't do you much good if you have to look up every word."

She went on to explain her method. The dictionary was to take the pressure off us. That was a new concept. Every other teacher I had had, had tried to put the pressure on! The thing she wanted to stress was translation, and she began to distribute our reading text for the term, *Le Livre de Mon Ami,* by Anatole France.

That was great with me. My strongest point in French, if I could call anything about French strong, was translation. It was the irregular verbs and the grammer that did me in. When I opened *Le Livre de Mon Ami,* I stared at the illustrations. They looked familiar, and then I realized that they were by John R. Neal, the artist who'd illustrated the Oz books.

Just looking at them reminded me of Camp Harel and the Oz story I had been making up for Norman in camp and for Sonia Musikants in town. When I said good-bye to her on my last visit to town, her eyes had filled up, and she said, "You mean I won't see you again, Davey? What about the rest of the story?"

I said, "Next year, Sonia. I'm coming back next year, and I'll tell you the ending, honest!" And I was sure I would come back. In fact, leafing through *Le Livre* gave me some ideas about my story. The illustrations were great.

And then Miss Engels said, "Mr. Quinn, would you start?"

I looked at her blankly. "Start?"

"Yes, start translating. Page one. Have you been listening to me?"

"Yes, of course." I turned back to the first page, and as I stood up I could hear some of the girls giggle. My reputation in French had gone ahead of me. "I would like to get an idea of what level each member of the class is at," Miss Engels explained, sitting down on the front edge of her desk, book in hand.

Well, in a way this was what I had been looking for, a chance to start off with a good impression. I began translating, and it wasn't hard at all, but I had only done two paragraphs when I felt the book taken out of my hand. Miss Engels had come down the aisle while I read. "Where is your pony, Mr. Quinn?"

"Pony?" I looked at her blankly. What the hell was she talking about?

"I don't think it possible that you can read that well without a pony," she said severely as she leafed through the book. "I've been going over your past record in French." She handed the book back grimly. "I want you to stay after class and we'll have a little talk."

That little talk didn't sound so good. If she had been looking at my past French record, I could forget about a good impression. I had never heard the term "pony," and I wasn't sure just what it meant, but I didn't like the sound of it, and when the class left and we were alone, I didn't like the way she looked at me.

"I've spoken to Miss Applebaum about you, Mr. Quinn. I want the truth."

I said, "What's a pony, ma'am?" I knew what a real pony was, but I was sure she didn't mean a little horse—or did she? Some teachers were strange.

"A pony is a translation. I'm waiting for the truth, Mr. Quinn. It's not too hard to find out what text you'll get in advance, now is it?"

I drew a deep breath. "Honest, Miss Engels. I'll swear on the Bible if you want me to. I never saw any translation of this book before! It's just—well, I've very good at translation."

"David Quinn, you failed French the first term you took it, and passed the second time by the skin of your teeth, with a bare sixty-five. You failed second-term French and had to retake that, and then you only passed with a sixty-seven!"

"That's progress."

"That's disgusting! You failed third-term and fourth-term French last year, and now you try to tell me you can translate this well?"

"It was irregular verbs and grammar that killed me, Miss Engels." I put all the sincerity I could into my voice. "Honest, I'll do better this term. I'm really going to try hard. I have a good vocabulary. After all, I've studied French for three years!"

"And gotten credit for one and a half years." But she was smiling, and I drew a sigh of relief. I could tell she believed me. She looked down at some papers on her desk, and I saw that they were transcripts of my records. She frowned a bit, then opened the book to a paragraph in the middle. "Read this for me, David."

240

I was David now, and I knew I had convinced her. I read the paragraph slowly, but pretty accurately, and she listened and nodded. Her voice was much friendlier, and she looked me up and down. "You're a pretty big boy to be taking fourth-term French."

"Well, I'm a senior. I've just had pretty bad luck with French."

"I can see that." She tapped her pencil on the desk for a moment, staring at me thoughtfully and chewing her lower lip. Then she said, "I'll tell you what. I'll take a chance on you, David. I think that with some extra tutoring, you might do very well this term and next and even end up with two and one half years' credit when you graduate. That would be a feather in my cap."

It would be a whole Indian headdress in mine, I thought.

"I've been tutoring some students privately at my apartment on Saturday afternoons. Maybe I could fit you in."

I said, "Gee, Miss Engels, that would be swell, but I couldn't afford it."

She smiled. "I wasn't thinking of charging you. If I could make you realize your potential and pass, it would be payment enough— and I mean pass with better than a sixty-five or a seventy. You aren't stupid, David. You seem to be just—perhaps unrealized."

I walked out of there with her address and an appointment for early next Saturday morning, and I was feeling pretty good. This was going to be the term David Quinn turned himself around! I'd pull up my mark in French, and in eco too. Who knows, I might even do well in gym, especially if I didn't have Mr. Szylowski this term.

But with all my good intentions, I still had to start the new term with a detention period after school. I had some left over from last year and they weren't wiped out by the summer, my home-room teacher explained. Just like a jail sentence. I'd have to serve them in full.

I was settling down in detention hall with *Le Livre de Mon Ami* when Bob Wagner, who had about as many detentions as I have, and usually sat next to me, handed me a note. He was a good cartoonist, and had drawn a student with wings and a ball and chain and had written under it, "If I had the wings of an angel, right over these detention walls I'd do a Lindbergh!"

I grinned at him and went back to the book, then looked at his cartoon again. The student didn't look like a boy at all. In fact, it looked very much like Marcia. Maybe that was significant too. I folded it up and put it in my pocket, but I couldn't study. I kept thinking of Marcia and the ride home from Catskill on the Hudson River Day Line.

I had been up in front on the top deck, alone, watching the dark-green hills on either side of the river slide by, trying to spot the Bear Mountain Bridge up ahead, when Marcia came up and leaned against the rail next to me. "Hello, stranger."

I turned and looked at her and realized that she had changed during the summer. She seemed somehow—well, fuller now, and her breasts weren't quite like marzipan anymore. I said, "Hi, Marcia," and I couldn't help adding, "Where's Squeak?"

She shrugged. "With your friends, I guess. I'm surprised you're alone."

I said, "Well . . ." and there was a long pause, then we both started to say something together, and then we stopped and laughed.

"I've missed you, Davey," Marcia said very softly, looking away toward the river. "I thought this summer—well, we'd be kind of, friends."

"We were friends, Marcia, until you began going out with Squeak."

"That's not so, Davey! I went out with Squeak—well, in self-defense. You didn't seem interested in me—that way."

I tried to act annoyed, but I couldn't do it convincingly. "Marcia, you spent all last winter telling me we should just be friends, that I didn't have to hold your hand or get personal. We could have, what do you call it, a platonic friendship. And now you're upset because I didn't keep taking you down to the haystack!"

"Oh, Davey, you're such a dope! Do you know what's wrong with you?"

I said, "No, Marcia! And I'll tell you something else, I don't want to know. I'm really tired of people telling me what's wrong with me. I spent a whole summer finding out what's right with me!" That sounded a little strange. "What I mean is . . ." I hesitated, because I wasn't sure what I meant. I felt very confused about

242

Marcia, very unsure of just what I wanted. "We'll see each other in the City," I finished lamely.

She looked at me very intently, then took my hand, and for one awful second I thought she was going to repeat that silly stunt of putting it on her breast right there out in the open on the top deck, but instead she just squeezed it and said, "Maybe you'll come to dinner soon?"

I said, "Sure," and she turned away, then turned back and grinned. "I really don't like Squeak that much. He's all mixed up— not like you, Davey." And she hurried off. I didn't see her for the rest of the boat ride, or at least alone. She was always with a group of other waitresses, singing camp songs.

After detention I walked down the hill from high school lugging all my textbooks. I wasn't going to leave them in my locker this term. They'd stay at home and I'd really crack them. This was a new Davey. Maybe I would call Marcia this weekend and go there to dinner. I even thought I could handle Mr. Beck, especially if he offered me one of his cigars. I'd try it and see how he liked that! I'd learned a few tricks during the summer, like how to smoke without inhaling and still pretend you were.

I'd also learned how to make noodle kugel, and I decided to make one that evening for dinner. Sam and Rhea were coming over, and it was going to be something of a celebration. Pop had found a job in a shop on 125th Street.

"It's nonunion," he had told me a few days ago, the first night after I came home from camp. "But don't let Sam know. He'll carry on about the hours and the pay. He doesn't understand that when work is this hard to get, you don't worry about hours or pay."

We were sitting at the kitchen table that night, Pop reading the *Daily News,* and I was looking through back issues of the comics from the past two months. Pop had saved them for me because I'm a real fan of *Terry and the Pirates* and I wanted to see what had happened to Burma and the Dragon Lady. I have a soft spot for the Dragon Lady. I was sure she wasn't as bad as everyone thought.

"And I think I have something for you, Davey," Pop said. "I was by the fruit store today and there's a new owner, an Irisher, Mr.

Fogarty, and he can use a delivery boy. I want you should stop by after school and talk to him."

Well, I did that the next day, but Mr. Fogarty, when I introduced myself, shook his head. "What do you want delivering orders, a big strapping lad like you?"

I said, "Because we need the money, Mr. Fogarty."

"Sure, and don't we all?" He was a very fat man with a great big belly and a round, pleasant face and a big red nose. He reminded me of Santa Claus without the beard. "What I can use, lad, is someone to help out in the store, lift boxes and unload the fruit. It's hard work, but you look like you got the build for it, and it pays better than delivering orders. I'll tell you, what do you say to fifty cents an hour?"

So we settled on that, and I felt pretty good about it. We agreed I'd start next week, and we shook hands on it after I explained that with detentions I'd be an hour late for the first two weeks. Mr. Fogarty seemed to get a kick out of it when I explained what detentions were. "I was never much of a scholar meself. You'll just work an hour later those days."

So that was that. With five hours on Saturday and three hours each weekday, I could pull down ten bucks a week! That was pretty damn good!

When I told Pop about it that night, he was pleased but doubtful. "You don't have such a good job record, Davey."

"I've changed, Pop. You just wait and see."

"Believe me, Davey, I'm waiting. What I'll see is a different story."

Then, the day I met Miss Engels, I came home and decided to make noodle kugel from the recipe Jenny had given me. It wasn't hard, even though I spent my own money on it. I had held back five dollars from the summer's tips. I gave Pop a hundred dollars, and that was in addition to the hundred I had given him up at camp. He was very pleased, and even suggested I keep two dollars for myself. I didn't tell him about the five I had held back, and he was surprised when I refused the two. "You deserve a few dollars, Davey."

I said, "Don't worry, Pop. When I need it I'll ask you." Now I was a little sorry I hadn't asked. The cheese and noodles and eggs

244

and cinnamon had cost almost a dollar, but I figured it would be worth it when Pop tasted the result.

We had our usual salmon salad for the main course, with all the stuff Pop chops into it, celery and cucumber and onion and lettuce, besides the mayonnaise. Pop is the only one I know who chops lettuce into salmon salad, but it sure stretches it. Rhea said it was delicious in that polite way that means, "Not this again!" But Sam wasn't polite. "For Christ's sake, Pop! Can't you make anything but canned salmon for dinner?"

That wasn't fair because sometimes Pop makes tuna salad, and once he made a salad out of canned tomato herrings. But that didn't turn out too well. Even I couldn't eat it.

"Wait till you taste the next course," I told them as I went into the kitchen for the kugel, which smelled pretty good.

"Davey's famous Jell-O?" Sam asked, but then I brought in the kugel and he stared at me. "You made that?"

"I sure did."

"And you expect us to eat it? Forget it!"

"Now, Sam," Rhea said. "At least taste it."

I served Pop and Rhea and gave Sam a tiny portion to taste. I knew if he liked it he darned well wouldn't admit it and ask for more. Anyway, even I was surprised at how good it tasted. It was a little burned on the bottom, but I didn't serve the burned part. Pop tasted it and lifted his eyebrows. "Davey, it's good. So where did you learn such cooking?"

"Jenny, the camp cook, taught me."

Rhea tasted it gingerly and said, "It's very rich." I didn't know if that was praise or criticism, but when Sam, without asking, took another helping, I knew I had a success.

After dinner, while I was clearing the table and he was shuffling the cards for the pinochle game, Pop said, "Sam, spill me a glass water."

I saw Sam's face turn red. Every time Pop said that, he'd yell, "Pop, Pop! It's pour, not spill! Spill is an accident. Pour is deliberate! Damn it, it's pour!" And Pop would tsk, tsk mildly. He just couldn't seem to get them straight, maybe because in Yiddish the two words sound alike. But Sam wouldn't accept any excuse.

This time he deliberately picked up the water pitcher, poured a glass of water, and then knocked it over. It spread all over the table, and Pop jumped up as it hit his pants. "Sam! What are you doing?"

"I told you it's pour! That's spill, what I did."

Pop went into the kitchen to get a dish towel, and I lost my temper. I shouted, "Goddamn it, Sam! That's no way to treat Pop!" I'd never yelled at Sam before, and I was a little surprised myself, but I was angry too.

Sam stared at me. "What?"

"You heard me," I shouted. "Pop deserves some respect. He works hard and he's been a father and mother to both of us. If you can't treat him with respect, you don't have to come here."

From the doorway where he was dabbing at his wet pants, Pop said, "Davey, shah! Shah!"

Sam stood up, his face furious, and he shook off Rhea's restraining hand. For a minute I thought he was going to take a swing at me, and I put up my fists, but Pop yelled, "Sam! Davey!" and I put my hands down.

Rhea stood up and took Sam's arm. "We'd better go, Sam," she said, and to Pop, "I'm sorry, Pop. Sam's been under a lot of strain lately. Things aren't too good at work. Come on, Sam."

Sam grabbed his jacket and walked to the door, and Pop said, "David, say you're sorry to Sam."

I said, "How about he says he's sorry to you?"

"Never mind. Say you're sorry."

I shrugged and grudgingly said, "I'm sorry, Sam."

Sam put his jacket on and had his hand on the doorknob, but Pop stopped him. "Sam, I want you should shake Davey's hand."

We both stood there without moving for about a full minute, then Pop said, "In my house brothers don't fight. I want you should both be friends. Shake hands now, come on."

Reluctantly, both of us put out our hands and shook, but Sam looked at me as if he wanted to squash me. After they had gone, Pop shook his head. "Davey, Davey, what's come over you?"

"I don't care what you say, Pop. He has no business treating you like that. Who the hell does he think he is?"

Pop sat down in his easy chair in the living room and patted the daybed next to it. "Come, sit down, Davey. Sam respects me. I know that. Sometimes he seems, well, a little tsedrayt, but he's a good boy, like you. You mustn't fight with him. It's a terrible thing when brothers fight."

"I don't fight, Pop. I just don't like his attitude."

"Attitude, shmattitude—so I'm out a pinochle game. Someday I'll have to teach you two-handed pinochle. Now calm down already. Tell me about school. Are you going to get more Fs this term?"

"F doesn't always mean failure . . ." I started automatically, and Pop looked at me and said, "No bobbe-mysehs. Last year you failed French. What about this year?"

I should have known. I yell at Sam and I'm on the spot! "This year I'm going to pass," I said earnestly. "Pop, I've got a swell teacher. She's not like Miss Applebaum. She's young and pretty and real nice."

"Young and pretty and nice is one thing. Is she going to put something into that head of yours, Davey?"

"Listen, Pop. I translated for her today, and she said she'd help me by tutoring me."

"What's tutoring?" Pop frowned.

"Giving me private lessons on Saturday so that I can learn my irregular verbs and grammar."

Pop said, "What?"

"At her apartment, Pop. That's how great she is, and she won't charge me."

"Oy vay!" Pop put one hand to his head and groaned. "Davey, Davey! What am I going to do with you? Private lessons at her home already. You'll start the whole thing again!"

"What whole thing, Pop?" I was really bewildered.

"First it's deliveries, and you fool around with the customer, then it's the library, and then at camp, that nurse! Davey, you'll never learn! If trouble isn't there, you'll go and find it!"

"Pop!" I was really shocked and I jumped up. "How can you even think that? She's a teacher. My God, do you think I'd ever try anything like that with a teacher, or that she'd do it with a student?

247

That's terrible, Pop, just terrible! I don't know how you can think that."

Pop spread his hands. "Davey, who's crazy, you or me?"

Well, we argued about that for half an hour, and by the time I had cleaned up the dishes and straightened out the kitchen and put up the pot I'd made the kugel in to soak, to soften the burned part, I had finally convinced him that he was acting crazy.

"I'm sorry, Davey," he said when I was getting ready for bed and pulling out the daybed in the living room. "I guess I misjudged you."

I told him it was all right. I could understand how he felt, and I said good night and closed the hall door, then put out the light and lay there in the dark watching the street light through the fire-escape window. How could Pop think that about me? A teacher! Who in his right mind would try anything with a teacher, even one as young and good-looking as Miss Engels?

Then I remembered her blue eyes and the lips that looked like a Tattoo Lipstick ad, and I smiled in the dark and thought, well, who knows. Maybe Pop is right!